FADE TO BLACK

FADE TO BLACK

A REQUIEM FOR THE CBC

WAYNE SKENE

DOUGLAS & McINTYRE
VANCOUVER • TORONTO

Copyright © 1993 by Wayne Skene

93 94 95 96 97   5 4 3 2 1

All rights reserved. No part of this book may be reproduced in any form by any means without written permission from the publisher, except by a reviewer, who may quote brief passages in a review.

Douglas & McIntyre Ltd.
1615 Venables Street
Vancouver, British Columbia V5L 2H1

Canadian Cataloguing in Publication Data

Skene, Wayne, 1941-
  Fade to black

ISBN 1-55054-089-0

1. Canadian Broadcasting Corporation.
2. Public broadcasting—Canada. I. Title.
HE8689.9.C3S54 1993   384.54'06'571
C93-091598-4

Cover design and text design by Tom Brown(WORKSHOP)
Editing by Brian Scrivener
Cover photo by Bruce Law
Typeset at Vancouver Desktop Publishing Centre
Printed and bound in Canada by D.W. Friesen and Sons Ltd.
Printed on acid-free paper ∞

This book is dedicated to my sons,
Cameron and Christopher.
The price they paid for the odyssey was as high as anyone's.

CONTENTS

Preface and Acknowledgements

THIS IS NOT *THE* BOOK ABOUT the Canadian Broadcasting Corporation. This is *my* book about the CBC. It is a book about my experiences, my frustrations and my interpretation of Canadian public broadcasting—what it was meant to be, how it was to serve us and what happened to it along its path. There will be people who will disagree with many of my premises. What they cannot disagree with are the events I witnessed as I watched this once-proud organization thrash its way to the edge of irrelevance.

The issue of who should be entrusted with something as valuable as our most important cultural entity is the book's central theme. Public broadcasting, from its inception, has seldom enjoyed a consistently applied philosophy. It has been made up, largely, as we've gone along. Thousands of people have come and gone—politicians, board members, presidents, management, executives, employees, consultants, supporters—and all have moved the tuning knobs for public broadcasting one way or the other as they saw fit.

If we could not agree on a philosophy, I felt like many others that the institution of public broadcasting had to at least be scrutinized. It was too important to be left without criticism, in the hands of people who walk in and out of the organization every five years or so, and while within it, often try to tailor it to suit particular biases or beliefs. It is not, as a friend pointed out, an unquestioned theology put together by management or a Board of Directors, and defensible as unassailable truth. When we arrived at Black Wednesday, December 5, 1990, I decided it was time to leave what remained of this truncated organization, perhaps write a book about my experiences.

My goal was to increase public awareness of the CBC, to open up the doors on a much too cloistered public organization and allow citizens a chance to decide if it is worth their allegiance and support any longer.

In writing this book I was fortunate to be able to rely on a number of significant books by other authors. This book would not have been as complete without their scholarly advance work, in particular: Frank Peers for his two learned volumes, *The Politics of Canadian Broadcasting — 1920–1951* and *The Public Eye: Television and the Politics of Canadian Broadcasting — 1952–1968*; Marc Raboy's *Missed Opportunities: The Story of Canada's Broadcasting Policy*; Mary Jane Miller's *Turn Up the Contrast: CBC Television Drama Since 1952*; Herschel Hardin's *Closed Circuits: The Sellout of Canadian Television*; Richard Collins' *Culture, Communications and National Identity: The Case of Canadian Television*; and Roger Bird's *Documents of Canadian Broadcasting*, among many others. Thanks to them all.

The process was two years of talking and listening and worrying and travelling and thinking and testing and discovering, and it could not have been accomplished without the help of my family, friends and associates. There are almost too many to thank and for those I miss, I would hope you forgive me.

My agent, Linda McKnight, deserves the *croix de guerre* for stubbornly believing, in the face of passing indifference from much of the publishing industry, that a book about the CBC was important to Canadians. My publisher, Rob Sanders, restored my faith in the publishing business with his patience, his cheerful support and his selection of Brian Scrivener as my editor. With great tact and skill, Brian tempered the rage, treated the syntax and, like Merlin, made it all better than it started out to be. Thanks to my son, Cameron, and his wife, Pauline Pelletier, who helped with the research and who must have suffered public broadcasting withdrawal after transcribing those hundreds of hours of interview tape.

Tellingly perhaps, there are many people within the CBC I spoke to who chose to remain anonymous, people who provided me with background, insights, information, stories and enlightenment. I thank you all for what you shared, especially my friend, "The Bladerunner."

Thanks to those inside the Mother Corporation, on their way in or out, as the case may be: Denis Harvey, Margaret Lyons, Cathy Chilco, Brian McKeown, Vicki Gabereau, Alex Frame, Rudi Carter, Ken Johnson, Andrew Simon, Brian O'Leary, Lionel Lumb, Gerry Janneteau, Ron Devion, Peggy Oldfield and Harold Redekopp, for holding the asylum door open just wide enough for me to escape. Also, I must express my appreciation to Gérard Veilleux, Patrick Watson, William Neville and numerous senior managers for their cooperation and candour.

Much thanks goes to the folks in Windsor who poured out their hearts and souls over the loss of their CBC station; to Mayor Al Duerr, Wendell Wilks and Doug Lauchlan, among many others, in Calgary; to former CBC presidents, Al Johnson, Pierre Juneau and Bill Armstrong; to Marc Raboy, Peter Pearson, Sarah Jennings, Bob Blakey, Ross Perigoe, Jack Gray, Paul Audley, Gerald Caplan, Daryl Duke, David Ellis and Ian Morrison, spokesperson for The Friends of Canadian Broadcasting, for all the time, courtesy, information and moral support.

When the nights got long and cold, and my resolve wavered, there always seemed to be good friends providing support and encouragement: Jo and Eric Moncur, John and Anne Lysaght, Robert Sunter and Cynthia Fung-Sunter, Cammie and Ged Ayotte, Roxanna and Jim Aitken, Larry and Helen Shorter, Bob Spence, Robb Lucy, Michael Lebowitz, Derek McGillivray, Lawrie Seligman and Marion Hyde, for their encouragement and assistance; Jack McIver and Gerri Grant for the wine, the laughs and blessed moments of space; Jane McCauley and Ted Barris for advice, direction and proof that good guys finish first; Mrs. Merle Seligman for graciously providing me with a roof over my head when the winds were coldest; Sean Rossiter for pushing me out of the conceptual ditch; and Paul and Audrey Grescoe for endlessly trying to convince me my words might make sense.

I must recognize the kids of the CBC Calgary television station, 1984-87. You made those years some of the best of my CBC-life. You did something unique. You took your talent and skills, and with little money but lots of energy and imagination, crafted a pretty good replica of what public broadcasting was supposed to mean. Bless you all.

A special thanks must be expressed to Edie and Bill White, the former vice-president of CBC's regional broadcasting operations. Canadian public broadcasting has seldom had a better friend than Bill. A much-belated thanks to my parents for quietly teaching me the mysterious value of The Word, and for showing me how a journalist can, by simply paying attention to it in print, spot those moments when reality deviates from truth.

While the writing of this book was coming to an end, an old and valued friend unfortunately passed away. Bill Jones was a dedicated public broadcaster whose conscience never let him forget who was boss—the Canadian taxpayer. We will miss his wisdom, his insight and his guidance. I also hope that someday someone else will get a chance to read this book—Joan Donaldson. A small tribute to both of them: to Bill Jones, who knew; and to Joan Donaldson, who would understand.

And to Connie, for whom thanks cannot be enough. For years she watched the emotional elevator called "the CBC" go up and down, and always knew when it was time to tell me to get off. More than anyone, it was Connie who knew what we had to do. She made sure I had the time, the space and the support to do it. It would not have happened without her. 'Love ya, Babe.

1 / Saying Good-bye to the CBC

"Vanity, rather than wisdom, determines how the world is run."
—Kurt Vonnegut, Jr.

THE UGLY NEWS ABOUT WHAT was to happen arrived on a December 4, 1990 managers' conference call. The CBC's Board of Directors had decided that they would primarily meet their $108 million budget problem by gutting regional operations—cancelling more than 2,000 hours of programming, closing three television stations, severely downsizing eight others and putting as many as 1,100 public broadcasters out of work. It was, without a doubt, the saddest day of my life with the CBC.

The following morning I arrived at my office earlier than usual. I needed time to figure out the best way to break the news to a bunch of bright and talented producers, writers, hosts, researchers and production staff—that their public broadcasting days were probably over. I caught myself staring out the window. The sky was growing lighter. The sun was coming up. Staff had begun to make their way across the concrete and brick patio that formed the front entrance to CBC British Columbia's Hamilton Street offices, oblivious to what awaited many of them inside. As I stared out the window, I imagined the faces of those who would gather shortly in my office, trying to judge the scope of the shock and anger they would feel. Suddenly I realized what was wrong with the CBC.

From researchers and script assistants, to producers and executive producers, these people were the living, creative embodiment of the only product the CBC should be committed to—the making of programs. I would have to tell them they were expendable. They would not be needed in the CBC's brave, new "renaissance" world. At that moment, out the window, I found myself watching one of our maintenance personnel who reported, not to the Vancouver managers of this CBC station, but to the CBC Engineering department. He was wandering back and forth across the terraced entrance, leisurely raking dead leaves and picking up bits of paper off the concrete, tidying up. And then it struck me. In an hour I would be telling producers and production staff that they no longer had jobs with Canada's public broadcaster. But the man who raked the leaves on the terrace, and who would later busy himself filling toilet dispensers with paper, would still have a job with the Canadian Broadcasting Corporation.

As I took my daily notes from December 4 onward, listening to the cross-Canada management conference calls, my heart just got heavier and heavier—the confusion, the lack of understanding, elements of corporate venality, the laboured justifications, the unnecessary personal damage, and, of course, the death of corporate purpose. It appeared as the days unfolded that the Board and the new administration, headed by former secretary of the Treasury Board Gérard Veilleux and chairman-designate Patrick Watson, were being compelled to restructure the venerable and bulky CBC without a precise understanding of what its history had truly been, how the organization was structured and how it operated. They did not, it seemed, fully understand what they held in their hands. A number of assumptions about the corporation were made, a number of decisions guided by flawed information. Much of the plan, if one could call it that, for the largest budget cut in CBC's history, was based, not on a consistent philosophical orientation, or vision, for the nation's public broadcaster, but on fiscal expediency, glossed over with a sad and thin veneer of rationalization.

For all Canadians, what was at stake was not just another troubled government department or crown corporation. This was the near mortal flailing of the nation's last, best hope for protecting the shaky elements of our culture and identity. Each move on the Board and the administration's part was as if a group of strangers had hold of the family album and, print by distinctive print, was innocently flipping the contents into some roaring homogenous hearth. When the fire cooled, we would have little left with which to identify ourselves.

Shortage of money was only one of a multitude of issues swamping the corporation. CBC management was passive and ossified, with roots and style stuck deep in the 1960s and 1970s. It was reactive rather than bold and inventive, inert and resistant rather than radical in thinking and planning. The initial advice provided to the Board for budget action was timid. Primarily because of the overwhelming need to retain commercial advertising revenue flow, the information tended to distort the true history and state of public broadcasting. As the days passed, and conference call after conference call added to the miasma, I began to realize that the process was being made up as we went along. This was a game about bureaucrats and numbers, not about public broadcasting. And it was done in an environment of chaos. The entire post-December 5, 1990 budget cut environment had a confused, contradictory, almost surreal feel to it, as if it had all been made up on the back of a half-dozen envelopes the night before in a smoky bar in Hull, Quebec.

The debilitating and expensive effect of single-year funding with which Parliament had saddled the CBC was finally blowing up in everybody's face. The ridiculous cycle of a billion dollar corporation trying to make programs and balance the books every twelve months—and now, cut hundreds of millions of dollars out of its operations—squeezed senior management into the situation where most of any fiscal year was spent frantically trying to figure out how much money the CBC really had. The desperate annual search for badly-needed funds meant the corporation was forced into a commercial advertising feeding frenzy, especially with its English television network. The network had become bloated with commercials. The move, which had been underway for decades, also meant the ETV network had been making programs as much to satisfy advertisers and co-production partners as to meet the cultural needs of Canadians. That meant *au revoir* to regular prime time programs catering to minority tastes or anyone over fifty. Culturally important programs— Canadian stage plays, reviews of books and literature, dance, performance, music, historical documentaries and drama, regional drama and even a truly Canadian soap opera—were out of the mix. It also meant a news and current affairs service that presented depth and perspective less and less frequently, tending to rely too often, like most North American television news services, on the glib and insubstantial.

We had arrived at a state of affairs where Canada's public broadcaster was virtually indistinguishable from Canadian and U.S. commercial networks and cable systems. By 1992 the CBC would be forced, with each promotion break between commercial messages, to *tell us* we were watching "public broadcasting," rather than allow us to witness the pictures, words and images that would convince us.

> *"There are times when nothing is better than something."*
> —Glenda Jackson, in *Sunday, Bloody Sunday*

As beautiful as it was to most of us, the CBC had always been a strange and troublesome place. It was full of conflicting opinion, streaking personal emotions, frightened bureaucrats and sometimes surly, rebellious people, all looking for their own particular creative haven within a corporate womb called "national public broadcasting."

For some of us the CBC was a cultural church. It was a place to go to feel more Canadian, to learn more about being Canadian, to contribute our little bit to national purpose. It did not matter whether we were technicians or clerks or reporters or production assistants; being part of the CBC placed us all in a higher calling than just broadcasting. We were the lucky Canadians who held jobs with social purpose.

I had grown up in Winnipeg eating lunch and listening to *The Happy Gang*, and in the evenings watching *Festival*, *Close-Up* and *Hockey Night in Canada* on CBWT. I was a complete CBC devotee, even as a teenager, because this was a broadcaster which seemed able, and eager, to put what I was learning as a student about Canada into some easily-understood context. Stanley Burke and Norman Depoe analyzed the national and international news of the day. Lister Sinclair and Fletcher Markle related the stories of our regional histories. Giselle Mackenzie, Wally Koster, George LaFleche and Juliette wove marvellous masques of national entertainment, using faces we recognized on Winnipeg streets.

When I was offered the chance to come on board in 1973, I felt as if I had been selected for the clergy. It was a bit like going home again. It was a trip that took me through the making of local and national radio and television programs. It took me back and forth across the nation. It provided me with stimulating insights into the true Canadian character, that we were not one, indivisible nation. How could we be? We had been French and Brit and Scot and Jew and Galician and East Asian and Native and Ukrainian and Irish and Indian. Hell, our history was not smooth and seamless. It was an awkward pastiche. We were a nation of individuals huddled together like a family of tired and irritable canines looking less for trouble than a quiet place to rest.

The CBC also introduced me to hundreds of intelligent and talented Canadians, most seemingly hell-bent on learning and putting to use the same catechism. Sitting in editing booths as the morning sun broke over the streets outside, tired yet exhilarated after a night of working with tape and images, I used to think how very fortunate I was. I had embarked almost unknowingly on a career path to public broadcasting, one that eventually intersected with circumstance. The CBC was letting me learn about Canada, and they were paying me for it. Each interview was like receiving a free lecture. Each documentary was like a Master's degree in another subject. I felt, as Bill Moyers once wrote about journalism, that "we are the lucky ones, allowed to spend our days in a continuing course of adult education."

The whole experience—perhaps it even defines the CBC—was a repository of ideas and dreams and beliefs, all woven into sounds and images of ourselves as a culture—from talking about human survival on the Barrenlands of the Territories, to staging an authentic Winnipeg "North End Social"; from listening to Sir Bernard Lovell talk about the mysterious quantum glass that hid God from Science, to watching our Vancouver news producers have the courage to go to air with "Dr. Peter," the weekly diary of an AIDS sufferer; from the 5,000 Calgarians who used to crowd into the station for Open House or our Stampede Breakfast, to the Calgary crew laughing together on location, tears rolling down our cheeks, as we tried to shoot the story of Nellie McClung with a single actress, because we could not afford a larger cast; from listening to James H. Gray sketch the essential characteristics of a diverse and angry pool of western Canadian settlers, to laughing at a bunch of kids called "Three Dead Trolls in a Baggie" doing crazed comedy from the back streets of Edmonton.

The drawback, the frustration for me, was the bureaucracy, some of it at the English television network, a bit of it in the English radio system, and most of it in Head Office in Ottawa; that and the whole damaging issue of centralized power. Toronto and Ottawa always wanted to control things, as if they alone could divine the deepest traits and idiosyncrasies of being Canadian—from their cultural aeries on Bay Street or Bronson Avenue. I carried the perhaps naive belief—as the authors of Canadian public broadcasting did in 1929—

that you could not properly depict or define Canada unless you did it from the provinces or regions. As things evolved to 1990, the visceral shots for national public broadcasting ended up being called by people whose view of Canada often came from the Executive Class cabin on a flight from Toronto to Vancouver and back again.

These were not malevolent or foolish people, nor were they lacking in talent. Most worked long and hard within their personal version of public broadcasting. But they were often the kind of people who had seldom got close enough to feel the calloused hand of the country. Even if they could claim roots in Sidney or Fort St. John, they could not help but begin to define "Canada" from the confines of Bay Street or the Toronto Broadcasting Centre.

I doubted they could remember the last time they had ridden a bus through southern Saskatchewan or northern New Brunswick, and remembered what the person next to them looked like, where they were from or what troubles they were carrying. I doubted that many of them had ever been forced to wait on tables or tend bar, understood the morning vista on the Trans-Canada from behind a truck's windshield, knew what it was like to try to hike a ride in winter near Nipigon, rode a combine in the hot August sun, mended fence, hauled a gill net, cleaned someone else's house. I wondered sometimes if they knew what it was like to raise teenagers, to cope with the surges of pride, confusion, passion and thank-God-fullness when it was over.

Had they listened to teachers talk about the mystery of the young? Had they ever slept on a warm grate on a cold night in the fall? Had they ever experienced that moment in your life when all you had was the sad jingle of a few coins in your pocket? Had they worked in a foundry? A fish plant? Pruned trees? Planted them? Lived with new immigrant Canadians? Delivered mail? Fought in a beer parlour parking lot? Lined up for UI? Watched the bank call your small business loan? Tried to make your staff's payroll? Mortgage your home the second and third time? In short, had they shared much of what life was like for most Canadians?

I will always remember the time I met an ETV network executive for breakfast in Edmonton one morning in 1983. He had arrived to discuss the possibility of co-producing a network series. He was young, bright and dressed in the pastel-spring colours all the rage in downtown Toronto that year. What he decided in his area of programming—what he liked, disliked or thought would be suitable for Mr. and Mrs. Canada—became the final say on what his division produced for the CBC network. It could have been his first visit to Edmonton. He returned from a morning stroll around the city's Churchill Square with a large question for me. "Why," he asked with a dismissive wave of his hand, "are the people here so homely . . .?" He did not understand—who these people were, where they had come from and how hard life had pushed most of them.

Most of us came to the CBC to make programs about our regions and to trade them with other regions. But the process of trying to explain to people in Toronto that they were not Canada, led many of us into management positions because, like officers at Khartoum, we felt that we had no choice but to stay and do battle with the bureaucracy, in the hope that what we did would make it easier for other creative souls to do their jobs, to tell the correct stories. Under the circumstances for me, coming back to the CBC, not once but twice, was like Camus' premise in *The Plague*, where one gets meaning out of life by fighting the absurd.

> *"Minerva's owl begins its flight only in the gathering dusk."*
> —Georg Wilhelm Friedrich Hegel

The CBC has always been an organization that has lived by a multitude of tensions: creativity versus order, programs versus bureaucracy and public service versus politics. The directions being handed down in December 1990 to senior network and regional managers across the country put the skids to a national broadcasting system that was originally meant to strengthen Canadian cultural awareness and national identity by tapping the stories and images and reflections that originated in the regions of the country. The corporation would now start changing very quickly, moving further away from the people it was meant to serve.

In the two-and-a-half years between December 5, 1990 and June 1993, the CBC would go from trouble to chaos, from facing a bleak future to hardly having one at all, from respect for its journalistic standards to accusations of being a toady of the Mulroney Tories and a progenitor of state broadcasting, from claiming there was no fat left in the corporation to discovering it is always there, somewhere. By 1993, the CBC seemed to be in constant turmoil. Hope ebbed with each new frantic corporate initiative. Decisions announced so ruthlessly on December 5, 1990, especially about shutting down local news operations in places like Calgary, would eventually be reversed in the light of stupefying audience and advertising revenue losses. Accusations of insensitive management practices were hurled at Veilleux and Watson. Accusations of kowtowing to political pressure were tossed at the Tory-appointed Board. CBC staff were signing protest petitions, and management morale was at the edge of despair, and getting lower with every new, fanciful edict that came out of Head Office. The administration's style would turn from mistrustful and secretive to bellicose. Incessant demands were made for CBC journalists to be "more accountable," but it was interpreted as meaning to Ottawa, not necessarily to the public. The ETV network began taking its major programming and scheduling cues from Ottawa. Audience ratings plummeted. By March 1993 the average share of the adult prime time television audience was tracking very close to CBC English's AM/FM radio share. The possibility now hit that audiences for the two media services might intersect, as television's kept heading downward and radio held relatively steady. The CBC would then be spending $565 million for the English television portion of its national broadcasting service and $181 million for radio—to attract roughly the same share of audience. The corporation as a whole had become a blur of falling audience ratings, stalled advertising revenues, controversy and public indifference. And as a corporation it would still cost Canadians more than a billion dollars a year.

The one thing to keep in mind in all of this is that Canadian public broadcasting, at its inception, was not meant to be an institution run or controlled from a place like Toronto or Ottawa. The CBC was meant to perform a national service by encouraging expression—self-expression—from the regions. The parts would contribute the images which made up the whole.

Today, Canadians express a growing sense of regional identification. A 1992 Environics public opinion survey found that unifying symbols like the CBC were less important than ever to Canadians, especially western Canadians. More than 60 percent polled felt more citizens of their province than the country. They were defining national identity through the optic of their region. On December 5, 1990, the CBC publicly had announced that it would be hereafter, and irrevocably, marching in the opposite direction from the nation.

2 / Sayonara Windsor

"No time for farewells as screens fade to black"
"Blink! They were gone. Windsor's local CBC news show went off the air without so much as a goodbye. In Toronto, sombre French broadcasters were told: 'Ce soir, there will be no ce soir.' And in Goose Bay, Nfld., they changed the locks on the door. The CBC axe was merciless and immediate yesterday. 'We can't even say goodbye to our viewers,' said Percy Hatfield, municipal affairs reporter for the CBC station in Windsor. 'We've been muzzled. We don't even exist any more . . .'."
—Bill Taylor, *Toronto Star*, December 6, 1990

IN THE AFTERNOON OF SUNDAY, December 16, 1990, thousands of citizens gathered in Windsor's Dieppe Park. They mingled together, ready to begin the march through downtown Windsor to protest what many of them saw as the most devastating event to ever effect their community. There were mothers with babies tucked into strollers. There were senior citizens, kids from inner-city schools and women in fur coats leading dogs on leashes. A high school band oompah-pah'd in the background. As the main body of the crowd snaked its way through downtown Windsor, they were joined by hundreds of other citizens, until the protest swelled to a number estimated to be between 8,000 and 10,000.

"I took my son and ran ahead of the crowd to get a better view," Jane Boyd recalled. "I turned around and saw this sight. Well, I almost cried. I could hear the band playing 'Oh Canada.' People were literally streaming from out of the side streets to join the protest. I mean, almost 10,000 people! It was remarkable. Here was the entire gamut of Windsor's population. Here was our community. And they were outraged. Really, really angry! And they were going to let the country and the federal government know that they weren't going to take this sitting down."

On that particular December afternoon, the citizens of Windsor,

Ontario, with an area population of more than 500,000, were protesting because they had just lost their only local CBC television station (CBET), and more importantly, their only source of local television news. Of all the decisions the CBC Board of Directors announced on December 5, 1990 in an effort to escape its $108 million budget dilemma, the closing of local CBC news operations and the downsizing of the Windsor television station to a tiny news bureau was the most perplexing, the most telling and, probably, the least courageous. It was perplexing because it confounded public broadcasters across the country; if you were not in the business of providing a public broadcasting service where it did not exist, what were you in the business for? It was telling in the sense that the decision to disenfranchise Windsorites from local news service seemed to say a mouthful about the hard-line thinking of this Tory-appointed Board. And short of courage in the sense they had an opportunity to correct the error but apparently did not have the pluck to admit they were wrong.

From the other side of the cultural divide, members of the Board, including president Gérard Veilleux and chairman Patrick Watson would later argue quite forcefully that they had been left with few options. Other options might have been more damaging to the structure and concept of public broadcasting in the regions of Canada than just shutting down a handful of television stations. But the decision to axe Windsor would stand out as the Board's Black Hole—drawing most of the light, purpose and matériel out of the fast-fading public broadcasting galaxy. Two-and-a-half years after the decision, still smarting, they would reach apologetically into the horrible maw their decisions had generated and talk about "doing something for Windsor."

Although the closing of CBET would end all local programming and theoretically mean about $5 million in annual cost savings to the corporation, Windsor would continue to receive a full schedule of CBC network programs—as opposed to locally produced—from *fifth estate* to *The National* and *The Journal* (later to be *Prime Time News*), from *Fresh Prince of Bel Air* to *Man Alive*. But being able to tune into *Fresh Prince* or *Golden Girls* or *The Road to Avonlea* was not the issue here. Beginning the evening of December 5, 1990, when the citizens of Windsor pulled up their favourite living room chairs to catch the news at 6 P.M., what they would see would have little or nothing to do with the events of their community, no matter where they turned the dial. They would be forced to watch another city's news—maybe London, possibly Toronto, probably Detroit, but not Windsor. It was this unnerving reality that set them marching in the streets.

Certainly the loss of eighty-four jobs was a significant blow, but the crux of the issue was local news; not just words and pictures about traffic accidents and corner store crime, but images of the very community itself. CBET local news was Windsor's "umbrella of protection against cultural acid rain," as then-Mayor John Millson put it. To anyone in Windsor fighting the day-to-day battle against the deluge of American culture, the loss of CBC local news was like being Canadian one minute and being disenfranchised the next. In Calgary and Saskatoon, where local CBC news operations were also cancelled, disgruntled citizens could at least change the channel to either their local CTV network station or a local independent station. Both provided daily news.

But what irate citizens of Windsor knew from living across the Detroit River from the American cultural monolith, and trying day in, day out to retain something resembling a Canadian identity, was that the absence of local television news would make it more difficult to find out what was going on in their community and, perhaps more importantly, how to define themselves culturally. Endless surveys reveal that the majority of citizens receive most of their news via television. They also claim that "local" news is their most popular form of information—providing viewers with a daily imprint of their community. It tells viewers, as only an electronic reflection of community events can, what the cost of life is and will be, whether they are safe or threatened, and whether their children will be able to grow up healthy, happy and wise. Everything else—the change of government in Peru, starvation in Somalia, genocide in Bosnia-Herzegovina, or even the debate over the nation's constitution—is secondary. "CBC local news was a lifeline for all of us," claimed University of Windsor communication studies professor Hugh Edmunds. "It was only through the local news that we had some contact with the community and the country. It was absolutely vital here."

It is not easy being Canadian in Windsor. You not only live in Canada's most southerly point on the map, you actually live south of Detroit, putting that U.S. city—half again larger than Toronto—literally and figuratively between you and the rest of Canada. After years of watching and listening to American broadcast media, your accent is different from that of other Canadians. Your pronunciation skews American. Your sports heroes tend to be Tigers and Red Wings instead of Argos and Blue Jays. Media, especially television, have been the widest pathway to Windsor's cultural confusion.

The CBC Board's decision to close down production of local programming in Windsor meant that the fourteenth largest city in Canada would be the only city of its size in North America without local television news. Even tiny Charlottetown, Prince Edward Island, with a population a quarter the size of Windsor, would end up with local news. Operating a Canadian private television station in Windsor was just not commercially viable because American program distributors set the value of any program on the basis of the size of the Detroit market. The price for an American-produced program in Windsor can often be greater than the cost for distribution in the rest of Canada. Enter the only alternative left for Windsorites to see anything substantively Canadian on their television sets—the CBC.

A 1985 University of Windsor study revealed that the longer you lived in Windsor, the more likely you were to succumb to watching U.S. television—and to begin adopting American ways and interests. On the other hand, the study revealed that if you resisted and remained a steadfast CBC viewer, you would be less likely to visit Michigan, vacation there and be more inclined to think "Canadian" on issues such as free trade. You would even root for the Blue Jays rather than the Detroit Tigers. A follow-up study by Dr. James Winter tested the use of American media and anti-government feeling among Windsorites and concluded that more frequent viewing of CBC television news "was found to strengthen pro-Canadian attitudes," and cutting back on the CBC, including the local Windsor CBC-TV news, would adversely affect Canadian enculturation.

Within days of the CBC announcement, the threat of the permanent loss crystallized Windsor's spirit. In addition to the rally supporters, 57,000 citizens signed a petition of protest for submission to Parliament—the largest petition ever gathered in Windsor's history. Almost one-quarter of the city's population signed the petition—a figure higher than the voter turnout in some Canadian municipal elections. A sixty-member "Save the CBC" committee was organized by the mayor's office. An "Other Options Committee" was formed, chaired by former Manitoba premier Howard Pawley, teaching at the

University of Windsor, and well-known Windsor lawyer, Charlie Clark, Sr. Pawley and Clark were responsible for negotiating between the CBC and the various parties interested in taking over CBC's local broadcasting responsibilities, including a bid from laid-off CBET employees. More than $40,000 was raised through voluntary donations to finance the protest movement and to intervene at public hearings of the Canadian Radio-Television and Telecommunications Commission into the CBC's decision to close regional stations.

Although in the early stages CBC Ottawa Head Office managers encouraged the Windsor committee activities, the only concession CBC offered to cover Windsor's loss was a hastily-conceived new approach to news programming that had been devised by the Board. After squeezing most regions down to one station, and slicing off hundreds of local personnel and production resources, the Board of Directors decreed that CBC news would now have a "regional" coverage mandate, rather than being primarily "local" as before. In Windsor's case, they were informed they would now receive their official CBC news from Toronto.

In Tom Stoppard's play, *Rosencrantz and Guildenstern Are Dead*, Rosencrantz asks, at one point, of his partner's bull-headed intentions:
"Is that what the people want?"
Guildenstern, as if to admonish his friend for such a simple-minded inquiry, replies with a puzzled but superior look, indicating that "the people" had nothing to do with it:
"It is what we *do*!"

As upsetting to Windsorites as the closing of their station was, just as unsettling was the manner in which the CBC senior management group seemed to conduct negotiations over the remnant-future of local news operations. Some locals called the style "duplicitous" or "bizarre" while others were convinced the CBC had "lied" to them, that the entire exercise was a "cock-and-bull story."

"The CBC essentially led us on that there was a chance of something taking place," claimed former CBC producer Jerry Wisdom, a support member of the mayor's Save the CBC committee. "They even held out the hope that at some point the CBC might cobble something together. They'd drop a few hints about doing a half-hour news, things like that."

"In our meetings, they were saying things like: 'Well, things are open . . . give us some options'," Jane Boyd, then assistant to the mayor's office and a member of the committee, recalled. Encouraged by the Board and CBC senior management's overture, Windsor's Other Options Committee looked at three basic options: a private company, Great Lakes-Riverton, with a plan to produce a nightly local news program for about $2 million a year; London station CFPL, which wanted to operate as a CBC affiliate with a Windsor news bureau; and the Windsor TV Employees Group, in which twenty-five of the eighty-four laid-off employees would produce a nightly half-hour news for CBC in Windsor—at a personal initial investment by each of the twenty-five of $10,000.

"We were preparing for a meeting of the Other Options Committee," Jane Boyd recalled. "CFPL did a video presentation, and the employees did a presentation, and what Charlie and Howard were looking at was putting the two together and saying to CFPL: 'Okay, you can do the newscast but we've got [the former CBC employees] we want to take care of and we want you guys to sit down and work something out.' Well, what happened was about an hour before we were to meet, the mayor got a call from Veilleux. He said there is now a Board policy that there will be no other options and we are not going to allow anybody else to use the signal. It was devastating. Everyone felt like they'd just been 'had'."

"It was a con's game," said Wendell Wilks, president of the Alberta Television Network. Wilks entered into negotiations with Head Office managers to purchase television station CBRT in Calgary. "They wanted it all. They wanted us to cover all the expenses of running CBC Calgary's station and indicated that they would keep all the revenue from the station's television advertising. It made no sense at all, unless you were just stalling for time or trying to look to the public like you were bending over backwards to try and work out a deal to save the station. It was B.S., frankly. They'd sit there all prim and proper and ask me: 'If we take all the revenue and you have to pay all the costs, how will you possibly make a go of it?' Well, under those kind of terms, of course you can't make a go of it."

"The terms and conditions they talked about were ludicrous," said Doug Lauchlan, general manager of the Calgary Centre for the Performing Arts and one of Mayor Al Duerr's committee to have CBRT local programming service restored. "They just created a situation where local people would assume all of the liabilities associated with the broadcasting, with essentially no opportunity to raise any revenue. It was obviously designed to pay lip service to the notion that there were options to the station closures."

"In Windsor, the Options Committee was led to believe that there was a possibility of something happening," *Windsor Star* television critic Ted Shaw recalled. "They were holding out this candle of hope and Howard Pawley came back from meetings with them all excited. He felt he had been encouraged, when in reality there was no intention at all of rejuvenating Windsor."

In Saskatoon, a committee of laid-off employees energetically pursued a possible purchase of that city's CBC local news operations, with $40,000 in help from the provincial government. But the CBC had no intention of ever selling operations to its former employees. "But we have to go through the motions," a senior CBC executive admitted on the front steps of CBC's Bronson Avenue Head Office in February, "to make it look good." It was lose-lose for the bidding groups from the start, a charade to avert growing public criticism and the demand from other centres that their local CBC service be restored.

Hearings before the CRTC held in Ottawa between March 18 and 26, 1991 were primarily over revenue and politics, not necessarily stations or public broadcasting. It was an event called to hear why the CBC made the budget cuts it did and to weigh the CBC's request to continue to sell local television advertising, as opposed to national advertising, in a market where it did not provide a local programming service. A 1988 CRTC decision prohibited access to a local television advertising market unless broadcasters provided a local program service. The CRTC was just as interested, on paper at least, to see how much damage the budget cuts had done to the CBC's "Promise of Performance"—essentially the oath a broadcaster swears before the CRTC to be able to receive or renew a broadcast license. The history of the CRTC is replete with broken promises and forgotten oaths, especially where Canadian private broadcasters are concerned. But in this case, an impartial observer would have to say there was very little relationship between the CBC's last promise and its new performance. CBC's Windsor license had most recently been renewed based on a promise to deliver at least eleven hours of local news programming a week. Now they would not deliver any. It seemed a simple open-and-shut case. But Canadian broadcast regulation has more to do with Alice in Wonderland than with reason. As the broadcast regulator for the nation, the CRTC did not have the regulatory power to call the CBC on an obvious violation of its terms and conditions of license. Other than a ruling on the single issue of local market advertising sales, the whole process was an expensive daytime soap opera.

The hearings were an irritant to the CBC. Having "downsized" television stations and abandoned local programming in places like Windsor, Calgary and Saskatoon, the CBC still wanted to be able to collect rents from the locals. They also hoped to eventually sell off property and equipment in closed centres. With national polls showing that two-thirds of Canadians opposed the CBC budget cuts, the hearings were not short of interested parties. There were seventy-five interventions—individuals, unions, Members of Parliament and former employees—presented before the CRTC, out of a total of 213 submissions—a list the CRTC admitted was "unprecedented." In preparation for the hearings, the CBC had provided written answers to CRTC questions. Management skirted the issue of "regional programming" and talked about "a national service, rooted in all parts of the country"—except they had just lopped off some of the parts. The CBC claimed that it would actually "increase the volume of network capacity in the regions" even though production capacity had been significantly reduced. To say, under these circumstances, that the CBC was now "rooted" more than ever "in all parts of the country" would be like saying a Mexican *maquiladora* factory assembling door panels for Dodge trucks just across the border from El Paso, Texas, meant that the Chrysler Corporation was now a wholly-owned Mexican enterprise.

In a document prepared for those taking part in the presentation before the CRTC, CBC managers were informed that the CRTC could not order CBC stations to be reopened, staff to be rehired or revoke licenses. The strong implication was: 'Don't worry. Be happy. They can't hang a thing on us.' The reality was that they were correct. The CRTC could not order the CBC to restore service for Goose Bay, Matane, Rimouski or Windsor. The managers were informed that CRTC commission members would, of course, play to the crowd in their opening remarks. They were told they could largely forget the need for any detailed follow-up, and the general tone of the advice was to let the commissioners and the intervenors get emotional but, above all else, don't get involved in a regulatory food fight. Keep your powder dry. Answer the questions. And we'll ride this thing out.

> *"Commissioners deliver tongue-lashing to* CBC*"*
> *"*CBC *president Gérard Veilleux said Tuesday he considered resigning in December after letting the axe fall on the* CBC*'s budget. . . . His comments came after the* CBC *received a tongue-lashing from* CRTC *commissioners for presenting its plans for service cuts as a fait accompli that couldn't be reversed . . ."*
> —Kathryn Young, *Ottawa Citizen*, March 20, 1991

Day One of the CRTC hearings heard Veilleux repeat his vision of a strong national service, "rooted in the regions"; the CBC had not abandoned local television service (despite the fact that more than 2,000 fewer hours of regional programs would be produced); and supper hours would be redeveloped with a "provincial" focus, a move which he claimed would not lose any audience for the regional news shows. Patrick Watson said the CBC would never go back into local programming "even if there was more money made available." However, Veilleux was on record saying that whenever financial resources were available, "we will reinstate regional programming other than news."

Day Two heard that the CBC intended to recycle redundant equipment and sell off surplus buildings to increase savings. CBC planning and corporate affairs vice-president John Shewbridge told the hearing that he did not think it was true to say the CBC was providing "no local" programming, even though there was not to be any more non-news local programming on CBC television by Board edict. Commissioner Beverley Oda tore a strip off Veilleux and the corporation for not seeking prior approval from the CRTC before announcing the budget cuts (although they did not really have to). Veilleux admitted that things were getting so harried around the CBC and the criticism so personal, that he had considered quitting the CBC, after little more than a year on the job.

Day Three heard a bitter rebuke of the CBC by Calgary Mayor Al Duerr, who called Veilleux's promise to Calgary of maintaining a "window" on Canada for Calgary a "shoddy peep show." But it was Windsor Mayor Millson's day to shine. Patrick Watson later called his performance "brilliant." Millson told the story of how Windsor was about to sign an agreement with the CBC to restore news programming to the city when the CBC did an about-face and the deal was killed by the Board of Directors. It was the case of the bride and the groom being at the altar and somebody called off the wedding, he said. He speculated correctly that the Board changed its position because it was concerned that other cities would demand similar treatment. Millson covered the litany of problems Windsor faced without a local news presence—the cultural threat from Detroit, the fact that CBLT Toronto's new "regional" news show concentrated on "bad" news but did not cover essential community events or issues. He cited a recent fire at a paint factory in Windsor where, because the city no longer had a local television news program, the city was forced to appeal to a Detroit TV station to broadcast details of possible evacuation routes for Windsorites. And, perhaps most significantly, he argued that the CBC had a legal responsibility, not just a cultural responsibility, to maintain a station in Windsor and produce local news for the city.

The CBC had originally been instructed by the CRTC to establish a Windsor station. CBET was opened in 1975 with 119 employees and the promise of fourteen hours of local programming a week. The decision was recognition at the time that if the public broadcaster was not in existence to protect the cultural environment of citizens under the sort of clear threat that Windsor felt daily from Detroit, why would you even bother to have a public broadcasting service? For what fundamental reason would the CBC exist other than to protect Canadian citizens from becoming cultural road-kills? In any other court of reason, a precedent that compelling would have won the day. But this was not a court. This was the Canadian broadcasting system in action.

Day Four heard Toronto economist John Crispo say he wanted less CBC and that he held the corporation "in contempt." The budget cuts were "nothing" and should be considered "a warning to the CBC," said the outspoken Crispo. Figuratively within hours Crispo would be appointed to the CBC Board of Directors by Brian Mulroney.

Day Five saw former CBC president Pierre Juneau make a compelling case that the closing of regional stations was against the law and that the CBC was just kidding itself if it believed that it would have more money now, after the budget cuts, to do more network drama. It is "going to have less money" he maintained—quite prophetically. Juneau also pointed out that CBC's plans for regionalized or provincial news was an "artificial distinction" that was not supported by legislative interpretation. The association of Toronto CBC producers and directors told everyone that, "research shows that people want a local news package . . ." and in a mammoth understatement, argued that the new "regional" or provincial approach to news had not been adequately defined.

On Day Six, Alberta entrepreneur and independent broadcaster Wendell Wilks called Gérard Veilleux and the Board of Directors "an inexperienced CEO and Board trying to make sense of an incredibly bad bit of advice they have received from their staff." Wilks likened the current CBC situation to the sinking of the *Titanic*. The ship "has hit an iceberg," Wilks claimed. "The captain's telling us 'we shouldn't be afraid, there's nothing wrong.' They're deceiving us. They're throwing away the lifeboats. . . ."

Patrick Watson highlighted Day Seven by denying allegations that the CBC had become, despite the closing of regional stations, more centralized; "The exact opposite is true," he said to some disbelief across the country. Gérard Veilleux claimed, in a jingoistic arabesque, that by choosing between regional and network programs, the CBC was choosing national programming, and that "choosing national programming is choosing Canada," although there is nothing specifically called "national programming" in CBC's portion of responsibilities under the *Broadcasting Act*. The CBC is considered the "national public broadcaster," but the priority emphasis for the corporation is on reflecting "Canada and its regions to national and regional audiences, while serving the special needs of those regions."

Veilleux went on to explain that the new definition for CBC regional operations was that "a region is a province (with one station in each) . . . with two exceptions": Ontario and Quebec would have two stations each. But then, of course, there was the "Maritime Region" composed of Nova Scotia, New Brunswick and Prince Edward Island. This style of reasoning no doubt led the CRTC to the conclusion that the CBC was having trouble getting the regions-are-provinces definition worked out in its head, pointing out that "its current structure is not consistent with the provincial model it espouses."

And Patrick Watson, as they say in vaudeville, took us out, by saying that one of the ways the CBC was changing things in the long term—in reference to building news bureaus where stations once stood—was to place more people out in the communities "so they could become advocates for stories there," even though in eleven communities staff with those same duties had been laid off. They would be saying, according to Watson, "we live here, we know this is a good story"—which was exactly what CBC employees were doing in the regions before they were given their lay-off notices after December 5, 1990.

CBC management's main argument to the CRTC was simple: they were going to be short of revenue and needed the cash from local advertising sales in locations where they had decided to eliminate program origination, a matter of $5-6 million (out of $23.8 million gained from local advertising in 1990, out of a corporate gross total of $350 million). Pleading future as well as current poverty, the CBC even projected, for the edification of the CRTC, that "it did not forecast any appreciable growth [in television advertising revenues] until 1993/94." Depending on what "appreciable" meant that statement did not turn out to be quite true.

The CBC also warned the CRTC that if it played around with its "existing revenue structure" (read: cut us off from that $5-plus million in markets like Windsor) it "could render it impossible for the CBC to discharge its mandate." The fact that it had already arbitrarily, and without consultation with the CRTC, chopped off a whole hunk of its mandate when it dispensed with regional production—closing three stations and downgrading eight to bureaus—was, of course, neither here nor there. The "mandate," it seemed, was whatever CBC senior management, like Alice's Red Queen, wanted it to be.

To some, the March 1991 CRTC hearings into the CBC's local sales request, corporate restructuring and budget cut dilemma, not to mention the off-stage antics of the corporation itself, were the funniest thing they had seen on cable television for some time. For the CBC, protecting access to local advertising sales revenue would be a waste of time. By 1992, the combined local advertising revenue in Windsor, Saskatoon and Calgary would be down by more than $2 million. In Calgary, total local and national advertising losses would be $2.3 million. For the people of Windsor, who had fought so hard and paid such a price in time, money and passion, their efforts ended in a fast pump or two of adrenalin, a spasm of heightened expectation of victory, followed by the devastation of an incomprehensible and crushing defeat.

"We had been given the feeling that the face-saving way out for CBC was for the CRTC to simply tell them that they had to do it—do a nightly half-hour news show in Windsor," said Jane Boyd. "Then the CBC could say: 'What can we do? Windsor is a unique situation.' We had every argument [before the CRTC]. What we did with our presentation was to try to craft it in such a way that it gave [the CRTC] a way out." There had been "a real fight" at the CBC Board over Windsor before December 5, 1990. They had been warned by some senior management that closing the station would "come back to haunt us." The Board debated the issue at length but finally refused to reconsider Windsor's unique situation, insisting that it could not break the illusory "pattern"—one station, one province—of allocated station closures.

The big talk at the hearings was about how the CBC was not only now prepared to give in to such a CRTC order, but was actually lobbying to get the CRTC to do just that—give it marching orders so everybody could get out of this ugly mess that was the Windsor closure decision. The tone of everyone's position seemed to change with the Millson presentation. It was humorous, convincing and made it hard for anyone who was paying attention not to try to think of ways to help the city out of its unique predicament. "His presentation got to all of us," former ETV network vice-president Denis Harvey recalled, "so I said to Veilleux at one of the breaks: 'why don't you get a quiet word to the CRTC . . . if they tell us to go back into Windsor and open up a half-hour of news, we'll do it.' I had Peter Kretz [CBC's ETV network head of sales and marketing] look at the numbers. Could we finance a half-hour news show in Windsor? We could pretty well with the extra revenues we were going to get. We couldn't *offer* to go back—the worry was we'd have to then go back into the north shore of the St. Lawrence, and Sydney, Calgary, whatever. But if they *ordered us* back into Windsor *only*, because of how unique the situation was, we'd do a half-hour news. . . . He didn't say anything to me then, but about the end of the day he came up to me and said, 'I got the message through to them'."

"I sort of had the feeling that they understood our situation and were somewhat sympathetic," Windsor's Boyd recalled. "And Mr. Veilleux was always very respectful of the mayor. It was almost as if there was a real friendship there. . . . That thing about the half-hour news was conveyed to us by CBC staff—the fact they were just waiting for the CRTC to order them back into Windsor. It was certainly conveyed to the mayor, that it was 'the way out' for them." In retrospect, Veilleux says he would not have closed Windsor. "I tried everything else to find ways [to reopen Windsor]," he admitted almost two years later. "I even pleaded with the CRTC to tell me to open it. In my closing statement at the CRTC, I told the CRTC, look, help us, tell us. Tell me. I'll do it."

The decision the CRTC rendered on June 28, 1991 crushed hopes that the courage would be there to provide Windsor with some semblance of local nightly news. Like a beat-up, tired old circuit fighter coming out of retirement with a $50 bill tucked into the back of his trunks, the CRTC stepped into the ring for a reputed comeback and went into the tank on the first soft right to the belly. It had no more appetite than the Board of the CBC did for going back into Windsor. "They wouldn't [do it]" Veilleux recalled in January 1993. "[CRTC chairman] David Colville said, 'look Gérard, I heard what you said to us. You told us to ask you to do it and you'd do it. We took that literally. We went back and we were making decisions around the table and the guy from New Brunswick said, well, what about Sydney? And the guy from eastern Quebec said what about eastern Quebec? . . .' He said, 'we're unravelling the whole goddamn thing!' So he said, 'look, we said no.' They had faced exactly the same problem we did."

The CRTC gently touched CBC's wrists with little slaps about not being as "rooted in the regions" these days as the corporation might like to think; about too much news and information programming on the network schedule; and admonished the CBC for not providing enough "details regarding the orientation of its [new] provincial supper hour news." The CBC could not provide details. It had not thought it through yet. News and current affairs staff were still scratching their heads over how they were going to make it work—and would continue to do so for as much as a year or more afterward. Rearing back on their tiny, timid horse, the CRTC declared "strong disapprobation" over CBC's failure to seek prior approval for changes in the status of CBC stations, admonishing the public broadcaster that its "failure falls well short of that expected and required of the public broadcaster."

The CRTC could have provoked a political crisis by refusing to modify the corporation's license, a function that falls within the CRTC's responsibilities to regulate the broadcasting system. It could have just thrown the ball back into cabinet's court, and the cabinet would have been left swinging on its ideological ropes, deciding whether or not the CBC could close the regional stations. But that would have put the blame in the lap of those largely responsible for the CBC not being able to carry out its mandate—the Mulroney government. Instead, the CRTC, using lashing terms like, "has serious concerns" and "will be watching with interest," approved CBC's request to change the status of its stations and program sources, meaning that it was okay to program news for Windsor from Toronto. It also told the corporation it could not "solicit sales" of local advertising. But, the rule simply meant, or was eventually interpreted as such, CBC sales staff could not telephone or drop in on local advertising clients. However, if the client called them, they could do business. "[The ruling] was like the laws of prostitution," said University of Windsor's Hugh Edmunds. "There's nothing wrong with them selling 'local' advertising as long as they don't solicit it. Like the girl in the street: 'I'm not naming prices, but you know why I'm here . . .'."

Only commissioner Paul McRae, a long-time Liberal, in a dissenting minority report, said the CBC's licence amendments should be refused. He recognized Windsor had been unfairly abandoned by the CBC. He slapped the CBC for arguing that the recent massive restructuring of its television programming was not a "fundamental change" in its operations. He obliquely addressed Patrick Watson's argument that the new CBC was more decentralized than the old, pointing out that no matter how you slice it, what the CBC was doing was centralizing, not decentralizing. Pure and simple. As if to drive home a universal point to Watson, McRae pointed out the seminal irony: "At a time when the concepts of regionalism and community are being promoted by government and being strongly supported by Canadians, it strikes me as being strange that the CBC, which is one of our most important institutions, is moving in the opposite direction."

The CRTC decision devastated the Windsor committee. "Everyone thought the Windsor case before the CRTC was so strong. There was a sense we had done it," said Jerry Wisdom. "We were all in the mayor's office. Millson opens the manila envelope. He pulls the decision out. He sits there, skims and reads through for two or three minutes to get to the meat of the thing. He gets to the paragraph. His face falls. Everybody sags. Cameras are rolling. And John's first reaction?

"'Ah, shit!'

"Then he sits there for a couple of more minutes without saying another word, reading to see whether nor not he was reading the right thing. The devastation for the rest of us was just enormous. Disillusioning. Disheartening."

Most citizens of Windsor have gone on with their lives—minus local news. Most do not bother to watch the CBC any more, even network programs. Audience ratings showed that CBC's share of the Windsor supper hour period audience dropped a whopping sixty-three percent between the fall of 1990 and the spring of 1991—from a thirty-eight share to a fourteen share. CBC's share of television viewing overall in Windsor plummeted to a mere seven percent by the fall of 1991—compared to fifty-six percent for Windsorites watching U.S. stations. If there is any doubt that Windsor was punishing the CBC network for bailing out of local television news, that minuscule seven percent figure was less than one-half the audience the original CBC station, CKLW-TV, received—in 1974. Net local advertising revenues dropped a dramatic forty-two percent by 1992. Back in 1974, gross revenues at CKLW-TV were almost $4 million. In 1992, after the decision to stiff Windsor finally sank in to the business community, gross local advertising revenues for the CBC station were $112,000 less than in 1974.

The CBC was also taking it on the chin in radio. A market focus group study held in Windsor, which interviewed listeners and non-listeners of CBC to see what was of interest to them and why they listened or did not listen, revealed that deep-seated feelings of bitterness still existed toward the CBC. Results of the study paralleled the television audience ratings and seemed to indicate that Windsorites were so angry at the CBC over its television decision that some refused to listen to CBC radio as well.

"I seldom watch CBC news any more," said Dr. Marjorie Armstrong-Stassen of the University of Windsor. "Why watch Toronto? The Detroit stations have more Windsor news on than CBLT. For me, there is no incentive to watch CBC. I used to watch religiously, but now I primarily watch Detroit news."

"This was our only TV station!" Jane Boyd pointed out bitterly. "Were we naive in believing all along that the CBC was trying to show us good will? I don't know. I do know that all the good will in the world ended up getting us, at the time, absolutely nothing."

For the Board of Directors, the corporate poltergeist called Windsor never slept. More than two years later, it still noisily stalked their deliberations, jangling the haunting chains in search of a solution. "I have to tell you, Windsor was the peak of awfulness," chairman Patrick Watson admitted in January 1993. "In retrospect, I underestimated the issue," said Gérard Veilleux. "That's one of the few little things I would do differently."

By June 1993, two-and-a-half years after the Windsor gaffe, the corporation was still trying to summon the courage to provide the city with local television news. It was attempting the usual awkward CBC deal—a bit of the CBC, a bit of private sector and a whole lot of caution. The irony was that a "deal" to provide Windsor with local news was never necessary. The funding the CBC needed to re-start Windsor news was there all the time. They just did not see it. The money was there. The will was not.

3 / Making It Up As They Go Along

"The heat is on the CBC: to flatter politicians, to get ratings, to make money, to carve itself up so that the competing private network can make money. The higher the heat the harder it is for the CBC to put good television programs on the air."
—Ken Lefolii, *Maclean's* magazine, February 9, 1963

THE EXERCISE OF TURNING A BUDGET cut target of $108 million into reality, and abolishing an eventual total of 1,216 jobs, was not as orderly and rational as CBC would have the public believe. The confusion, lack of information and loss of purpose that preceded "Black Wednesday" continued for almost three months. Some would say the destructive flailing never did end. In the February 15, 1991 *Globe and Mail* columnist Brian Fawcett took CBC management to task for trying to convey to the Canadian public the impression that the massive television cuts to the regions were "part of an orderly process of restructuring." Without really knowing the details, or how close to reality his suspicions were, Fawcett ended his column by recalling the scene in *Apocalypse Now* where it is suggested that the methods of the mad Colonel Kurtz might be unsound. The reply by Captain Willard was closer to the reality of the CBC situation than any movie fiction: "I don't see any method here at all."

There was no plan to accommodate the Board's direction to cut $108 million. "There was nothing in place," admitted one senior Ottawa manager. "Zip. Zero." As another said to a manager who inquired in some agitation on December 4, 1990 where "the plan" was for the next day: "Read my lips," he instructed the stunned manager. "There is no plan. [Your vice-president] doesn't know what the fuck is going on. But we are going to pretend. . . ."

Time was a big problem. The Board of Directors had not made its final decision about what to do until barely forty-eight hours before the word hit the streets. A staff committee had been quickly formed to oversee the cutting process, but its members had no clear idea of how to do it. They were not even sure if they understood what the Board was after. They would pretend they knew what they were doing—"a lot of fleece and a lot of shit flying around," as one senior manager put it. They would oversee chaos, and add it to the indignity. They would make it up as they went along.

Veilleux publicly cited five major reasons for the projected 1991/92 budget cut: The Tory government's ongoing expenditure reduction program would cost $32 million. Lack of funding for inflation would cost $18 million. A drop in television advertising revenue projections would add up to $30 million. A pay-back to the CBC pension fund would cost $12 million. And there was $16 million in taxes, regulatory and statutory requirements to be covered. To meet these anticipated fiscal challenges, the CBC would quit funding Radio-Canada International ($20 million) and the Parliamentary channels ($5 million), find $7 million in non-program expenditure savings, slip radio services a one percent hit, save $18 million under the "other" category, reduce network television budgets by $12 million and, as the *coup de grâce*, tear $46 million out of regional television operations.

"From the beginning," the annual report for 1990/91 reads disingenuously, "every effort was made to ensure equity and fairness, to minimize involuntary departures, to limit the number of employees with job security but not assignment, and to maintain optimal skill and flexibility in the workplace." From the beginning, in reality, there was confusion, disorder, bickering, in-fighting, power posturing, errors, misjudgement and the odd bit of character assassination thrown in for good measure. One moment Toronto's CBLT news operation was gone, the next it was back. One moment Ottawa's was gone, the next it was back. One day there was one station per province, the next there were two in Ontario and Quebec. The CBC was out of the production of telethons for good. A couple of months later, CBC would be doing telethons. When all the reversals and mistakes were added up, the "shortfall" as it was referred to, or the amount between what they could realistically hope to get back from the cuts they applied and the $108 million target, would total about $13 million. Depending on what day, the number could go higher or lower. Who knew?

On December 6, managers discovered the Board's philosophy of one station per province meant targeting Calgary technicians for lay-off—but ten of them had always been part of the western Canadian crew that produced network sports events such as *Hockey Night in Canada*. "How do you fire a crew and still keep them on staff?" asked an incredulous Toronto manager thinking about the next hockey game in Edmonton. The error would eventually be solved by transferring crew members and their families to Edmonton. The cost—roughly $100,000, not to mention the dislocation to the families—would eventually be added to the bubbling "shortfall." On December 7 it was discovered there was no master lay-off list. Except for staff on programs summarily cancelled, no one really knew which of the original 1,100 positions we were talking about. On December 10, somebody woke up to realize the networks did not know what production capacity they now had across the regions. This was embarrassing because the Board was saying publicly there would be more regional production now than ever before. On December 13, Head Office managers admitted there was no corporation communications strategy in place for these budget cuts—more than a week after the first public announcement. And somebody wanted to know, quietly and timidly, with the extra room now projected to be available in the Windsor station, whether the corporation could store some PCBs there. . . .

On December 14, management posted lists of the positions to be eliminated by the budget cut. The list would change day-to-day, sometimes be redone every few hours. The costs of the lay-off procedure at this point were estimated at $75 million . . . or maybe $100 million . . . or perhaps $125 million. It was also learned that some CBC employees were getting advice from consultants—hired and paid for by the CBC to provide out-counselling services—that they should see lawyers and sue the CBC. On December 17, Head Office finally realized that if you close an operation that has sales people in it, but you want to continue selling commercial advertising in that market, it might be a good idea not to lay off the sales personnel. The costs of these little oversights now added up to a $15 million short of the target. The confusion over who would finally be laid off would result in what amounted to chain-letter termination notices. Managers would hand one out, but if the employee was able to bump someone else, or someone resigned, or there was a management decision that changed the employee's status, the manager would take the letter back, stroke off that name on the list, and fill in someone else's. By December 20, a program for severance packages was finally put in place, allowing certain employees to volunteer to resign, thus saving a job for an employee targeted for lay-off. Line ups for this option started forming immediately. In Vancouver, thirty-five employees came forward on the first day the program was offered. By March 1993, nearly half of all staff affected across the corporation would take the opportunity to get out while the getting was good. Even if you survived the lay-offs, staying around the CBC would not be fun any more.

On January 2, regional managers awoke to the reality that there were no rules for making programs for the ETV network. No one knew how, exactly, to get a program produced under this new "restructured" television operation. Two days later, the budget shortfall was now quoted at $10 million, with still no idea where the estimated $75 million to cover downsizing costs would come from. By January 15, Head Office still could not decide about "equity and fairness"—it was insisting that some staff would get two weeks severance, others three and maybe some four weeks. Regional managers were furious at the inequitable treatment and said so. Head Office also admitted that day that no one really knew how they had arrived at the $75 million estimate for downsizing costs. On January 25, more forgotten costs were built back into the remaining Windsor model, raising the estimates by $1.2 million in Head Office "oversight errors." There would also be added costs for transmitting French programs between Ottawa and Toronto now that the Toronto French station, CBLFT, was gone. Somebody had forgotten that.

By January 26, the shortfall was a definitive $12 million, but three days later it was up to $13 million again. It was estimated the result could be another 200-225 lay-offs. In arriving at the estimates of where to find cash, someone in Ottawa—who had no real idea how programs were put together in the regions—thought the technical crews for supper hours news programs and late evening news programs were two different crews. Often the same crew covered both shows, meaning the dollar estimates were out of whack by hundreds of thousands. On January 30, 960 employees were earmarked to be out of work and 140 positions were to be cancelled. By early April, the number would wilt to 630 laid-off, retired or leaving voluntarily, with

220 shifted to other jobs. The same day—almost two months after Black Wednesday—some managers across the regions finally received copies of the "master plan" for carrying out the downsizing process from the Industrial and Talent Relations department at Head Office. It had few details, no numbers, just time/performance graphs showing who would do what to whom for how long.

While researching material for this book, I wandered into CBC Ottawa's Lanark offices. In addition to my own horror stories, I had been criss-crossing the country, picking up even more sad tales about the damage that had been done to other regions and what the loss of their programs would mean. I was taking the pulse of a mortally wounded organization. No one kidded themselves, though. Many of us knew the CBC's capacity for doing unbelievably stupid things would still remain intact. So, I was not particularly surprised to witness accidently the inauguration—on February 27, 1992, fourteen months after Black Wednesday—of a $100,000-plus renovation of the Ottawa building's cafeteria.

For a moment, with my packsack of budget cut stories and tales and numbers, I thought I was caught in some mocking time-warp. People were laughing and smiling. One wall was adorned with a new, original mural. Tablecloths glistened. Cutlery was clattering and glassware was tinkling. A separate, floor-to-ceiling glass-enclosed area had been constructed exclusively for smokers, like the transporter room out of *Star Trek*. The highlight of the event was a free lunch for employees—a choice of fine beef or poached salmon flown in from one of the coasts, with wine and beer served by smiling, black-tied waiters. A maître d' stood at the entrance to welcome everyone. Like the man in the Engineering department who still raked leaves and filled toilet dispensers in CBC Vancouver, the cafeteria episode was another snapshot of everything that was wrong with the CBC. Producers, journalists and editors went jobless, fewer programs were produced, and cafeterias got renovated. The CBC now only existed marginally to make programs for Canadians; it had its priorities monumentally backwards. After decades of stunted growth and lost purpose, it existed to exist.

Something could eventually rise out of these horrible ashes. Organizations, even crippled ones, can spawn other organizations. But the gene pool of national public broadcasting was now too confused. There were now too many broken DNA floating about to

30   FADE TO BLACK

be able to put back together what had been dismantled. There would be no hope that this battered body could now survive. The Tories were not totally to blame. Their cuts had only made things bloodier. Throughout the late 1970s and early 1980s, governments were demanding the CBC do more with less and less money. The absence of full funding for inflation meant the corporation fell further behind with each fiscal year. New regulatory and tax costs were added every few years. The annual Parliamentary appropriation arched downward, in real terms, as costs went up. The corporation started living day-to-day on the fragile hope that advertising revenues would go up forever. The corporation began to dip into its pension fund surpluses, the equivalent of a householder buying groceries on the strength of a bank overdraft. It was all symptomatic of an organization that could never regain a healthy equilibrium.

What we saw by December 5 was a new administration, urged on by a tense and distracted Board of Directors feeling somewhat hung out to dry by management, trying to make the venerable CBC fit circumstances over which they had very little knowledge or control. The decisions the Board made in the late fall of 1990, to ravage the regions and close stations and cancel programs, were made in distress and panic. But their options had been few. By the time senior management finally came around with the Big Surprise—that commercial revenue estimates might be off as much as $40 to $50 million, according to Veilleux—there was little time to do anything but go for what remained of the gut.

The presentation of options—you could not call it a plan—also reflected a lack of understanding of how the corporation was supposed to work, as much on the part of some senior Head Office managers as the Board. In their bureaucratic frenzy to make the budget trains run on time, they lost sight of what "public broadcasting" was all about, what it was originally meant to be, what its role was and where it fit into the cultural niche of the nation. With little time to reflect, both parties were forced down the path of least resistance by the misbelief that prevailed, that ultimately what really mattered was preserving the network centres. The regions were an expendable element. But this was not the railways of 1930s Italy. This was the CBC.

There are many Canadians who argue that the CBC had it coming. With the kind of public money the corporation was throwing around, and the tight financial times facing everyone in the 1990s, it was just something the CBC had to do. But the CBC had been effectively cutting its budgets since the late 1970s. To properly preserve public broadcasting, without changing the basic purpose, the deeper the cuts went, the more intelligent the cutting exercise had to be, the more precise the planning should have been. But the most frequent fall-back was to cut all budgets a percentage across the board—a penalty on everyone. Programs were cut the same as travel budgets. Drama departments were cut the same as the department that supervised shipping-and-receiving. News department budgets were cut the same as budgets for office cleaning. The process said that, in effect, there were no real and identifiable priorities—in a corporation principally responsible for providing Canadians with unique, public broadcasting programs. Within an organization as complex and complicated as the CBC, the wisest approach to gathering knowledge for decision-making was by speaking with the programmers. But in December 1990, the lowest priority on the corporate scale, unfortunately, was given to conversations with programmers or the preservation of programs.

Unfortunately, it took until the late spring of 1993 before the corporation admitted it had a monumental organizational problem on its hands, and it had better start talking about it. "Opportunity for Change" was a much-overdue effort to get all staff involved in making changes in the way the CBC was fundamentally organized and did business. It solicited input from everybody. It sought ideas on everything from work assignments to training and development, from employment security to how the CBC workforce should be structured. Somewhat ironically, the discussion document referred to the staff as the corporation's "reality check."

When things were coming to a head in the fall of 1990, CBC president Gérard Veilleux, the former secretary of the Treasury Board, had been in office barely a year. Patrick Watson had not yet been installed as chairman. He was given chairman-designate status and acted as special consultant to the president. He would not be sworn in until June 14, 1991. In terms of hands-on leadership and intimate knowledge of the inner workings of the CBC, they and the Board placed themselves at a disadvantage when they decided to rely almost solely on the counsel immediately available to them within the CBC's Head Office, and from the four main networks—English and French radio and television—in Toronto and Montreal. Some of the information the Board would receive came from senior managers with little understanding or experience in public broadcasting, in regional television or, strangely enough, in the structure of the CBC outside Ottawa and Toronto. The counsel they would eventually receive, especially on where in the Corporation $108 million might be found—or whether $108 million was even the number—was not totally misleading or incorrect. It was just that, as sociologist Max Weber wrote about actions within bureaucracies, the initial information will have a tendency to preserve and protect those elements or parts of the organization that are complex and difficult to grapple with—or have to do with your own bailiwick.

What the CBC Board needed from management during 1989 and 1990 was an outline for a bold new corporation, a draft-vision based on historical knowledge and detail—knowledge from recent experience that the CBC could not continue to stumble from fiscal crisis to fiscal crisis. This was the time for a radical view of the future of public broadcasting in Canada. The vision had to take into account programs as a first priority. But what it got as its road map out of the threatening fiscal disaster was a bureaucratic outline of possible options for the Board. These contained some false assumptions. One set of data prepared by Head Office on regional supper hour audiences was referred to by some senior managers as "The Big Lie." The options tried to interpret the public broadcaster's maze through the eyes of administrators in Head Office and, to some extent, Toronto. It helped distort the very essence of what public broadcasting was supposed to be in Canada—a national public service with the origination of its programming rooted deeply, not marginally, in the regions. The summer and autumn of 1990 was a turning point in the history of the CBC. And the folks in Ottawa pointed in the wrong direction, to a passageway, as the Spanish say, with no exit.

> "There are times, however—and this is one of them—when even being right feels wrong."
> —Hunter S. Thompson, *Generation of Swine*

I'm told that George Santayana once wrote, about the working of humans in organizations and institutions, that they were mainly the result of "a vast mass of routine, petty malice, self-interest, carelessness and sheer mistakes. Only a residual fraction is thought." When one tracked the CBC decision-making in search of $108 million, Santayana's dictum seemed to apply. It raised serious question about the quality of management guiding the CBC. It raised the issue of why a corporate leadership felt little need to consult with a wide array of its senior regional and network management. The former Ontario regional director, William Armstrong, who also had been executive vice-president and president between Juneau and Veilleux, was left out of the embarrassing Windsor decision. His only role would be to fly to Windsor and inform the locals that their CBC station was toast. The vice-president of the ETV network, Denis Harvey, the most influential of the corporation's media vice-presidents, had to request that he be present at senior management deliberations over the final decisions for the nation-wide budget cuts. For regional supporters, Harvey's attendance would be a mixed blessing. When push came to shove, he advocated their elimination.

Feedback on options and an assessment of potential reaction from across the system had not been widely solicited by the Board or Head Office before the downsizing went into effect. Directors of television—the people responsible for managing more than $100 million in programs and facilities in the twelve major stations across the country, and responsible for the jobs of more than 2,200 employees, were not consulted at any stage of the process. The result was, for the two months following December 5, an embarrassing and costly confusion of instructions that sparked a widespread sense of paranoia and fear among staff and contributed to the erosion of whatever spirit might have remained after this sad exercise was over.

"So we went to the meeting," Harvey recalled. "Veilleux started [explaining the plan] across the country from Vancouver: 'No problem from Vancouver.' So we get to Calgary and Alberta and he said: 'We decided that we are going to close Edmonton; leave Calgary. Everybody agree?'

"Just hang on a second. I don't agree. You can make an argument with anybody that we are leaving a station in every capital. You're breaking that pattern here. You are going to have tremendous criticism. You are leaving something in Calgary anyway. You've got Newsworld there. So move to Edmonton. That's the capital.

"Instant decision," Harvey recalled with a snap of his index finger and thumb. " 'Fine. Fine.' said Veilleux. Anybody disagree? Everybody agree?' It was just like that," Harvey went on, snapping his fingers six times. "We get to Ottawa and I said, 'you cannot close Ottawa. You just can't. You are going to be accused of blackmailing politicians. Ottawa is your window to the politicians.' Well, he got mad at me at that point and he said: 'Alright. If you are not going to close Ottawa you have got to close Toronto!'

"I said, 'Toronto is too significant a place. How can you close Toronto?' So, I finally said, 'You're leaving Quebec City and Montreal, why can't we be allowed one station in Toronto and one in Ottawa'?"

Everyone was desperately trying to hold to the Board's desired principle of "symmetry"—one station to a region or province. Despite the structural damage the cuts would do, they were trying to apply a consistent philosophy to give their actions some believability. "We were trying to anchor our decision in some principles," Veilleux later explained. "I didn't want this to be just a simple expenditure exercise." But the symmetrical overlay could not hold up in the face of intra-CBC politics and the need, as expressed by Veilleux, laudably enough, to leave a CBC standing with a modicum of regional production capacity. But the principles got contaminated by reality and corporate politics.

Sixteen days after Black Wednesday and the implementation of the first step of the $108 million budget cut, and after numerous conference calls with senior regional managers, staff finally received a formal memo outlining some of the details and guidelines on separation options they were asking for, quite logically, immediately after the budget cut announcement. Because of regulatory requirements set down by the Minister of Labour, various collective agreement clauses and the general lack of planning, few employees to be affected by the lay-offs were aware their jobs were finished on December 5. Head Office was unsure about, and very frightened of, the cost of the entire downsizing exercise. It could go from $75 to $125 million. Each employee's severance situation was different. Each change of a name on the lay-off list changed the total.

They also had no idea where the $75-125 million might come from. If the federal government did not provide extra funding, or some creative alternatives, the CBC was facing the Kafkaesque possibility of being caught in the perpetual motion machinery of endless budget cuts. If they had to find the $75 million from existing budgets, that would mean even more budget cuts and even more staff laid off. This would increase the cost of downsizing, and more cuts would have to take place, more staff be laid off, increasing the costs of downsizing, and so on. "We were looking at a never-ending, downward spiral—cut to finance those cuts, then cut to finance . . ." said Veilleux. The CBC was saved, strangely enough, according to one CBC source, by Ontario's Premier David Peterson's cancellation of the construction of the Toronto Opera House. Part of the money earlier earmarked by the federal Tories to support the project was turned over to the CBC to fund $50 million of its downsizing costs. Nevertheless, it took more than two months after the December 5 announcement for most employees to know whether or not their jobs were eliminated. Staff morale plunged. People avoided talking to one another in the hallways for fear they would find out things about their status they did not want to hear. Confusion reigned— about jobs, about what programs would remain in the network schedule and what ones would not, and, most of all, just where in the hell was the CBC now going?

What helped stir the general state of confusion throughout the entire budget cut process was the lack of any operational plan. A major Canadian corporation was going to suddenly shed about a tenth of its body weight and had little clear idea of how to go about it. Of course, the philosophy of how the CBC would now change as a public broadcaster was stated easily enough by the Board, and endlessly repeated, as if the message's redundancy would somehow help solve the problems piling up at the operations level. But that was the easiest part—making up philosophies.

As part of an effort to anchor decisions in some principles, the Board had trotted out "principles" which restructured media respon- sibility based on certain phantasmagoric notions of how Canadians watched TV and listened to radio. Radio would look after things 'local.' Television would look after things 'regional,' 'national' and 'international.' And the remnants of CBC regional stations would look after 'provincial' or 'regional' news matters. Someone even came up with a catchy new term to accompany the philosophy—'complemen- tarity.' They innocently assumed that if Canadians wanted a local news fix they would just dial up CBC radio. Later in the day, thirsting for news from across their province, they would turn into television viewers and switch on their CBC 'regional' supper hour news. Unfortunately, life in front of the tube and speakers seldom works that way. The demographic profile of CBC listeners is decidedly different from CBC television viewers.

"I thought the idea was horseshit," said one blunt-speaking former vice-president. "I can remember saying at meetings: 'This is nonsense. There is no cross-over between radio and television audiences. You've got to stop thinking that there is 'complementarianism.' There isn't'." But he was fighting against the Board's need to come up with a justification for the damage they had done to the regions, one that would sell to Canadians and look neat and business-like despite the chaos.

Six o'clock supper hour programs—the last vestige of local production—were declared to have a 'regional' mandate. But what did 'regional' mean? There were no guidelines handed down. Did it mean one program per province, as some said? If so, why was Ottawa getting its own 6 P.M. news as well as Toronto? Did 'regional' mean to expand local news from predominantly urban coverage to encompass a whole province? How could this be done? Supper hour budgets were being cut, not enriched. Or did 'regional' mean exchanging local or provincial material inter-provincially?

Veilleux told the CRTC the new regional news mandate would mean "a more focused role for regional television," and would not lose audience. In fact, it diffused the focus. There is no such thing as regional news the way CBC defined it. The assumption would be terribly ill-advised. It would help fracture morale even beyond the impact of the cuts, confuse and sometimes amuse veteran news personnel, be inconsistently applied across the country and drive almost half the news audience away from CBC. A year-and-a-half after the decision, news producers and local station managers were still struggling with the concept. Staff were shifted here. Cameras were added there. Eventually, more staff were even hired to, ironically, replace some of the news personnel despatched on December 5, 1990. Tens of thousands of dollars were spent on conferences and meetings to discuss the changes. The philosophy was debated among news executives and its application in some markets simply ignored. The 'regional' news philosophy ended up being whatever local producers wanted it to mean. It certainly was not a policy uniformly applied across the country. And CBC regional news ratings plummeted.

In places like Calgary, tens of thousands of viewers would abandon

CBC supper hour news. By 1993, the Calgary audience for their regional CBC news—produced out of Edmonton—had fallen to less than 14,000 viewers, from a 1985/86 high of 126,000 viewers when CBC's *The Calgary Newshour* had been the most popular supper hour news program in the city. By the summer of 1993 corporate embarrassment would be so great that they would backtrack from their regional news edict and begin to stuff extra manpower and resources back into the station. News staff complement would rise by 15 to 20, masking the fact that there would now be as many news camera personnel as the station had in 1985. But the ultimate humbling about-face was the announcement that "local" news would return to Calgary in the fall with a half-hour portion of the early evening newscast hosted, not by CBC Edmonton's Bob Chelmick, but by a yet-to-be-named Calgarian. Across the country the 'regional' concept would be so alienating to CBC viewers that by the end of January 1993 the national audience for all CBC supper hour programs would drop from a late-1980s high of 1-1.2 million to about 600,000—a figure roughly equal to the audience for *one private news operation*—Vancouver-based BCTV. The decision also had severe commercial revenue implications for the CBC. While overall advertising revenue inched up, net advertising income for English community stations dropped by $14.5 million between 1990 and 1992, largely in response to the 'regional' news decision.

Other rules or guidelines which did exist for the downsizing exercise kept changing. The hard-and-fast doctrine laid down so emphatically on December 5—absolutely no regional programming in the future except in news, for instance—became more fluid and subject to change as time and lobbying pressure marched along, and as the unexpected public backlash to the cuts began to sink in at the Board's doorstep in Ottawa. One of the most embarrassing corporate spins for regional managers to digest was the flip-flop on the order that all regional television stations would cease production on *local* programs immediately—*verboten*, full stop. This instruction included telethons produced by the regional stations. Regional managers began telling staff and the public who inquired that telethons were cancelled. But by December 10, the future of regional telethon productions mysteriously evolved back into a "maybe" category. By December 13, Head Office informed everyone they were a definite "no" again. By December 19, they had graduated again to the level of a "could be." By January 3, the "no telethons" decision was reversed. What confidently and emphatically had been relegated to the history of Canadian public television on December 5, found its way—along with the potential for other types of regional production—back into existence. The telethon incident was followed by the resurrection of the Maritime region series, *Land and Sea*, as a "network" series in the summer of 1992, thanks to strength of the outcry from the public and politicians.

At various points in the turmoil Gérard Veilleux was quoted as saying that the CBC—presumably meaning the president, the Board and chairman-designate Patrick Watson—had "no choice" but to deliver the blow to the corporation in the way in which they had. Senior management and the Board had been forced to opt for the quickest fix for the corporation's financial plight. But a potential blueprint for restructuring had existed for over a year. "The English Media Consultative Process," or "Committee of 600" as some named it, after the number of employees estimated to have taken part in the process, was a product of the 1989 twilight period of the Juneau administration. It was a bottom-up effort to plan ways of meeting the start of the four year, $140 Mulroney government slash of CBC funding. In the words of Pierre Juneau, the process was set up to look at "everything we do, how we do it, and how we can do it less expensively, or whether we need to do it at all." Most importantly, it was staff-driven. It utilized people who knew how the CBC worked down at the shop floor level.

Its most passionate affirmation was that programs and stations were the very heart of why the CBC existed, and had to be protected at all costs. The entire system would have to be drained dry of options before programs were touched. Why else would you be in public broadcasting if it were not to make programs? The committee had maintained that the CBC must remain a national service, "rooted in the regions, with the capacity for local, regional and national production." The committee's report took aim at Head Office elements of the corporation and recommended severe cuts or elimination of non-programming services. The report also called for a review of the then-estimated $381 million Toronto Broadcast Centre and for the CBC to consider alternatives, "up to and including abandoning the project and selling the site" it was being built on. As estimated all-in costs of the Centre began to bounce above a billion dollars in 1992, the foresight and wisdom of the committee would seem to greatly exceed that of the CBC's Head Office planning and engineering arms. These were not people who endorsed the Board's Neutron Bomb philosophy of budget cutting—eliminate people and leave buildings standing.

"It was the beginning of a process to try to get people on board, to buy into a common set of solutions," said one regional manager bitterly. "I think there were people [in Head Office] working hard to make sure that the process didn't continue because it wasn't in their best interests. They discounted the process. That was the message they were giving Veilleux: 'This is a bunch of whiners, a bunch of complainers. This is just bitching. Its all finger pointing. . . .'"

To Veilleux, the consultative committee report was enlightening, although he admitted that in the end, the recommendations did not influence him a great deal. "I was frightened by what it told me more than what was written," he said obliquely. "The amount of rivalries and lack of corporate will and corporate view was just frightening. There was no sort of cohesion." Welcome to the CBC. But for Veilleux, the most significant revelation, even at this early stage in his tenure, was that "the networks would want to dominate my life, particularly television"—to the fatal detriment of the regions. The official response was that the report had been taken fully into account during the 1990 budget cut deliberations, but, in fact, very little of the report's major structural recommendations ever did see the light of day. The consultative committee was correct on one point: cuts to stations and programs would be "short-sighted and wrong."

"When we get public disputes about broadcasting, they always seem to be about politics or administration or advertising or some kind of manoeuvring. Seldom about the things that count, which is what comes out of the box and what it says and does to people. . . . The CBC is full of . . . bureaucrats determined to keep everything tidy and neat . . . it's not much wonder the CBC is in trouble."
　　—anonymous CBC producer quoted by Ralph Allen in
　　Maclean's magazine, February 9, 1963

Thanks to a sclerotic bureaucracy, divisional competition and in-fighting between the networks and Head Office, and a national economy on the downslide, the CBC got caught with its fiscal pants down. A public corporation that spent almost $8 *billion* in public funds throughout the 1980s, not including over $800 million in capital funds, simply misjudged how much money it might have—not would have—by a wide margin.

One of the problems was that the corporation had been playing cute with its advertising revenue projections for years, pushing the outside of the envelope each year, cockily gambling that spectacular growth in advertising revenues would go on forever. During the 1980s, advertising revenues grew faster (thirty-six percent) than the Mulroney government could cut CBC budgets (a little more than eleven percent). "It is one thing if you're happy raising revenue as 'found money' and investing it in one-time things," said Board member William Neville. "It's another to convince yourself that this money is there forever, and build your base of operations on that premise." Neville was one of the members of the Board frustrated over the corporation's continued effort to paper over its expenditure shortfalls with commercial revenue. "I kept saying not only that I thought this an odd sort of accomplishment for a public broadcaster. We were sowing the seeds of a serious problem, because booms come to an end. There's always retraction and we're going to get caught by it."

Although management projections as early as the spring of 1990 called for roughly a $50 million total shortfall for fiscal year 1991/92, most in Head Office felt the problem was "manageable." In May the senior staff were instructed to draft a set of options for the Board to review. The networks had factored in the usual revenue growth percentages, but during the late summer, network sales managers reworked their projections, figuring in new, bleaker economic information, and reported to Head Office that sales revenue projections might be off a bit.

Out across the country, the weeks between October and December 5, 1990 were full of rumours but no real information on where the Board and senior management were going to find the millions needed to meet the 1991/92 budget problem. Regional supper hours programs, representing about $50 million on the hoof, were high on the list of suspected targets. Many ETV network managers, Head Office officials and some Board members had for years asked the rhetorical but unresearched question: "Why not just get rid of the supper hours? They look just like the competition, and they don't attract much audience, and they cost a lot of money and . . . ." But CBC regional supper hour programs were one of the last physical links between CBC-TV and the citizen. They were exceptionally well-received in their communities and had a better "reach" (more people tuned in) than *The National*. Combined supper hour audiences on the owned-and-operated CBC stations were actually outdrawing *The Journal* by eleven percent. Supper hour shows were one of the largest contributors of audience tuning to the CBC network. But their detractors never let the facts stand in the way of a good lobby.

Conventional wisdom had it that you could not get that kind of money from staff support departments—Engineering, Human Resources, Communications—because these departments had arguably been cut in the past. Head Office was apparently no longer a target, having been cut by about twenty percent the previous year. A major budget cut might have initially handicapped both television network systems, located in Toronto and Montreal. But a cut administered to the networks would probably have been less disruptive in the eyes of the Canadian public. The economic impact might have been felt in the two urban centres. The emotional impact of the cuts would hardly have been felt at all. The move would not have generated the nation-wide backlash that the decimation of regional programming did. But the networks were where the power was, and power was the name of the game at the CBC, as it is in life.

In fact, Veilleux seemed so smitten by the intractability of this thing called 'networks' that he wrote to the CRTC's David Colville (or the text was written for him by Head Office officials) on January 11, 1991 that deep cuts to network budgets had been considered as one of many options but rejected "because national network programming is the most essential and distinctive component of the CBC's television and radio mandate." CBC network television? Essential? Distinctive? Who was he kidding? Radio? Its distinction lay in its regional programming. Veilleux was seemingly prepared to defend a concept that fractured rather than reinforced Canadian public television. He hinted at it even more strongly when in the same correspondence he wrote that wiping out the regions down to simple bureau status had some "attractive features." Beyond generating "the largest savings," saying good-bye to the regions would preserve and strengthen "the CBC's distinctive network services, and would clearly represent a new vision for the Corporation." A new vision alright—in the rear-view mirror. Where was he getting his counsel?

So of course the first item on most menus of potential entrées to meet the corporation's 1991/92 fiscal diet was to close down all regional operations—every station, all the staff, every regional program, every last manifestation of the CBC, other than tiny bureaus, in places outside Toronto or Montreal. Like hungry dogs growling over a skimpy bone, the big ones were baring their fangs first. The idea was attractive alright, to bureaucrats. But it had nothing to do with the ethos of Canadian public broadcasting.

Two years later, Gérard Veilleux's version of events had him playing defender-of-the-regions. "We had long, long discussions about that," Veilleux remembered. "And they'd say, 'Ah, now it's time! Finally! Let's solve the goddamned problem [and kill the regions].' I'd said, 'look, we do that and we kill the CBC. I didn't come here to kill the CBC. So we anchored the principle of radio being 'local' and television being more 'regional' to try to preserve the regions. But all the advice I was given—pfffft!—the regions, gone." In a strange, almost incomprehensible twist of public service logic, some of these same Head Office and network management advisers eagerly telling him to axe the regions were also vocal in their support of two inconsequential peripheral services—the financially haemorrhaging CBC Enterprises and Radio-Canada International—the voice of Canada in such 'regional' places as North Africa and Ukraine. Is it any wonder Canadian public broadcasting was in trouble with these guys in the driver's seat?

"Those people don't understand this country. They've never seen half of it," claimed a former Toronto producer, now a regional manager. "They're basically Toronto-types or Montreal-types who have not experienced what it means to be a 'regional broadcaster'. I can remember working in news and having the Toronto national assignment editor telephone me and ask me if the 'well-head' price of gas was the price you pay at the gas pump! He was the national assignment editor! Another national assignment editor asked, 'what is potash, anyway'? It is a clear sign that they are out of touch with the rest of the country."

"The TV business is uglier than most things. It is normally perceived as some kind of cruel and shallow money trench through the heart of the journalism industry, a long plastic hallway where thieves and pimps run free and good men die like dogs, for no good reason. Which is more or less true.

For the most part, they are dirty little animals with huge brains and no pulse . . ."
—Hunter S. Thompson, *Generation of Swine*

There were other parallel forces hard at work, seeking to change irrevocably the face of Mother CBC. One was the continuing influence of commercial advertising on the ETV network. Federal government funding for the CBC had always been a carrot and stick affair. Tied to one-year funding and legally unable to borrow money or carry over deficits, the CBC had to rely on massive amounts of commercial advertising revenue to get by each year, mostly from its ETV network cash cow. More than a quarter of CBC's total expenses were covered by advertising revenue. In 1992, net advertising revenue was $320 million, up from $160 million in 1984 when the Tories took office. Another $57 million came in the form of "miscellaneous" revenue, from Newsworld cable fees, interest, rentals and program sales. Under the Tories, Parliamentary appropriations fell from seventy-eight percent of CBC's total operating budget to sixty-nine percent by 1989. The difference was covered by turning up the burners on television advertising sales.

The dependence on commercial advertising revenue was a huge, double-edged sword, especially where the corporation's single most noticeable entity—the ETV network—was concerned. It was both saving and killing the CBC: saving in the sense the money was needed to keep the corporation running; killing in the sense it corrupted the function, operation and look of public television programming. As William Neville put it, undue reliance on more and more revenue was just "putting off the day of reckoning," a sort of mesmerizing dependency that would inevitably "come back and bite you." It also solidified program decision-making in the hands of Toronto network television executives dedicated, as much as anything, to making CBC-TV meet the needs of advertisers as much as those of the Canadian public. Network programs had to become more "urban," hip and popular, eventually distorting the image the audience and public had of the CBC, and of themselves. By January 1993, when the new *Prime Time News'* demographic profile—age, gender, education level, average income, employment status—skewed younger than the old *National* and *The Journal*, ETV network officials sounded pleased, even though the audience rating share for the re-jigged evening news show was less than that for *The Journal*.

This huge thirst for increasing commercial revenue opportunities would also help drive Canadians away from CBC television. By the end of March 1991, audience share for the ETV network had dropped to an all-time low of fifteen percent. The prime time programs ETV network program head Ivan Fecan confidently claimed "worked" for Canadians in 1991 would lose six percent in the first quarter of the new season—while CTV gained thirteen percent. Patrick Watson's pronouncement that the new program changes announced before the CRTC in March 1991 would mean an "electrifying new direction for the CBC" was dismaying, if not pathetic, rhetoric. By the time the network schedule did change drastically in the autumn of 1992, their audience share had tumbled further into the low teens.

By March 1993 the ETV network's share of all-day adult viewing dropped another eighteen percent from the previous March. At the same time as the audience was marching away from the ETV network in battalion numbers, the CTV network was enjoying an audience resurgence unparalleled in North American network circles. Where once CTV parried with the CBC in the twenty to twenty-two percent share range, the private network was now revelling in a prime time share touching on a full one-quarter of the Canadian audience. After the ETV network introduced *Prime Time News* in 1992, CTV *News* ratings shot up twenty-two percent.

Despite the happy talk about attracting a younger audience, by the spring of 1993 an embarrassing drop in audience was beginning to be seriously felt on the revenue side. Panic was beginning to set in. Except for the advertising revenue expected from the Stanley Cup play-offs, the chances of being able to charge advertisers the same high commercial rates for CBC programs that were losing massive audiences were slim and none. "Unless they do something drastic the bottom is going to fall out of their commercial revenues when summer comes," said one private station sales manager. The summer of 1993 would be the time the CBC would have to go before advertisers and agencies—not unlike Olympia and York going before its bankers—to try to convince them they should still pay the same high advertising rates for programs that had lost huge numbers of viewers.

"I think it is one of the sad things that's happened to the CBC—the commercialization," Denis Harvey admitted. Under Harvey, CBC's reliance on advertising revenues almost doubled. "There is no question it started to affect our programming, without any doubt." Harvey talked about the loss of performance programming on the ETV network—opera, ballet, symphony, major variety specials—as a direct result of the need to achieve large audience ratings, satisfy advertisers and increase commercial revenues. "When Ottawa would give us our budget target we would look at it and say: 'Well, are we going to spend $1 million out of it on a [producer] Norman Campbell ballet or opera?' And we know we can't get any revenue from it, and it's prime time, Sunday night, two hours . . ." said Harvey, thinking of the poor ratings the program might attract. "The combination of the cost of these kinds of programs and no [commercial] revenue . . . there was no question that performance programming was lost as a result of the commercial pressures."

This impulsive hunt for advertising revenue also meant the network would grab opportunities to buy specific U.S. programs with no other goal in sight than the money that program would bring in. "We bought U.S. mini-series every year for one reason only—to make money—because it allowed us to 'package' it, run it in simulcast [with the U.S. release] even though it would mean we would have delayed *The National* and *The Journal* for three or four nights in a row . . . because those series were running [on the U.S. network] between 9 and 11 P.M." Harvey admitted. "And we did that every year for three or four years because the revenue was several millions of dollars. And again, it was because we were trying to reach those *goddamn* revenue targets that we set, because we knew that otherwise we would have to cut our budgets."

Through much of the 1980s, the ETV network entered each fiscal year facing large operating shortfalls. In 1988/89, the first year of television's "Canadianization" plan, the estimated shortfall was as much as $27 million. To do all it wanted to do the network could either cut budgets by that amount, or turn up the burners on its advertising sales. In the first official year of the cultural repatriation plan for Canadian content on English television, some of the "All-Canadian Specials" displayed on the ETV network included *Down and Out Donald Duck, Trapper John MD, Garfield's Nine Lives, Garfield's Christmas, Meet Me in St. Louis* and *The Disney Easter Parade.*

In the mid-1980s, commercial time was also increased in the regional supper hour news shows to a maximum allowable of twelve minutes in the hour, turning these local news programs into little "cash calves." The move to capture more commercial revenue cut total local news content for viewers across the country to roughly forty-five minutes and raised millions of dollars of untapped revenue for the CBC—the only reason it was done.

Prime time ratings, not public service or authenticity, were the hormones driving the urges of the Toronto-based ETV network. This was not just a distortion of CBC's public television responsibilities. It was also a fool's game. Pursuing the advertisers' need for the young-and-restless did not represent the interests, tastes or the reality of the rest of Canada. This public-broadcaster-as-shill mentality reached one of its low-water marks when some network management tried, unsuccessfully, to get the Ottawa producers of the folksy, heavily-rural regional series, *On the Road Again* to give the show a more "urban" or "city" look. Even though the series had been extremely popular, drawing 100,000 viewers in the Ottawa area alone, network programmers wanted changes before the show played across the country. They wanted the name changed. They also wanted the producers to make their popular host, Wayne Rostad, look more "downtown"—interpreted to perhaps mean they should have Rostad dressed by Harry Rosen. "I think we make a mistake playing the numbers game," said one eastern-based regional manager. "To me, the CBC isn't a numbers game. It became a numbers game for commercial reasons. We were never supposed to be a populist service. We became a populist service because we needed the money. And now, we are driven by commercial interests."

This drive to make most CBC entertainment programs marketable by urban, American television standards simply sped the spiral of the corporate deathwatch. The less the federal government contributed, the more commercial revenue the CBC had to chase after. The more they caught, the less the government had to contribute. The more they chased, the more the network had to stylize programs and series to look like the competition. The more the CBC looked like the competition, the less Canadians were able to distinguish their public broadcaster from the rest of the North American television chaff. Until, finally, one study revealed most Canadians could not tell the

CBC from CTV or anybody else. The CBC's famed *Road to Avonlea* co-production was considered by a majority of those polled to have been broadcast on CTV, because of all the commercials in the show.

A 1991 CRTC-commissioned survey revealed that Canadians found CBC English-language television programming the least appealing of any television network. Only sixteen percent thought the CBC's English programming "very appealing" while a massive forty-three percent ranked PBS programming, the American public broadcaster, just that—very appealing. The CBC's own data showed that commercials in programs could negatively affect the size of your audience. A tracking of the history of viewers to commercial-free programs such as *The National, Marketplace* and certain children's series revealed that audience levels stayed relatively steady for more than a decade for these programs, while audiences for heavily commercialized programs such as *World of Disney* and *Hockey Night in Canada* declined by half over twenty years.

To add to the viewer's confusion, the CBC maintained as many as twenty-eight affiliate agreements with private television stations across the country. These affiliate stations carried part of the CBC network schedule and any other program from any other source they chose. In some affiliate areas "the CBC station" could broadcast *The Nature of Things* the same evening it broadcast the seediest U.S. sit-com, or follow *The National* and *The Journal* with a twentieth-century version of Back-to-the-Bible Hour. Somewhere in that video jungle of cheesy furniture warehouse commercials, David Suzuki and born-again religious programming was, in the minds of confused viewers, "the CBC." The only other image that seemed to materialize in the minds of many Canadian viewers and taxpayers was one of a public broadcaster that looked little different from the private broadcasters—except that, to them, it cost a billion dollars a year.

4 / The Potemkin Village

"In the beginning the Corporation attracted two types . . . people who were creative and people who wanted to work for a nice organization and dig themselves in. These second people dug in and assumed control. In the old days people sacrificed titles and offices for the sake of programs. But titles are what a bureaucracy lives for. See, the only thing now they will sacrifice is the talent. They'll cut down on that to save money. Some of these people would be much happier if there were no programs."
—Harry J. Boyle, *Maclean's*, April 2, 1966

THE CBC IS AN ENIGMA, a large and not terribly efficient enigma. To some Canadians "the CBC" is simply a channel on their television set, not significantly different from the private stations, or a comforting and intelligent spot on the radio dial. To others, it is a baffling host of programs, people, buildings, trucks, cameras, politics, personalities, controversy and dollars—hundreds of millions and millions of them, year after year. To say you understand the CBC and how it works is similar to saying that you understand with clarity the theory of quantum mechanics. Its structure is distant and labyrinthine. Its spending and accounting of public funds is mysterious and bordering, as some managers laughingly admit, on the occult. "I'm a professional accountant," said one CBC financial manager, "and I can't understand the way they break the figures out." The financial statement used to build the annual report is "more of a political document than a financial responsibility document."

The CBC is an organization that is loved, despised, ignored, admired, resented, treasured and reviled. It is seen as a reassuring and friendly neighbour, or an arrogant and aloof bureaucracy. It is Peter Gzowski gently drawing word-images of life in Whitehorse, or it is three different CBC television crews arriving at the same event, at the same time, to cover the news in three different ways. It has been our "national theatre" and an "electronic bridge connecting the country." It has also been "a drain on the Canadian taxpayer" and "a haven for socialists and left-wingers." It has been a six-decade long vehicle of creative expression for literally tens of thousands of talented Canadians—writers, actors, performers and musicians. It was, at times, a source of uniquely Canadian information, entertainment and enlightenment. To many of us who have been allowed inside, the CBC has been a wonderful way to express yourself creatively and intellectually—your own personal sandbox of cultural ambition.

People talk and write about the CBC as if it had a single production function—what a fine "CBC documentary," what a moving series by Newsworld, what a wonderful "CBC television movie"—as if it were making massive numbers of television programs and sending them out over the public airwaves. In fact, these days the odds are the documentary was produced by an independent producer or the National Film Board, the Newsworld series came from the BBC and the movie was probably produced by an independent, largely with Telefilm Canada funding. The CBC was the broadcaster. In so far as tying us together is concerned, the only creative linkage Canadians outside of Toronto and Montreal have their hands on is seven hours a day of CBC Radio and an hour-and-a-half of supper hour TV news.

The CBC is still a multitude of component parts, modules that move back and forth awkwardly, in and out, like the shifting colours of a cultural kaleidoscope. It has so many different shapes and forms and duties that it resists definition by the simple use of the term "the CBC." It would be like saying that we all share the same image when someone uses the word "neighbourhood."

Some days it is an organization that best resembles the Roman Catholic Church. It has a literal dogma that almost defies time and change. It has aloof and distant cardinals, and offended and angry bishops. It has a Vatican that is rich and powerful, and it has congregations who keep feeding the wooden collection plates yet are told, not asked, what it is they want out of life and worship. It is an organization designed and managed like something out of the early 1960s. The CBC operates with a heavily centralized management structure—today more than ever before—where communication and ideas come top-down and whole layers of staff are left out of the deliberation process. The public, the people who pay the bills and listen to the radio and watch the television programs served up by the corporation, are most often an abstract part of the deliberations. It is a place, as mythographer Joseph Campbell has said, like a "wasteland" where "people are fulfilling purposes that are not properly theirs but have been put upon them as inescapable laws."

The CBC is either an entertainment bargain or a public company that squanders the better part of a billion taxpayer dollars a year. It is the last gasp of a national culture, or a public corporate trough with television producers who have gone as much as two years without producing anything, and unionized staff running up hundreds of thousands of dollars in needless overtime and meal displacement allowances. It is said to be the single most influential force for culture in Canada and yet its share of the English television audience is marginal, and falling, and its English radio audiences are small, loyal, but aging. It holds more than a billion dollars in assets, or it only costs thirteen cents a day per Canadian. It is an organization that is too fat, or one trimmed so lean it cannot perform the tasks Parliament and the public demand of it. It is a broadcaster that is too close to government, or one that refuses to do the government's bidding.

The CBC spends $1.35 billion a year, which works out to $3,698,000 a day, seven days a week; $154,000 an hour, or $2,568 per minute. After December 5, 1990, it eliminated 1,216 jobs and yet, by 1992, the annual budget for salaries and wages went up $38 million, from $520 million to $558 million dollars. While the CBC made fewer programs between 1988 and 1992, expenditures for the administrative bureaucracy of the National Broadcasting Service portion, referred to as "Operational Management and Services," and not including corporate Head Office and Engineering costs, went up fourteen percent, from $96 million to $109 million dollars.

For the fiscal year 1991/92, the CBC received a total of $1,031,037,000 from Parliament (down from $1,078,430,000 in 1990/91) in the form of operating funds ($900,562,000), capital ($126,475,000) and working capital ($4,000,000). The balance came from television advertising sales and other revenues. The annual amount of money Parliament provides to the CBC would subsidize 86,000 Canadians at the poverty line for a year, or cover first year university tuition fees for 500,000 Canadian kids, books included. On the other hand, the CBC's current annual billion dollar appropriation is only one-fortieth of the interest paid each year on the national debt, and its $49 per year per capita cost is light years away from the roughly $17,000 each of us shares for that same debt.

The CBC is not the largest broadcast organization in the world, but it is one of the most complex. It delivers its program services in two official languages, plus native languages in the North. It operates or manages ten networks—three in English (TV, Radio-AM and Stereo-FM) and three in French, as well as Newsworld, Radio-Canada International, the Northern Services for the Territories and the Yukon and the National Satellite Channel (the Parliamentary channel). It does this over five time zones, or roughly the geographic distance between London and Karachi. The British Broadcasting Corporation has twice the budget of the CBC and operates in one time zone, in one language.

Reading through the bulky mass of money spent by the CBC and on what, the extent of corporate holdings, the tonnage of programs produced and the analysis of cash, expenses, liabilities, depreciation and equity figures probably ranks up there with the report of one of the former Soviet Union's five-year plans: harvests in billions of hectares, millions of gallons of fuel used, hundreds of thousands of labour hours, transportation and shipping costs in carloads and rubles. The numbers are imposing, sometimes shocking. They are not of a magnitude that reflects a light, fast creative organization capable of responding to the emotive impulses of a culture.

According to CBC statistics, in 1992 the CBC spent $697 million in salaries and related expenses ($108 million of that figure in salaries for its nearly 2,000 managers alone); an additional $308 million in payments and royalties to writers and performers; $70 million to distribute programs; $44 million in overtime. Its pension fund was the twentieth largest in the country in 1991 with assets valued at more than $2 billion. Perhaps just as stunning in their simplicity are numbers such as $1.2 million a year for postage, $2 million for office equipment rentals and maintenance, $2 million for videotape, almost $1 million for grounds maintenance, $1.5 million on entertainment and receptions, $4.1 million on consultants, $3.9 million for stationery and a $14 million corporate light bill.

According to government estimates for 1991/92, the CBC costs about four times more than it cost to operate the House of Commons and the Senate combined. What the CBC spends in one day would have covered the annual cost of the Advisory Council on the Status

52   FADE TO BLACK

of Women. The $2.5 million annual cost of the defunct Court Challenges Program would have been covered off by what the CBC spends on books, papers and periodicals. Salaries and wages for CBC employees in Ontario alone ($148 million) would more than cover Parliament's appropriation for Telefilm Canada's support for a nation full of independent television and film producers. CBC's bill for surveys and ratings in 1992 ($5.4 million) would have easily covered the estimated cost of the Law Reform Commission ($4.9 million). The corporation's $8.9 million for consultants, legal and professional fees would cover this year's cuts to the Canada Council. The Art Gallery of Ontario's $4.5 million operating deficit could be covered by the amount the CBC increased its spending on advertising and publicity in 1992. The Toronto Symphony's $3.7 million 1992 debt could be covered by what CBC spends in an average year on computer lines and PC software. The estimated cost of sending 311 athletes and 169 officials to the 1992 Barcelona Olympics could have been covered by what the CBC spends on building cleaning services.

Although the number of employees on CBC rolls fell between 1988 and 1992, the total cost of salaries went up, with the average salary going from $41,300 to $53,400 a year. Union salaries increased an average of 5.2 percent. Management salaries went up 4.3 percent on average. Senior management payroll—the executive and other Head Office managers—increased by 5.4 percent. Yet expenditure on training in an organization with close to 2,000 managers and over 10,000 employees was disgraceful. Officially, the CBC spent only $2.48 million, or about $230 per employee on training—an amount that included $356,000 in membership fees and tuitions. In late April 1993 the CBC finally announced, in tandem with the release of its report on media accountability, that it would boost the budget for training and development $4 million each year over the next two years. But the money was primarily for journalists. There was no word on training for managers. In the private sector, companies can spend from $500 to $2,500 per employee each year on training and development. Based on broadcast industry standards, the CBC should be spending closer to $40 million a year on training. According to officials of the European Broadcasting Union, anything less than three-to-four percent of total expenditures spent on training would mean a broadcaster would be locked into "a descending spiral of incompetence." I have seen the spiral.

"CBC pension fund aims to buy brokerage: firm would trade on its own account"
"The CBC Pension Fund is seeking permission to buy a stockbroker, becoming the first of that industry's major clients to take its business in-house. . . . The purchase of the firm, which is inactive, would give the pension fund a seat on the TSE."
—Dan Westell, *Globe and Mail*, July 21, 1992

In 1992 the CBC sat in the middle of Canada's top 500-rated companies, according to the *Financial Post Magazine*. It was ranked No. 251 by sales or operating revenues. According to *Report on Business* magazine, it is the ninth largest crown corporation by revenue (Canadian National Railways is No. 1) and the third largest by staff complement. The CBC has a staff about the size of a standard army division. And like an army division, it has precious few fighters and an unhealthy number of people working in rear echelon. The 1992 Organization Chart reveals that, just in the two television networks, there are 769 clerks and secretaries. Well over a quarter of CBC's staff are involved in giving orders, planning battle strategies, moving supplies, typing memos, counting tape and pencils, changing light bulbs and moving filing cabinets. If it was truly an army division, it would be one of the few armies in the world to have one officer for every four soldiers.

The 1992 average staff complement was listed at 10,457. The exact number of CBC employees is a shell game. The figures shown in the annual reports represent permanent positions occupied by a warm body. In the 1990/91 annual report, "permanent" staff totalled 10,131, yet the "corporate total" averaged out to 11,290, a number which did not include the creative backbone of a broadcast organization—writers, actors, musicians, performers. As the employee numbers continued to hover annually in the 10,000-to-11,000 range, even with the many position cuts and lay-offs, the total salary expense for the CBC went up between 1990 and 1992 by $45 million. As staff salaries rose, freelance payments for actors, musicians and others went *down* $15 million in the same period, from $159.7 million to $144.6 million. One might conclude that fewer creative people are being put to use by the CBC, while those inside the corporation have their salaries raised with comfortable regularity.

CBC's corporate organization chart—tracing who is who and who reports to whom—is a book an inch thick. But it does not include the names and positions of unionized workers. If every staff position were to be included, the book would probably measure five inches thick. In the 1992 book, the Société Radio-Canada organization chart included a managerial position ("Officer Organizational Charts Management") whose sole responsibility appeared to be to update the French division's organization chart.

In 1992, the total salary expense for CBC was $697 million. Add the cost of performers, writers, musicians and talent rights, and CBC's "people cost" amounts to over $1 billion. There were 386 producers on staff status, down from 485 in 1990. When contract and freelance producers are included, the estimated total is about 1,300 producers. Producers are the people who design, plan, cost, organize, supervise and produce programs. They are the creative heart of a true broadcast organization yet most have the skimpiest version of job security. About 1,000 CBC producers are on contract, often one year at a time. Their employment can be terminated with sixty or ninety days notice. Contract producers have no pension plan, although their contracts allow for a 12.5 percent compensation payment. They do not receive overtime, although they can claim days-in-lieu for extra time worked. Few producers ever had the luxury of working nine-to-five.

At the same time as these producers toil in sometimes embarrassing compensation conditions, the vast majority of all other CBC employees enjoy full salary and benefits, access to one of the nation's wealthiest pension plans, guaranteed holidays, overtime and generally a pretty good nine-to-five life. The CBC in 1992 employed 1,920 managers, 2,490 clerical employees, 1,275 script and production assistants and 3,139 technicians. The CBC had more "confidential" employees on staff (481)—most often secretaries or assistants to managers—than staff producers (386). In 1989, the salary total for CBC clerical staff ($135 million) was twice as large as the combined total of salaries for artists, authors and musicians employed by the CBC. The total for management salaries was two-and-half times the salary total for journalists.

It is naive to say there is "no fat" inside the CBC. If it is not fat, then the corporation is hugely over-administered. Some of the excess is easy to spot. But most of it is buried in an archaic management structure, an antiquated corporate decision-making process and a distorted system of priorities that places higher emphasis on maintaining the organizational structure than on making programs. One of the most frequently asked questions about CBC finances is: "How much of the money goes into the actual making of programs?" If you follow the official corporate line, the vast majority of the $1.3 billion in expenditures is devoted to making and distributing CBC radio and television programs. Those costs are lumped into what is termed the "National Broadcasting Service." In 1992, the National Broadcasting Service category added up to a very impressive $1.2 billion. A detailed breakdown is hard to arrive at because the accounting system allows for an extremely liberal interpretation of what costs can be applied against the making of programs, and because Head Office occasionally changes the way it lays out the allocations on the administration side. Most of the fat within the CBC exists in these chunky folds of the corporation's structure.

The present organizational structure of the CBC actually can encourage waste, frivolous expenditure and inefficiency. There are few incentives for managers to find creative ways to operate their stations and departments more efficiently, or to keep programs on the air. Budget innovation and savings are seldom rewarded. Managers are encouraged by practice to use the amount of money allocated to them in their budgets—use it or lose it. Although we disliked talking about it, the "fourth-quarter burn-off" of budget funds has been a way of life within the CBC—and still was after the 1991/92 budget cut.

Fourth-quarter burn-off involves the spending of surplus funds before the books are closed for the fiscal year on March 31. Admittedly, the practice was more prevalent in the past, but it is still in modest vogue today. The spending is seldom on programming or production. Most of the money is spent on 'things'—more computers, printers, software, extra cellular phones, office furniture, some travel, a cafeteria or office renovation or two, a new switchboard or security desk, repainting the washrooms, spare tires for vehicles. As one regional manager put it when asked whether things were any different in 1992 from the profligate "old days": "Are you kidding? We've got trucks lined up outside shipping-and-receiving that can't even get to unload their [deliveries]. It's embarrassing!"

"I can't spend enough of the money offered to me," one regional manager said with some sadness in March 1992. He was budgeting for a year-end deficit but was being offered extra funding from Head Office and network sources—money to spend before March 31. "I can't remember a year when there hasn't been money to spend in March." But not on programs. "The embarrassing part is after cutting the shit out of the place, this is the first year we have been able to renovate our washrooms for handicap access—in the year of the most major cuts ever seen! And we've had no money to do that for ten years!"

I received a call in late March 1992 from a friend who worked as a sales representative for an equipment and systems supplier. He did a lot of business with the CBC and was curious about "what the hell was going on inside" the corporation. "I thought they were having big financial problems?" he asked. He had just finished signing a "pretty good" contract with one CBC office and was shocked about how easily the sale was made. Taking the CBC's fiscal plight into account, he had cautioned the buyer that the system involved was really a luxury product. The CBC could get along adequately with what they had. But the CBC response to his sexy system up-grade was like a hot flash frenzy. Money was no object, it was implied. By the time he closed the deal, he had been on the telephone to fellow suppliers across the country. The word was out: the CBC can still be had for a big score.

Ironically, part of this built-in budget waste—and admittedly it is not as prevalent now as in the past—is a direct result of Parliament's insistence on keeping the CBC on single-year funding cycles. The inability to marshal money and resources to plan program production beyond a single year makes for a very unbusiness-like environment, and the cost is placed directly upon the taxpayer. The other major impediment to cost efficiency is the centrally-controlled structure of the corporation. Decision-making is centralized in Ottawa and Toronto and Montreal. An individual station manager has no real authority to make hard, tactical decisions when it comes to his or her budgets—what to jettison instead of programs. You might see the sense in laying off non-program related personnel—let the leaves pile up—or cutting back in other administrative areas to save a regional program, but you have little say in the matter. The result has been the growth and preservation of a still inordinately large administrative infrastructure, while programs are cancelled across the nation and television stations closed.

The $1.2 billion depicted as the cost of the National Broadcasting Service rounds out at eighty-eight percent of all corporate expenditures and masks a huge working management bureaucracy. It includes thousands of employees whose work has only a marginal relationship to the production of programs. It includes overlapping, parallel and even competing functions. And it also includes administration costs that certainly exist in support of program production, but are highly peripheral. Many of these costs would simply not exist in the private sector. The functions, the jobs, would have been cancelled or creatively absorbed into other parts of the organization long before major cuts to programs and stations ever took place.

It looks like it cost about $120 million to administer the CBC in 1991/92—corporate management, selling expenses, restructuring costs. The costs, if considered as the price of supporting the production and distribution of CBC programs—which should be the essential reason for the corporation's existence—are deceptive. On first glance, it seems there are only a couple of thin administrative layers to peel off the billion-plus onion, like the $9.1 million for "corporate engineering services," $48.6 million for "corporate management and services" (the costs of Bronson Avenue-centred Head Office), $45.7 million as the cost of selling advertising and services and $16.2 million as "expense reductions and restructuring" for instance. When the cost of Engineering is taken into account, the minimum cost of corporate administration rises. When you add in the total administration costs at each network—French and English, radio and television, network and regional—the figure jumps to a CBC administrative total cost of more than $230 million.

Some CBC managers do not manage, they just exist. The 1990 French television network organization chart had seven "managers" of publicity in their network communications department—Manager of Publicity (Promotion), Manager of Publicity (Sales Promotion), Manager Printed Publicity, Manager of On-air Publicity, Manager of Publicity (AM Radio), Manager of Publicity (FM Radio), Manager of Publicity (Television). Only one managed any staff. The rest were all on their own. But by 1992 that embarrassing problem had been solved. More staff were added to the department, providing a number of those solitary managers with someone to manage. In 1990 the department had thirty-seven positions. In 1992, the same department had fifty-one positions. The department head's title also changed, perhaps in keeping with the expanded non-programming responsibilities, from "Director French Network Communications" to "Director-General Communications French Services."

In the CBC, programs and their planning are supervised by managers. The outright purchase of an independent producer's film is done by managers. The negotiations for Telefilm funding are carried out by managers and the details and contracts processed by managers. There are managers in the design department and managers in the arts, science and music creative departments. There are managers overseeing the technical departments and managers in the news departments. Throughout the entire organization, there is a quiet web of management administration that helps make the system work, and, often, duplicates cost and effort. It also helps keep shirt, tie, suit and briefcase manufacturers in business.

"Under the 'Crown Corporation' syndrome, a creative Corporation culture has tended to become converted through time, budgetary pressure and other constraints into a bureaucracy managing creative capabilities. The general perception is that the process of this conversion has resulted in inadequate and costly administration coupled with an eroded capacity for innovation."
—*A New Beginning,* CBC-TV producers, February 1983

Before one gets too carried away with tirades against a CBC "top-heavy" with management, it has to also be pointed out that these people, by and large, are not really allowed to manage. They are mostly told how to manage. In many cases, they admit that they have ended up being highly paid baby-sitters for corporate assets. Regional directors are a case in point. Their freedom to exercise senior experience and wisdom in decision-making is largely held in check by a very rigid central ruling structure. The tentacles of authority run to Ottawa in policy and administrative matters and to Montreal and Toronto in programming matters. CBC regional managers struggle to survive in an unhealthy environment that has them situated between the emasculating policies and practices of Head Office, and the domineering influence of the networks. The evolution of management within the CBC—the process of selection, training and development of the most professional and skilled people to supervise and administer money, staff and resources to achieve the lofty goals of public broadcasting—is a quiet but unmitigated disaster.

In a billion dollar corporation, there was, in my time at least, no program dedicated to the overall training, tracking and development of managers. Recruitment for these positions was almost random. No comprehensive training program existed to prepare managers for new duties and responsibilities, regardless of the size of the challenge or the scope of their financial or personnel responsibilities. The whole concept of professional development for managers has been ad hoc, intermittent and definitely haphazard. I worked for the CBC for roughly fourteen years—as a producer, executive producer, program director, director of television (twice) and regional director, with two networks, in seven different locations, managing hundreds of staff at a time, and responsible for spending millions of dollars—and was never offered a single day's training or development in executive management, in financial administration or in supervisory skills. My queries about development opportunities were most often greeted with the statement that Head Office Human Resources, which controlled training policy, plans and dollars, did not have the necessary funds.

Except in certain areas where technical complexity demands that new employees be given instruction to allow them to master new duties, training is usually done on the job. A lot of the costs of necessary training, certainly at the regional level, simply came out of programming and production budgets. As a former vice-president admitted, "the majority of our managers received very little training and if we did get training it was very superficial." Audio technicians can become supervisors, then production managers, then directors of radio, then regional directors, even vice-presidents—responsible for thousands of employees and hundreds of millions of dollars—without a single substantial course in management techniques, budgeting, personnel administration or executive operations. Occasionally, some managers and staff are offered introductory courses, most often in human motivational techniques—the assumption perhaps being that you need a lot of that working for today's CBC—or basic management theory. But inside the CBC it is an exception, right up there with the odds for winning a provincial lottery, when a manager is given the opportunity to take part in a serious development program.

With little recruitment of new talent, and no comprehensive training, a debilitating kind of stasis develops. Stenographers, mail persons and office clerks are promoted to production assistants, who are then promoted to producers, who then become managers. "Suddenly we have a stenographer mentality running a program or a station," said a former regional director. As former head of ETV network sports and director of television in B.C. Ron Devion put it: "One day somebody was an executive producer and the next day they were head of a bloody station! Nobody told them who was who, how to do what. And you learned by making eight million mistakes until you made enough of the right mistakes that you got some results. We did this time and again—to hundreds of people's careers—and you didn't know your ass from a hole in the ground in terms of how the corporate ethos worked."

CBC managers are often selected for major responsibilities with only perfunctory scrutiny of their abilities and needs. Worse yet, they are then often cast into their roles without firm objectives for their jobs and seldom are properly evaluated on their performance. "I've never had a performance appraisal in my career," admitted one Ottawa manager who has worked in a number of centres and in a number of production and managerial jobs. "Except once my supervisor wrote on a piece of paper—'Excellent!'—complete with exclamation mark. I've never had anyone tell me I fucked up and never had anyone tell me I had done well beyond 'good job'."

"I've never had anyone hand me a written job description as I entered a new position," said one senior radio executive. "I always made up my own job description once I got into the position and started to figure out what was required. I don't know how many job descriptions I made up as I went along. In my first job as head of a creative department with a $6 million budget I was told: 'Welcome. Here's your office.' And that was all! The only training course I received was one week—an introduction to management styles."

To the credit of the Veilleux administration, efforts were made to raise managerial efficiency within the CBC and the management structure, according to Veilleux, "delayered." The total number of managers has fallen from 2,100 in 1990 to 1,920 in 1992, although the total cost of their salaries only fell less than a half-million dollars. A new system of management objectives was also introduced. "Memorandum of Understanding" (MOUs, or "Moo's" as staff irreverently liked to call them) is a system meant to be a simple but formal set of objectives and expectations between managers and their superiors. The documentation was supposed to be a page or two, with a couple of signatures at the bottom. But many managers complained that by the time Head Office was finished with the MOU process, it was confusing, cumbersome and often out of sync with the corporation's annual planning process. MOUs became the subject of great derision across the corporation and were often considered "totally meaningless" or "just a joke."

With little support in management basics, and no advance management training to speak of, it is probably to the credit of CBC managers that most have taken their jobs and their duties seriously. If they had not, the CBC would certainly be in more of a mess than it is today. When Head Office 'lost' $55 million in its new accounting system (incorrect coding put the $55 million into a suspense account), it was the personal cuff records of regional and network managers that saved the corporation from even further expense, humiliation and derision. They were the ones who kept the books balanced, as the auditors recognized in their report.

Many of those same managers consistently applied themselves to their public responsibilities with an amazing amount of honesty, common sense and good will. They have made it up, too, as best they could, as they went along. Managers—throughout the regions and in the networks—have been one of the key ingredients in making this desultory corporate universe function at the level it does. By and large they have worked with dedication to the basic tenets of public broadcasting, guided by what former regional broadcasting vice-president Bill White called "an alliance of trust"—between them and the people who produce the programs on behalf of the citizen paying the bill. And they have done it in spite of the immense lack of trust and respect Head Office has shown them.

The CBC is also a very large corporation in terms of capital assets, holding fixed or capital assets—land, buildings, equipment, transmitters—valued on March 31, 1992, at cost, at $1.4 billion. The net book value of these assets was almost $787 million. The asset figures never go down year-to-year. They just stay on the books and get bigger—while the CBC makes fewer programs and lets production staff go. It is probably reasonable to assume, given the inflation of property values over the past thirty years, that the value of some of the assets has risen to remarkably high values since the properties were first purchased. But assets do not make an institution. People do.

The CBC is a corporation that just loves bricks and mortar. Its land holdings at cost are over $36 million. In addition, the net book value of its buildings was over $161 million. The value-at-cost of those buildings was $301 million. According to the 1992 statistics, the

CBC owned and operated nineteen television stations and sixty-five radio stations. (The 1991 statistics stated that the CBC operated thirty-one TV stations. But many of the missing twelve are still standing, still cost money to operate, but after the 1992 downsizing exercise are now considered simple, but expensive, rebroadcasting facilities.) The corporation also operated 1,148 radio and television rebroadcast facilities. In 1987/88 the CBC had fifty-one different buildings housing production studios, with staff in ninety-six different building locations across the country. If transmission sites were included, this meant it owned 505 properties. Building cleaning and maintenance costs alone average more than $5 million a year—or more direct dollars than the corporation would need to operate the Calgary television station.

CBC buildings range from antiquated to modest, from converted 1950 auto showrooms to architectural monuments, complete with art work (another capital asset on the books in 1992 at an acquisition cost-value of $603,000). Of course a broadcasting organization with the sweeping responsibilities given to it by Parliament requires buildings, property, production equipment, transmission equipment and vehicles to perform its tasks. On the other hand, these inflexible resources are only capable of expanding, seldom contracting. By their intractable presence they mesmerize Head Office thinking, contributing to corporate paralysis: "That particular building or system has always been there. We needed it before. We must need it now." Buildings have to be heated, even if they are not fully functional. And people have to be employed to patch leaky roofs, design policy and fill toilet dispensers. Over time, the presence of this hardware asset structure will inevitably grow while the 'software'—people and programs—are let go because of financial constraints.

Between 1988 and 1992, the net book value of the CBC's fixed assets increased over thirty percent. In the same period the number of employees across the corporation dropped by over six percent. And the number of hours of regionally-produced English television programs fell by thirty-two percent. The CBC is now in an advanced state of ossification.

It has often been argued in the hallways of Head Office that these are capital assets and they "belong to the Crown" and are therefore not that easily disposed of. But the *Broadcasting Act* allows the corporation to pretty much do as it pleases up to a limit of $4 million with real property, and with some vision, a little politicking and approval of the Governor in Council, the sky would be the limit. The other argument has been that it is not easy, maybe impossible, to convert capital assets into operating funds. But anyone watching how easily capital can be converted into operating dollars any time there is a financial crisis knows that where there is an administrative will, there certainly has always been a political way.

The CBC owns a blue and grey concrete warehouse in an industrial park in Burnaby, on the eastern doorstep of downtown Vancouver. It stretches the better part of a city block and contains about 100,000 square feet of floor space. More than one-half of the facility is rented, most to B.C. Tel, the provincial telephone utility. Engineering staff take up a small amount of office, garage and storage space and once or twice a year one of the network's movie crews will use a portion as a production office. The remaining space is jammed with an eclectic assortment of production sets, costumes, props, spare lumber and boxes of outdated financial files.

Few people within the CBC even know this facility exists. Sets and props and costumes take up most of 40,000 square feet. They are relics of a once energetic and glorious CBC British Columbia production past, dating from the 1960s, 1970s and early 1980s when the west coast region was a major producer of drama and variety programming. The costumes include nineteenth-century crinolines from the *Red Serge Wives* series, World War I and II uniforms and cowboy outfits, perhaps left over from the popular *Cariboo Country* series. The props, backdrops and sets are expertly catalogued and neatly stacked in industrial bins that rise almost to the ceiling. Each bin is a time-reflection of some major production that the B.C. region undertook in the past. Staff say that the original sets from the Paul Anka and René Simard variety *Superspecials* are still around somewhere. There is also a dungeon set, complete with torture rack. Staff joke that the rack was once part of a certain manager's office furniture.

The value of the material and costumes is debatable, but in 1989 the estimated market value of the building was over $5 million. The facility is superfluous to the present programming needs of the B.C. region. Hundreds of hours of regional programs have been cancelled. People laid off. But a warehouse full of memories and relics remains on the CBC books. It begs the questions: How many other underutilized facilities exist in the new, downsized CBC? Could they have been converted to operating revenue—rented, sold off, leased, disposed of—before more program cancellations or lay-offs had taken place?

Part of this embarrassing problem lies in the CBC's awkward and inefficient organizational structure. Media managers, the people who have traditionally managed the corporation's program operations across the country, have little flexibility to make simple business decisions about what costs to cut and where, in the interests of preserving program production. In fact, the organizational structure at the CBC is quite ridiculous. Imagine being responsible for and managing a CBC regional television station, spending $20 million a year and supervising more than 500 staff, ostensibly to make programs. But you cannot make final decisions about programs. The network can overrule you at any point and make whatever business decisions it likes, at whatever cost to the station. Imagine a general manager of a private television station having to ask his plant engineer for the money to renovate a studio because the engineer, not the general manager, supervised studio renovations and buildings. Imagine having to check with Toronto before using your own studio. Is it any wonder the man who rakes leaves remains employed but producers are not?

"People are terrifically busy at Head Office all the same. They are drawing up Reports and Flow Charts and things like that and making appointments to confer with each other and sitting brightly in board rooms while bilingual secretaries with alert backsides hurry down corridors carrying messages of interest and importance . . ."
—Jon Ruddy, *Maclean's*, April 2, 1966

During a tour of management offices on the first day of my 1987 visit to CBC's Head Office, as a member of a three-person task force trying to figure out what 'Head Office' was, how much it cost and where we could cut it, I walked into two managers' offices whose desks were clean of paper and clutter—except for the crossword puzzles sitting, poised for instant use, in the middle of each desk.

The CBC Head Office on Bronson Avenue in Ottawa is probably the most enigmatic part of this enigmatic organization. It is housed in a 1950s tricorn-shaped building, built, so rumour has it, adjacent to a geologic fault line. It requires, so the fable goes, a special suspended foundation to keep the building from collapsing. There are more than a few who would argue that Head Office has been functioning in suspension for longer than just the life of the Bronson Avenue building.

"It is like a Potemkin village," said one Toronto television manager, of Head Office. "Everybody looks busy doing jobs they don't know anything about. I attended a meeting there in the board room and I was astounded by how 'white-male-middle-class' the place was. It has been a long time since I've been in a room like that. The composition of the faces was bizarre—no women, no minorities. It was like a scene from the 1950s, something out of *Father Knows Best*."

Some Bronson inhabitants do good work—setting up labour negotiations, tracking spending, liaising with politicians, seeing to the mountain of federal regulations and standards, travelling to international television and film festivals. But Head Office, occasionally aided by network senior management, has also been quite capable of bringing down goodly amounts of public embarrassment upon the corporation. More than any one group in its history, they have contributed their share to a number of gaffes that ring in the memory of many Canadians: the $55 million National Financial System 'disaster'; the Victoria, B.C. television station built at a cost of $4.5 million, then allowed to sit vacant for four years until it was sold, for far less than the construction price, to the private sector competitor, CHEK-TV; how to implement the $108 million 1991/92 budget cut. The last of these may have been their second finest moment. The Toronto Broadcast Centre might yet be their finest.

In appearance, the Head Office edifice gives no indication that it is the Vatican of the country's most important cultural entity. It looks more like the offices of Revenue Canada. One could wander the corridors for hours, as the Fowler committee observed in its 1960s broadcasting report, "without having the slightest reason to believe he was in the headquarters of a broadcasting organization." A goodly number of the people who work there could care less about public broadcasting—or would know what it was if it fell on them. Like the young lady at the security desk who, when told I was there to see the President—asked me three questions: "President of what . . .?" "What did you say his name was . . . ?" And could I spell it? "V E I L L E U X . . ." Pause. She began searching the telephone directory. Fourth question: "Do you know what floor he is on?"

Security personnel aside, it is the home and breeding ground for a particular species of corporate acolyte. It is the place you migrate to, corporately speaking, if you enjoy pretending you have power. By itself, it is just a building in Ottawa that houses a few hundred people who, according to the annual report, only spend about $48 million a year to make sure the corporation's $1.358 billion is well-spent. But it is also the locus of control for an elaborate and tangled administrative structure. Head Office has nothing to do with making programs and everything to do with the preservation and expansion of authority over them. It is not the cost of its existence that should be looked at, but the cost it imposes on other sectors of the corporation and, ultimately, on the taxpayer.

One of the first discoveries our little 1987 Head Office task force encountered—beyond the crossword puzzle talents of two Head Office managers, one of whom was later promoted to new corporate heights—was how far the tentacles of Head Office reached into the organization and how much money and how many people they actually controlled. CBC is definitely not a decentralized organization. Rather than look at a simple and benign "head office" costing less than $50 million, one has to keep pulling the Russian dolls out of each other until the overall administrative numbers climb to $200 to $300 million and staff that counts in the thousands.

The 1987 task force discovered that just staff or administrative departments reporting to the senior vice-president, not including radio and television networks, represented over $190 million out of the CBC budget and involved over 2,400 staff—accountants, engineers, clerks, personnel officers, computer specialists, lawyers. If you tossed in the 320 people working in communications and public relations, the administrative staff number crept over 2,700, indicating that more than one-quarter of the CBC staff complement worked under the Head Office administrative umbrella, and had nothing to do with the making of programs. As a microcosm test, in 1990/91, roughly twenty-eight percent of the average region's costs were tied up in administration and overhead.

One doll the task force could not pull from the enigma, just as others had failed in the past, was "Engineering Headquarters", or just Engineering. EHQ is one of the most expensive and enduring riddles in the CBC administrative structure. Engineering is a large part of the Head Office empire and a deceptive one. Although "Corporate engineering services" show up in the 1992 books as a $9.1 million annual expenditure (even though corporate engineering salaries and benefits alone totalled $15.2 million), the cost of engineering services swings wildly between the $9.1 and the sky. In 1991, Engineering salaries expenditures alone were $38 million. Extra money comes from regional and network engineering budgets and from the capital pot appropriated by Parliament, a portion of which Engineering uses to pay salaries and other costs in relation to capital projects. In 1986, a private study conducted by the Board of Directors pointed out that this method of funding—dipping into capital funds to pay salaries and overhead—"distorts the perception of the cost of services delivered by CBC Engineering." It also recommended the CBC should contract out much of the then-$68.4 capital budget to the private sector.

In 1990, corporate engineering costs did not include almost 170 engineering employees working in the ETV network, the more than 175 engineering employees scattered throughout the regions and the roughly 130 engineering staff in Société Radio-Canada—including eight air conditioning mechanics at the SRC headquarters on René Lévesque Boulevard, and the three mechanics-in-charge responsible for supervising the other eight. By 1992, the number had risen to nine. Their salaries, like the salary of the maintenance employee in Vancouver who raked leaves and kept the toilets amply supplied with paper, are considered part of the cost of making CBC programs.

CBC Engineering is an outdated and costly anachronism. It grew out of the late 1950s and 1960s along with the introduction of television. The lack of broadcast engineering skill in the private sector made it necessary for the CBC to have its own in-house engineers—advising the corporation what equipment to buy, supervising it, even building some of it, figuring out where to put it, how much to spend and what current research and development would do for CBC's future. Today, the market is flooded with private sector equipment manufacturers and other engineering firms doing research, development and providing services that might challenge or surpass the CBC in sophistication and cost.

In 1985, the technical managers of the CBC Calgary television station decided that if the station was to perform more efficiently, produce more and better programs, and attract a larger audience to its regional programming, it would need a new block of tape editing suites. The official Engineering estimate of what the project would cost was in excess of $100,000, *not* including the cost of equipment. In effect, the project was a home renovation—turning one large area in the building into four functioning edit suites. The Calgary managers were appalled at the estimate—which included the standard ten to fifteen percent capital work order surcharge to cover Engineering costs and expenses. The local managers refused to pay.

Breaking all sorts of corporate protocol, they decided they would do it on their own. They had pictures taken of similar editing suites in Vancouver and Toronto, reviewed their plans against Engineering standards, called for competing bids from local building and electrical contractors, supervised the renovations themselves, and, with the help of the regional director, diverted funds from administrative and other non-programming sources to pay for the project. The total cost of their efforts came to a little less than $60,000. Standards were met. The edit suite complex eventually contributed to a dramatic increase in production efficiency, many more regional news stories, documentaries and entertainment programs, and an almost instant jump in audience ratings for the station—not to mention a sizeable leap in staff morale. And the Canadian taxpayer was ahead in value by $40,000. Free enterprise at work in public broadcasting.

CBC Engineering's *raison d'être* is to spend money. They are responsible for the continuing technical and physical health of a wide range of buildings, sites, facilities and transmission systems. In 1989/90, while B.C. television management were desperately short of funds to make more regional programs, the Engineering group was able to come up with more than $40,000 to renovate and modernize office space. More often than not, they do a good job and know what they are doing. But Engineering operates on a five-year expenditure treadmill, setting spending objectives in the tens of millions of dollars on new premises, replacement equipment or the refurbishing of a television mobile studio, with what sometimes appears to be only passing reference to the need or appropriateness of those expenditures to public broadcasting.

Engineering ends up a largely self-directed, perpetual motion machine, spending tens of millions of dollars of the CBC's annual Parliamentary capital appropriation. Between 1984 and 1992, while program budgets were being slashed and regional program operations closed down, the amount of capital money available to Engineering went up a startling 89 percent—from $66.8 million to $126.4 million. Occasionally, the criterion they use to explain the expenditure on the upgrade of a new sound studio, or a television camera or the replacement of a part in a remote broadcast transmitter in the far reaches of northern Alberta, is an abstract professional standard: the technical "life" of the part is decided by engineers, whose advice is scrupulously followed by other engineers, who sometimes look puzzled when it is argued, theoretically, that the money might be better spent making a program rather than replacing a part which *might* fail in the years ahead. To many CBC programmers, those were the kind of professional standards which would help do-in public broadcasting.

> *"CBC's building boondoggle"*
> *"The Canadian Broadcasting Corp.'s dreamy new Broadcast Centre in the heart of Toronto is now set to cost the Crown corporation as much as $1.6 billion in rent over the next 35 years. On an annual basis that will be nearly triple what they are now paying for office space around the city, and far costlier than CBC executives stated publicly before construction began."*
> —Adam Corelli, *Financial Times*, June 29, 1992

The construction of the Toronto Broadcast Centre was a project eagerly supported by Engineering, as well as Head Office, partly because it allowed the department to hone its technical expertise—and its existence—for years to come. Nothing wrong with that. Unfortunately, the TBC may, like a giant ten-storey tombstone, mark one of the largest administrative and organizational blunders in the CBC's history. It could also stand as a cenotaph for the death of regional broadcasting.

The Centre began rolling as a project in the early 1980s. The 9.3 acre Front Street property, one of the most valuable in Canada, had been acquired in the late 1970s for $19.5 million. The TBC was designed to be a combined office and production centre containing, unfortunately, large elements of almost automatic obsolescence. The idea lived inside the CBC on puffs of mouth-to-mouth resuscitation for so long that, when it was finally brought to life, it was already an old idea whose time had passed, whose function had largely changed, and whose financial numbers would not add up.

The Board promised in the 1988/89 annual report that the cost of the project "will actually be less than the continued use of existing [Toronto] premises." One unnamed executive proudly proclaimed in 1991 that the deal "made and saved a fortune of taxpayer's money," based on the belief at the time that CBC could end up paying as little as $15 million a year for its new premises, compared to $23-24 million it was paying for twenty-three locations around the city. Unfortunately, it appeared the CBC signed a deal that would see the corporation pay an estimated $28.5 million in TBC rent in the first year, escalating to over $31 million in year two and escalating, as one knowledgeable observer put it, to "God knows where thereafter." The 1991/92 annual report stated the CBC would opt to commence rent payments earlier than the September 1993 due date. They had earmarked $58 million as an advance to keep down future interest costs associated with the lease.

There was no disputing the need for newer, consolidated premises for Toronto operations. But ETV network and Head Office planners were warned by people working in the initial project group in 1984 that the Centre would mark the "death of regional broadcasting," because there just was not enough money in the system to construct and operate the Centre without financially stripping the regions. "It was clear to us in 1984 that the CBC just didn't have the necessary funds for the project," said one former project group member. But year after surreal year, the project pushed ahead, cobbling gullible aspirations together with outdated methods and needs, until the go-ahead was given for a construction project that had, as a former project group member put it, "a divergent path from reality."

Financing for the project was largely based—not unlike the ETV network's annual advertising growth aspirations—on "huge increases in the value anticipated from inflation in the Toronto real estate market." The CBC was going to build the Centre and pay the bill by syphoning off, year after year, the profits from increases in real estate developed adjacent to the Centre itself. The deal was brought in with a financial liability attached to the project that had banks and trust companies eager to take part because, as confidential bank documents stated, all "the financial risks of the project are for the CBC." Canadian taxpayers would pick up the tab for any economic surprises or management misjudgements.

The Centre sits in front of the entire CBC like a huge political time bomb. It has been said in some close quarters that the decision to move on the project was partly "rammed through" a dubious Board of Directors by management; that they had not been given adequate information and were forced to make decisions they did not feel comfortable with. The topic was now "a little cancer" that surrounded the nervous Board. The very mention of it would cause them to erupt—blow "the whole place apart." The Centre is the perfect metaphor for the contemporary problems of the corporation. As a project, it will cost hugely more than was estimated, or what it is worth. It has lots of empty space. And it has no core—the centre of the structure is a huge, empty atrium. By the end of its lifetime, it may turn out to be one of the most expensive structures ever erected in Canada. Its rolling costs could eventually exceed those of Montreal's Olympic Stadium.

Head Office, EHQ and ETV network managers consistently seemed to underestimate the actual risk-cost of the project, always maintaining that it was only costing the CBC $381 million, while confidential documents laid out a deal with the developer, Cadillac Fairview, that had the CBC responsible for a $800 million loan over the term of the agreement, not including taxes, operating and equipment costs. The true extent of the future liability to the taxpayer, not surprisingly, has never been addressed by Head Office. The deal, signed on September 30, 1988, had the CBC backing an initial $550 million construction loan to Cadillac Fairview, and an additional $250 million "roll-up facility" as a subsidy on the centre's rent for the first ten years, more than doubling the Head Office cost estimates of the project right up front. These costs did not include the cost of equipping the building, estimated between $150-180 million. Over the next thirty-five years, it has been estimated the ten-storey Centre could end up costing the CBC $1.6 billion.

The CBC gambled that private partners—Cadillac Fairview and Bramalea Corp. Ltd.—would be in a financial position to undertake construction of a multi-use commercial, residential, shopping and garage complex on the remaining 5.3 acres of adjacent property, and share profits from the complex with the CBC. But the commercial sod had definitely not been turned by early 1993, and with a collapsed commercial real estate market, twenty percent-plus office vacancy in Toronto and some developers projecting no recovery for the rest of the decade, chances of any 'offsetting revenues' for the CBC were not on any immediate horizon.

To make matters worse, in late 1992 Bramalea Ltd., a real estate development arm of the financially troubled Edper empire, reneged on a $92 million mortgage the CBC had accepted to back Bramalea's portion of the adjacent complex construction. The money would have helped the CBC reduce its financing costs. Although Bramalea paid about $20 million before it went into financial freefall, instead of the cash from the deal, the CBC was forced to launch a court action and had to accept shares in Bramalea—a company that lost $937 million in 1992. The Bramalea failure meant the CBC—which claimed damages of $100 to $200 million—would now have to stretch the Centre's financing over a longer period or pay higher annual costs. And in late April 1993 it was reported Dominion Bond Rating Service lowered Cadillac Fairview's debt rating from single-A to triple-B because of fears about Cadillac Fairview's ability to refinance a large loan that matures in November 1997. In the event anything serious were to happen to Cadillac Fairview, the CBC would have to assume responsibility for the repayment of the TBC's $800 million loan. Even if the commercial complex had been built alongside the Centre, the share of revenue was estimated by some to be insignificant when compared to the huge loan costs and indebtedness for the CBC.

The CBC took possession of the Centre in July 1992. As the numbers added up in the spring of 1993, the corporation could eventually end up paying three times what it was shelling out for rents in the twenty-plus locations around downtown Toronto. The project will now cost more, not less, than "the current situation," as the Board hoped. And the rental costs being "offset by commercial revenue" are still more mythical than real. If Canada survives long enough, any commercial complex built on the vacant part of the property will revert to the CBC ninety-nine years down the road. As one CBC employee who helped program the project said to the *Globe and Mail*: "Ten years from now, this could look like the most brilliant piece of planning ever accomplished. As is, right now, it looks like somebody made a terrible mistake."

5 / A Pearl Among Swine

"We have to insure [public broadcasting] against destruction by private interests, but the private interests have been very vigilant. They have determined . . . to destroy this publicly owned facility."
—Conservative R.B. Bennett, in opposition, 1936

THE HISTORY OF THE CBC is the stuff of bad soap opera. The opening has our heroine arriving full of high-minded promise and virtue, carrying support for something unique—the preservation of national unity through the enhancement of cultural understanding. The first act struggles through an introduction of purpose, with lofty speeches, lots of principle, but no money to achieve them. The villains—parsimonious governments, usurious and greedy private broadcasters and cablecasters, spineless regulatory agencies—hover in the sinister shadows waiting for their cues. The second act focuses on the making of a tragedy, with threats to the very existence of public broadcasting, not to mention the possible suicidal tendencies of the heroine. The final act is a battlefield scene. Adversaries join together, surrounding the beleaguered star, poking sharp sticks of criticism, taunting mercilessly, edging in like jackals for the kill, promising charity in return for surrender. The heroine fights badly and alone. As we fade to commercial block three, she is mortally wounded, short of tradeable assets, promises or cash with which to pacify her attackers. Looking left and right for constituents and supporters, she discovers that most have long departed the field, thanks in part to her indifferent treatment toward them over the years. The soliloquy has the heroine, mortally wounded and on one knee, reflecting on the directions life has taken, wondering if there is a purpose to it all, and what the future might look like with even fewer friends.

As veteran broadcast lobbyist Graham Spry, one of the fathers of Canadian public broadcasting and a founding member of the Canadian

74

Radio League, put it in his 1961 article, "The Decline and Fall of Canadian Broadcasting": "The CBC has been maligned, misrepresented, savaged, nagged and subjected to meanness and indignities by hostile and sometimes greedy competitors or ill-informed politicians [until it was] out-flanked, surrounded and hemmed in to a subordinate place in the structure."

It was not meant to be this way. At the genesis of public broadcasting in 1929, with the tabling of the report of the Royal Commission on Radio Broadcasting (the Aird Commission), Canadian broadcasting—all Canadian broadcasting, not just the CBC—was meant to be a *public* service, operated by one *national* company, with control of programming and the stations in the hands of *provincial* authorities. Ideally, it was to be non-commercial, with revenues coming principally from license fees, indirect advertising and a subsidy from the Dominion government. Faced with the rising tide of U.S. domination of the airwaves, public broadcasting was to be a force for national unity, a system that informed, enlightened and entertained Canadians with predominantly *Canadian* programs.

It might be hard for some Canadians to grasp—especially private station owners and assorted members of the Canadian Association of Broadcasters—that Canadian broadcasting was not originally meant to be a commercial system controlled by private broadcasters. In fact, the first run at broadcasting by private stations was so crass and revolting, even to Conservative MPs, that they were almost legislated out of existence. In the hands of the private sector between 1920 to 1929, the Canadian broadcast system had been an embarrassing adulteration of lowest-common-denominator American entertainment programming, commercial greed, along with heavy doses of propaganda and religion. In English Canada, right into the 1930s, Canadian airwaves were flooded with programs depicting American values, lifestyle, culture and commercial products. But as Frank Peers points out in the first of his two vital histories, *The Politics of Canadian Broadcasting: 1920-1951*, Canadians still thirsted for their own means of identification and they sincerely "wanted a broadcasting system that would allow them their own modes of expression, their own means of talking to one another, their own ways of discussing public affairs—with a Canadian accent."

In the hands of private broadcasters, the Canadian radio environment had been so abysmal that it even prompted former Tory prime minister Arthur Meighen to tell the Aird Commission, somewhat awkwardly, that the "amount of fodder that is the antithesis of the intellectual that comes over our radios is appalling while the selection of material for broadcast remains in commercial hands." R.B. Bennett, the Conservative prime minister who eventually introduced the *Canadian Radio Broadcasting Act* of 1932 into Parliament, spoke, not in favour of free enterprise in Canadian broadcasting, but in favour of public ownership, a system that was to be, according to Bennett, an effective instrument for nation-building, with "an educational value difficult to estimate." Even the Conservative Bennett could not see "leaving the air to private exploitation."

The government appointed Sir John Aird, president of the Canadian Bank of Commerce, to chair a commission. Aird was originally inclined to support private ownership and development of radio broadcasting. But after travelling widely and investigating working broadcast models in various countries with his two fellow commissioners—Charles Bowman, editor of the *Ottawa Citizen*, and Augustin Frigon, director of l'École Polytechnique de Montréal— the commission came away impressed with the publicly owned British Broadcasting Corporation model and intrigued by the German broadcast model, where each *lander* or state was responsible for developing and producing its own programs. The anarchic American model, with no holds on programming and the cowboys of commercial enterprise dead-set on little else than private gain and profit, turned out to be the least appealing of the lot, and was sweepingly rejected.

The Canadian Association of Broadcasters, formed in 1926, predictably opted for the American model but, as Marc Raboy points out in his 1990 broadcast history, *Missed Opportunities: The Story of Canada's Broadcasting Policy*, not just for brave, entrepreneurial reasons, but for the possibility of government subsidies to be made available for privately-owned stations. Given the growing support for public broadcasting at the time, private broadcasters doubted they would get to own the broadcasting farm, so they at least wanted to ensure they got some space at the public trough.

Aird quickly came around to the view that if the system which prevailed before 1929 was allowed to continue—private stations broadcasting U.S. programs and, in some cases, ownership of the Canadian stations by U.S. radio networks—Canadians would likely never hear a Canadian program on their airwaves. Those powerful

American signals would carry no Canadian stories, no Canadian news, no Canadian dramatic presentations and no Canadian artistic performances. There would be endless American soap commercials but little or no news about what happened in Ottawa or Winnipeg.

By the 1920s, Canada had been putting itself together, culturally speaking, after forging a stronger sense of nationhood during World War I. Under the circumstances, the nurturing and growth of a national identity was a major preoccupation for Canadians. Who owned Canadian broadcasting and what message was to be transmitted on the system became paramount in the minds of many politicians—Tory and Whig alike. This was not a debate over business opportunities or the formulation of industrial strategy. This was a recognition that the health of Canada as a nation could actually hang on the strength or weakness of its broadcasting system. This was, in effect, what would distinguish the Canadian broadcasting model from others: it would be a public system, yes, but one that would be imbued with national purpose. And the debate over a distinctive Canadian broadcasting system was one of the few occasions when national unity and a belief in a shared culture would win out over free enterprise ideology and narrow partisan interests. Aird was a victory for Canada, without question. But, unfortunately, it would turn out to be more pyrrhic than permanent.

It took Aird and his colleagues less than a year to gather their thoughts. The commission travelled to twenty-five Canadian cities and received 288 submissions. What the commission proposed was not just a radio broadcasting system. It was a "public" system that wrapped itself around the whole concept of nation-building. It would, to the commission members, conceivably be one of our more important cultural and national building blocks. In sculpting this new, lofty role for radio communications, it also reinforced a picture of the evolving structure of Confederation. Canada was not a unitary state like Great Britain. It was not a federal state like the United States. The Canadian federal system reflected the coexistence of several states or provinces within a nation, each with its differences and distinctiveness.

Canada was a mosaic, not a melting pot; a nation of competing interests, not a single-minded, united nationality. The Fathers of Confederation recognized, despite Sir John A. Macdonald's longing for a legislative union, that there would be no nation *a mare usque ad mare* unless the provinces were left some degree of autonomy, some allowance for reflecting regional diversities. Over the decades, time, circumstance and the Judicial Committee of the Privy Council made certain Canada would not be a single-minded, unitary state. And one of the fundamental lessons Aird would impart, in implying that Canadian broadcasting should have a nation-building, unifying responsibility, was the further recognition of Canada as a pluralistic state. The commission talked of "one national company," not a broadcast organization centred in one part of the nation. The regions, or the provinces, would be the suggested key to a truer reflection of what this nation called "Canada" was all about. It had nothing to do with a concept that said control of program ideas would come exclusively from some yet unnamed centre, such as Toronto, Montreal or Ottawa.

The Aird Commission tabled its recommendations for government action in September of 1929. In the eyes of the commissioners, Canadian broadcasting—all of it that existed at the time and would develop in the future—should be based on "public service." The nation, not private broadcasters, would own the broadcasting system. Canadian broadcasting was proposed as a public monopoly. The stations belonging to that public service—the only stations allowed to have licenses—would be owned and operated by a single, national company called the Canadian Radio Broadcasting Company (in legislation, "Commission"), the predecessor to the CBC. And provincial representatives—provincial radio broadcasting directors, assisted by public advisory councils—would be responsible for programming the system. They would, according to Aird, have "full control over the programs of the station or stations in their respective areas."

It was a strong, visionary document. The Aird Commission's recommendations were "the first principles" of Canadian broadcasting. They were, or should have been, a constitution for our national culture, built through broadcasting.

Aird had become, as Marc Raboy cites, "a strong supporter of the view that broadcasting should be primarily a means of education and not of commercial exploitation." Writing in 1931, Graham Spry argued that broadcasting "is no more a business than a public school system is a business. . . . Broadcasting, primarily, is an instrument of education in its widest significance, ranging from play to learning, from recreation to the cultivation of public opinion, and it concerns and influences not any single element in the community, but the community as a whole." This fervent belief in broadcasting's potential was a long way from *Boston Blackie, Amos 'n' Andy* and the incessant advertising offered in the private perception of broadcasting. And it would be light years from *Fresh Prince of Bel Air, Empty Nest* and *WKRP in Cincinnati*—programs Canadians still had to watch, complete with twelve minutes per hour of commercials, on their national public television network in 1993.

To the Commission, the concept of "public" in broadcasting was paramount. It meant a system that was enlightening, worthwhile and truly capable of nation-building. There was no room for private broadcasters, other than as part of a "provisional service" which might operate until the entire public system was up and running. All other private stations would then be closed down and dismantled. The question of the proper development of national broadcasting could even "include television," the Commission wrote presciently. This new public enterprise would have a mission to unify the nation by making programs that would come from the parts or the regions of the country. These programs would be more truly reflective of what Canada was all about.

Then, with barely one turn around the block, the wheels started falling off the little red wagon marked, "The Dream of Canadian Public Broadcasting." A month after the Aird Commission's recommendations were tabled, stock markets around the world began tumbling, sparking the Great Depression and fears about where the estimated $3.2 million in capital and $2.5 million in operating costs might come from to get the CRBC up and running. The Aird Commission had recommended that revenues should come from three sources: license fees, rental time on stations for programs carrying indirect advertising (as opposed to commercials) and a subsidy of $1 million a year for five years from the Dominion government. By the time R.B. Bennett became prime minister in the summer of 1930, he now preferred, given the tough economic times, a broadcasting system that cost the federal treasury next to nothing.

Private broadcasters, facing expropriation and the loss of their lucrative businesses, and supported by any company or individual who believed in the mantra of commercial advertising—newspapers, magazines, some politicians—were not about to take this usurpation of their profit pipelines in the name of the nation's culture sitting down. This temporary rump of Canadian broadcasting began an energetic lobby effort that would never ease—to this day, unfortunately. If Aird did not succeed as planned, it was, in large part, thanks to these captains of commercial radio and their skill in manipulating the political process to their demands—always, of course, in the name of "giving the Canadian public what it wants."

The 1932 *Canadian Radio Broadcasting Act* that eventually evolved out of Aird's recommendations and created the Canadian Radio Broadcasting Commission, was neither as impressive nor as nationalistic as Aird's report had been. The act talked about public ownership and gave the CRBC the power to regulate Canadian broadcasting (subject to the "approval of Parliament" the commission could "take over all broadcasting in Canada"), but it left room for private stations to receive broadcast licenses and set up private, commercial networks. The legislation hinted that private stations might simply be a minor or temporary phenomenon (they could be "expropriated" under the act), but this was not legislation that closed the doors on private commercial radio stations. It opened them almost as wide as any contemporary CRTC decision could ever do.

Instead of following Aird's bold new vision and avoiding the worst aspects of the BBC and the American broadcasting models, the 1932 legislation helped combined them. Canadian broadcasting ended up half-British on the public side (we'll call it "public" but not make it a monopoly), and half-American on the private side (everybody will eventually get to sell commercials). Some historians call it a "hybrid" broadcasting system, a typical genetic print-out of our North American cultural duality. In fact, the act gave birth, not to any hybrid in the sense that Canadian broadcasting would evolve better and stronger than its progenitors, but to an hermaphrodite—a body carrying two sets of competing sexual organs, capable of being whatever anyone wanted at any one time but forever confused and disoriented about its gender, and what its role should be in the household of Canadian broadcasting.

The deepening depression meant that government funding for quick expansion of the new public broadcast stations was not available. The fledgling CRBC would have to rely on the private stations to carry much of its programming if it was to reach as many Canadians as they planned. That was not the only problem. Before the CRBC was even functioning, private broadcast licenses were being issued to Tory supporters, effectively cutting the CRBC out of one-half of the country's English-language network market. The Bennett government restricted the license fee at $2 and provided a mere $400,000 for the CRBC's first fiscal year of operation; hardly suitable considering that Aird had estimated a start-up operating cost of $2.5 million.

The refusal by successive federal governments to provide the CRBC, and then the CBC, with suitable, long-term stable funding would do as much damage to the dream of a national public broadcasting system as the persistent and damaging lobbying by private broadcasters. By not providing public broadcasting with the money with which to achieve the goals Parliament set for it, the CBC would be forced to make immense compromises in its coverage plans and programming philosophies. The government kept license fees much too low (they were still $2.50 in the late 1940s). Not able to expand coverage because of the shortage of cash, the CRBC and CBC had to rely on private broadcasters to carry the public broadcaster's programs. But the private stations needed to sell commercials to stay alive. So did the CRBC and the CBC. Commercial advertising in public broadcast programs would prove to be a long-term corrupting influence. Many programs would eventually be designed and produced, as we now know so well, not for their enlightenment value, but for how much commercial revenue they brought in. The increasing size of the commercial pie for public broadcasting would be a running point of conflict with the private broadcasters. And when the CBC entered television in 1952, the lure of huge revenues was too much to resist.

The embryonic CRBC, perhaps deservedly, had a short and undistinguished life. It was accused of being wasteful, inefficient and politically partisan. National public objectives went out the window. The CRBC did not have the necessary cash to acquire the private stations, as the act suggested, and because it was unable to set up a national network, it was forced to pay private stations to carry its programs—triggering, of course, not the eventual demise of the private stations but the growing reality of their power and influence. By 1936 there would be seventy-three radio stations in Canada. Only eight of them would be publicly owned. That year, Mackenzie King's Liberals quickly brought in a new broadcasting act to change the shape of Canadian broadcasting.

The *Canadian Broadcasting Act* of 1936 established the Canadian

Broadcasting Corporation and said good-bye to the sad CRBC. Although the act set out the CBC as the preeminent player in Canadian broadcasting, it did not endorse public control as the 1932 act tried to do, and did nothing about the matter of nationalization of private operations. By formally defining the working relationship between the public broadcaster and the private station owners, the 1936 act recognized and legitimized the latter's role in the broadcasting firmament. The concrete had set. The private broadcasters would now have a firm foundation from which they could start twisting the system to suit their own interests.

The CBC was born in a cradle of confusion, familial conflict and mistaken purpose. The swaddled tyke of Canadian public broadcasting, five years in a difficult gestation, opened its eyes to a life-scene of parents squabbling over the doctor's bill and what profession she might eventually enter, siblings complaining about another mouth to feed and where would they all live, and cousins sniping from outside the doorway, arguing that the new kid would just make it harder for them to get a job and get rich when they grew up. It would be enough to make the kid wonder whether she wasn't better off back in the womb.

> "The power and importance of 'private' broadcasters in Canada have grown steadily and without interruption, but the role of the 'public' element of the system has ebbed and flowed. . . . The public sector has depended on the particular importance attached to broadcasting by the party in power and its attempts to master the political context, while the private sector has grown with just a little help from its friends."
> —Marc Raboy, Missed Opportunities: The Story of Canada's Broadcasting Policy

Not deterred by all that Canadian content, national unity and cultural interest stuff, the private broadcasters started out on a five-decade pillage of the founding principles of Canadian broadcasting. They ended up being the biggest, baddest, richest pigs at the public trough. They manipulated the broadcast system, lobbied and coerced politicians, whined, kvetched and received massive public subsidies, engaged in propaganda against the CBC, curried favour with MPs, counted exorbitant profits, got themselves elected to Parliament, made

82

FADE TO BLACK

it onto Parliamentary committees overseeing broadcasting and into cabinets, influencing the emasculation of the CBC, its mandate and its budgets, and eventually were able to twist and destroy the broadcast intentions of an entire nation. Not bad for a half-century's work.

Throughout the 1930s and 1940s, with the CBC in the lose-lose position of both needing the help of the private stations and being their regulator, the private broadcasters demanded and received larger pieces of the commercial pie, almost always complaining that they were losing money when, in fact, they were making massive profits. They howled for concessions in Canadian content and programming standards and received them. They were allowed by the CBC to set up lucrative high-powered radio transmitters, which shut out the corporation from some large urban markets. By 1939, with these captains of free enterprise enjoying monopoly market protection, many of them heavily subsidized with free CBC programming—as well as cash payments to carry those free programs—there was now, once again, as much American programming on the Canadian airwaves as Canadian. By the start of World War II private broadcasters out-numbered CBC stations seven-to-one, with the latter providing its affiliates with as much as eight free hours of programming a day and, by 1945, $1.2 million in annual payouts, a form of "corporate dole," to carry those programs. At the end of the war, private station revenues were growing twice as fast as CBC's, and by 1948 their combined assets would be valued at three times the CBC's.

But they did not let up. Backed often by large and powerful lumber, mining, transportation and newspaper interests, the private broadcasters began forging strong links with opposition MPs, and began to swing opinion in the House of Commons in their favour. Strangely enough throughout this period and into the late 1960s, various Parliamentary committees and Royal Commissions and task forces would persist in not only trying to circle protective wagons around the CBC, but also would constantly remind these commercial savages that they had a social (not to mention moral) responsibility to uphold as well as the manna of net profit. They were frequently reminded that the airwaves were a public utility and that they did not own their licenses as they thought. They were reminded that the broadcast system was constructed to achieve national unity and cultural awareness, not to be a purveyor of commercial entertainment and line their pockets. They were also prompted to recall that none of them had ever gone bankrupt, yet they contributed embarrassingly little of their windfall—only that which they were forced to—to the making of Canadian programs.

The private broadcasters responded, certainly in the 1940s and 1950s, with an anti-CBC propaganda campaign that would have made members of the U.S. House Committee on Un-American Activities smile. They accused the corporation of "purloining the airwaves," carrying out a "campaign of suppression" and of nationalizing radio. They howled that CBC "talks" programs (the precursor to public or current affairs programming) were "leftist" and, in crying for an independent regulator, painted the beleaguered and ever-indulgent broadcast regulator as "the government's CBC." They never seemed to mention Canadian programs, public service or national unity. And as they started sharpening their knives for the kill in the early 1950s, they paused in their work to stare at a strangely attractive glow on the business horizon. Television was coming.

Buffalo television was spilling over into the southern Ontario area and by 1951 there would be 60,000 television sets already in Canada, going up to 150,000 by the end of the year. Canadians were lining up to buy sets, to be able to grab an eyeful of that entertainment cornucopia from south of the border. The Royal Commission on National Development in the Arts, Letters and Sciences, known as the Massey Commission, after Vincent Massey, chancellor of the University of Toronto and a future Governor General, was established by the St. Laurent Liberals to try to set ground rules for the introduction of television in Canada, among other things. Its report was tabled in 1951. Scornful of private radio broadcasters as a whole, it called the programs they had produced and carried over the years "regrettable": "Private station interests have spent much money and energy on campaigns to change the laws of Canada. It would appear to be more in the public interest if the same money and energy were applied to developing better live broadcasting by private stations and a greater use of Canadian talent and opinion." They reminded them they were even lucky to exist. They denied the Canadian Association of Broadcasters' argument that broadcasting was a dual system with a clear allowance for private stations, pointing out that two broadcast systems were never contemplated in the legislation. They rejected their request for a separate regulatory body. The commission pointed out, with a glimpse of the future under the CRTC's control, that a stand-alone regulatory board would just enforce minimum allowable standards. They recommended that no private networks should operate without CBC permission but rejected the idea of the CBC becoming a non-commercial network. They wanted the CBC to receive $14 million a year, from license fees, commercials and the rest from Parliament. And they wanted more original production to come from places other than Toronto and Montreal.

The CAB responded by calling the Massey recommendations "unwise" and attacked the CBC as a government agency and "propaganda machine." Conservative MPs called the corporation a purveyor of "atheistic propaganda," and the advent of CBC television as "a giant step on the road to socialism." By September 1952 the CBC had television stations up and running in Montreal and Toronto, with plans for stations in Halifax, Winnipeg and Vancouver. These were not to be simple program relay centres either. They were production centres, meant to follow the Aird path and produce programs from and to the regions—in keeping with the original legislative intent of how best to reflect a nation.

By 1954 there would be 1.4 million sets in use in Canada and the national television network would consist of five CBC stations and four private stations, with the CBC providing ten-and-a-half hours of programming a week. While the CBC was busy building the few stations they had money for, the Liberal government opened the back door a crack and started handing out private station licenses, which Massey had recommended not happen. By the end of the year, seventy-five percent of Canadians would have access to television. By 1955 there were seven CBC stations and seventeen private stations.

Of the seventeen private television stations in 1955, nine of them were making profits in their first year of operation—a phenomenally quick return on investment. Advertisers were lining up to buy commercial space. Private broadcasters enjoyed monopoly protection in their markets. And as Canadian "programmers," they did not really have to produce many of their own, filling their schedules with programs from the CBC, and especially from south of the border.

Faced with rising costs of expanding the Canadian television system, the Liberals appointed another Royal Commission—under Robert Fowler—in 1955. Fowler's recommendations helped turn the screws on the CBC a bit tighter, arguing for a new regulatory body for broadcasting to replace the CBC in that role, accepting the concept of a mixed or dual system, and encouraging the CBC to cover its financial shortfalls by getting more aggressive in the commercial sales department, although the commission did call for a more stable form of grant funding to support the corporation—which was turned down by the government. Fowler also noted that, whatever "the disabilities under which the private broadcasters labour, they are not difficulties of financial distress and lack of profits." Of 144 radio stations enjoying twenty percent net income of sales, only 100 showed any expenditure on Canadian artists or talent. Of the 100, the average was only $8,600 per station. Fowler wrote kindly that: "We have been forced to the conclusion that free enterprise has failed to do as much as it could in original programme production and development of Canadian talent, not because of a lack of freedom, but because of a lack of enterprise."

Fowler was the start of more than a decade of fast political decline for the CBC, a time when it seemed to be losing friends left, right and centre on the political spectrum. By 1957, Liberal caucus support for the corporation was slipping with every public affairs program presentation or news story about the latest government problem. Many Liberal MPs resented the CBC's reporting. To some extent, they saw the CBC as "theirs." They had protected it against the Conservative and Social Credit hordes. How come the CBC was on the Liberal's case now? On the other side of the House, the Conservatives were criticizing the corporation for weighting their programming in the Liberals' favour. MPs were also receiving complaints, on the one hand, from citizens saying they were not getting their promised CBC coverage and, on the other, static from those offended by CBC programs they felt were a bit racy, or which questioned traditional religious beliefs. The corporation began to feel the long arm of the Liberal government trying to intervene in programming matters. The good news was that they were saved by the arrival of a new government. The bad news was that it was John Diefenbaker's Conservative government.

While the CBC was fending off its political foes, its launch of a distinctive Canadian television program service was drawing kudos from all points. Its Canadian television programs in the arts, drama, performance and variety began to draw attention and rave reviews: Arthur Hailey's *Flight into Danger*, Bernie Slade's *The Prize Winner*, *Front Page Challenge*, Canadian personalities like Wayne and Shuster, Juliette, Nathan Cohen, Tommy Tweed, W.O. Mitchell, Frank

Willis and René Lévesque. It was the dawn of the CBC's golden era in television, and it was spectacular while it lasted. In 1957, $11 million was paid out to 15,000 artists and performers. According to CBC figures, the corporation's television network was pumping out more programs than either NBC or CBS—on one-fifth the budget.

> *"I find it difficult to understand why the* CBC, *having available to it the best outlets in Canada, is continually in the red. . . . Private stations make money. . . . [The* CBC] *should make profit."*
> —John Diefenbaker, House of Commons *Debates*, 1956

In 1958, the Tories did what Tories alone can do so well: they turned back the clock. The 1958 *Broadcasting Act* stripped the CBC of its regulatory power over broadcasting and gave it to a Board of Broadcast Governors, which largely went out its way to protect and nurture the private broadcasters at the expense of the CBC. The private broadcasters got equal billing in the system. They were given even more opportunities than ever before to get rich. And Canadians ended up watching more American television than ever before. The Diefenbaker Tories also cut off CBC's license fee and statutory grant funding and forced it to go each year to the federal government, cap in hand for funding, begging the question of future political influence in CBC policy and programming intentions, and making administration less efficient and more costly. The Tories and their private broadcaster friends would try to twist the mainspring all the way back to the wild, woolly, no-holds-barred broadcasting days of the 1920s.

Diefenbaker wanted the CBC in place to ensure that broadcasting would look Canadian. He knew he could not rely on the private broadcasters to opt for Canadian rather than American programs. He also wanted to see the national service expand (in its myriad parts rather than its whole) to the regions and communities that could not support private stations. He opened the house for his buddies to bring in their U.S. programs, and he made sure the CBC would look after that tattered thing called a "national service." They would fill in the gaps where the private stations could not make a profit or attract a government subsidy.

In the early 1960s, the Diefenbaker-appointed Glassco Commission found major weaknesses in the CBC—in the organization's structure, in responsibilities and in a top-heavy Ottawa head office operation. Glassco recommended the Corporation should be reorganized and decentralized into the regions if it was to do its job right. While the CBC was otherwise distracted, the BBG increased the amount of commercial time stations could carry on radio, opened the door to second stations in a market, and to a second network to compete with the CBC—CTV. The BBG established fifty-five percent Canadian content requirements for all broadcasters, and then said the "Canadian content" could include "special events" of interest to Canadians—like the World Series and addresses by the President of the United States. To ease the price of being Canadian, the BBG allowed broadcasters to take more than two years to meet the Herculean goal of being "half-Canadian." The BBG also discovered that none of the private stations were living up to the promises they had made about doing more and better Canadian programs for Canadians. Some of the private stations even argued that the CBC should start providing *them* with Canadian programming, as it did for its affiliates.

The Diefenbaker government protested, not unlike the Mulroney government would later, that its goal was not to weaken the CBC. Yet the corporation was leaning farther into the financial ropes. The march of the private drummers into heretofore unchallenged commercial markets cost the public corporation $10-12 million each year. Revenues were off an average of twelve percent a year. Add this to the Diefenbaker austerity budget cutbacks and the result was a dramatic erosion in the production of CBC non-commercial Canadian programming, especially in prime time. The country's public broadcaster started jettisoning mandated programming in favour of programs that would attract large audiences and large amounts of advertising revenue.

By 1965, the private broadcasters were in charge. Every large Canadian city had a private television station, as well as the CBC. In nine years, private TV stations had blossomed from twenty-nine to fifty-nine. Profits for private broadcasters in 1965 were $22 million on revenue of $146 million. All nine of the second stations the Conservatives had let in the door were making a profit, but less than five percent of their gross revenues were being spent on Canadian talent and writers. And Canadian prime time, for all those lofty dreams and desires of a meaningful and culturally significant broadcasting system, was filled with American entertainment programming, the majority of which the United States' own Federal Communications

Commission chairman Newton Minow called "a vast wasteland."

Robert Fowler was brought back by the Lester Pearson government in 1965 to direct an advisory committee on broadcasting. The committee's report rubbed the CBC's collective nose in its record of shabby management but conceded that its programs were not that bad. In all, the CBC was still the essential element in a confused broadcasting system. The committee's harshest criticism was reserved for the private broadcasters, calling the few programs they produced "at the cheapest possible price," systematically mediocre and "deplorable." Fowler criticized them for running too few Canadian programs, for the little use they made of Canadian writers and performers, and for their refusal to do anything with their gross profits for "the further development of a Canadian consciousness." And Fowler's deliberations seemed to strike a tone of surprise when it was discovered, as well, that the addition of so many private stations to the Canadian broadcasting system over the years had actually *increased* viewing of American programs.

The Fowler Committee began its 1965 report by stating grandiloquently: "The only thing that really matters in broadcasting is program content; all the rest is housekeeping." And then, as Marc Raboy points out, proceeded to pay attention to housekeeping rather than programming. Canadian broadcasting was in a mess and another developing infant, cable television, would soon only make the play-pen messier. Recognizing that the CBC was short of cash, and with morale falling, Fowler called again for long-term stable funding for the CBC, principally to allow them to keep a healthy distance from Parliament Hill. And, the committee maintained, Canada needed a better version of a broadcast regulator than a BBG dedicated, it would almost appear, to stuffing concessions into the pockets of private broadcasters. According to the Report of the Special Senate Committee on Mass Media, in 1965 the return on equity for Canadian television station owners was a whopping 64.4 percent. In 1967 all B.C. CTV affiliated stations spent the embarrassing total of $4,446 on talent payments. In 1968, private television operating profit would be $17.5 million on $100 million in advertising revenue.

The CBC was still on the defensive. It was getting pilloried in the streets for its "avant-garde" programming, and petitions were circulating to clean up the smut on CBC television. Told by the legislators to keep expanding television coverage across Canada, costs were mounting along with the criticism over them. MPs seemingly could not make the connection between their instructions to bring television to the entire country and the cost of those instructions. One day they would praise the CBC in the hope of seeing expansion of service into their ridings, and the next they would blast it for showing cleavage. Finally, it was left to everyone concerned—politicians, the Board, CBC management, even CBC producers (the only group missing was the CAB and the private broadcasters)—to gather together, join hands and all fall on their own large sword at the same time. The wound would be self-inflicted, messy, very public and would leave a scar on the face of CBC for decades. It was called *This Hour Has Seven Days*.

As a television series, *Seven Days* was one of the industry's most innovative, most popular, most courageous uses of the medium. As an event in the history of the CBC, along the development path of national public broadcasting, it was an unmitigated disaster. The fight over one of the CBC's most watched programs ever took less than two years between October 1964 and May 1966, exposed a huge fracture between CBC management (who wanted more control of programming) and its creative staff (who wanted more freedom), wounded staff morale, caused a wild public outcry across the country, and, most importantly, invited the government to get involved in the decision-making of the nation's public broadcaster. It involved almost everybody who could be involved. It had management trying to manipulate programmers; programmers using MPs, cabinet ministers, even the Prime Minister, to manipulate management; it had a Parliamentary committee trying to pretend it was the CBC Board of Directors and a Board of Directors who just wanted it to all go away. Looking back from 1993, it was the *Fawlty Towers* of Canadian broadcasting issues.

For two seasons, *Seven Days* trapped the CBC and the Liberal government—but most importantly, the CBC—in a sort of hunter's jacklight. No matter what seemed to come out through the tube, what subject covered, the program froze the corporation in the public sights and revealed all its weaknesses, bickering and internecine warfare. *Seven Days* was the introduction of guerrilla television. It tried to poke fun at the Queen, interviewed politicians, convicts, homosexuals and the leader of the American Nazi party, satirized the Pope's visit, defended "the little guy" against Big Business and Big

Government, showed its biases and shoved its cameras wherever the producers felt that goodness and justice could be served. And the audience loved it. *Seven Days* drew 3,000,000 viewers weekly during the winter and spring of 1966, second only to the enormously popular Saturday night hockey games. The unconventional nature of the program's topics, and the subjective treatment given them by the producers and hosts, drove the staid CBC management into a control frenzy. With pressure from politicians and some viewers, management tried repeatedly to censure *Seven Days*, and finally threatened to close it down unless the program's two controversial hosts—Patrick Watson and Laurier LaPierre—were removed.

Buoyed by huge ratings successes, the producers short-circuited management by going directly to the government and the press. "Save Seven Days" committees sprang up across the country. MPs and the CBC were bombarded with letters and calls. Producers threatened to strike. The Parliamentary Broadcasting Committee called for hearings (they would eventually hold eighteen hearing days versus just fourteen hearing days on the entire future of broadcasting in Canada). The Prime Minister met with the producers' association in an attempt to mediate the issue. By comparison, the brouhaha that surrounded *The Valour and the Horror* had the measured tone of a discussion of the Oxford Debating Society.

A report commissioned by the Liberals blamed management and the producers equally for the fiasco. Management stuck to their guns: no *Seven Days* unless LaPierre and Watson were out of there. Producer Douglas Leiterman refused. He was dismissed. Others resigned. And the sad episode of *Seven Days* edged into the history books. One thing was very clear. Mother CBC had just washed all her dirty laundry in public, and the audience-as-taxpayer did not miss much. It was not what one would call a public relations coup.

> *"You know, you read the Broadcasting Act, it's like reading the constitution of Mars. It doesn't correspond in any way with what is taking place in the broadcasting environment. So, since nobody conforms to it, then everybody gets away with it."*
> —Marc Raboy, March 4, 1992

The *Broadcasting Act* of 1968 tried to reaffirm the CBC as the dominant player in the national broadcasting system. It was an improvement, but it was not a monumental one. In some cases the 1968 legislation just manufactured whole new problems for the CBC. The Diefenbaker act had gone too far. The BBG had devalued the currency of broadcast regulation. The bones of a national public broadcasting system had been rudely tossed aside in favour of feeding the hounds of free enterprise. We had more Canadian radio and television stations than ever before and dramatically fewer Canadian programs. But there were now too many players fiddling with the system to re-make first principles. The cable industry was growing, with revenue growth poised to rocket from $70 million in 1970 to $360 million in 1980. "Communications" was now a bigger catch-phrase than "broadcasting." Led by Quebec, the provinces were carving out pieces of the public broadcasting turf out themselves with the establishment of educational television. The CBC was given back a bit of its former authority but no solution for its perennial funding problem.

The 1968 act also saddled the CBC with the largest millstone possible for the time: to be the Liberals' main cultural cudgel for national unity. The act proclaimed that the corporation should be a balanced service of information, enlightenment and entertainment and should contribute to national unity; it should provide for a continuing expression of Canadian identity. Stated in the atmosphere of simmering Quebec independence, the initiative looked and sounded ideological and politically expedient; that the Liberals were shifting public broadcasting toward the dreaded concept of state-controlled broadcasting to support their social and constitutional policy positions. Others argued that it made balanced journalistic coverage impossible. How could a CBC journalist report objectively if she was also responsible for preserving the unity of the nation, maybe even mouthing the defences of the government of the day? More ominously, others stated that once the issue of national unity was settled, there would evidently no longer be a role for the CBC. Secretary of State Judy LaMarsh plumbed the depths of the Liberals' commitment to public broadcasting by stating that she did not think there was "very much more time left for public broadcasting to prove itself, to prove to Canadians it is worthwhile spending the money on."

The act replaced the Board of Broadcast Governors with a tougher regulatory agency in the Canadian Radio-Television Commission ('Telecommunications' was added to its name and mandate in 1976), and five-year statutory funding for the CBC once again slipped through the cracks in the debate in the House. LaMarsh indicated that a second bill was in the wings, which would smooth out the issue of long-term funding for the corporation. The CBC, and Canadians who believe in public broadcasting, were still waiting in 1993.

After 1968, industry issues would no longer be bound up in a search for a definition of a "national broadcasting system." The issue was now more complex. It was now "communications"—radio, television, educational broadcasting, cable transmission, cultural policy, telecommunications, satellite transmission and the early stirrings of the marvels of information technology. The major cultural issue—the fight of good (public broadcasting) against evil (private broadcasting)—would be overshadowed by the growing separatist movement in Quebec and its ugly incendiary events in the 1970 October Crisis.

During 1969, CBC president George Davidson was under fire from federal politicians for harbouring subversives and separatists and for allowing them to slant the news coverage of Radio-Canada. Davidson fought back. If you are talking censorship, he challenged, then legislate it. Yes, there were separatists within the CBC, but so long as they did not propagandize, the delivery of the news became more important than political intention. But the new Liberal millstone—to be responsible for contributing to national unity—got heavier with every attack or incident.

The October Crisis of 1970 further blurred the CBC's role as innocent national unity middleman. The Front de libération du Québec wanted to manipulate the Quebec media by having them broadcast the group's manifesto. Trudeau's office reached across from Ottawa and refused to allow Radio-Canada to carry the manifesto, relenting only when it was evident the FLQ message was public knowledge. The declaration of martial law and the implementation of the *War Measures Act* further obscured the distinction between the public broadcaster and the government's messenger. With Trudeau's shadow hovering behind them, management claimed that the CBC's coverage of the October Crisis had been cautious, fair and balanced. But the growing impression among other media and the public was that the CBC was becoming more and more sensitive to the government's position.

In 1971, the CRTC held hearings on cable television. Cable growth was estimated to have already siphoned off $35-45 million from the traditional broadcasting industry. Two delicious ironies evolved out of the debate over cable television. The first presentation to the CRTC, by the cable industry, used the same script its competitors and objectors—the private broadcasters—used to chip away at the CBC in days of yore. Wrapping themselves in the sackcloth of "the public interest," the cable operators set about trying to convince the CRTC that they were only providing Mr. and Mrs. Viewer with "more choice." The CAB countered by showing all its long-faded nationalist tattoos. Broadcasting was part of "our national heritage," it proclaimed. It warned that, left in the hands of the cable operators, there would be a "dramatic invasion of the cable system by American programs" that could eventually destroy the Canadian broadcasting system. The CAB started babbling as if it was the CBC circa 1936—about the national interest, the need for Canadian programming (there was no mention, of course, of the dearth of that commodity in their hands) and support for loftier public policy objectives over carpetbagging cable technology.

Fast forwarding ahead through twenty-two years more of cultural rape and pillage to the March 1993 CRTC hearings on the ominous threat from "death star" satellites, digital compression and another invasion of American signals via the marvel of fibre optics, it would be amusing to see all these former adversaries—the private broadcasters, the cable operators, and the CBC—eventually gathered together like musk oxen, their butts firmly interlocked, peering nervously outward together at the latest version of the U.S. communication threat. In the story of Canadian broadcasting and culture, the only thing funnier than the dance are the strange partnerships.

6 / A Fandango for Lunatics

"This is a fandango for lunatics who can't get along even after they've made their revolution . . ."
    —Simon Bolivar, in Gabriel García Márquez, *The General in His Labyrinth*

THE 1974 CRTC LICENSE RENEWAL hearings for the CBC were a pivotal, and traumatic, point in the post-1968 period. They marked one brief, shining moment for the broadcast regulator. A confident, beefed-up CRTC would now be the agency the original Board of the CBC should have been: a regulator of the cultural direction of broadcasting, not just the overseer of an industrial strategy and the economic well-being of private broadcasting stations. It was also one of the few times that Canadian public voices spoke loudly and passionately about "their" public broadcasting system. The briefs presented to the CRTC were overwhelmingly in support of public broadcasting. The public's message was a protest vote—in favour of public broadcasting and an intelligent broadcast service. And it showcased the CBC for what it had become, administratively speaking: timid, bureaucratic, short on vision, tied to the hind teat of commercial television, its creative arteries clogged and hardening. Where protection of the tenets of public broadcasting were concerned, the CBC now had all the courage of the Cowardly Lion in *The Wizard of Oz*.

The 1974 CRTC hearings were a watershed opportunity for the CBC. The corporation was sitting in front of a sympathetic, if challenging, regulator, led by a chairman, Pierre Juneau, who had also been a member of the BBG from 1966. He understood both the genesis of public broadcasting and the factors that inhibited its development. The private broadcasters had been placated with power, recognition and numerous opportunities to make money—the production of Canadian programs, of course, being another matter altogether. Except for the odd, calcified breath from the back benches about a "leftist" CBC, MPs were preoccupied with a range of other matters from the Quiet Revolution in Quebec to the oil crisis in the Middle East, from the advent of new technologies to the repercussions of the social revolution the 1960s had bequeathed us.

The experiences of the late 1960s—from Expo 67 to the election of Pierre Elliott Trudeau, from the explosion of international radicalism in 1968 to the long view of an America locked in the Viet Nam experience—had crystallized strong cultural expectations in many Canadians. They were looking for Canadian things to believe in and a public broadcaster to reflect their images, their stories and their differences from their neighbours to the south. Another of the sensitizing agents was the 1970 Report of the Special Senate Committee on Mass Media. The "Davey report," named after its chairman, Senator Keith Davey, helped focus an extremely strong light on the state of Canadian mass media—newspapers, radio, television, magazines, periodicals, minority press, alternative press, even student newspapers. The section of the report on broadcasting clinically dissected the industry and helped provide, indirectly, much of the framework for the 1974 CRTC hearings.

The fifteen-member Senate Committee report began by calling broadcasting "The Beast of Burden"—an institution saddled unlike any other media with responsibility for holding the country and its culture together. It immediately took a jab at the private broadcasters, pointing out that they, too, were expected to help carry this great burden on at least one shoulder: "After all, the other shoulder is often employed in carrying quite heavy bags of money to the bank." It went on to remind them that the 1968 *Broadcasting Act* declared the airwaves to be public, not private, property and "Canadians had a right to expect that broadcasters would use that public property to strengthen our culture, rather than dilute it."

This Senate committee—light years distant from the reactionary and ossified rantings of *The Valour and the Horror* group in 1992— thought the CBC was "a national institution in a country that lacks national institutions." It was a unique institution, made vulnerable by an unfortunate reliance on commercial revenue and annual appropriations from Parliament: "The CBC is like a housewife, obliged to pay the costs of running the home but never certain how much her husband will give her out of the pay packet each week." To make ends meet, she occasionally had to "take in washing." The committee pressed Parliament to provide five-year grant funding for the CBC. They quoted then-CBC president George F. Davidson about the dangers of reliance on commercial revenues: "My personal belief," said Davidson, "is that we are excessively dependent on commercial advertising now. It is showing signs of affecting the quality and nature of our programming in prime time." The committee wanted an "alternative" programming role for the CBC with programs that were unique and different from what private broadcasters might provide. Pointing out that there are large English-speaking centres outside of Toronto capable of producing Canadian programs, the committee wanted more production to come out of other regions if the corporation was to be a true reflection of Canadian culture.

Turning its guns of national passion on the private broadcasters— and particularly the CAB—the Senate Committee felt "driven to conclude that the private broadcasters, no matter how sophisticated their individual thought, seem by group interaction to achieve a level perhaps best described as neanderthal." It called their performance "strip-mining." It ridiculed the private broadcasters' position on the steady concentration of station ownership as a natural phenomenon and a sign of operational efficiency: "One is struck in considering this position that it reflects a belief that we have encountered before: the belief that operational efficiency must be served at all costs, that the system must be strengthened and perpetuated regardless of human needs or values, that the machine's needs must be satisfied. The idea that the public might not be best served by having all Canadian broadcasting owned by about a dozen groups seems simply to be considered irrelevant."

The committee went on to ridicule the CAB's position that it was good that our cultural heritage was safeguarded and developed through public funds: "The notion that a private broadcaster might spend some of his *own* funds for these purposes just doesn't seem to be even thinkable." And the CAB position, that if left in a world minus Canadian content regulations, an appropriate number of Canadian programs of a suitable quality would be produced by the private broadcasters, drew this caustic response from the committee: "We feel there is simply not a shred of evidence to support the C.A.B.'s protestations that the private broadcasters, if left to their own devices, would produce plenty of high-quality Canadian programmes. Some private broadcasters have produced high-quality Canadian programmes. We feel this country should recognize them for what they are: persons so exceptional in the private broadcasting world as to be virtually of another species."

As for the rest, they went on, "the fact is that the vast majority of private broadcasters have done the minimum required of them by law, and no more. They have been content to let the networks fill the prime-time hours with imported programmes; they have been happy to take whatever the networks would supply free; they have filled the rest of their hours with as much syndicated material as possible, producing themselves as little as possible. They have been content, as one of the exceptions once noted, 'to sit at the end of the pipe and suck'."

Not quite finished mopping the floor with our captains of the private broadcast industry, the committee went on to point out that "One reason it is so profitable is that broadcasters have been protected by successive regulatory agencies against competition." This was the sort of scathingly critical environment that helped fuel the demands of cultural nationalists and people just simply fed up with what private broadcasters had perpetrated upon them. They would go before the CRTC seeking a return to a worthwhile Canadian broadcasting system.

Over 300 intervenors expressed their views in writing and twenty-nine made oral interventions to the CRTC about what they wanted, in some cases demanded, in public broadcasting. As Herschel Hardin pointed out in his book *Closed Circuits: The Sellout of Canadian Television*, the people raising their voices were the supporters of public broadcasting and "the idea of the CBC." Canadian broadcasting, in general, had gotten off the tracks. Canadians were angry over the English television network's loss of purpose, the blatant ugliness of commercials on public broadcasting, and the loss, as Hardin put it, of "intellectual fibre" now replaced by programming timidity, blandness and triviality. Private radio was wall-to-wall popular music mixed with inane chat and news in "bulletins." Television had evolved into simply being a merchandising mechanism for distributing syndicated U.S. entertainment programs. Despite the BBG's brave fifty-five percent Canadian content rule, by 1970 about eighty percent of prime time television was taken up with U.S. programs. Canadian private television stations in 1968 made an astronomical fifty-percent return on equity before tax—and were putting beans-all back into the broadcasting system in the form of indigenous programs. Most Canadian content was slipped into the dog-hours of the schedule when few people were watching—on both the private stations and on CBC. The hope in 1974 was that a renewed CBC could make all things better for the national broadcasting service. It certainly would not get better left in the hands of the free-wheeling private carpet-baggers.

The 1970 effort by the CRTC to further stiffen Canadian content regulations—sixty percent of television prime time to be Canadian and thirty percent of all music on radio had to be Canadian—had shocked most private broadcasters. They had been the villains who had dragged the purer concepts of broadcasting into the ditch of commercialism, split the system to their own ends and undermined the objective of a system meant to contribute to greater national understanding. "Their ideology was the American ideology," Herschel Hardin wrote in *Closed Circuits. Broadcaster* magazine, the CAB's unquestioned supporter, speculated ridiculously that the CRTC might be laying the foundations for the same uses of Canadian broadcasting that the Nazis had before World War II. The CRTC's determination to implement new Canadian content regulations was "a shaft pointed right at the heart of the democratic system." The CAB went on a rampage against the CRTC and anyone who did not support the CAB's position: Canadian programming was bad programming; the talent was not there; private broadcasters would lose millions of dollars. It boycotted part of the hearings. The performance was so odious, some private station members resigned from the organization. *Broadcaster* also asked a number of rhetorical questions that made one wonder if private broadcasters lived in the same country, or resided on the same planet, as the rest of us, or valued the same beliefs: "Why must there be more Canadian content? . . . Can the CRTC provide documented proof that U.S. television programming has an adverse effect on the people of this country?"

Intervenors supporting the CBC at the 1974 CRTC hearings seemed to feel that now was the time to set things straight. Their themes were consistent with Aird. The CBC must be a national institution, but it must be minoritarian, seeing to the regions, the parts, and perhaps even a multitude of cultural interests—labour, consumers, children, women, natives, rural citizens. If the CBC didn't do it, who would? The private stations? The CBC was, as Juneau put it, "the central nervous system of Canadian nationhood." It was the argument that Sir John Aird, Dr. Augustin Frigon and Charles Bowman crafted in 1929: there was no reasonable way to reflect the true nature of being Canadian, and preserving Canadian culture, other than to ensure that the programs came from the regions. A number of intervenors wanted programming for Canadians to be designed by others than the "Toronto-Ottawa-Montreal mafia." The CBC internal forces of program centralism, ones that admired American-style programs and carried a focus on urban as opposed to rural Canada, had to be checked. The intervenors wanted the CBC out of commercial broadcasting. They wanted the public service of Canadian broadcasting to be unique. The issue was public broadcasting as a means of building for social and cultural purposes. The CBC did not exist, many believed, to build an audience for commercial purposes.

The CBC opened the hearings on February 18 by stating that it had only three options. It could adopt a working model that was totally commercial, but abrogate the current public service mandate. It could be different and Canadian but aim its programming at an elitist, specialized minority. Or, it could be different and Canadian and aim its programming at a "mass" audience—meaning concentrate on being popular and stay predominantly commercial. It picked number three. The CBC felt it was the only reasonable strategy, given its responsibilities and funding. But the direction the corporation was now prepared to pursue would irrevocably alter CBC's role. As Marc Raboy points out: "The distinction was important, because it established the CBC's perception of Canada as a mass society rather than a community of publics. . . . This was a departure from the position the CBC had taken before the Massey Commission twenty-five years earlier, when it said that it saw itself serving different segments of the society at different times."

Looking into the future all the way to the chaos that was the CBC after December 5, 1990, mass would come to mean less rigorous, less distinctive programming on the CBC. Mass would mean a continuation of American-style, mainstream programs and commercials on public broadcasting. Mass would mean a preoccupation with audience ratings to the detriment of distinctive programs. Mass would eventually mean fewer regional programs, less reflective of the diversity of Canadian lifestyles. Mass would eventually mean the end of regional programs, other than news. If option No. 3 was supposed to be a strategy for the future, CBC management were riding in the wrong direction.

That mass audience they were going to rely on for ratings and commercial revenue was already eroding under their feet. It was as if they had not been paying attention to the forces at play within their own industry. It was a time when television audiences were already beginning to fragment and diversify their tastes with the increasing number of program options cable had started to deliver. To begin marching toward a goal of mass audience attraction just as the industry was beginning to splinter, was not unlike the Light Brigade's charge into the "Valley of Death." It was glorious, to be sure, to know where you were going, and to believe in such a cause. But technology was against you, the odds favoured the other side from the start, and the timing, to say the least, was very bad. The outcome would be inevitable.

This was at a time when Canadians were beginning to cry out for more substance—more Canadian shows, better public affairs presentations, more programs that utilized Canadian writers and performing talent—in their broadcasting system, especially in the public broadcasting sector. The CBC was opting for less. The public, and to a great extent, the CRTC, would challenge the corporation to think courageously, step out of form and grasp the future with Canadian programs that did not vie for ratings. The CBC went into hunker-down mode and started pretending the past was the future.

Intervenors attacked the centralist programming biases of the CBC television networks and, once again, argued for stable, multi-year funding from Parliament. Some sought a broadly-based, commercial-free public television system. Some argued that chasing a mass audience was wrong, that the CBC had reached an incorrect assumption about its national role and should be seeking a role that was different and diversified. Radio-Canada producers reminded the CRTC of a reality that CBC management have never been able to comprehend, that the "network" audiences they relied upon did not really exist. People watched television in the context of their neighbourhoods, their communities, their regions—not some administratively convenient abstract called a "network." Some called the CBC a "closed system," where the public had no involvement with the making of programs for their consumption. The CBC's technical union, NABET, called for citizen participation in programming, in effect taking public broadcasting back to the Aird Commission and the recommended provincial citizen advisory councils. As Raboy reflected: "The CRTC hearings . . . demonstrated the gulf that had arisen between the public broadcaster and its supporters."

The decision handed down after the hearings was probably less earth-shaking to intervenors and the public than it was to the CBC. The CRTC had heard the call of the Canadian public and suggested that the CBC increase regional production, increase Canadian content in prime time, spend more time serving the diverse needs of the regions of the country, get out of commercials in radio, and start reducing commercials in television. "We proposed that advertising minutes [per hour] be reduced by one minute a year for five years, down to about five minutes," said Juneau in 1992. "The idea was that the size of advertising in CBC programming should be reduced drastically." The CBC objected to that "very vigorously." The CRTC had done extensive research and analysis about the CBC's program schedule and were able to see clearly that the corporation's program strategy was as much as anything determined, as Juneau puts it, "by the obligation toward money." In its summary, the CRTC pointed out that "commercial activity deflects the CBC from its purpose and influences its philosophy of programming and scheduling. It must, in the Commission's considered opinion, be reduced or even eliminated."

The CBC told the CRTC that it intended to continue to maintain its policy that certain classes of television programs would be commercial-free. And it would voluntarily get out of radio advertising. But the CRTC had been inundated with complaints about all CBC commercial policy. Articles had appeared in national magazines before the hearings berating the corporation for being in the commercial business. The secret was simple to most concerned Canadians—get the CBC out of commercial advertising. Management balked. The cost might be $100 million a year. With the Liberals holding tight on the purse strings, they could not see a way out. They were not about to take the hint—from the public, from their own staff, or from the CRTC. "They just said, 'the hell with you'," Juneau remembered. "Nothing happened. The idea was dropped."

In parallel with its push to get CBC television out of the commercial advertising business, the CRTC tried to block the CBC's goal of chasing a "mass audience." The corporation should treat its audience, the CRTC said, not as a "mass" but "as an active community of people, with real and varying communication needs." The CRTC laid a hand on another sclerotic artery—the distance the corporation preferred to maintain between itself as the public servant and the public. The CBC seemed to be following a philosophy that reflected less the needs of the public "than the need for institutional survival." The programming process was clearly "inimical to a free flow of ideas especially for those geographically removed from production centres." The CBC had evolved into what Raboy called an "administrative broadcaster"—caught up in its own version of what the public wanted in programming, secure in its pursuit of commercial revenue and ratings as guidelines.

Ironically, while the corporation argued heatedly against the efficacy of a non-commercial lifestyle for CBC television, its initiative to free its radio networks from the clutches of the merchants of soap, sedans and toothpaste forged a model for a fine and respected version of Canadian public broadcasting to come—commercial-free CBC radio. Opting out of radio advertising was not the fiscal challenge television advertising would pose. Rid of unseemly commercials, the CBC English radio network went on to become everything that the ETV network could not be: distinctive, Canadian, with programs based solidly in the regions of the country, reflecting the reality of what life in Canada is all about, not just what advertisers would like to see. The solution for television was sitting right beside them.

The CBC also shackled itself to the past by not recognizing and taking advantage of the massive transition the broadcasting industry was beginning to undergo at that very time. Escalating industry fragmentation—to cable, to educational television, to Pay-TV, to home satellite dishes and to video cassettes—did not seem to mean much to CBC management. Getting out of commercial television would have been only half of the equation, a very important half to be sure. The underlying reasoning was that a non-commercial public broadcaster could, in a fragmenting world, perform as Canadian public broadcasting was intended to. It could be distinctive. It could stand out from the dregs of North American television and attract solid audience support. The moment called for vision, for more channels to deliver programs, providing more options for serving the Canadian public. Without a CBC-2, or a similar public channel governed separately, the corporation would always be hopelessly trapped. Lacking the necessary vision, as Hardin wrote, the CBC "tied it self into a straightjacket of its own making and kept pulling the knots tighter."

Although the next CBC president, Al Johnson, would lobby aggressively for a CBC-2, the CBC would, when the moment eventually came, be denied its modern distribution solution. The exception would be the successful battle for an all-news channel—Newsworld—which the corporation was able to achieve in 1989 by putting the service, on paper at least, on a no-cost, user-pay basis and decentralizing operations to Halifax, Winnipeg and Calgary. One thing would be constant over the next nineteen years. The CBC would become more dependent, not less, on commercial revenues derived from the ETV network—to the point where those thirty and fifteen second annoying slices of unreality would help choke the last breath out of Canada's national public broadcaster. By the fall of 1989, when Gérard Veilleux walked in the door, commercialization was growing at a faster rate than the Tories could cut the CBC's budget.

Even as the CRTC hearings were being digested at the end of 1974, the spectre of industry fragmentation was already becoming a reality. There were more than 400 cable operators in Canada with access to eighty percent of the homes in the country. Subscribers were lining up to get in on this cornucopia of mostly foreign TV signals. Cable revenues were already one-half those of the television industry. It was becoming a wired, not a broadcast, world. By 1979, Vancouver would have cable penetration close to ninety percent. A year after the CRTC and the CBC picked up their files and headed home, Pay-TV (feared by private broadcasters, loved by cable operators) loomed on the television horizon. Satellite transmission, direct broadcast satellites and the fibre optic doorway were all part of the new, rapidly expanding technological future. Private broadcasters were no longer overly concerned about the status of the CBC. They had other things on their mind, like delaying, or controlling, the introduction of Pay-TV in Canada. This benign neglect from an industry foe which had worked so effectively at mauling the basic precepts of public broadcasting over the years hinted at an even spookier reality for the CBC: it was becoming less and less relevant—to its competitors, to audiences, to politicians. The eclipse was already well underway.

"It was a Liberal government that began the process of undermining and eroding public broadcasting. They made it extremely easy for the Conservatives, when they came into office in 1984, to implement their historic policy with respect to broadcasting."

—Marc Raboy, SCAN magazine, March/April 1991

The political tensions which boiled between 1970 and 1980, and the possibility of Quebec turning its back on Confederation, put the CBC again under the hot lights of political and public scrutiny. Fuelled by the emotional ride of the Quiet Revolution, Quebecers opted in November 1976 to test their relationship with the rest of Canada by electing the Parti Québecois government of René Lévesque. The PQ's commitment to a referendum on independence would lead indirectly to four years of very public CBC-bashing and 'whose-side-are-you-on?' baiting from federal politicians and the press. Sweeping allegations of a pro-separatist bias within Société Radio-Canada would peak in 1977 with the tabling of the CRTC's report on its investigation into the allegations. The CBC's basic dilemma was that after 1968 it was firmly carrying the responsibility for contributing to national unity and Canadian identity. But even the most disciplined and objective of news reports about happenings in Quebec—in the context of their responsibility to contribute to national unity—were construed by many Parliamentary critics as not doing the unity job. The CRTC report found that, by and large, there was little clear evidence of distortion in SRC's news and public affairs programming. But regardless of the findings, the CBC would be under constant pressure and criticism, especially from Quebec Liberal MPs. Al Johnson, CBC president during this time, would latter recall quite seriously that, "they made my life hell."

Al Johnson became the CBC's president August 1, 1975. He was a Harvard Ph.D. in economics, professional civil servant, a former deputy minister of finance and secretary of the Treasury Board. Johnson brought a new enthusiasm to the CBC—for public broadcasting and for what he saw as the traditional role of the CBC as a leader in both programming and nation-building. Johnson found it hard to visualize a Canada without the CBC. He believed it was needed to reflect the attitudes, beliefs and values of Canadians across the country: "I was quite clear about the *importance* of the CBC. There was no question. I had been brought up on it. I was raised in the Prairies.

The CBC had introduced me to Canada."

He was shocked at how few hours of Canadian programs actually appeared on television—certainly on the private stations, but on the CBC as well. "We were awash in American programming," Johnson recalled. Canadians were still being inundated with U.S. values, beliefs and history. Considering how long the road and how hard the journey toward a national broadcasting system had been, Canadians actually seemed to be in a position that was as bad as or worse than before 1929 and the Aird Commission. Less than one-third of the programs Canadians were receiving on the system were now made in Canada. A mere four percent of that was Canadian drama—the programs most responsible for helping to shape national consciousness. "So how could you blame people for not watching Canadian programs when they didn't have Canadian programs to watch?" Johnson asked.

The "Canadianization" of television was his goal. CBC radio would be his model. It was a unique broadcast service, commercial-free, with a distinctive sound. It was predominantly Canadian. CBC radio had developed a very close relationship with Canadians and their neighbourhoods. Many of the programs that helped to make the service so popular were produced in the regions, not in Montreal and Toronto. Radio was delivering an authentic, unfiltered version of Canada to Canadians. It was hoped CBC television would, once and for all, start to look like the national, public model that had been sculpted in 1929. The only issue was: who would pay for it?

If Parliament was ever in a mood to pony up the approximately one hundred million dollars it might take to see Johnson's dream become a reality, it would not have been in the 1976-77 period. The main preoccupation was national unity. And to many MPs, especially those from Quebec, the national institution they saw responsible for national unity was not doing its job. Give it more money? Not likely, at least not until the CBC started toeing the party line and supporting the federalist side of the debate. "The dilemma of getting more quality Canadian programming lay, of course, in finding funds—getting along with the government," Johnson recalled. "There was no way we could get along with a government that was in such a state of distraction, to put it very mildly. When you feel your country is threatened, and you are fighting for your country, and you have a CBC that doesn't respond by saying: 'Ready, Aye, Ready,' you say—if you are a Quebecer—'What the hell is going on here'?"

The guts of the problem lay in opposing interpretations of the 1968 *Broadcasting Act*. The legislation requiring the CBC to act on the behalf of national unity and national identity stated that the corporation should "contribute" to the development of national unity. Quebec MPs and many others saw it as a responsibility to "promote" national unity. This would be an interpretational dichotomy that would continue to haunt the CBC, even after the referendum was settled. "Contributing to the development of national unity means reflecting our country," Johnson pointed out. "Out of that emerges a sense of country and a belief in a country and a passion for the country that transcends by any measure the political arguments that take place when you are trying to argue people into being Canadians. But when it comes to news and current affairs, that clause does not apply. In the context of a free country, where freedom is the prevailing value, you contribute to the development of national unity through good journalism."

The national unity issue, the CBC's role in it, and the unforgiving and hostile reaction of the Liberal government toward the public broadcaster, would poison the well for any future development or restructuring of the corporation. As Laval's Marc Raboy pointed out, after the referendum of 1980, "there was a feeling that there really wasn't a political reason to go on pouring huge sums of money into the CBC." The CBC's refusal to play a more politicized role leading up to the referendum would be a bitter taste Liberals would carry in their mouths. The first chance they had to get even, they would see that the corporation slipped even further into institutional irrelevance.

Shortly after the CRTC inquiry into Radio-Canada and CBC's public affairs programming was underway in the spring of 1977, Johnson launched "Touchstone for the CBC," his revitalization plan of action, wrapped around a philosophy that the CBC was really all about the creation of national consciousness. Touchstone would spark the move toward Canadianization of the English television service. It would be a means of enhancing Canadian identity and would broaden French language television to reflect the full diversity of the nation. The strategy depended on two new commercial-free, satellite-to-cable channels: "CBC-2" for English and "Télé-Deux" for French language broadcasting. The CBC-2 concept would offer

Canadians "distinctive, thoughtful, alternative programming." It would carry repeats of successful CBC programs appearing on the main networks, as well as new programs produced specifically for CBC-2. Johnson saw clearly that "you can't fulfil the mandate of the CBC with a single channel."

The new, revitalized public broadcaster would include public advisory councils, a complaint commission and the holding of public forums to draw the audience closer to its broadcaster and involve it in program deliberations. Johnson thought seriously of moving the new second network's head office to Vancouver, to prove that the CBC could be a regionally-based, national network. Johnson was betting that a more popular CBC could be "the single most powerful instrument for strengthening Canadian nationhood." Touchstone was Johnson's personal gamble on greatness for the CBC. All he needed was $25-30 million from Parliament.

While Johnson was hoping to save public broadcasting and, perhaps, the nation, the CRTC inquiry into the CBC and Radio-Canada's alleged biases tabled its findings on July 20, 1977. It found no nefarious plot by separatist-leaning journalists. CBC's big problem, according to the inquiry report, lay in the facts that: programming and production were too centralized in Toronto and Montreal; the French and English language networks were isolated from one another; and an excessive reliance on U.S. programming caused the English TV network, particularly, to end up more or less in "self-imprisonment in the North American mould of entertainment and commercial sponsorship." It also found the usual CBC problems: low morale within the organization and complaints about not enough regional programming input. But the important thing to note is that the CRTC, in what should have been a simple sidebar inquiry into suspected CBC journalistic indiscretion, was really running up, once again, the red flag of cultural and constitutional warning. Not unlike Johnson's Touchstone effort, it was saying to the Liberal government: your major problem in the national unity debate is that you have failed to provide support for the one institution capable of binding the country together. You have been so blinded by the attraction of the weeds on the fringe, that you missed seeing the forest.

The CRTC inquiry report seemed to echo Johnson's solution for a more meaningful, responsive and valuable CBC: public broadcasting, to be an effective force for national identity, had to get back to its roots in the regions, had to get out of the commercial television rat race and had to quit trying to play "the ratings game" with the rest of the industry. It stated this very clearly: "It is not the number of people watching a program that matters, but the importance of that program, and the cultural situation of the people who are watching it."

The main argument in Johnson's unorthodox approach to mainstream public programming and greater audience attraction—and one that some of his English television network program managers tried to buck—was "authenticity." To Johnson, the CBC had to make television programs that were "authentic" and recognizable and appreciated by Canadians—as being Canadian. Nothing else. No American sit-com rip-offs. No "Canadian drama" that looked like it came from L.A. To be "authentic" meant you took risks. You went with programs that would mean more to Canadians culturally than commercially. As he would say with some passion fifteen years later: "*Pigeon Inlet* [a very folksy, down-home look at life in Newfoundland] means a hell of a lot more in terms of Canadian identity than *Street Legal!*"

Johnson found that many of the ETV network management group—as many still do to this day—were measuring their definitions of Canadian public broadcasting by an incorrect model. Their standards were not cultural standards; they were North American, commercial television standards. But with Johnson the higher standard was tied to an effort to be authentically Canadian. This meant crafting programs that were full of stories, images, people, names, places, reflections, issues, thoughts and sounds that were recognizably Canadian, and in a lot of cases, more rural than urban. *That* was what public broadcasting in Canada was supposed to be about; not a Nielsen rating point or "reach" or advertiser's cost-per-thousand. Johnson wanted more programs like *The National Dream* and *The Last Spike*. He got fewer. In the midst of Canada's most important constitutional debate, Johnson almost pleaded for a dramatization of the Battle of the Plains of Abraham, to provide some historical context to the running French-English debate. He was led to believe the theme was not entirely suitable for contemporary television. Who knows what ETV network management were thinking? Presumably, the program might not attract a large audience, might cost more than the commercial revenues it brought in or would not do well in the ratings. It would never play in L.A.

Johnson needed time, money and political support for the key to Touchstone—CBC-2. He got lots of time, and the rest is history. A stripped-down version of CBC-2 would cost a little more than $25 million, a "Model-A Ford" version as Johnson put it, and still a fraction of the total cost of the CBC. But at this moment, the corporation's main network also needed more money as well. Johnson wanted to get out of commercial advertising, but that would mean $97 million more in 1979-80 dollars. He knocked on the big, oak door of "the most senior people" in the Liberal government. Inside, he found a spiteful Liberal government. "They were in a state of distraction [over Quebec]," Johnson remembered charitably. The Liberals, all the way to the major power-brokers in cabinet, were not prepared to hand out money to finance Johnson's dream. Hell, they wanted fealty. More than that, given the CBC's behaviour to date, they wanted penance. This was a testy and reactive Trudeau government. Under intense pressure to keep the country together, they resented the fact that the corporation would not do their exact bidding. Johnson argued that the best force for unity and understanding was sound, balanced reporting—a principle seemingly beyond the Liberals' collective cerebral grasp. He stood his ground. "And my strategy therefore had to be to get the CRTC on-side. I could not conceive of the CRTC, charged with the mandate that had been given in the act, of saying 'no' to our license request."

Faced with the intense pressure of exploding communications technology, a neolithic Liberal government, the national unity crisis, the gluttonous ineptitude of the private sector, the forces of centralization in broadcasting, a new set of whine-and-win twins in the cable industry and the seemingly relentless invasion of U.S. programming schlock hammering against the country's cultural shores, the CRTC between 1974 and 1977 tended to point to a healthy CBC as our national salvation. But just as the CBC was starting to get the message—that it relied too much on North American commercial standards and the mass audience—the years of Liberal enmity and vengefulness crossed currents with a new wave of supply-side thinking on the CRTC. The interflow of the two murky waters would turn the one brief shining moment of public broadcasting back into a slough.

"The Pay-TV Fiasco was not only predictable, it was predicted. Pay-TV never made Canadian sense."
—Herschel Hardin, *Closed Circuits*

Under new leadership, the broadcast regulator once again developed a decidedly private sector bias. One case in point was the introduction of Pay-TV in 1982. It would be a disaster—from a cultural point of view, a business point of view and a Canadian programming point of view. After trying for years to sensitize Canadians to the need to circle the protective wagons around their fast-dwindling culture, the CRTC opened up the tent to a circus of private sector clowns, their pockets mostly bulging with U.S. programs. Somehow, God only knows how, this latest CRTC saw Pay-TV as, "our last chance to get Canadian content right." As Hardin wrote: "Trying to re-Canadianize television with Pay-TV was re-Canadianizing it by Americanizing it even more thoroughly."

Pay-TV, the CRTC said, must be "a predominantly Canadian programming service of high quality"—but without the CBC as a player. They were going to introduce a new toy in the sandbox of Canadian broadcasting for only the private sector to play with. This CRTC actually believed—after over fifty years of private broadcasters fiddling with the cultural objectives of the system—that you could trust the private sector to concentrate on filling the Pay-TV cables with Canadian programs and films.

The concept of Canadian Pay-TV was ill-advised, poorly planned, ridiculously licensed and did almost nothing for Canadian culture, identity or national unity, even though it took the better part of a decade to get it up and running. The CRTC's own research revealed that there was little demand for the service. Only fourteen percent of those surveyed said they would be "very likely" subscribe to the service at $9 a month (the price would end up being closer to $16 a month on average). Pay-TV turned out to be everything Canadian private broadcasting had always been—too many players, broken promises, a white lie or two, shabby regulation and a pipeline for more U.S. programming into Canada. Licenses were handed out like popcorn, after years of delay. Six Pay-TV licenses were given out at the first pass, with two others pending, and the CRTC was calling for more. Licensees went broke, one after another, within figurative minutes of getting their licenses. Independent producers did not get the work that was expected. Canadian content regulations were thrown out the window. The survivors did what any good Canadian free enterprise broadcast spirit would do. They lobbied, divided up the territories and received monopoly status from the CRTC.

A month after calling for license applications for Pay-TV, the CRTC shot down Al Johnson's dream—a request for a license for CBC-2—because, "we did not think it was good enough," claimed CRTC chairman John Meisel. Looking back, a mildly bitter Al Johnson called the CRTC's reasoning on CBC-2 "gutless" and "my blackest moment in the CBC." Johnson could not imagine being turned down by the CRTC. He had synthesized recommendations from over the years, studied the direction broadcasting was being pushed in, and, in effect, come up with a plan that would meet all the CRTC's critical requests for a unique public broadcasting service: totally Canadian, commercial-free, a truly alternative service, regionalized production operations and catering to individual tastes, not a mass audience. Admittedly, he still had a large liability or two. The main CBC television network still chugged along, chock-a-block full of commercial messages and U.S.-made programming. His argument for a new, purer version of Canadian public television was hard to digest as long as the family's biggest embarrassment, the ETV network, went to air with their made-like-America colour bars each day.

That aside, the CRTC still failed to see the merit in the CBC-2 concept. They also had it on good authority that the CBC was not going to get the extra money from the Liberals for CBC-2, even if they had received a license. "[The CRTC] had a different view, I think, of their relationship with government," Johnson theorized. "If the money wasn't there, how could they appear to be telling the government to give the CBC money? Well, if I had been chairman of the CRTC, I would have relished that, because the government kicks you in the shins all the time. Why not kick them in the shins once? But they said 'no'."

The referendum issue, but not the constitutional issue, had been settled in May 1980 with the narrow defeat of the separatist forces in Quebec. The CBC seemed to crawl out from beneath the constitutional wreckage in a win-lose position. On the one hand, Johnson's principled stand on the independence of CBC journalists to do their jobs as professionals, rather than shills for the federal Liberals, won many votes. On the other hand, his stand helped sour the last few ounces of traditional support the corporation might expect from an angry and resentful bunch of Liberal MPs, especially those from Quebec. If you were not my friend in time of trouble, went their reasoning, Mother Mary was not going to comfort you when you were short of cash. The NDP were supportive but short on numbers. Tory backbench mouths had remained open and breathing all these years in anticipation of getting even with the CBC for the perceived slights going back into the Diefenbaker years. There were fewer and fewer friends on the Hill. From 1981, life, broadcasting and the importance of the CBC would move downhill quickly.

The Liberals were about to stir the slough, making public broadcasting just another part of the industrial strategy mix called "culture and communications." With national unity out of the way, the CBC's main justification (in the eyes of many MPs) as the nation's cultural cornerstone was expiring. The pressing sweep of new communications technologies forced the tired, old public broadcaster into the back seat of broadcasting and cultural significance. Some of CBC's power splintered off to a CRTC pressing for more regulatory influence over the CBC. Some of it went to the Department of Communications for planning reaction and policies for new forms of communication. And a trunkful of film and television production money, which would have been earmarked for the CBC in the old days, went to the new cash dispensing machine, the Canadian Broadcast Program Development Fund (Telefilm Canada), revved up in 1983.

Telefilm Canada, or just "Telefilm," would be the government's pay-off to a mess of Canadian private production companies and independent producers (many of them former CBC employees) who had been haranguing the Liberals over what they saw as a doddering old CBC getting in the way of their making major productions—and major profits. The independent producers were typically Canadian. Eventually, many of them would go on to produce millions of dollars worth of Canadian programming—using comparatively little of their own money. They would risk a lot of their time, and worry occasionally about the odd second mortgage hanging over their heads, but the Canadian taxpayer was the one who put up—and still does—most of the money to have these Canadian programs made.

Telefilm would turn out to be the big investor in the Canadian programming mix, providing, in later cases, as much as forty-nine percent of the cash needed to produce a program. Although Telefilm's "investments" were originally meant to kick-start production projects—get them up and running to attract replacement non-public funding—in many cases Telefilm stayed around in the barnyard filling and refilling the trough for the independent producers, for three and four years in some cases. The CBC would throw in cash license fees and often thousands of dollars in manpower, facilities and production resources. Provincial film and television funding agencies, and occasionally a domestic or foreign distributor, would toss in the rest. Voilà: creative Canadian entrepreneurs at work.

At the same time, the Liberal government continued what was to become a relentless tightening down of the budget screws on the CBC. The Parliamentary appropriation had jumped to $650 million by 1981 and the Liberals slapped constraints on further expansion. The Liberals also launched the Federal Cultural Review Committee, known as "Applebaum-Hébert" after the co-chairmen, composer Louis Applebaum, and writer and publisher Jacques Hébert. They tabled their report on November 16, 1982, which helped further slick the skids for the CBC, reinforcing life's reality that the private broadcasters, now accompanied by their junior partners, the independent production sector, were on top of the system. The committee's recommendations, as Toronto communications consultant Paul Audley would predict, would lead to a decline in Canadian programming. Its recommendations ranged from the repetitive to the radical. They called the CBC the "key element in the system" and reminded Canadians for about the eightieth time in fifty years that we were at a "critical moment in our history." We needed a "better, more vital, more courageous CBC," but, the committee poked, "too many Canadians are beginning to question the very need for a public broadcaster such as the CBC."

They recommended that the CBC get out of commercial advertising, the lost revenue to be replaced with multi-year funding from the federal government. Commercials on CBC television and restrictions on annually funding, they said, had led to disastrous pressure to buy U.S. programming and produce look-alike U.S. programs. The CBC should diversify and carry alternative programming. A fixed proportion of its budget should be allocated to producing programs strictly in the regions, decentralizing the program decision-making apparatus and getting the programming power out of Toronto and

Montreal. The most controversial recommendation was to privatize CBC assets and farm out all television production to the private sector, except news. The committee wanted CBC television to become simply a carrier of independently produced Canadian programs.

Pirouetting over to the private side of the broadcasting ledger, the Applebaum-Hébert committee pointed out, in understatement, that the private broadcasters "had been well-served by the protection afforded them by regulation." It noted that the industry was healthy, sales were up and profits steady. If the CBC were to get out of commercial television, it pointed out, there would be about $100 million more in the pool for the sharks to feed on. The committee discovered, like almost every committee before them, that "there is little to indicate a relationship between [private] industry health and improved Canadian programming in either television or radio." Its solution was to have the CRTC, that wild beast of broadcasting regulation, force the private broadcasters to spend more money on producing and broadcasting better Canadian programs. It was more of a plea than a recommendation, given that the CRTC had only failed to renew a private broadcast license once, and had never penalized a license holder for not producing the Canadian programs it said it would to receive its license.

The Liberals walked 180 degrees away from Applebaum-Hébert. They would rely on the cable industry, not broadcasters, to provide the public with more "choice." Telefilm would stimulate production of Canadian programs. The fund would eventually help boost independent industry revenues from $124 million in 1980/81 to $623 million in 1988/89. Although observers would be hard-pressed to make a direct connection, it was clear that if this was public money going to produce more Canadian programming, it had to be coming out of money that normally went to the CBC. Telefilm's expressed purpose would be to "stimulate the development of Canadian television drama, variety, children's and documentary programs," a mandate that could just as easily have been run off on a CBC photocopier.

But the largest irony for Mr. and Mrs. Canada would be the eventuality that between 1986 and 1990, Telefilm would hand out $173 million for English language production, $81 million of which would end up supporting production associated with private broadcasters. The Liberals, ever more creative than their reactionary buddies across the House, had found a way to redirect money normally earmarked for public broadcasting, not just to independent producers, but to the private broadcasters as well. The culture bandits were now being subsidized with taxpayer cash. In return, the bandits called the Telefilm initiative "being flexible."

Adding irony upon irony, the public money that would eventually find its way through the Telefilm bank account would probably do as much to continue the trend of making Canadian programs "look American" as anything the private broadcasters could have thought up. Telefilm projects must be available to the largest audiences possible, meaning they have to be aimed at a place in the prime time of a broadcaster's schedule, achieve high ratings and make everybody a profit, if possible. Telefilm values are not necessarily public broadcasting values. Its priority is programs that are popular and sell, in the distribution vernacular. The more American values the product possesses, the more likely the sale. A Telefilm office would be opened in Los Angeles. There they could keep in close touch with the U.S. film and television nabobs, attend endless cocktail parties and film festivals, and "do lunch."

> *"Costner teams up with Canadians: Toronto company developed project"*
> *"Toronto—Excitement was running high yesterday at the offices of Toronto's Paragon Entertainment after an announcement that Kevin Costner has agreed to star in and co-produce a major Hollywood movie developed by the company. 'This is the biggest coup for a Canadian production company in the history of film,' said Margo Raport, vice-president of worldwide marketing for Paragon Entertainment. 'We have affiliated ourselves with a major, major star.'. . ."*
> —Christopher Harris, *Globe and Mail*, December 17, 1992

The Liberals were signalling that broadcasting was just another business. It no longer would be a platform for social and cultural purposes. When the Mulroney Conservatives kicked the Turner government out of office in September 1984 there was hardly any difference in the two political philosophies toward the CBC. The only difference would be in style. The Liberals played for high indifference. They were smoother at making life difficult for the CBC. The

Tories—true to the memory of the Diefenbaker government and its reactionary, get-even roots—would try to make the corporation hurt. The neoconservative wave of deregulation, privatization and denationalization had arrived. By the time the PCs had finished, you would not, as Brian Mulroney liked to say, recognize the place.

Finance Minister Michael Wilson started the ball rolling downhill again with an $85 million annual budget cut to the CBC in November 1984, followed by a six percent salary cut beginning in 1986, and a Department of Communication $10 million annual reduction—followed in 1990 by a further $140 million in budget cuts to take us up to 1993/94. You may remember the November budget moment from television. When Wilson announced the CBC was going to take an $85 million hit, he had to pause in his speech until the standing ovation from the Tory benches abated. The minister responsible for the CBC, Marcel Masse, declared that the Tory government "intends to ensure that public broadcasting not only survives, but prospers in the coming years." In April 1985, Masse announced the formation of a task force to recommend a new strategy for broadcasting's future into the twenty-first century. The Mulroney government would then ignore the task force recommendations and continue to do whatever it wanted with the broadcasting system, and the CBC.

The task force, called the Caplan-Sauvageau Task Force after its co-chairmen, former NDP national secretary, Gerald Caplan, and Florian Sauvageau, a Laval University communications professor, held extensive public hearings across the country. They began their odyssey for answers to the question: "Whatever happened to national broadcasting?" in an atmosphere of more sweet irony. Brian Mulroney had just started his free trade shuffle. Canada's private broadcasters, as well as the cable operators, immediately leapt out of their profit stupor to realize that their industry's interests—and all that cushy and profitable regulatory protection they had enjoyed for decades, like simultaneous commercial substitution for broadcasters and tax exemptions for Canadian advertisers—might get bargained away as cultural trade-offs at the free trade table. 'Hold on just one nationalist minute!' these born-again cultural-capitalists might have cried out in unison. 'What about sovereignty and protection of Canadian culture?' 'There must be a way to stop all those horrid Americans from cutting into our pie?' The irony for the rest of us, of course, was while the private broadcasters were whining once more, one was hard-pressed to find a single, notable Canadian program or series in the prime time schedule of the Global network, or anything meaningful and Canadian between 8 and 11 P.M. on CTV.

Caplan-Sauvageau would turn out to be a woeful dirge for Canadian broadcasting and for the CBC, very little of it new or enlightening. All the old themes were touched upon: U.S. programming dominated our TV screens, the private pirates were still talking Canadian, broadcasting American and raking in large profits, although the gross numbers were falling slightly from the pre-cable days; a continued reliance on commercial revenue and the production of U.S.-style "Canadian" television drama on CBC was killing the corporation and keeping it from being healthy and distinctive; it was hanging by a fiscal thread; production was centralized in Toronto and Montreal and there were not enough opportunities for regional images to be reflected on the CBC.

In a strange, fading requiem, the task force would spend an inordinate amount of time on issues concerning the health of the public broadcasting component, at a time when it was no longer the lodestar in the Canadian broadcast heaven. Reading the 1986 report, one would think that the CBC was still a fixation for Canadians. It was really small potatoes by then, given all the other players who had been able to wrestle away large chunks of the broadcasting pie. The text read like a learned debate among the survivors of a nuclear bombing; each trying to make a point about the precise dating of radioactivity half-life ("Now, was that ten million years or fifteen million years . . .?") while everything around them had melted. CBC English television, to be realistic, was a cultural skeleton in need of a decent burial.

The report was really the last gasp, as Gerald Caplan put it in 1992, "of traditional public broadcasting." Had the task force been formed two or three years later, "we would have come out with a qualitatively different report which would have recommended some sort of downscaling and narrow-casting function for the CBC." A noticeably discouraged Caplan, with the advantage of six years of hindsight, now saw the task force report as the *grande finale* for public broadcasting: "I don't think [the strengthening of public broadcasting] is ever going to be possible again. Nobody is ever going to give the CBC back the money to make it what once we pretended it was."

Caplan-Sauvageau was a convergence of all the forces arriving at the same time as the nation's fight for a unique broadcasting character petered out. It was like a convention of the seven deadly sins of broadcasting. The CBC was in attendance with Pride, for its failure to fight courageously for public broadcasting, and Covetousness, for relying on commercial advertising for revenue. The private broadcasters were there with Lust and Gluttony. They had taken those two iniquities to new, higher levels of effectiveness. Cable operators hung in with a huge dollop of Envy and had designs on Lust as well. The federal government—Liberal or Conservative—had Anger, at the CBC, all to themselves. And the CRTC hung around in the background, attaching itself quite comfortably to Sloth. We had travelled in turmoil and debate for almost six decades and had arrived back at exactly the same spot from which we embarked. It was the concourse of myriad historical paths of influence, indifference and lack of purpose.

CBC English television stood in front of Caplan-Sauvageau as hardly a unique public broadcaster; it looked like commercial television, smelled like commercial television, but pretended to itself that it wasn't because it did not allow commercials, at the time, in the twenty-two minutes of nightly national news, or in a handful of children's programs. Without a character that stood out, or a close relationship with the public, Canadians had become increasingly indifferent to CBC television, migrating to other stations and networks, including PBS and the various provincial educational broadcasters. New technologies were helping the broadcasting industry pass the corporation by. Stuck with a single television network in each official language, on which they were compelled to deliver the broadest range of programming in the industry, the CBC had no chance of competing for a healthy future. Government, the CRTC and its own lack of creative management contributed to the CBC being stuck as a one-trick pony in a circus of hundreds.

The owners of the circus were now the cultural clowns—the private broadcasters and the cable operators. The first had started out as a temporary act, supposedly filling in until the public broadcasting star could get her balancing act together, and they ended up owning the tent, the ponies, the wagons and the elephants. The second got rich by riding the backs of their distribution monopolies. By 1986, much of the audience hardly even cared if the CBC stayed in the circus business or not. There was too much entertainment competition across the street with programming-on-demand, videos and VCRs and a whole new generation of entertainment opportunities packed inside those marvellous little fibre optics. Who cared about an act with one tired pony and a bunch of baggage?

The Caplan-Sauvageau task force noted that "Sir John Aird would feel very much at home with the issues and dilemmas with which the Task Force has attempted to come to grips." After all the argument and effort, U.S. programs inundated Canadian television screens. It was almost endless commercial schlock, often violent and insulting, with little that said "Canadian" on it. Private broadcasters had scalped the system clean and then indignantly claimed to be giving Canadians what they wanted. They did it in the 1920s and we had let them do it to us again, in spades, by 1986. We had played around with the system for nearly sixty years and confused the national purpose, adulterated our culture and muddied the opportunity to understand each other better. In terms of cultural, linguistic and regional understanding, we had actually grown *farther apart* as Canadians, thanks in large part to the failure of the "national broadcasting system."

Canadian children recognized Bill Cosby but not Gordon Pinsent; Arsenio Hall but not Brent Carver; Oprah Winfrey but not Margaret Atwood or Maureen Forrester. They could not find New Brunswick on the map but knew who was running around on whom in *Dallas*. They watched American characters, American history and American social problems—and thought they were ours. They followed the NFL and NBA instead of the CFL. They thought the Manitoba Schools Question was a college entrance exam. They guessed that Rowell-Sirois was a vaudeville troupe, Pierre Berton was once married to Elizabeth Taylor, subscribed to *People* magazine but not *Saturday Night* or *Maclean's* and believed Orangemen were the Syracuse University football team. Their parents thought the Miranda Rule and the right to bear arms were all part of being Canadian. It was enough to make you ashamed of "being Canadian"—whatever that phrase meant.

Sir John Aird & Co. had given us the greatest plan for a cultural head start of any modern, twentieth-century nation. And we turned a massive, powerful learning experience—one that might have helped to make us wiser, better educated, more thoughtful, more understanding citizens—into *Disney, America's Funniest Videos, Hawaii Five-O, COPS* and the 'tits'n'ass' of *Three's Company*—seen for years in the 5:30 P.M. "family viewing" slot on CBC English television. "English Canadians are virtually strangers in the land of the imagination,"

Caplan-Sauvageau wrote while pointing out that only two percent of drama seen on English television was Canadian. In answer to the standard myths, most of them perpetuated by the CAB and private broadcasters, Canadians tended, the task force found, to watch Canadian programs in proportion to their availability. Canadians did not watch Canadian programs because there were not that many to watch. When Canadian programs did appear, we could be "insatiable" viewers. Not surprisingly, the task force discovered that children were ill-served by Canadian television, that the system had incentives for private broadcasters to buy American rather than produce Canadian programs—and the worst offenders were the independent stations. As a group, these stations spent fourteen times as much on foreign programs as Canadian. The task force also found that distribution on Canadian cable systems actually *reduced* the viewing of Canadian programs.

For the CBC, with a 1986/87 budget already at $1.1 billion and $848 million of that from Parliament, Caplan-Sauvageau called for a retrenchment, a non-commercial operation (when the money was available), and for CBC to "Canadianize" the television schedule. It would cost about $30 million. The CBC should start an all-news channel, get involved with a new public, non-commercial broadcasting venture (TV CANADA—an expanded version of Al Johnson's CBC-2) which would include the NFB, consolidate its regional operations into five "super regions" (to the task force, regional broadcasting was "the most vexing single question in the current debate on the role of the CBC") and convince the CBC's thirty-one affiliated stations to take the full network television schedule.

Caplan-Sauvageau wanted the system corrected. It wanted more Canadian content, especially drama, on private television stations. It wanted tighter and tougher regulations to back that up. The task force somewhat naively called for the entire broadcasting system, not just the CBC, "to serve Canadian culture." The task force report—once thought of as the broadcasting game plan for the twenty-first century—made its way on to the shelf, to be covered by years of Tory dust. "It just petered out," Caplan said of the report's impact.

7 / Drinking Kool-Aid in the Deerhurst Jungle

"We all stood up at Deerhurst to testify: if what our decision means is saving the CBC, we were willing to give up our regional air time and resources to do it. We were willing to give up our ideals to save the CBC. But the whole effort was hi-jacked."
—Cathy Chilco, regional television producer, February 11, 1992

IN APRIL 1987, roughly one hundred CBC managers and staff from the ETV network and regional television offices across the country gathered at Deerhurst, Ontario, at a place brochures told us was the "largest all-season resort east of the Rocky Mountains." Along with a handful of observers, the group met for the better part of three days to deliberate on what appeared to be the very bleak future of CBC television. The Tories had already made it known that annual budget cuts to the tune of at least five percent would be applied to the CBC over the next four years. They were also not prepared to pony up for the annual cost of inflation, an extra four-year cost hit of more than $70 million. The grand total looked like $200 million. Much of the Tory slash would have to come either from the largest sector of the CBC—the ETV network—or from the regions. As the discouraged patrons of the upscale Ontario resort were unpacking their bags, not many of them could discard the thought that the body of CBC English television was surely dying, and that they had been invited to help draft the arrangements for the funeral.

What they could not have known is that not only would they be able to keep the poor monster of Canadian public broadcasting alive, they would put the pieces back together in such a way that when the electrodes in the forehead started sparking, this miscreated mummy—which they would eventually name "Canadianization"— would stand up and loyally follow whomever had a hold of its hand.

The original idea was a CBC English language television system that increased the reflection of Canadians living in the regions from Halifax to Vancouver. But when it finally lurched off the operating table, Canadianization staggered in the direction of someone who was not even present at Deerhurst—the ETV network's soon-to-be head of programming, Ivan Fecan. It ended up being his pal. He nurtured it, gave it things to do, and it did exactly what he said it should. And with the concurrence of senior network management, Fecan would proceed to define Canadianization—and public broadcasting—largely in his own way.

Fecan's interpretation of Canadian public television for the 1990s would little resemble the consensus arrived at by all those corporate proselytes gathered in the Ontario woods. He had missed the epiphany. The people with the most to lose—regional broadcasters—had lined up at the CBC's version of Jonestown tables. They had been the ones with tinges of true-believer's Kool-Aid at the corners of their collective mouths. Fecan had not been there to understand what drove the gathering to take on the political and professional risks inherent in charting a new future for Canadian public television. When he did arrive, he did what almost everyone does in the CBC, he started to make it up—Canadianization—as he went along. "The CBC has a history," said one disgruntled Toronto senior manager, "of always being capable of being taken over by one person."

The overriding problem facing everyone was that a large piece of the CBC's $200 million-plus shortfall might have to come out of English television, as much as $40 million. Then vice-president of the ETV network Denis Harvey wanted an opportunity to tell everyone how serious the future budget situation looked, and to see if the group had any bright ideas of how to escape this fiscal conundrum. One alternative, where Harvey was concerned, was to cut the regions, perhaps close down millions of dollars of regional programming, operations and stations. He was the head of the ETV network and it was not in his mind to commit divisional hara-kiri, to see the brunt of any cuts fall on the ETV network. To Harvey, if you did not have a Toronto-based network pumping out programs, "then you might as well close the CBC."

The opening day at Deerhurst turned into a desultory affair. Hands were wrung. Insults were hurled at the Mulroney government. Snarling but general attacks on the corporate state of things were often

DRINKING KOOL-AID IN THE DEERHURST JUNGLE   123

received by the crowd with shrugs and silence. They-can't-do-that-to-us protestations and what-if scenarios echoed off the walls. The room was awash in defeatism. The financial numbers were so imposing, the options all so drastic, that by the time the meeting broke up into study groups later in the day some were talking about just slipping out and heading for home as soon as it was politically polite.

The practical reality of what damage the Mulroney government budget cuts might do—programs cancelled, hundreds of staff laid off, stations closed, whole services curtailed—was both hugely depressing and, strangely enough, encouraging. The downside was so bad that it started people thinking about radical solutions rather than the usual tinkering-with-the system ideas. If there ever was a need to 'blue-sky' the future of public television, it was now. The alternative was cloud and rain and incessant storm. "We needed a vision to follow," recalled Alex Frame, former television program director in Vancouver and later head of radio network current affairs.

The vision most participants focused on was a purely Canadian television network. The presence of so much U.S. programming in the network schedule had always been a major irritant to producers and managers. The 1987 fall network schedule called for an average of thirty-five hours of U.S. programming per week, five-and-a-half hours of it in prime time alone—from *Dallas* to *Slap Maxwell*, from *Oldest Rookie* to *Facts of Life*. As CBC broadcaster Mark Starowicz pointed out in a perceptive analysis of Canadian television in the mid-1980s, only twenty-two percent of all English television available to Canadians was "Canadian." By the time a child reached the age of twelve years, he or she had watched 12,000 hours of television— eighty percent of it American. Canadians were spending half their television time watching popular drama, but only five percent of it was Canadian. The Deerhurst vision that evolved was to make the CBC distinctive, to "Canadianize" Canadian public television.

"It soared from being one of the most depressing conferences I was ever at, starting off with an earnest attempt to save the corporation by saving on paper clips, and turning into this passionate cry," said former executive producer of *Beachcombers* Brian McKeown. "And the cry was: 'If we were going down, let's at least be distinctive before we go—or by the time we go."

Passion seemed to overcome common sense. Vision obscured

reality. Enthusiasm overcame costs. The decision to finally be a fully Canadian television network carried the day at Deerhurst. And the traditional CBC cautions—about the tenuousness of power relationships, about the delicate but volatile balance of influence between the network and the regions, and the partisan instincts of corporate survival—melted as quickly as the spring snow blanketing the woods around the resort. "I still compare the meeting to almost a church revival," Denis Harvey recalled. "The meeting just took off and rolled and rolled and rolled and rolled. . . . Some people had tears in their eyes. It was incredible. It was very moving."

"The message that came from the group was:'You've got nothing to lose. You are going nowhere. You are going to die anyway, if you don't do something about it'," former B.C. regional director Eric Moncur recalled. "All of a sudden it flooded the room. Everybody got up and started making speeches or said something about going Canadian. There were others who fought it to the death, but they were in the minority."

A "study team" was put together to investigate whether it was even feasible to try to Canadianize the network. The team represented a national cross-section of CBC television interests, regional and network. The team's mandate was to develop a plan that would eventually result in an ETV network schedule in 1990/91 that contained ninety-five percent Canadian content in prime time, and ninety percent Canadian content overall. But just as important, the team members were responsible for designing a system that would "provide a stronger reflection of the regions to the whole country." The idea was to spread production responsibility—not just production, but responsibility for production—across the country, primarily to five major production centres, in the hope of manufacturing a more honest picture of Canada. The plan was to get the production out of Toronto and let the regions sculpt their own vision of Canada.

The team tabled its findings at the end of July 1987. The proposal met the call for ninety-five percent Canadian content in prime time by 1990/91. Members wanted a stronger reflection of the tastes and interests of the regions on the network. It would be a popular network television schedule, with high quality a priority in information programming, drama and children's programs. Production of Canadian drama would double. There would be more programming for teens and youngsters, as well as pre-schoolers. And as much as forty-three percent of the network schedule would originate, in substance as well as style, from outside of Toronto.

"And suddenly, what seemed like a terrible problem for years—getting to a higher level of Canadian content—looked like not that big a problem," said Bill White, vice-president of regional broadcasting at the time. "My sense then was it really meant that we could start doing more production *in* the regions." But there was a very scary catch for the regions in the plan. They would have to collectively hand over much of their money, production resources and schedule time to the ETV network. The transfer, or redirection, from existing regional budgets, in the interests of funding the new, expanded initiative, was a delicate and potentially dangerous *quid pro quo*. It was delicate in the sense that the regions were trading their cash, their skills and their hardware—and, in effect, their traditional community-based role in Canadian public broadcasting—on a promise. It was like two gunfighters facing off with each other and promising, in the interests of both having longer lives, that each would be the first to pull out his six-shooter and place it peaceably on the saloon bar. The one to go first was either going to end up being the initiator of a new, friendlier relationship or, if he guessed wrong, be the next delivery to Boot Hill.

On paper, the regions were going to have to give up $23 million worth of money and resources, and would receive in return about $28 million worth of network production. The crucial part of the trade-off was the recommendation that the regions were to share in the decision-making that set the tone and direction of the television schedule. This was the key to the whole deal, and the one that frightened the death out of most regional supporters. Regional managers were supposed to have access to a "national offers system" that acted as a creative doorway into the network schedule. To try to ensure that the whole plan did not simply develop into a network fully controlled by Toronto, the team drew up a list of regional "superstation" production assignments models. In addition to most of its current production activity, St. John's would produce a new national children's show, drama and a national outdoor show. Halifax would do drama and a national quiz show. Winnipeg would contribute a medicine and health series, a national version of the successful regional children's series, *Switchback*, and more drama. Edmonton would do a teen series, contribute to national drama and continue its *Par 27* golf series. Vancouver would coordinate drama production throughout the west and produce an afternoon Canadian soap opera, among its other production duties.

Increasing dramatic programming was considered the key to the success of Canadianization. The team recommended that the area head of drama have "senior lieutenants" or "deputies" located in the two largest centres outside of Toronto—Halifax and Vancouver. These regional drama specialists would be responsible, not to the network program director, but to the specialist in charge of all drama. They would have their own money and a "large measure of autonomy" in choosing the dramatic production projects that best reflected the interests of the regions. The study team never spoke of these drama deputies ever having to obtain prior permission from the Toronto network about what drama projects they wanted to pursue. The study team report constantly emphasized a Canadian public television network that was strongly situated in the regions. Phrases such as "increase in regional reflection," "new, national programming, most of which will be produced in the regions" were not placed there idly. Members were aware of the sensitivity of the mandate given them by the Deerhurst participants. Uppermost in their minds was the need to make sure that the two parties—the regions and the ETV network—followed the text that had been orchestrated at Deerhurst: the regions were prepared to give up resources and money for the greater good of the CBC, but they wanted—and this has always been the root cause of distrust between the two factions—the right to make the decisions about what programs best represented the distinctiveness of their particular region. What they foresaw would be the essence of a 'Canadian' Broadcasting Corporation. It would not be—as it unfortunately is today—a 'Toronto' Broadcasting Corporation.

The consensus was that there could never be enough safeguards to protect the regions from a blatant power-grab from Toronto. To that end, the study team recommended that a new senior manager, reporting directly to Harvey, be appointed, responsible for monitoring the implementation of the Canadianization plan. This was the study team's sheriff at the saloon bar. He or she would see that the rules of Canadianization, as understood by the regional staff and managers at Deerhurst, were followed. "This is the biggest undertaking in the history of the English network," the report stated in support of this recommendation. "It will require appropriate management." The report also warned that the plan "is an integrated plan. We expect it to succeed. If parts of it are dismantled or disconnected from the overall structure, the chances of successful implementation will be diminished," the team wrote prophetically. But the one major recommendation that never made it into the 1988/89 ETV network operating plan—the initial year of Canadianization—was the one for a senior manager to see that the Deerhurst rules were followed.

"The network cherry-picked the report," said study team member Alex Frame. "We said: 'This is not a document that you can just use what you like. Don't forget that this report was done with and by the stakeholders. They gave up a lot to make this happen.' [The study team] was working for everyone. But the network didn't see this; that it wasn't just *carte blanche*. We saw the report on Canadianization as Fecan's mandate. He was the new program director. We put forward the report as a package. It was reasonable that Fecan had to be free to develop his own variations on the general theme. But what we needed was the implementor we had recommended; someone to oversee and manage the recommendations."

Freshly arrived from NBC, Ivan Fecan took the Deerhurst dream of renewed Canadian public television and moulded it to suit his interpretation and the circumstances he felt faced with. In the initial stage, he made some concessions to the study team's recommenda-tions, testing some of their proposals for program origination against the station's creative and resource capability. But he quickly moved away from the Deerhurst plan and began programming Canada's national public television system based on his instincts and interests. He was reminded "constantly" by senior network management that, politically, he had to understand that the regions were not going to survive unless the network gave them the opportunity to develop their own talent and their own ideas. But he did not feel strongly enough about the agreement that had been reached. He took control of everything—the program ideas, the schedule, the productions, the resources—and started defining public broadcasting by his own definition.

"What we had was a very strong centralist in Toronto, who seized the opportunity to centralize what was never meant to be centralized," said Eric Moncur, the senior member of the study team. "What [the team] said was that you set up three or four or whatever number of regional centres there are, and each of those has a level of power that makes sense for them; a level of money, a level of funding, and a level of independence. And out of that will come a stronger regional picture and much better regional focus for the network.

"Ivan walked in the door. He was fresh. He had no baggage. We gave him the [Deerhurst] plan. And he took the plan and worked it to suit himself. And partly, that's why that disastrous budget cut went the way it did in 1991/92. Because those who made [the December 1990] budget cut only saw how things were working then. They didn't think there was any regional programming going on, and they literally killed the Canadianization structure in one fell swoop, without consultation, because they felt that Fecan was responsible for everything. He had just walked into a vacuum—a change-over vacuum—and took over. . . ."

> "The problems underlying the CBC's crisis are profound. First, the constraints imposed by commercial considerations make programming and scheduling decisions unacceptably dependent on revenue criteria. Second, the CBC's distribution system, which partly relies on privately owned affiliated stations, leads to distortion of programming priorities. These two problems intertwine, making the mandate entrusted to the national broadcasting system impossible to carry out. . . ."
> —CBC television producers' report, "A New Beginning,"
> February 1983

The ETV network operating plan for 1988/89 that kicked off Canadianization touted the fact that Deerhurst provided new vision for the network and that "regional and network programmers are working together to achieve that vision." It also tooted the horn for its particular interpretation of Canadianization by informing everyone that the plans would "provide each region with at least as much—in most cases, more—production as before." It just did not let anyone know that Toronto would now call the shots on what was produced in the regions.

As well as being short one senior manager to monitor this historic deviation in Canadian public television, this bold new venture, the operating plan revealed, was short of cash right from the start. Weaned on ratings and commercial revenues for decades, the ETV network almost annually met any projected budget shortfall by simply boosting commercial sales activity—putting more commercial advertising on the air or charging more for it. This time the shortfall nut would be larger than ever before—between $24 and $27 million. But to very few people's surprise, the network intended to close the gap primarily by selling commercial time more aggressively.

All the hoopla aside, Canadianization of the ETV network schedule was to most observers a qualified failure. 'Qualified' in the sense that the real plan never materialized after Deerhurst. Canadian content on the CBC increased, but never to the ninety-five percent prime time target that was set. Little of the content increase was in the important area of Canadian drama. Much of the increase was in the cheaper information programming—news and current affairs. So much so that Canadians would be subjected to one of the highest information-to-entertainment television ratios in the world. Instead of getting to watch, learn and be entertained, most Canadians got talked at.

Ironically, Canadianization just escalated the thirst for ratings and commercial revenues. The former began to fall in 1988/89 and the latter could not keep up with growth projections. The vision of authentic public broadcasting programs many of the people at Deerhurst were hoping for got replaced with *Mosquito Lake, Material World, Danger Bay* and more and more stuff that looked like it came from The Disney Channel. Without those authentic programs to reflect what Canadians were doing and thinking in places like Gooseberry Cove, Newfoundland, and 100 Mile House, B.C., Canadians got to see less and less of themselves—and more and more of what the folks in Toronto thought Gooseberrians and Hundred-Milers looked like or wanted in the way of public broadcasting programs. By 1991, Head Office and ETV network management were beside themselves trying to figure out why fewer and fewer Canadians now thought the CBC was distinctive and, worse yet, why fewer and fewer were watching the ETV network. They could not understand that there might be a strong correlation between fading audience allegiances and the loss of authentic, regionally-based programs.

"Our thinking was clearly shaped going into Deerhurst," said one regional manager. "We wanted nothing less than the Canadianization plan. Where we were disappointed was, first, the eventual definition of Canadianization and, second, the way the definition was applied [by the ETV network]. Regional programmers stood up and said,'I'm prepared in the interests of a national service to do less programming about myself to myself, and do more programming about myself to the rest of the country.' That thought carried certain assumptions. And if it shifted, it shifted as a product of implementation, not as a product of Deerhurst."

Many of the Deerhurst participants were drawing their cues for a renewed CBC from a document entitled, "A New Beginning," composed by corporation television producers in 1983. Just as significantly as the corporation's television producers were already eons ahead of the CBC's management in foretelling the future, they were almost hauntingly able to predict where the ETV network was going to end up if it continued operating in the fashion it insisted upon. "A New Beginning" began by stating that "public broadcasting had lost its way." The ETV network prime time schedule was too full of U.S. programs (then as much as eight hours out of twenty). Fewer and fewer programs were being produced in the regions. CBC Halifax had gone from producing thirteen to fifteen hours of network production a year in the late 1960s and early 1970s to one hour by 1976. Regional production was being curtailed by the network. Each year "more and more money is taken from the regions in an attempt to pool resources for network production." Ratings and the thirst for more commercial revenue drove management decision-making, not the needs or tenets of public broadcasting and public service. As a result, the CBC now concentrated on programs that "delivered the biggest bang for the buck—news and current affairs and sports." The network schedule had become rigid and inflexibly commercial.

The producers also warned that the introduction of independent co-producers into the CBC production process, and the reliance on their money and programming concepts that accompanied it, would lead to added distortion of programs. The need for co-productions to look commercially acceptable south of the border would lead, as many projected, to the "Disneyfication" of the CBC. The public broadcaster's future would be shaped by outside commercial forces, not cultural ones. Those commercial forces were in combat with the CBC's cultural responsibilities "to ensure that different parts of the country truly communicated with each other."

The producers called for a return to public broadcasting basics: an all-Canadian public broadcasting service with programs the audience could not receive elsewhere. The programs—and the ideas for them—should come from across the country, not just places like Toronto. The regions should share their programs with one another.

Their goal was to have a distinctive television service that served the mandate of public broadcasting, not the interests of advertisers. The days of management-by-budget "and its handmaiden"—ratings— had to end. New corporate objectives should address, not the tastes and interests of network managers on Bay Street or Head Office bureaucrats, but the communities across Canada and their cultural interests.

The producers were calling for a "bottom-up" approach for public broadcasting, not a top-down approach, a new democracy that would give the citizen back the public broadcasting system they had originally been promised. Decision-making had to be rudely decentralized back to the regions with the introduction of "responsible production units" and "autonomous production teams." It was as if the modern techniques of Japanese design and manufacturing were to be applied to Canadian public broadcasting—with a similar degree of intended success. "A New Beginning" was what many of the people at Deerhurst had in mind, and in their hearts, when they were arguing about a successful future for Canadian public television.

To some extent, the plight of the regions—and the erosion of public broadcasting that their demise represented—was of their own making. Although regional programs were often good reflections of the communities, some looked cheap and contributed little to the CBC's overall reputation. Internally, the regional production efforts, especially those that eventually made it into the ETV network schedule—*The Canadian Gardener, Best Years, Urban Peasant* from Vancouver, *Disability Network* from CBLT in Toronto, *Land and Sea* from Halifax—were referred to derisively as "mushrooms." They were small ventures. The network had no great expectations they would bloom into award-winning, prime time productions. They grew in the shadows of the more heavily-funded network series. They were always short of cash. Life expectancy was year-to-year. And they existed on a steady diet of network indifference and the broadcasting equivalent of night soil.

It is true that some of the CBC's English television regional programs were popular, and many of them were award-winners— even when matched up against ETV network-produced programs and series. But too many of these regional or community-based programs looked marginally better than cable offerings, cost an inordinate amount of money and resources to produce on a per-viewer basis and drew low, sometimes pathetic, audience numbers. For the most part, the cause was simple: for over ten years, starting in the 1970s, the regions had been systematically stripped of their money, schedule time, resources and ability to make high quality programs by the Toronto-based ETV network. The situation was exacerbated by the absence of any real strategy for the production of regionally-based programs. Each region was, by-and-large, allowed to go its own way and spend on productions it felt best fit the needs of their particular region or province. The result was a kaleidoscope of life in Canada: programs about kids, dogs, fire safety, the environment, potters, the family, business, politics, flowers, pick-up trucks, immigrants, religion, exercise, country-and-western crooners, fishing, books, personalities, folk dancing, wheat, potash, oil, forests, freeways, education, crime, cooking, eating, ethnicity, history, travel, events, institutions, government, islands, mainlands, lakes, weeds, snow and life. It was costly. No other broadcaster was doing it. It was anarchic. But it was about communities, and it definitely was 100 percent Canada.

However, without access to prime program time in the ETV network schedule, much of that helter-skelter view of an authentic Canada never got shown outside the region that produced the program. The ETV network had taken away their prime schedule time. As the scythes were being sharpened in Head Office in the fall of 1990, this disparate crop of mushrooms became a much too easy target for the Head Office harvest. "The wheels started falling off regional television in the early 1980s, as soon as the CBC became pinched for cash," said one former regional manager. "You didn't have to be brilliant to see what was happening. There was just a lot of shit being produced out there across the country. Shit with no audiences. And expensive shit. And so the siphoning started, to set up *The Journal*, for instance." Before the major cuts began, the regions had a comfortable existence. There were no rules, no real strategy for how to spend those millions. There were no real evaluations of how effective the programs were. "Part of our job was to fill the holes in the network schedule. We didn't operate on a program filling strategy. We operated on a 'time filling' strategy. When we did have a strategy for spending all that money, it was when we concentrated on the supper hours."

In 1984, the CBC went in search of a new, meaningful role for the regions. A "Focus for Quality" task force reported that the regional broadcasting infrastructure produced more than 10,000 hours of locally-based programs a year at a cost of about $110 million. That regional figure represented thirty-eight percent of the money the CBC spent on English television production. But spread out over nineteen stations, the money devoted per program was tiny and, as a consequence, the programs ended up with low production values and lower audience ratings. The task force found: "Local programming is far and away the most expensive CBC-TV produces, and it's still not doing the job, simply because the economics of production will not permit it."

Much of the problem was caused by a major deterioration in the regions' position that took place during the 1970s as the ETV network began to control the CBC television agenda. In the 1950s, 1960s and late into the 1970s, the corporation spent millions of dollars building and equipping regional production centres. As much as thirty percent of the schedule was produced in the regions. As more and more stations opened, the emphasis slowly shifted to local production, a phenomenon that was accelerated by developments in the late 1970s. Regional program budgets began to decline rather dramatically, while the ETV network went on a competitive spending binge, siphoning off millions of dollars to support new network initiatives. By the time "Focus for Quality" came along, only two regionally based productions sat in the ETV network schedule—*Beachcombers* from Vancouver and *Hymn Sing* from Winnipeg. The regions "were left to their own devices," and with less money available to program at the high quality level and compete for schedule space on the ETV network, the regions—individually and collectively—did what always happens in the CBC. They started making up a role for themselves as they went along. Without any overall announced corporate strategy, they decided that they would "be local."

Rising out of the ashes of this horridly expensive and inequitable experience (one former regional manager likened the task force's discoveries to stumbling across a leper colony in the family summer recreation compound), the task force pushed for a bigger and more meaningful role for the regions in CBC English television—more dedicated prime time on the network schedule, regional programs with the same handsome budgets that Toronto-based productions had, and for network television production to be decentralized to the regions.

The entire effort collapsed, like most efforts within the CBC to effect structural as opposed to cosmetic change. The corporation, as it would later after Deerhurst, cherry-picked the task force recommendations, leaving out the significant, happily introducing the insignificant. Critics of regional operations used the opportunity to say "I told you so . . ." about the expensive, poor quality programs being produced in the regions. The network half-heartedly opened up some early prime time slots for "national" programs, which were eventually taken away from the regions. The budgets set for these programs were far less than what the task force had considered "minimum" amounts. Denis Harvey had long been convinced that "Focus for Quality" indisputably established that programming being done in the regions was terrible. "It was a waste of money. We were just pissing [money] away in the regions. I always argued that no country in the world tries to produce drama in twelve centres. And all those awful variety shows coming out of the regions . . ."

"When we analyzed the audience in terms of cost-per-viewer, the irony was that—and what was not picked up by many—award-winning [network] shows did not necessarily have large audiences," said "Focus for Quality" task force chairman Ron Devion. "Shows in certain regions had extraordinarily large audiences, in spite of modest budgets. St. John's was producing variety shows which had larger audiences than variety shows that were on [all the CBC-owned stations]. It was embarrassing for the network, and everyone tried to find out if there was some magic formula Newfoundland had for attracting larger audiences. [The formula] was the relationship that existed between the people of Newfoundland and the CBC; that's what the special chemistry was."

Devion's point is the essence of what the CBC is all about—television and radio, French and English—and what Canada is all about. "I didn't understand it until I had an opportunity to travel the country from coast-to-coast. This is really a country of regions. Until you've had a chance to live and work in different parts of the country, you don't really understand the nature of how different we are. Northern Alberta is as different from the southern part as B.C. is to Manitoba. It's hard to understand if you are sitting in the east, in the Golden Triangle. . . . I have to admit that the media headquarters and the action is in Toronto, but the CBC is different from the media. It's a public broadcaster and the trunk of the tree may be in Toronto, but the roots and the branches are all across the country."

"CBC's directors of TV, the people who manage the local stations, saw it coming. Eighteen months ago, when they saw the axe looming over their local newscasts, they put together an internal document to save their shows. They argued that their programs are a 'unique reflection of this country . . . represent the essential spine of news and information for [CBC's] national news and current affairs service . . . [and] provide a broader range of regional, national and international news—reported by Canadian journalists.' Nobody listened . . . Calgary's news now comes from Edmonton. Windsor's from Toronto, Saskatoon's from Regina . . . but all of CBC News is hurt. Its spine has been, if not broken, seriously weakened. . . ."
—Antonia Zerbisias, *Toronto Star*, December 12, 1990

If there was one small glimpse of reality that proved the argument that public broadcasting can only exist in good health if it had strong ties to the community, it was—until 1990 at least—through the amazing success of the combined regional supper hour news programs. In the catty, internecine CBC management circles, their success had often been denied or derided by Head Office and some ETV network management. Regional supper hours actually represented millions of dollars in commercial revenue. In audience loyalty terms the collective regional supper hour shows were one of the most important program entities on the CBC—as important to Canadians as *The National, The Journal, Avonlea, Hockey Night in Canada* and *Fresh Prince of Bel Air*. Combined regional supper hours delivered more audience to the network of CBC-owned stations than any other single program offering.

The gross audience effect of these programs was startling, and should have been sobering to network and Head Office officials preparing their options for the Board in late 1990. Even CBC marketing managers admitted that regional supper hour news shows might be the most important programs in the overall commercial revenue mix. They were used in packages of programs to attract advertisers with an appetite for local impact. The regional supper hours made millions of dollars for the CBC, and yet, up until a puny change-of-corporate-heart took place in the spring of 1992, their budgets had been systematically cut. It was only after Head Office surveyed the extent of the damage their policies had done to regional audiences and their commercial revenue base after December 5, 1990 that they began to slowly realize how important regional news was in the corporate scheme of things. After watching net advertising income of regional stations plunge $14.5 million between 1990 and 1992, they quietly started returning some of the money and schedule time to regional supper hours in the summer of 1992.

But by then it was too late. Thanks to the Board's 1990 decision to "regionalize" supper hours, Canadians turned away from this CBC service in astounding numbers. By the end of 1992, the average total regional supper hour audience across Canada would plummet to barely 600,000 viewers from 910,000 on Black Wednesday, and down from a 1980s high of 1.2 million. Although, at the time, close-mouthed ETV network executives in Toronto would not estimate the extent of damage this awesome audience meltdown was causing to their commercial revenue projections, industry estimates had the potential loss in the millions of dollars by the year's end.

Regional supper hours were also the backbone upon which the entire ETV network news programming operations rested. Although programs like *Prime Time News* kept reporters and cameramen in most locations, they relied on local newsrooms, reporters, researchers, even local camera, sound and editing personnel to get their stories out to the network. The same held true for other network news and current affairs programs. Newsworld, one of the great smoke-and-mirror efforts of all corporate time, could not have existed comfortably until 1992 without the regional news structure. Touted as a network entity standing on its own and living bravely off its commercial revenues, Newsworld worked out of regional stations, with much of its news gathering cost subsidized by regional operations. Newsworld used regional station office space and studios, regional equipment, heat, light and electricity—often free of charge. Many of the stories used by the news network came, not from an elaborate string of Newsworld reporters, but from the newsrooms of the regional supper hour programs. Any further shrinking of regional news resources and it would start to "kill" Newsworld, Denis Harvey admitted in the spring of 1992.

The central purpose of the CBC networks has always been to contribute to cultural awareness and national identity by reflecting life and issues in and from the regions. The CBC's roots were in a pluralistic Canada, not a centralist Canada. Its programs were supposed to be culturally authentic and come from places like Halifax and Regina and Calgary, not necessarily Toronto. If the CBC was seen by critics to be leaning over backwards, spending huge dollops of money to try to catch a broad enough panorama of what the country was like—as opposed to churning out programs that simply had the same entertainment values as NBC, ABC and Fox Broadcasting—then the corporation was simply doing its job. The problem was that the CBC, especially in television, was neither doing much of that job any more, nor would it in the future.

"There's only one person standing up for the regions' survival at this point in the history of the corporation," said one Ottawa manager close to the Head Office scene in the summer of 1992. "And that, strangely enough, was Gérard Veilleux. No one else around that Head Office table [cares]. When the cuts came these people just followed their philosophy, which was that the centre of the CBC is what counts. But the only reason the regions exist today is that Veilleux said they must exist."

The fact that the regional rump that remained could no longer function effectively in anything but news programming was an error in comprehension. To begin with, Veilleux and Watson carried somewhat derivative interpretations of the role of the regions. Watson's was based on his personal experience as "an old network guy" who focused on the issue of quality—the regions could play a role but the network [read: Toronto] had to be there to coordinate skills and keep standards high so the result would be good television. To Watson, the network was "the custodian of the national mandate."

Veilleux's interpretation was embedded in his personal sense of federalism. He agreed there would be no CBC without the regions. Kill the regions and you "kill the CBC," he told people many times. And he was proud of the fact his first major act as president was to visit the regions, not the networks. The trip was his way of sending a message about his priorities. Yet he had no hesitation in telling Board members—who were traditionally supposed to represent regional interests—to "check their regional concerns at the door." The Board was a 'corporate' board, a 'national' board, to him. But if the Board took his advice, it would be eliminating the natural tensions the regions might rely on to protect their interests. The networks knew who they were and where their best interests lay. If the Board went 'national' in its thinking, who would act as individual regional counterweights? It would be a bit like telling the provinces that they had to check their individual aspirations at the door to constitutional conferences.

The problem with this kind of determinism is that it conflicts with a basic reality of political life in Canada. We achieve what we achieve and define who we are by allowing for competing diversity, not homogenizing the place. By touching your finger on the conflicts and bickering and competing factions—but ensuring the factions were in the same weight category, fought fairly and understood the rules—that was life inside the CBC. And by letting the tensions work out a 'national' compromise, you were emulating Canada. Those tensions were symptoms of how the CBC, like the nation, worked. Without strong regional pressures and open advocacy, we were reduced to a semantic hypothesis about CBC being "rooted in the regions."

What Veilleux and Watson would eventually come to understand was that regional broadcasting was worse than a siamese-twin tar baby. They stuck to everybody who hugged them. They also were almost impossible to pull away from. Senior management informed the CRTC that they intended to "recycle equipment and sell buildings" they had closed. But aside from some minor dealings, they could not. The structure of regional broadcasting was so intertwined with and around the networks, with radio, with French language services, that one just simply could not cut-and-run, or cut-and-sell. Each component used a piece of regional broadcasting, so much so that some of the network functions would find it hard to exist—or find it very expensive to exist—without the regional centres located across the country. Without the elaborate regional production structure, the costs of sports production would escalate. Many of the crews and much of the production equipment are located in the regions. The regions were the babies' organs—heart, lungs, kidneys, ears, eyes and mind. The network was the skin, and acted occasionally as distribution orifice. You could not logically have them all sharing a heart and lungs, unless they remained stuck together. Separate them and you had a major organ shortage.

The regions were also the CBC's pipeline into the community. They were the cultural mirrors Gérard Veilleux and Patrick Watson liked to talk about. The regional stations connected to the community as no network television show, producer, or executive could ever do. The regions were the place where the public received its one true view of what the corporation is and stands for. Without it, the CBC was just another television network, rising and falling in popularity with the ratings strength of its latest program hit or failure.

Without a powerful place at the corporate table—without Board representatives refusing to check their regional aspirations at the door—the regions naturally became, over time, the disposable element of the CBC whenever financial trouble struck. Myths circulated about their effectiveness. Information about their contributions was parcelled out selectively. Myths were piled on myths. After the December 1990 budget cut announcements, chairman-designate Patrick Watson crossed the country arguing, among other things, that the closing of CBC Calgary was a reasonable decision, based on the economics of the situation, admonishing those who said that the CBC brass were closing a station that actually *made money for the* CBC. Speaking to the employees of the B.C. region on February 1, 1991, Watson categorically denied that the CBC Calgary television stations had been a "profit centre." He said that Head Office finance data were "incontrovertible," that Calgary had not been making a profit for the CBC. Yet, regional staff and management knew for some time that the Calgary station did make a sizeable real profit for the CBC. Watson was relying on shaky data provided to him by Head Office.

Head Office operating statistics showed that in 1990, CBC Calgary made $3,245,000 more in revenue than it cost to run the regional television station. Even then, the $7 million in "expenditures" applied against the station's $10.3 million in net income were almost $3 million more than the station's operating budget. Head Office then added in even more expenditures—arbitrary proportional costs for corporate administration, transmission and things like network distribution. The revised Head Office data then showed that, not surprisingly, the Calgary station "lost" almost exactly one million dollars that year. Left on its own, as a cost-revenue analysis undertaken by regional management showed in 1987, the Calgary station could actually deliver a complete CBC mandate to southern Alberta, support all the network and other production ventures required, produce its pre-1990 agenda of regional information, entertainment and even dramatic programs, and still make a profit.

Head Office applied paper 'costs' to Calgary not unlike how a foreign multinational corporation with Canadian branch plants uses 'transfer pricing'—spreading corporate costs across its holdings, building in costs to a chosen subsidiary plant to ensure that any eventual profit shows up primarily on the books in the country with the lowest taxes. By allocating wholesale, arbitrary costs to each station, expenditures can be piled up high enough to snuff out any possibility of station 'profit.' And to tip the scales even further, the cost to the Calgary station of subsidizing Newsworld operations, network news and current affairs programming or supporting the network sports department with personnel and resources was seldom tallied on the credit side of the station's ledger.

There is no CBC if there are no properly functioning regions. The regional structure that remained after December 1990 is a mirage; the buildings are there, people come and go, but any television programs made are either from the insignificant mushroom patch or heavily subsidized by outside non-CBC funds and labour. Some mushroom co-productions were so heavy with direct sponsorship and commercials—car and tire manufacturers financially supporting a series such as *Driver's Seat*—that they were referred to by staff as "infomercials." There no longer is enough money to produce programs that reflect regional Canada. Veilleux's check of the rabid Ottawa-Toronto push in the fall of 1990 to eliminate the regions entirely left the corporation with less than half a loaf—they still have the expensive costs of the national regional infrastructure to pay for and very little in programming terms to show for it. "They are losing their constituency across Canada," said Toronto communications consultant Paul Audley. "With the demise of regional programming, with every disappearance of another regional program, there is less and less reason to support the CBC. December 1990 was probably the last straw."

The programs went. The audience are going. By the spring of 1993, ratings for the ETV network and regional supper hour programs tumbled downward with embarrassing regularity. Commercial revenues would follow south with ugly predictability. Corporate morale dipped to almost neurotic levels. The dream of Canadianization was on hold, perhaps forever, although the pace of the "Torontoization" of English television was on target. That last big shake of the dice during that weekend in Deerhurst in 1987 was now as sour a memory as the Kool-Aid we ended up sipping. The dream of a unique public television network—built around a house of shared regional and network interests—never had a chance.

8 / Anne Murray in Disney World

"The CBC is a very depressing place to work because they aren't given enough money to be commercial, and they aren't given the mandate to be PBS with the lower audiences that would entail. . . . And there's one committee after another studying them, meanwhile, everything's on hold. You can grow 200 years old waiting for somebody to finally have the guts to decide what to do."
    —Ivan Fecan, *Vancouver Sun* interview from New York, October
        23, 1985

TO MANY CANADIANS the English television network *is* "the CBC." And by that refraction, by the way it operates and the way it is perceived, the network has helped distort the purpose of public broadcasting in Canada. The ETV network has been the CBC's political stalking horse, its commercial knight errant, the country's high priest of news and information and its entertainment clown. It has become a highly commercialized network, making it almost indistinguishable from private broadcasters—in Canada and the United States. Other than through its news operations, it has few physical links with communities across the country. It does not encourage public involvement in its programming. It has an innate urge to cater largely to the hip, the young and the urbane. A handful of ETV network people in Toronto act as gatekeepers of public broadcast taste and mould the decisions about what Canadians will see on national public television. Protests aside, ratings are the most important single determinant of a program's value in the network scheme of things, yet the network has been losing viewers at a disturbing rate.

When all operating expenditures were taken into account, the English television network—news, current affairs and entertainment—cost about $418 million in 1991/92 (for programs, administration, distribution and payments to private stations), the corporation's largest single unit of expenditure. Its salary bill alone was $167 million. The network also brought in the most money, with net advertising revenues totalling $220 million out of a corporate total of $320 million.

Canadians have two primary images of the CBC, through the filter that is the ETV network, as a reliable source of news and information, and as the nation's "national theatre"—the main hub of dramatic and entertainment production activity in the country, presumably a place where millions of dollars are spent and thousands of employees are busy churning out hour-after-hour depictions of life in Canada. But between 1988 and 1992, the total of CBC-produced programs on the ETV network fell from 3,293 hours per year to 2,637 hours, while hours of procured program rights went up from 1,764 to 2,870. The network was acquiring more programs and making fewer.

Many Canadians assume the network is solely responsible for producing the thousands of hours of indigenous programming we presume we need on the CBC to help know who we are. Although the network produces a prodigious amount of news, current affairs and sports programming, its primary role, where drama and entertainment are concerned, is no longer the making of programs. Almost three-quarters of the drama seen on the ETV network is produced by independent producers. In-house CBC production of drama programming dropped from about forty-nine percent in 1985/86 to roughly thirty percent in 1992 while the total cost of all network programs went up twenty-one percent. The network produced fewer expensive drama programs, yet cost more to operate.

On the French television side, although its costs went up by almost the same percentage, Société Radio-Canada produced *more* in-house hours of programming in 1992 than in 1988, and unlike its English brethren, it bought substantially less programming from outside the corporation. What the figures and trends seem to indicate is that a very well encased bureaucracy has been growing steadily within the structure of the ETV network.

The 1992 Toronto-based ETV network organizational chart showed it employed roughly 2,700 people. Twenty percent (533) were managerial level and confidential employees. Another 306 were secretaries and clerks. The aggregate figure did not include term and casual contract personnel, or actors, writers, performers and musicians. Some of the 2,700 were located in regional sales and communication offices, but their reporting lines were through Toronto. About fifty-eight percent of the cost of the ETV network is taken up with overhead and management. The remaining forty-two percent goes, in an accountant's manner of speaking, into the making of programs. The ETV network produced a lot of programming that was relatively inexpensive (more than sixty-five percent of the weekly prime time schedule was filled with news and information programs), and a large amount of programming that some would consider culturally frivolous.

In 1992, an Olympic year, the ETV network produced 772 hours of sports programming. By direct cost, this represented twenty-nine percent of the total number of in-house hours produced by the CBC. Again, in an Olympic year, the nation's public broadcaster produced more hours of sports programming than any other individual category—news, current affairs, drama, children's and entertainment. Between 1989 and 1992, direct spending on in-house sports production went up eighty percent, from $29.5 million to $53.1 million, while drama spending only went up thirty-one percent to $37.8 million. Of 'CBC' continuing dramatic series included in the 1992/93 network schedule, only *Street Legal* and *Material World* were produced solely inside the CBC. Productions like *Road to Avonlea*, *Northwood*, *North of 60* and *Odyssey*, for example, were co-produced primarily with other people's money and using, in many cases, non-CBC production personnel. In some cases, CBC's contribution in resources and staff was notable. In others, the CBC contribution was in the order of thirty percent of the direct cash cost. In cases such as these, the CBC was now receiving many programs for thirty cents on the dollar, while the cost of the network establishment continued to rise.

Co-productions have become another taxpayer's subsidy for the CBC. Contrary to popular belief, the ETV network did not produce *Road to Avonlea*. It was broadcast by the CBC. The CBC was a big creative player in the production, spearheaded by Sullivan Films, but so was Telefilm Canada ($2.5 million) and so was The Disney Channel ($8 million). In many cases, the federally-funded Telefilm puts up as much as forty-nine percent of the cash cost of production. In 1990/91, the ETV network utilized $20.7 million in Telefilm broadcast funds, almost $16 million for drama.

As well, advertising revenue success and program saleability are now, perhaps more than ever, the dominant guiding principles behind the making of drama and entertainment programs on the ETV network—whether done by the CBC or with independent producers. Independent producers, and often as not their foreign partners, now influence the manufacture of CBC programs. To make their investment worthwhile, everyone—the producer, Telefilm, Disney, the CBC, even the provincial funding agencies—wants to see programs that are both popular (receive high audience ratings) and a marketing success (sell a lot of commercial advertising and are purchased for rebroadcast outside Canada). Program concepts that are culturally important, perform strictly as a service to the Canadian public, or those which would be attractive only to minority audience taste seldom, if ever, make the production list.

In this distorted public broadcast environment, Canadians see no series of programs adapted from the Canadian or the classical stage, no series of plays from alternative theatre, no regular prime time performance series, no series on literature—Canadian or otherwise— no access programming, no major continuing series on specific human issues, no series on Canadian history, no series on multicultural Canada, no major information series on global issues and no continuing series showcasing new Canadian talent. But we did have Ralph Benmergui trying to emulate Arsenio Hall.

When "cultural" programming is mentioned, CBC executives are quick to point to *Adrienne Clarkson Presents* and *Sunday Arts Entertainment* in defence. These series do exist and they cover a fairly broad range of cultural happenings. But first, given CBC's huge public broadcast responsibilities, these are token offerings. As well, they tend to focus on Canadian cultural programming as defined by cultural gatekeepers in Toronto. While appearing on CBC radio's *Cross Country Check Up* on March 28, 1993 Adrienne Clarkson defended her role as the nation's "cashmere filter" for the network. To Clarkson, "good broadcasting" on Canada's public broadcaster could only be achieved through a central control authority such as herself, a position the network's vice-president, Ivan Fecan, supported on the same radio program. The fact that a multitude of Canadians might not share her views or tastes—or might define their elements of "culture" differently—was apparently beside the point where Clarkson was concerned.

Clarkson and Fecan, and too many others within the ETV network structure, unfortunately share an aberrant definition of Canadian public broadcasting. They believe that the commercial value of a program is more important than its social function. They talk about their criterion being "good television"—a commodity, presumably, only they in Toronto are capable of delivering. They do not seem to comprehend that this has little to do with the fundamental definition of public broadcasting as a unique service to the citizen. No one should be filtering perceptions of Canada but the people who live it, who see it every day and understand it from the perspective of their region of the country. Clarkson and Fecan's misinterpretation of Canadian public broadcasting is simply driven by the commercial imperative.

Because the ETV network can no longer act independently of the demands of the commercial television marketplace, it is inclined to make deals with cultural impostors. The public broadcast needs of Canadians are no longer the principal negotiating influence in the deal. For Canadians trying to find their way through the jungle that is now "Canadian public broadcasting," we end up with *Anne Murray in Disney World* variety specials, American film stars as principal actors in Canadian productions and U.S. television executives having a sizeable say in what the CBC would eventually get to present to Canadians in the form of 'public broadcasting' programs. The system requires that these programs have to 'look American' to make a return on everybody's investment. As *Avonlea* producer Kevin Sullivan pointed out about his multi-partner co-production in the January 9, 1993 *Toronto Star*, "Disney and CBC have been very good partners, creatively. This is very unusual that you have a Canadian broadcaster and an American broadcaster trying to do something like this. They recognize where the audience is, and their goals are the same. . . ." February 1993 episodes of 'the CBC's' *Road to Avonlea* would include American stars Treat Williams and Meg Tilly.

The ETV network also operates in some program areas as if it were bankrupt. With all its millions, and with all the cash help the CBC now received from Telefilm and other government funding agencies via the independent producer, the ETV network still cannot make ends meet. In many cases, it was unlikely the network would broadcast certain series in the schedule—*Street Cents, Disability Network, Driver's Seat, Urban Peasant, People and Dogs, Road Movies*, just to name a few—unless someone else, most often the independent producer, came up with cash by making deals with commercial sponsors and supporters to finance the direct cash costs of production.

By the spring of 1993, a whole new generation of these "mushroom" ideas were popping up—proposed new series on wellness, cycling, parenting, interior design, pets and cottages. Most of these ventures—which are highly questionable in the context of public broadcasting to start with—would be produced with other people's money. "If anyone walks in these days with a bag of cash, they can do public television," one CBC Vancouver producer lamented.

Road Movies existed thanks to the huge amounts of 'contra' (goods and services provided by suppliers in return for mention in the series) and sponsorship involved, from airline passes to cameras used on the series. The innovative and award-winning teen show, *Street Cents*, would not have existed if it were not for the more than $1 million in cash the executive producer hustled, all by himself, from the Canadian Bankers' Association, provincial governments and other cash sponsors. There was no CBC cash in *Street Cents*, although CBC got to keep the commercial revenue that the series generated. *Best Years* relied, in part, on the cash supplied by the federal and some provincial governments to meet annual cost increases. These might be considered shrewd business moves but the end product often has little or nothing to do with public broadcasting or unique Canadian programming.

If the ETV network cost over $418 million and employed close to 3,000 people, what exactly were they producing for Canadians? Program spending on national news and current affairs, the vast majority of shows on the network by far, ate up only about thirty percent, on average, of the direct program budgets. The total hours of CBC in-house dramatic series production was miniscule and falling regularly. More and more documentary, children's and variety production was being largely underwritten by Telefilm or the NFB. To be sure, a large percentage of the ETV network staff would be involved in news and current affairs, as well as the production of children's and sports production. But during the 1991/92 budget cuts, the entire Toronto establishment, included in the number staff who worked for the Ontario region and were separate from the ETV network, lost fewer than 200 positions. Just as ominous, the hardest hit staff groups at the network were those Toronto employees who made programs—producers, technicians and design and staging staff. More than half of those employees laid off in Toronto were from these three production categories. On the original 'hit list,' distributed on December 12, 1990, only thirty-one "managers" were fingered for removal, compared to thirty-seven production and script assistants, thirty-one technicians, and thirty-eight producers.

One of life's great mysteries for regional managers has always been where all the ETV managers and production executive types came from and what they did for a living. It was not uncommon to attend meetings in Toronto and stare across the room at endless new managerial faces, whose names and identities you could never remember or reconcile. It seemed that every time a new network initiative was undertaken, a covey of fresh, new managers would appear. Many an evening the homeward-bound regional managers would gather in the airport lounge, asking each other: Who the hell were that bunch at the end of the table? What do they do? Who do they report to? The network management cadre grew with puzzling regularity—while lay-offs were taking place in the regions.

Finally, now that the CBC ETV network was no longer a presence with close ties to the public and the communities, who made the decisions about what it was Canadians would see on their public broadcasting network? And based on what criteria? By 1993, the entire network schedule was in the hands of Ivan Fecan, now vice-president for the English language television network. Surprising as it might sound, and as uncomfortable as it might make those who believe public broadcasting should be democratic as well as public, the entire menu of network production and scheduling decisions was made by the young former NBC executive.

> *"Far from being the dreamy, remote, undisciplined child of 'culture,' the* CBC *is in grave danger of becoming just another obedient child of Madison Avenue."*
> —Ralph Allen, *Maclean's* magazine, February 9, 1963

From the dotting of a financial "i" on a multi-million-dollar co-production deal to discussions on the rough editing of a Movie-of-the-Week, from the choice of a host on a new entertainment show to the way the make-up department combed his hair, from the decision on who would direct a situation comedy series to word changes on the scripts, from moving a program or series to another time in the network schedule to supervising the production of the annual sales launch tape, Fecan either oversaw the process, directed it, was consulted about it, okayed it or influenced it. To the extent that CBC's ETV network is the public's largest manifestation of public broadcasting, Ivan Fecan, alone, has defined what national public broadcasting in English television looked like. "Ivan has his finger on everything," Denis Harvey was quoted as saying by *Toronto* magazine in 1989, "and that's the way it has to be." Having risen even higher in the power ranks of the CBC, Fecan made it clear, on at least one occasion in 1992, that the entire English television network, as one regional director put it, "belongs to him—the schedule, the resources, the program ideas."

But Fecan's mission has been an impossible one. The subtext of CBC's mandate calls for the network to be totally distinctive from the competition, reflect "Canada and its regions . . . while serving the special needs of those regions," be a popular service in ratings terms and make more commercial revenue. Fecan has been able to achieve one out of four.

In Fecan's first full year as head of CBC's English-language television network, 1988/89, the ETV network's prime time audience share was 20.6 percent, compared to CTV's 22.8 percent and 3.8 percent for Pay-TV and specialty services. By the end of 1992, the ETV network's prime time audience share had fallen thirty-three percent, CTV's had risen by thirteen percent and Pay-TV and specialty services leaped 236 percent. When Ivan Fecan arrived back at the CBC, expected net advertising income on the network was about $152 million. By 1992, it was $220 million.

Fecan has set the tone and the direction for public television in Canada. Despite his career success in commercial television, his ultimate control of the nation's public television agenda raises serious questions about whether it is healthy to trust the entire future of the network to one person. *Toronto* magazine speculated in a March 1989 article that Fecan might be "too hip for the broad cross-section of the Canadian public that is the CBC audience. . . . Others insist that his instincts—and Fecan operates to a very considerable degree on his medium-cool intuition—are too commercial for a publicly funded network." His move to centralize power at the network disenfranchised the regions from the programming process and occasionally left a trail of management redundancy, confusion and, on occasion, questionable program spending practices.

Fecan's changes to the network's program management structure—

freeing creative heads from the worry of day-to-day budget matters and centralizing decision-making—tested a basic rule of public broadcasting, that the person responsible for building a program must also be totally responsible for how the money is spent. The decision to free the network creative heads from worrying about "adding up taxi chits"—leaving that job to administrative managers—and focus on creative decision-making, meant that the production process now had the potential for running on two parallel tracks—one for the money being spent, and one for the creative design.

"We are gathered here to wash away the face and memory of a staid old mother corporation and replace it with the new face of TV," executive producer David Marsden wrote to the staff of *Pilot* 1 on November 21, 1988. "And remember, the key to the show is 'us'." *Pilot* 1 was an interesting piece of entertainment television. Conceptually, it was the sort of thing CBC should always be doing—challenging convention, offering program alternatives. The original concept had been a relatively inexpensive, regionally-based, weekday afternoon series for teens. It ended up an expensive, Toronto-directed, one-hour series for the young, the hip, the trendy—lots of black leather, a little technicolour hair, earrings and pouts. It was also one of the first tests of Fecan's newly reorganized management structure. Although *Pilot* 1 was breaking new and interesting ground in youth television, from an administrative point-of-view, it was a debacle.

Pilot 1 was one of the first of the post-Deerhurst "regional productions" put together under Fecan—it was produced in the B.C. region, but the concept, the treatment and all the major decisions were made either in Toronto or with Toronto's concurrence. Although a number of B.C. producers were contracted to the show, B.C. regional managers were not a main part of the process, except to track the impact on the Vancouver plant—and watch the costs mount. The project was overstaffed (there were thirty-three people on the crew, an inordinately high number for a limited entertainment show scheduled for off-prime time) and even network administrators admitted it. But they had no control over the creative end of the production under the new organizational structure. Spending began almost immediately after the show went into planning in April 1988, even though a budget was not formally approved until less than four months before the series went to air, not an uncommon practice within the CBC. Cautions from B.C. managers were frequently passed to Toronto about how the money was being spent and how cheaper alternatives were available, but the message seemed to have trouble getting through the network bureaucracy at 1255 Bay Street.

The project became the embarrassment of the office hallways of CBC British Columbia. At one end of the building we were facing future budget cuts to regional programs and staff, and across the street and around the corner, money seemed to be no object. After much discussion over the availability of studio space within the main CBC building, the production crew, under the direction of an executive producer newly arrived from Toronto, decided to locate off CBC premises. Among the reasons given, the kids needed distance from "staid, old mother" CBC, needed a place to "hang out" we were told. It sounded to us as if the network was moving out of TV and into adolescent social services.

The *Pilot 1* crew moved a few blocks away from the CBC Hamilton Street site and set up production in a vacant building—agreeing to a year's lease at $15,000 a month. Office modifications at the rented site cost $126,000. Building renovations to make the rented site suitable for shooting totalled $336,000, with $66,000 of that for telephones, computers and typewriters—some of that available down the street and around the corner at the main CBC site. The bill for furniture was $24,000. An elaborate set was constructed on the rental premises at a cost of $100,000.

When *Pilot 1* went to air January 13, 1989, letters of protest started pouring in immediately. The show was aimed at the young and the hip and hit the rest of the audience right between the ethical and moral eyes. The rock lyrics, the sex-and-you segments and the general in-your-face tone of the show was perceived as pure Toronto. Mothers commented about the show (twenty percent of the audience turned out to be children between the ages of two and eleven) with "a mixture of disgust, anger and shame." Critics talked about "a new low in young people's programming." An angry B.C. affiliate station manager agreed that *Pilot 1* was definitely an example of alternative programming—"an alternative to good taste, good sense and good television." The series seemed to be drawing more angry mail than viewers. The average audience for the show was 105,000 viewers— 50,000 less than for the inexpensive music video program *Good Rockin' Tonite* it temporarily replaced. *Pilot 1* cost $66,000 an episode, or $10,000 more than was budgeted; *Good Rockin'*, one-tenth or less.

At a January meeting of regional and network managers, during a coffee and muffin break, Fecan sidled up to me. "What is this thing [*Pilot* 1] really costing me?" he asked, perhaps as much for confirmation as curiosity. On January 24, I had our regional managers total up the costs. The grand total was $1,418,517. On February 7, Fecan pulled the plug on *Pilot* 1. The series would run itself out to March, we were told, and it would be appreciated if we, the region, would clean up. Like bedouins slipping away in the night, everybody dispersed after the last show. B.C. regional management—which had no large hand in the show's creation or direction—was instructed to keep paying the $15,000 monthly rent until September (charged to the ETV network) on the soon-to-be-vacated site—on the off-chance the series might be renewed in the fall—hire security guards to watch the equipment, sell off assets the ETV network did not want and send the computers back to Toronto. We were also left to answer irate letters and telephone calls, and arrange for the formal laying-off of the Vancouver staff assigned to the series. This was an episode of "more production in the regions than ever before."

For whatever reasons, the *Pilot* 1 experience that danced so briefly and so expensively across our screens was the antithesis of what most of those gathered at Deerhurst had envisaged as more regional production. Left in the hands of the B.C. region, *Pilot* 1 would have cost substantially less and might have remained longer in the network schedule than eleven weeks. On one point there should be no debate. A Vancouver regional production could not have drawn a smaller audience.

Ivan Fecan has been called "the boy wonder," "the whiz kid of Canadian TV" and "one of those rare 30-year-olds who's going on 50." He watches television like others eat or read books. His television programming senses—steeped in the North American commercial TV marketplace—can at times be brilliant. He believes passionately in the CBC, but lives on another planet, figuratively speaking, as far as many other public broadcasters are concerned.

Fecan's principal preoccupation is in contemporary television. He believes in a sophisticated audience he told *Toronto* magazine in 1989, "an audience that grew up with TV—a smart audience who watches things like *Hill Street Blues* and *thirtysomething*, and that's why I think it's important to put quality on the screen."

Born in 1954, just as television was beginning to envelop Canada, Ivan Fecan was raised in Toronto and began his career with CBC radio, moving from there to CITY-TV where, at age twenty-three, he became the station's news director. He returned to CBC's Toronto station, CBLT, as program director in 1982, became the network's director of program development a year later, its head of television variety a year after that, and a year later was NBC's vice-president of creative affairs, by age thirty-one. He returned to the CBC in 1987 as the ETV network's director of programming, responsible for overseeing the Canadianization of the network, and in the summer of 1991 became vice-president, ETV network arts and entertainment. By 1993 he was vice-president of the ETV network.

He drew for all of us the creative impression he had of Canada and what its appetite for public television might consist of. Based on his professional judgement, he set in motion the machinery that told Canadians what they looked like and how they thought. Fecan admitted he saw public broadcasting as a one man show he was responsible for: "Someone has to make the decisions," he told *Cross Country Check Up* listeners in the spring of 1993. In a country so vast and different that it stretches five time zones and over hundreds of different cultural traits and social habits, one person brokered the ideas of what Canadians would see on public television. To say that, by comparison with the geographic and cultural breadth of the nation, Fecan's experiences were somewhat limited would be kind.

Ivan Fecan is probably without peer in Canada when it comes to understanding and serving the audience's appetite for North American-style television programming. But as good as his skills and talent are, the main thrust of Canada's public broadcasting—English language television—should not be left in the hands of one individual. As a senior Toronto manager commented: "If you look at someone like Al Johnson's perception of what public broadcasting is, given where he came from [Saskatchewan], and someone like Fecan, those are two different perceptions about the role of public broadcasting." The institution of CBC television has to be larger and more important than Fecan's perception of it, perhaps even larger than Johnson's.

Fecan argued repeatedly throughout 1991 and 1992, like Chairman Patrick Watson, that "more network production is now taking place in the regions than ever before." One regional director thought Fecan, "was going to come across the table and grab me by the throat" when he argued in a 1992 meeting that Fecan was using a different definition of regional production than most regional directors. Fecan seemed to assume that because a program was technically produced in a certain region of the country it constituted a regional production—complete with all the local cultural and unique social reflection of that part of the country. But to do it that way—to control the design of a program concept in Toronto and send the idea to Vancouver, along with the Toronto staff, to produce the program and call that a regional production on our national broadcasting service—reflected little more than Toronto's biases about the country and how it is constituted. Toronto, and to a large degree Fecan himself, would end up being our cultural filter.

When the 1991 Juno Awards show on the ETV network was 'produced' in Vancouver, forty-nine of the seventy-seven people involved in putting the show together came from Toronto. Only twenty-one of B.C. region staff were used on the production. Seven other staff flew in from Alberta and Ottawa. The Toronto fly-in list included all the necessary production creative 'heavies'—producer, director, writer, network executives, cameramen, studio directors, set designer, makeup artist. The Toronto list even included the show's hairdresser and an announcer—as if Vancouver hairdressers did not know how to properly fix hair, or one of the announcers on CBC B.C. staff rosters could not read words from a prepared script.

The concept for the show was developed in Toronto. All negotiations with sponsors and co-producing partners took place through Toronto. The show was designed in Toronto. The choice of participants and entertainers was made in Toronto. Most of the huge, dungeons-and-dragons set was built in Toronto, and shipped to Vancouver for the show. No consultation on the concept of the show, use of talent or the show's theme (even though it was loudly hailed as a "celebration of talent—west coast style . . .") took place between the show's Toronto producer and Vancouver-based program management. The entire Toronto entourage blew into Vancouver, set up camp in the Queen Elizabeth Theatre across the street from the CBC B.C. headquarters, produced the program and started to leave town the next morning. Yet, the Toronto-based English Television Network considered the 1991 Juno Awards show a regional production.

At the press conference announcing the new 1992 fall network schedule, Fecan made sure everyone in attendance knew that a "record number of shows were either from the regions or set in the regions." This was "a new crusade for us," he added. For what many of these programs meant to regional Canada, they could have been produced in Bangor, Maine. On the west coast, *Beachcombers*, cancelled in 1990, was the last vestige of a truly regional CBC production, and even that series was controlled and finally massaged out of existence by Toronto network executives in its last few years.

Another couple of Vancouver-based series that ran in the 1991/92 television network schedule—*Mom P.I.* and *Max Glick*—were about as close to being regional CBC productions as the various former Soviet states are to still being a Union. *Max Glick* was a Winnipeg-based production concept the network and the co-producer agreed to set in the B.C. Lower Mainland rather than Manitoba, where the original film had been produced. Although the network invested a cash license fee in the series, only two CBC B.C. technical staff saw regular work on the series. *Mom P.I.* was another closet regional CBC coproduction. The series set up production, was broadcast in the schedule, did not particularly do well in the ratings, eventually folded its tent and left town—never having anything substantial to do with the regional CBC offices. These series were loudly hailed by the ETV network as a net increase in the hours of B.C. regional production after the demise of *Beachcombers*.

Beachcombers was an excellent example of the application and need of pure, as opposed to adulterated, regional production in a national public broadcasting system. *Beachcombers* was conceived, nurtured and survived for nineteen years through the energy and creativity of CBC personnel, not in Toronto, but in Vancouver. *Beachcombers* was originally produced by local CBC producer Phil Keatley, who had been instrumental in pushing the concept to reality, often against the preferences of the network. If left solely to a Toronto network decision-maker, the folksy little program idea, about a bunch of happy beachcombers who spent most of their time either arguing in a leaky boat or sitting in a coffee shop, would never have made it to the small screen.

But *Beachcombers* went on to become the most successful Canadian dramatic television series ever made. Its over 400 episodes have been seen in forty different countries, in five languages. The series has made the CBC hundreds of thousands of dollars in sales revenue. It has played to a whole generation of Canadians and, until the 1989/90 season when it was moved in the schedule from Sunday to Wednesday evenings by network executives, *Beachcombers* averaged more than a million viewers a night. It went as high as 1.9 million viewers in 1981/82. The series was cashiered because of falling ratings. Ratings almost always fall when you move a program about in the schedule. The move to Wednesday evening immediately cost *Beachcombers* almost a half-million viewers. The switch, which made room on Sunday evenings for the very successful *Road to Avonlea* series, was the traditional mark of Cain for the series. With *Beachcombers'* audience share cut in half by the move, the network began discussing how the popular series could be phased out—without a lot of negative publicity or public backlash.

As a television program, *Beachcombers* was delightfully entertaining, reflecting life on the west coast—people, lifestyles, issues—injected into the Canadian social and cultural mainstream. It helped define a region to the rest of the country. And, by and large, it did that *authentically*. The people who made the shows lived on, and knew, the west coast, with all its particular quirks, personality and idiosyncrasies. As a consequence, Canadians received a pretty real and entertaining slice of Canada. Unfortunately, there will never be another series like *Beachcombers* on the CBC.

> "CBC *repositioning turns off viewers*"
> "*After only five weeks of the radically restructured* CBC *television season, some of the network's longest running and most popular shows have lost significant numbers of viewers while newer, more innovative shows are hemorrhaging because of too early or too late time slots.*"
> —John Haslett Cuff, *Globe and Mail*, December 10, 1992

Under Fecan, ETV network management understood, clearly, the value of a Nielsen rating point or audience share percentage. The network is driven by audience ratings, although depending on circumstances the addiction will often be denied. When ratings for programs are high, the audience measurement system tends to be acceptable. When they are low, the fall back is to talk about the CBC as "an alternative" to commercial television and the ratings race—despite the fact the CBC programs can look amazingly similar to those of private stations and networks. As one frustrated CBC reporter told the *Vancouver Sun* on February 13, 1993: "Some weeks ratings count and some weeks they don't. Some weeks we are the public broadcaster and ratings don't matter so much. Sometimes they do matter. It swings back and forth."

As the new repositioned 1992/93 schedule began haemorrhaging, the network announced it was no longer chasing ratings. In January 1993, as *Prime Time News* wallowed at a twelve percent share of the viewing audience, compared to fifteen percent for now-departed *The National*, regional supper hours down an astronomic forty-plus percent and due to fall further and *Designing Women* running short 600,000 viewers from 1992, Fecan told the *Globe and Mail*: "We want to get it out of our heads that we're competing with anyone. If you're just competing, then you'll behave like your competitors and then why have public broadcasting at all?" However, in the same January 30 article Fecan admitted he was pleased by *Prime Time*'s ratings to date: "He (Fecan) said advertisers like the new slot and a demographic breakdown shows *Prime Time News* viewers are younger on average than those of *The National* and *The Journal*."

Ratings not only serve to gauge the effectiveness of network decisions about which program should play and which should not. They are also the base statistics the network uses to compute how much to charge for television commercial time. But this preoccupation with commercial revenue has been a singular disaster for public television in Canada. Network management, and often corporate management at Head Office, also use audience ratings like peas in a shell game—moving from one measurement to another when the glow rubbed off a certain rating figure. If a program's "share" (the percentage of people viewing a particular program) seemed to be falling too drastically, they will either move to quote "rating" (percentage of the population watching TV) or, if bulk numbers looked better, quote the quarter-hour averages—nice, big juicy slabs of audience like 550,000 or 1.117 million. If none of this works as effectively as desired, they turn to EI—Enjoyment Index, or how much the viewer enjoyed a particular program. But with ETV network audience ratings falling the past few years on most if not all fronts, CBC executives began to quote audience "reach," or the percentage of those who tune into a show, but who do not necessarily stay for the whole presentation: "Our share may be down to a seven, but look at our reach: up to 79 percent!" What 'reach' can also tell you is that the audience passed through that particular show, 'grazing' its way to other more attractive program options on other networks or cable services.

Relying solely on ratings to judge program and corporate effectiveness is a house built with flimsy cards. Except as trend indicators, audience research data are unstable and often misleading. Yet major changes in CBC corporate direction, or ETV network programming philosophy, have taken place, based on those data. Major program decisions are made on those data. The introduction of the disastrous "repositioning" schedule of the ETV network—disastrous certainly in audience number terms—was initiated in small part because it was believed Canadians were going to bed earlier. They weren't. It would appear many stayed up—and tuned into CTV News at 11 P.M. The reality CBC researchers seldom ever discuss is that the numbers and the measurements used to decide if a CBC program is a ratings success are simply flawed.

The old diary system, in which families were asked to keep weekly written records of their viewing habits, skewed wildly. Memory lapses, wrong channel designations, family feuds, coffee spills and bald lies made their way into these presumably scientific measurements of viewer behaviour. One-half of the children involved in U.S. Nielsen 'people meter' reporting simply quit pressing the button from disinterest. Later people meters, using electronic sensors, scanned living rooms and reported that someone large and round sat on the sofa and watched unlimited hours of a certain channel. Unfortunately, the large and round someone often turned out to be the family dog.

Writing in the March 1992 edition of *The Atlantic*, Erik Larson pointed out that the margin of error in TV rating systems is so large that it is almost unprofessional, from a statistician's point of view, to use those data. A 1989 industry study showed that only thirty-seven percent of the targeted households sampled produced usable data about viewing habits on any given day; a rate well, well below any basic research standard. Larson concluded that the ratings used by Nielsen, and followed almost religiously by the CBC—from the Audience Research people to Ivan Fecan—are "inherently imperfect" as a professional measurement tool.

While attending university in 1970, I held a job as an 'assistant stationary engineer' for the City of Winnipeg waterworks department. I would sit up all night monitoring the city's water flow on moving charts. The engineer and I would watch in amazement on Saturday nights as almost half of the city flushed its toilets in unison—during the commercial breaks on *Hockey Night in Canada*. By watching the flow needles drop dramatically we could chart almost by the second when commercial breaks took place in any television program. Large drops between commercials meant fewer viewers watching the show. The "Winnipeg Waterworks Television Viewing Rating System" was about as accurate—maybe more so—as the current rating systems in use. And the CBC, the ETV network and Head Office, still insist that it is reasonable to base major deviations in programming, in policy— even to some extent set the agenda for public broadcasting of the future—on something scientifically akin to the flush of a toilet.

The thirst for higher and higher ratings became more pronounced in the mid-1980s as the ETV network raced harder on the commercial track to try to keep ahead of dwindling budgets. The network's producers warned presciently in their 1983 "A New Beginning" document that the use of ratings could be a major factor in the erosion of the CBC's identity as the public broadcaster: "Ratings are a measure, the lowest common denominator. Numbers are important, but they should be considered as one of the many factors in judging a program's success and performance. Criteria such as Canadian expression, specific audiences, subject matter and more, should receive strong consideration in tandem with ratings."

The persistent press for ratings success was driven by the need for larger annual advertising revenue to help CBC meet its yearly budget nut. But it also led to the self-Americanization of Canadian public television. As one western Canadian film industry representative put it: "You get a little tired and confused—and a little irritated—dealing with Canada's public broadcaster, when they start the [deal] conversation by wanting to know if we've got NBC on side."

Programs that lurk around the deep cultural fringe of Canadian public broadcasting—historical drama or documentary, performance, community issue debate, adaptations of Canadian stage plays, profiles of local performers or prominent Canadians—are not seen as ideal ratings winners. And they are a much tougher commercial sell. They would not make smiles break out on sales personnel faces. One might suspect that working for the CBC was also a bit uncomfortable for the sales staff. Selling commercial time in a television program about multicultural issues in B.C's Lower Mainland, or a half-hour regional drama about the life of suffragette Nellie McClung, or the plight of native people in Regina, or blacks in Halifax was certainly more challenging than selling time in *The Magical World of Disney*. Often, the commercial availability time in the former was filled with promotions for other CBC programs, or public service announcements—as an admission of the sales department's failure to sell Canadian—while in the latter the "SRO" signs went up. As one former regional sales manager said: "When I was hired from the private sector, not once was I given any instructions about anything to do with 'public broadcasting' programs. It was all simply *sales*. They told me to sell availability and if there ever was a debate over commercial policy or sales versus programming that might effect sales targets, I was to get right to Kretz [ETV network head of sales and marketing]," meaning he would work to fix the problem in favour of the sales department.

"I'm amazed when we go through discussions and the position taken by many senior management people who see no conflict between their definition of public broadcasting and relying for fully thirty percent of your revenue on commercials, even though they admit the distorting effect it has," said Board member William Neville, who evidently is powerless to do anything about it. Between 1982 and 1988, the share of the corporation's operating budget covered by sales revenues rose from 17.8 percent to 26.3 percent. By 1991, the percentage had climbed beyond one-third. Between 1983/84 and 1988/89, CBC's share of the overall Canadian advertising sales market rose from sixteen to twenty percent. By May of 1991 and the tabling of the Peters-Girard "Economic Status of Canadian Television" report, the $350 million-plus siphoning of the nation's advertising revenue pot into CBC coffers was a major source of irritation to private broadcasters. This chase after the commercial dollar occasionally reaches morally abysmal lows for the CBC, as on October 19, 1992, while Bill Cameron was interviewing Prime Minister Brian Mulroney. On the eve of one of the most important moments in Canadian political history—the referendum on the Charlottetown Accord—as a million or more Canadians were hanging on every word uttered by Mulroney, Cameron was forced to interrupt the conversation on Canada's national public broadcaster—for a commercial break. On the one hand, it was embarrassing. On the other, it was poetic justice.

To many, the ultimate contradiction about Canadian public broadcasting is CBC Sports. It has always been assumed that Sports was a huge, glitzy cash generator for the CBC, whether on the French or the English television network. But in 1990, the two network sports departments ate up $54 million to operate ($38 million in English, $16 million in French) just in direct costs. That does not count what they would have spent on overhead and administration. With all the human and public broadcast devastation that lay scattered across the country after December 5, 1990, the ETV network sports department escaped the budget cuts "unscathed."

Hundreds of creative public broadcasters lost their jobs and we still got the same number of hours-per-year of games, fights, race cars and Don Cherry commenting monosyllabically on the state of the universe. Decisions like that indicate that we Canadians either have a wholly unhealthy national fetish with televised sporting events or the CBC has its public broadcasting priorities all fouled up. According to the 1991/92 annual report, as of March 31, 1992, a year before the corporation would have to begin dipping into its employee's pension fund surplus to try to survive, CBC commitments for sports rights amounted to an astounding $140.8 million!

During the last decade, sports coverage on the ETV network averaged over 700 hours per year, much of it in prime time. Sports hours increased substantially with the introduction of wall-to-wall Stanley Cup coverage each spring. "In fact, I used to laugh because [the network program director] would wait to do his program planning until I finished acquiring all the sports rights," former head of network sports Ron Devion recalled. The public broadcaster's program schedule would be largely driven by games. Lured like a harlot looking for pocket change, the CBC tends to use sports, not for any fulfilment of public broadcast goals, but for the millions it brings in annually to corporate coffers. If you think that all those decades of being subjected to watching horrid Toronto Maple Leaf hockey teams on CBC had anything to do with a national love affair with the team, you have it wrong. The stumbling Leafs were there—Saturday night after unfortunate Saturday night—because of the role they played in attracting advertising interest in the large, southern Ontario market.

It certainly is not a matter that sports coverage opportunities are limited on Canadian television screens, as if CTV or TSN would refrain from televising sports events. Competing private broadcasters would dearly love to be able to wallow in the lucrative sports trough of *Hockey Night in Canada* or the Stanley Cup Playoffs. But CBC holds the rights—paid for with tax dollars. In 1991, the CBC spent $37 million purchasing the rights to sports events—an amount that would have neatly covered the $32 million the Tories cut out of CBC's 1991 budget. Add that $37 million paid out to televise sports events to the $50 million in direct costs for the French and English sports production activity for the year and the total—$87 million—is almost *twice* the amount cut out of Regional Broadcasting Operations. The CBC can spend $87 million on sports production but cannot afford $46 million to keep the bare essentials of public broadcasting alive.

The question, of course, is: What is more important in Canadian public broadcasting? Sports? Or authentic stories about life and people and being Canadian in places other than Toronto? I'll bet you picked the wrong one. This chronic distortion even has members of the Board scratching their heads: "I do not believe the people of Canada kick up a billion dollars a year so that we can carry a Blue Jays baseball game instead of [some other broadcaster]," said William Neville.

Between 1989 and 1992, the ETV network spent, on average, $13 million a year more on Sports production, in direct dollars, than it did on programs the network is best known for—news and current affairs. In 1992 alone, Sports direct costs were $26 million more, or double the annual average, than spent on news and current affairs. If the CBC is spending those millions on the production of programs that the private sector would take over in an instant, what, you might ask, is the CBC doing in the sports production business anyway? The answer, it would appear, is: "Making a ton of money."

The Winter Olympics opening ceremonies drew a thirty-seven share of the national audience. The men's downhill ski race, broadcast on a Sunday morning, captured a forty-four share. Sunday evening prime time viewing of the Olympics from Albertville averaged 1.7 million viewers and a nineteen share. But as one disillusioned senior network manager admitted: "Those numbers are not statements about public broadcasting. They are statistics about a televised event. That audience would be there no matter if these events were on CBC, CTV or the U.S. nets." Stanley Cup coverage, which obliterates everything on CBC's television schedule for three hours a night, for up to seven weeks each spring, is a veritable gold mine for the corporation. The Stanley Cup Playoffs can mean as much as $50 to $60 million to the CBC, or close to fifteen percent of the total annual commercial revenue the corporation rakes in.

Network sports managers love to parade their department as a huge profit centre. But true sports costs are another internal scam. The actual costs of producing sports programs lie hidden within the regional television infrastructure—where a sizeable portion of the base cost for crews and equipment is as unquantified as Merlin's projections. And no one has ever calculated the cost to the CBC in disaffected viewers—audience who have had their viewing expectations brutalized by night-after-night of Don Cherry playing commercial shill and drawing names out of a drum for a tire company. Stanley Cup hockey preempts *Prime Time News* in the schedule with impunity. In Vancouver during 1990 Stanley Cup action, the beleaguered regional supper hour news program, *The CBC Evening News*, was preempted or moved to a time other than its six o'clock slot twenty-five times between April 4 and May 22. How much audience loyalty does a show lose when it does not appear in its expected schedule slot for more than a month? And how much off-setting related commercial revenue do you lose from the subsequent drop in that regional show's following or ratings?

The scenario for the future looms where, someday, CBC's ETV network will, with great fanfare, announce that the Stanley Cup Play-offs made it to their maximum possible forty-nine games. For three hours each night, over almost two months, we will be told, the CBC was the most popular television network in the country. The commercial revenue 'take' totalled more than $60 million. And the next night, when hockey broadcasting overkill was complete, only a couple of thousand stubborn but incensed viewers will finally get to watch CBC's *The Nature of Things* in its proper time slot.

> *"Worried about Tommy Hunter going off the air? Or the future of Wayne and Shuster or Front Page Challenge? Well, rest easy. They'll be around as long as Ivan Fecan's around. These shows work, he thinks, so why toss them out? They get good, solid ratings. They reach the key audience. They're a success and he's not going to mess around with success."*
> —Peter Goddard, *Toronto Star*, February 29, 1984

When the ETV network started to chase more aggressively its commercial tail, it also had to start chasing a slightly different audience—the young and trendy. As ratings dropped, the network fine-tuned its audience targets in an attempt to satisfy advertisers, giving a higher priority to a few groups, a lower priority to others and all but dismissing some. Shoulder-to-shoulder in interest—the ETV network, the sales department and advertisers and their agencies—started marching, like a bunch of telegenic Jesuits ("Give me a child until he is seven, and I will give you the man for life . . .") after the kids.

Fecan's January 1993 comment about how the younger demographic profile of *Prime Time News* made it extra attractive to advertisers was not a slip of the tongue. A balanced public broadcasting service, proper regional reflection and minority audience interests were being nudged to the sidelines by the commercial imperative of advertisers. It was either that or drop its advertising rates and make less money, but the CBC would not do that unless forced to. Since the 1988/89 television season, the network has given a high priority to programs that attract audiences which are young, urban, hip and acquisitive.

Advertisers' research shows that youngsters are not as loyal to specific brands as adults and are more susceptible to messages about new products. They act like TV magnets, drawing other members of the family to the program they are watching, increasing opportunities for more viewers to witness the commercial message. Although the thirty-five-to-forty-nine-year-old audience group is the largest, single body of population, and holds substantial disposable income, it buys with more discretion and reflects a large degree of brand loyalty. If you are still with me at this point, you might be thinking: "What's this got to do with public broadcasting?" Precisely.

Young is beautiful on the CBC ETV network. *Tommy Hunter* is old. Before he bit it from ETV management, he had been on CBC for twenty-seven years. But in 1992 *Tommy Hunter* was "predictable and old-fashioned," even if the program still drew solid audience numbers. Bumped up against *Hockey Night in Canada* in the network schedule, *Tommy Hunter* drew an average audience over its last three years of 850,000 viewers. During his last dance in January 1992, the show drew almost an average one million viewers, very respectable numbers in anyone's television terms; *Prime Time News* would love to have them. But for the ETV network and the sales department, they were the wrong viewers: men and women over the age of fifty were dominant. The enjoyment of almost a million Canadians did not count when pressed against the need for demographics that would keep attracting commercial revenue.

By 1993, the issue that had chased CBC television since the 1960s—an overabundance of U.S. programs in our national public television broadcasting schedule—was no longer the central issue hovering over the heads of the ETV network. Canadian programs had largely replaced American in prime time. In the 1992/93 season, only two-and-half hours of American, not including mini-series, remained in prime time (although the week's afternoon schedule was loaded with seventeen hours of ancient American sit-com re-runs, from *WKRP in Cincinnati* to *Taxi*). The issue now was that much of the Canadian entertainment content on the ETV network had come to look as American as the programs it replaced. Much of it looked, felt and smelled like it had been made in Los Angeles. As CBC's producers pointed out long ago in "A New Beginning," co-production with an American partner "clearly dictates that the ensuing program is acceptable to the U.S. market." The producer's interests "will not in all cases coincide with the public service mandate of the CBC."

In 1988, the ETV network announced that Vancouver would be the production base for a new, made-in-Canada afternoon game show program. *Talkabout* was a three-way partnership between the network, a Canadian co-producer, Primedia, and Don Taffner of *Three's a Crowd* fame—a U.S. series of which *TV Guide's* Robert MacKenzie once wrote: "This show is so despicable that my main reaction is amazement." The interest of each party was simple. The network needed an inexpensive afternoon audience participation show. A game show concept had been recommended for the network schedule by the Deerhurst Canadianization task force in July 1987. They had in mind something that would inform Canadians about their nation and its history, and entertain at the same time. Primedia's participation would keep CBC's cash exposure low. Other than the assignment of a coordinating producer, there was no creative input in the *Talkabout* project from the B.C. region. The region was simply the base of production—the place where the series would be put together. It could have happened in Halifax, Toronto or Des Moines, Iowa. It had nothing to do with 'regionalism' or 'regional' production. As we would later find out, *Talkabout* would have little to do with Canadianization as well.

The first indication that this new production was skewing south came when one of Taffner's production people assigned to the project began asking for a number of the questions and answers to be recognizably American—presumably so the series could sell more easily in distribution on the other side of the border. Distinctive Canadian references—along the lines of "Wolfe," "Montcalm" and "Kicking Horse Pass"—hit the floor faster than you could say "free trade." In their place came the likes of "George Washington," "the Empire State Building" and "San Bernardino."

The second indication came when it was learned that hosts and guests would have to learn to perform "like they do on the game shows in the U.S." Participants were instructed to make sure that they always smiled—giggling, jumping up and down and rolling the eyes was even better—and got very excited whenever they answered the questions correctly or won a cash prize.

But the most telling indication that *Talkabout* was quickly losing what little identification with public broadcasting it had was when the ETV network informed me that they would not be using CBC Vancouver make-up artists on the pilot production. Instead, they would be using two from Toronto, artists sensitive to all the latest L.A. trends and styles. Host Wayne Cox had to be made-up to look like a U.S game show host. With the two make-up artists attending to things of great cultural substance—like teased hair and no-shine nose make-up—Cox was outfitted in the latest jackets and ties and his photograph taken for publicity purposes. It was explained that they were trying to get "the right look" for Cox. They wanted him in both still-photo and on the small screen to meet all the expectations of a Canadian audience used to watching American game shows. When I asked what exactly they were trying to achieve, and why the extra cost and effort, after all, Cox was already a handsome and respected west coast broadcaster and journalist, I was informed that the network was after a certain "look" that would drive the mostly-female afternoon audience into orgiastic distraction.

Talkabout lasted two seasons on the ETV network, averaging a little less than 250,000 viewers for each show. It did quite well with children and teenagers, generally drawing around an eleven or twelve percent share of that audience. *Talkabout* was replaced in the 1990/91 network schedule by a not-too-funny and definitely well-worn U.S. sit-com, *Alice*—the story about a bunch of people trying to survive life in a hamburger joint south of the border. When we later came forward with a subsequent proposal to substitute for *Talkabout* with a series that was substantially more "Canadian" and intellectually more challenging—a series based on the immense amount of information contained in Mel Hurtig's, *The Canadian Encyclopedia*—the ETV network set the proposal on the shelf, claiming that, despite how much they loved the concept—and baby, they *did* love it—the idea was just too expensive at the moment for the nation's public broadcaster, regardless of how much motherhood and Canadiana oozed from the idea. Not only that, it was clear that because the proposed Hurtig concept dealt exclusively with Canadian subject matter, unlike *Talkabout*, there was the embarrassing consideration that it probably could not, unfortunately, be marketed and sold in many other countries and bring in further revenue from sales. However, if Mel Hurtig could come up with a couple of million dollars of his own cash, maybe something could be done . . .

9 / Kafka's Castle

". . . by career and values, I am a good public servant: I do the job I am given to do . . ."
—Gérard Veilleux, *Globe and Mail,* July 18, 1992
"People here think they own the goddamn jobs."
—Gérard Veilleux, January 12, 1993

UNTIL HE ANNOUNCED his resignation on July 29, 1993, the country's single largest cultural entity was carried along on its corporate path to the future primarily on the instincts of one man, Gérard Veilleux. Perhaps more than any president, Veilleux was placed in time-and-space not just to face a corporate holocaust, but also, ultimately, to be free to mould the waning future of Canadian public broadcasting with his own clay and into his own form. What he ended up with might not always blend with the corporation's historic reality. It might not sit well with the needs, beliefs and understandings that many Canadians have of what the CBC should be. A great deal of what Veilleux did since he was appointed in the fall of 1989 was a sizeable gamble for national public broadcasting. If he was right, a stronger, healthier and more effective organization might be the result. If he was wrong, we could effectively, and finally, kiss the fading dream of Canadian public broadcasting good-bye forever.

Gérard Veilleux did not initially want the job as president of the CBC. He turned it down a number of times, only agreeing to take it when the prime minister—"the commander-in-chief" to Veilleux—made it clear he wanted the then-secretary of the Treasury Board installed at Bronson Avenue. He was so reluctant that he even suggested, just before the appointment was made public, that there was still time for Mulroney to change his mind. The move could "backfire" on the PM; it would "damage the institution" to be seen to be sending "the slasher" from Treasury Board to lead the CBC. He admitted he had no real concept of public broadcasting when he came. He watched little television and listened to radio even less. Although he read "everything he could assimilate" of what his Head Office managers made available to him, he had not read any major history on public broadcasting before assuming office.

He admits he did not know what he was getting into. The complexity of the CBC "scared him." The quality of the briefings he received from Head Office management when he arrived were "loose" and "not well organized," not issue oriented, in an organization being beaten and battered by myriad issues. The lack of order and precision "frightened the hell out of me," he said. He would begin to learn about national public broadcasting on the job—making it up, as best he could, as he went along. Unfortunately, his apprenticeship would coincide with one of the most consequential periods the CBC has ever experienced.

Gérard Veilleux is a very engaging person. In comfortable settings with people he enjoys, he can be expansive and chatty, his arms flailing about in emphasis, his face beaming with impish smiles and expressions. He comes across at first meeting with the cheery, hand-pumping personality of a politician on the election stump. He is bright—"a mind like a steel trap," as one Ottawa bureaucrat put it—articulate and clearly a dedicated Canadian public servant. He was an unknown quantity outside the corridors of political influence when he was appointed CBC president in 1989. It was Patrick Watson who was going to save the CBC. Who was this other guy? Well, he was a genuinely decent person who cared about his family and his country, respected and valued his friends, and carried a huge reputation among the professional civil service. He is proud that throughout his career he has been the good public servant, serving "my Minister" and the government.

The other Veilleux can be brittle, prickly and quick tempered, "going ballistic" when things do not go his way. Face-to-face, he can be tough as a stevedore. Senior managers openly feared his wrath. "Temper," "angry" and "rage" were terms that came up frequently when people talked about him. Stephen Godfrey wrote in the *Globe and Mail* on July 18, 1992 about Veilleux being so annoyed by statements being made by public members of a CBC focus group in Montreal that he came out from behind the one-way glass and instructed the participants on how misinformed they were. Producers came away from meetings with him reflecting on the lack of reserve he exhibited as a major executive—"losing his cool."

He spoke often of the secret of good management being open lines of communication and the opportunity to "let the managers manage," yet his office shared information selectively, and he was not reluctant to contact journalists or producers directly with questions and instructions, by-passing vice-presidents, senior managers and network managers. He apparently thought little of contacting CBC journalists and querying them on their coverage. He talked about the "arm's length relationship" between the Tory federal government and the CBC as being scrupulously adhered to, but seemed to be quite comfortable with the fact that CBC journalists and programmers were not at arm's length from him.

Veilleux made much use of the terms "trust" and "loyalty" and yet, as one west coast television producer pointed out, when the budget crunch came there was no communication from Head Office, no consultation, no "big picture" explained. "The ground was simply pulled out from under us. You can't build trust and loyalty when you treat people like that." Thirty-year veteran CBC manager Andrew Simon was marched out of the corporation and his job as head of Radio-Canada International when he simply confirmed to Ottawa media, when asked, that the overseas service was probably on a list of budget cuts being considered prior to December 5, 1990, a matter Veilleux did not want discussed publicly. Because of the secrecy surrounding the cuts it was reasonable to assume everything and anything was on such a list. But Simon was perceived to have gone public on the matter. Bloodied by personal confrontations with Veilleux after December 1990, some regional managers referred to his style as "fear-and-favour"—if you supported him, you'd be favoured; if you didn't, you would simply live in fear of losing your job.

He had been called "a faceless bureaucrat," a "mandarin" and a "tough negotiator." He had called himself a "hardened realist with a mild sense of optimism" and "the guy with the sharp pencil." The 1990 budget cut decision he orchestrated was termed "callous" and "criminal." There was a severe kind of school-master tone that surrounded his explanations of decision-making. A number of times, he had referred to the budget cut decision as a "success" or "strong and painful medicine." One of Veilleux's favourite quotations was about doing "constructive damage to the status quo." He was publicly berated after the cuts for displaying a "deputy minister mentality" and being insensitive to the needs of national public broadcasting. Yet, strangely enough, it was only his stubborn fight against a number of his own management advisers that preserved the tattered remnants of the regions—the now shallow and spindly roots of what is left of Canadian public, as opposed to network, television.

The scalding personal attack he received after the 1990 budget decision evidently turned a relatively optimistic Gérard Veilleux into a different kind of manager. He was pilloried in public. He lashed out publicly and angrily at his critics. By January 1993 he had the look, and talked like, a man who would just as soon be rid of the job. He had almost resigned, more than once. He had been on edge ever since December 5, 1990, suspicious of many, trusting few. The events of that date tore the final bit of heart out of the CBC. After he fended off the heat of criticism, Veilleux—hounded publicly, wounded professionally, appearing resentful down to his bones—then proceeded to restructure its soul—unfortunately, in a personal environment of mistrust, disappointment and suspicion.

Gérard Veilleux was born May 8, 1942 in East Broughton, Quebec, grew up in Asbestos, the youngest of five children. His father died when he was less than five years old. Times were tough for the family, but he went off on a scholarship to Laval University where he received his commerce degree in 1963, and then, in 1968, a master's degree in public administration from Carleton University. His work experience is an impressive read, step by promotional step, through the hallways of government power and prestige: the Manitoba Department of Finance, the federal Department of Finance, director general of Federal-Provincial Relations in Quebec's Intergovernmental Affairs department, a series of stints in the Treasury Board secretariat, Finance and Health and Welfare. He was seconded to the Privy Council in 1980 to work on constitutional reform, made secretary to the Cabinet for Federal-Provincial Relations in 1982, and in 1986, was appointed secretary of the Treasury Board—the man who oversaw government expenditures.

As Robert Fulford wrote after his appointment to the CBC, Veilleux was "all but universally admired by connoisseurs of the mandarinate. Like them, unfortunately, he knows nothing of broadcasting." It is a business, as NBC vice chairman David Adams explained in Ken Auletta's *Three Blind Mice: How the TV Networks Lost Their Way*, in which to survive "requires the reactions and sensitivities that grow from long experience in the field, and an outsider can be effective only after a period of high-level apprenticeship learning the nuances of a very singular business."

Veilleux inherited a six-decade mess. His CBC was a corporation hobbled by more than a decade of political siege, poor planning and hesitant direction—the end-product of years of refusing to face up to the corporation's creeping economic and organizational realities. The bureaucracy was big and fat and sloppy, with an arrogance and management immaturity born of decades of in-breeding. They had been living so long in the protective and predictable cocoon of civil service unreality—moving up, promotion by promotion, from the studio and the production office to the heights of Bronson Avenue and Bay Street—that they never expected a time might arise when they would be called upon to make bold decisions and manage with at least one eye on the horizon of a changing future. In fact, it was a management team that most often waited around to be told how and when to manage.

The corporation's funding was being choked off by the Tories. They were hot after the CBC to be 'accountable' in its journalism. Canadians were growing frighteningly indifferent to both its political and fiscal plight, not to mention its English television program offerings. His early reluctance aside, Veilleux began work at the CBC with some optimism. The lure was too seductive. He began to catch, as most people inevitably do, its elan, its self-perceived sense of greater purpose than just making programs for listeners and viewers. And before he barely had time to get to know and understand the corporation, he was led to a situation that called for its gutting.

Shortly after assuming command, Veilleux quickly toured the regions of the CBC, warming to the creative atmosphere, meeting staff and managers, effusively pumping the flesh, his right hand quick to the stretch, and a big smile breaking across his face. He called the staff "dedicated," "sensitive" and "creative." He was truly enjoying this. He even slapped "CBC" logo stickers on all his luggage, the sign to the more jaded CBCers that the new guy had fallen in love—and wanted the world to know who she was.

"The sad truth is that the CBC *is undergoing a profound transformation, but in an unsatisfactory, unsystematic and ad hoc manner, and directed by those who have magnificently proved how little they deserve our confidence."*
—Gerald Caplan, *The Canadian Forum*, April 1993

When Gérard Veilleux walked into his sixth floor Bronson Avenue office, among the briefing documents awaiting him were a number prepared by the CBC's finance department. Some of the numbers they displayed were innocently revealing: sixty-eight percent of the CBC's money went out in salaries and more money was being spent on clerks' salaries ($135 million) or managers ($143 million) than on artists', musicians', and journalists' combined ($122 million). More significantly, however, the data also tracked the impact Tory budget cuts had had on the CBC to date, and what future cuts and the cost of inflation would do to the operating side of the ledger.

This financial overview told Veilleux that up until his arrival, CBC budgets had already absorbed more than a half-billion dollars ($540 million) in accumulated Tory government cuts applied since 1985/86, plus an estimated $163 million in inflation for the same period. The CBC faced an additional $179 million in cuts over the next four years, not including inflation. And just as significant, without continued real growth in commercial revenues, the CBC would have "an almost impossible task" in meeting the fiscal challenges of the future. He was looking at neat, coloured bar-graphs that told him he was inheriting a severely crippled public corporation. But his reaction over the next eight or nine months, strangely enough, did not reflect the concern those numbers might have normally generated. He evidently felt he, alone, had aces up his sleeve. Although neither Veilleux nor Watson had been given absolute assurances from the Tories that the CBC would be protected from further budget cuts, both felt their conversations with the Prime Minister and the communications minister at the time, Marcel Masse, were "very positive" about protection the CBC might receive from any further slashes in the Parliamentary appropriation. "Masse was saying, 'I will do my best'," Watson recalled.

If Veilleux sensed a problem, it was not necessarily with his Tory bosses. It might have been the loose way things were managed within the CBC. Having now to work weekends seemed to be a bit of a shock to some Head Office managers. He received no advance briefing from Head Office officials before his first swing through the regions. His rather lax introduction to the CBC, especially with all the major issues outstanding, and the fiscal flailing the corporation had been going through, bothered him. It was one of a number of bad signs. The extent of the hostility that existed between the Board and senior management did not say a lot for the "CBC team." The least little mention of the controversial Toronto Broadcast Centre within ear-shot of the nervous Board "blew the whole place apart." The risky habit of allocating expenditures before knowing where revenues were coming from upset him and sent a shiver up his bureaucratic backside. The size of the annual gamble the ETV network, alone, had been used to taking through the late 1980s could run from $16 to $27 million a year.

He also resented the way the networks tried, early on, to manipulate him, pressing him to justify his decisions and trying to dominate his life. People were "playing games." He was concerned about the lack of cooperation between many departments, especially the confrontations between the Head Office planning department and the ETV network: "We were negotiating with ourselves. The English television team on one side and Head Office on the other side. It was like the goddamn Viet Nam War. I said, 'What the hell is all this about? This is one business. [Head Office] isn't out to screw you." The suspicion, rivalry and out-right arguments, particularly over revenue numbers, displayed "a lack of corporate will." Finally, this public servant of almost three decades was taken aback at the cavalier way CBCers had gone about conducting themselves as servants of the public. He saw among many managers an annoying tendency to think that public broadcasting "belonged to them" rather than the citizen who paid the bills and owned the airwaves. Veilleux was not impressed at the way business was being done.

In January 1990, Veilleux imposed a $35 million budget cut, taking $20 million out of the administration side of CBC, cutting twenty percent out of Head Office operations and reducing the overall establishment by as many as 500 positions. "We're looking to cut $8-10 million [in 1991/92]. I think we'll manage, but it's going to be tough," he told the *Toronto Star*. If the government did not come up with money for inflation the cut would jump by another $15-20 million. In a June memo to staff, he implied that the worst part of the budget cutting was over and that the future was now secure: "A year ago we had been questioning our very existence. Now we need no longer do that. The CBC is here to stay."

According to Watson, Veilleux had been "prowling the corridors of power," letting his old colleagues know the positive things that had been going on inside the CBC—improved efficiency, a more business-like management of public funds, restructuring—and within a short time "was beginning to get pretty good feedback from the deputy minister group" that if the CBC hit a major fiscal problem it could be "protected." In Veilleux's mind—given the numbers and issues he had been presented with—he could make the money problem a wash. Even when in the late spring of 1990 Head Office management began letting him know there might be slightly larger financial problems ahead than anticipated, Veilleux, so he claimed, was not particulary concerned. He felt he knew where he could find the pockets of necessary cash. During the summer, the staff were sent away to come up with options on how they felt the corporation could meet the budget shortfall, now estimated as high as $50 million.

A year after taking over, Veilleux circulated a personal document entitled "Mission, Values, Goals and Objectives." It was Veilleux's vision for the CBC and he thought it would be "useful to share" with the staff. His vision was centred on three main themes: the primacy of programming, the need for sound management and the creation of "a unified CBC team." People were "our most valuable resource. We intend to enhance the sense of unity, pride and mutual trust shared by everyone working for and with the Corporation, and to create an environment in which all our employees can make the maximum contribution to our common goals and objectives." With that lofty reassurance, he went on, almost in the next breath, to tell staff that there would be "No more 'splendid isolation,' no more 'whining and complaining,' no more 'surprises'."

In the nervous environment of annual budget cutting, the statement that people were the CBC's "most valuable resource" and that there was now a corporate commitment to "maintain, and if possible increase, the overall level of regional activity in CBC program services" helped calm the fears of some regional broadcasters. Managers and staff had been juggling almost daily rumours since before Veilleux's arrival about the death of regional supper hour news shows, the end to regional current affairs programming and the closing of certain stations, in television and radio. During the summer of 1990, rumours began to spread about a Head Office document called 'The Blue Book' and its perceived curse upon regional operations—that, in effect, the future CBC would be much better off well rid of these distant, trashy outposts of the Ottawa, Montreal and Toronto empires. Veilleux's words were reassuring: "It is vital that the CBC embody, to the best of its ability, the regional dimension of Canada," Veilleux wrote in "Mission." "We are a national service rooted in the regions. We must serve each region as well as possible, by reflecting it to itself and to the rest of the country in both official languages."

But by late summer, the Board began to get even more nervous. It now appeared it might have a major financial problem on its hands. No one was talking any longer about a $20-30 million problem. By October 16, the Ottawa Citizen reported that Veilleux, like his predecessor, Pierre Juneau, had approached his former colleagues at Treasury Board and tried to get the CBC's budget increased in return for a "revitalized" CBC. They reportedly stonewalled him. By the end of October, staff were talking about a shortfall of $80-105 million, and counting. A call went out from many managers and staff for a loud public outcry, a backlash against the Tories. What many would perceive as a major public policy issue—a malevolent Tory government helping to put the screws to Canadian public broadcasting—which should, for the sake of the institution's existence, be fought loudly in the streets of principle, Veilleux seemed to see as simply a management problem; a particularly ugly one, but a management problem, nevertheless. You were given an order, a job one was given to do, and you got on with it. The lid would be held down.

At almost the same moment the "Missions" document was circulated to over 11,000 staff in October, Veilleux suddenly told the Ottawa Citizen that we were certainly now talking about the end of the CBC "as we know it" if the federal relief wagons did not show. In late November, Veilleux warned the Standing Committee on Privileges and Elections that the CBC was now facing a resource allocation of the "most onerous nature" and may have to cancel its live coverage of Parliament. Rebel Tory MP Chuck Cook admonished the former Treasury Board bureaucrat for his past involvement in CBC's problem: "Having shot your parents, you're now pleading for mercy as an orphan. . . ."

Veilleux maintained the $108 million shortfall issue—as opposed to $50 million—was a complete surprise. "I have to tell you, people say 'You must have known?' I didn't know. Nobody knew the dimension of the problem." But the problem was not a shortage of money. That was the symptom. The problem was the Ottawa-Toronto-Montreal management system. It was dysfunctional.

Senior management had spent most of the summer trying to come up with alternative plans on how to meet the cuts, then suspected to be in the $40-50 million range. The hoary spectre of an additional $50 million shortfall was hiding, like a troll under the bridge to 1991/92, waiting to pounce. During this time, Veilleux had already noted things he could do to meet the $40-50 million target, including axing CBC Enterprises—a division which lost $20 million between 1986 and 1990—putting Radio-Canada International on a cost recovery basis, maybe skimming a two percent cut here or there. According to Veilleux, he left on an international business trip to Cyprus and the Middle East in late September. "I left . . . knowing we had to find $50 million," Veilleux recalled. He was not "unduly worried." Before leaving, he gave instructions to senior Head Office financial people where they might look to meet the shortfall. "The first day I set foot in the office after the Cyprus trip—the first hour in the morning—[senior vice-president] Tony Manera came in and said, 'Look, we have a serious problem' and he says, 'It's not $50 million. It's $100 million.' And I just about died!"

According to Veilleux, those risky advertising revenue projections had taken a nose dive, were down massively. "So we had to find another $40-50 million." Projected French network television revenues had collapsed by $20 million. It was now anticipated that for 1991/92, the ETV network revenue would be less than originally expected. And there were a couple of other non-commercial, multi-million-dollar surprises shoved onto Veilleux's plate. "Whoops," said one senior executive in 1993, to explain the Head Office reaction. Suddenly, they had over a $100 million problem on their hands with barely two months to do anything about it.

The first nut would turn out to be $108 million. The cost of letting an estimated 1,100 people go could reach $75 or $100 million, for a possible total dollar shortage of more than $200 million. The one non-surprise was how quickly the network sharks were able to turn on the regions as the solution. Armed with the planning department's recommendations, some pointing indelicately at the empire's last regional outposts for extinction, the Board convened at

Montebello, Quebec in mid-October to search for a solution to this massive problem. The tone of the recommendations said, in effect, the regions were less worthy than the networks in the current scheme of things. It was, as another vice-president put it, "basically unfair." Some of the data used "was a lie." But the idea of scooping $80 million in one reach, and wiping out the regions, was instantly attractive to many senior managers in the corporation's Golden Triangle—Ottawa, Toronto, Montreal.

According to Watson, the debt-clock was ticking at $2 million-plus a day. A final decision had to be made in six weeks. The solution was typically Canadian—a compromise. Take a bit ($46 million) but not all out of the regions. "I think to have cut $50 million out of the network at that point in time would probably have killed the CBC as well," said Veilleux. "There was a very delicate balancing thing that I had in mind." Almost everyone involved, except maybe the odd network and Head Office potentate, knew it was a deal made in hell. It reflected the overwhelming and embarrassing reality that this was a corporation that now—at this critical juncture in its history—did not have time to find out what to do and do it properly.

> *"Looking back on the way ABC bungled the compensation issue and other mistakes made at the three networks, ABC executive Mark Mandala astutely remarked, 'The longer I've been in this business the more I believe less in the cunning of Machiavelli than the bumbling of Sancho Panza.'"*
> —Ken Auletta, *Three Blind Mice*

Part of the problem that hit Veilleux and his Board stemmed from Parliament's single-year funding millstone. Part of it was attributed by him to the factional in-fighting between the networks and Head Office. Part of it was the corporation's dysfunctional history, a product of nineteenth-century CBC management thinking and processes. Annual expenditures were set in stone before revenues were assured. Even though the whole corporation lived on the razor's edge of one-year funding, Head Office—and therefore, the Board—did not have instant access to the status of those hundreds of millions of dollars in anticipated advertising revenue. The numbers most often rolled in rather casually a month at a time, sometimes, according to Head Office executives, only every three months.

"We would ask for the revenue numbers all the time," said Tony

Manera, "and they would come. Sometimes more frequently, sometimes less frequently [than once a month]. If there was a real problem it would be flagged, but if things were running smoothly then there wasn't too much worry about whether we got them monthly or quarterly. We were certainly getting revenue information but it wasn't always on a particular date. It varied."

That may have been an acceptable way to manage the financial affairs if the year-to-year history of the organization had been uneventful and revenue always arrived predictably and regularly from reliable sources. But Parliamentary appropriation had been going down since 1985/86. Each year new unanticipated costs were added to the struggling corporation's fiscal load. And it had already been exhibited that there was enough competing tension between the Head Office planning department and the networks to conclude that advertising revenue projections were probably shakier than a cease fire between Bosnian Serbs and Muslims. According to Veilleux, the planning department and the networks would "fight like hell" between themselves over what were the correct advertising revenue numbers when they met in planning and allocation sessions.

To boggle the mind further, Head Office management had spent the entire summer of 1990 working numbers for the Board and coming up with plans for the eventuality of a major budget shortfall. The possibility that advertising revenues would continue to soften through 1990 and into 1991 had always been a serious consideration. Surprise should not have been a factor. The fact that the Quebec TV advertising market was falling apart could have been gleaned from reading *Report on Business*. But added to this tranquillized unreality was the revenue experience CBC went through in the previous fiscal year. The advertising revenue target of the ETV network had to be adjusted downward significantly, after budgets had been allocated, because of the network's inability to bring in the revenue it had originally expected. If these events did not add up high enough to eliminate any surprise, it probably could be assumed that they should have at least made some people nervous enough to begin tracking a revenue picture as shaky as that on a daily basis, never mind monthly or quarterly.

"We didn't know how to ask the right questions [of the networks]," said one executive in mammoth understatement. "We had to go through that terrible crucible [of the budget cuts] to know how to discover how to ask the right questions [about the state of network advertising revenues]. This corporation has never acted very corporately," he added somewhat apologetically.

Less than two months after the circulation of assurances about the importance to the corporation of people and the regions, the Board of Directors chopped $46 million out of regional operations. No major network sports programs were cancelled. No large properties were put up for sale. No major cuts were made in the engineering infrastructure. No major capital projects were set aside and, evidently, no work orders for painting toilets or raking leaves were cancelled as a direct result of the decision.

In his official budget cut memo to staff, Veilleux sat the baby-of-blame on the doorstep of "outside circumstances: market conditions, the state of the economy, and government austerity measures." He went on: "The CBC has no choice but to adapt to these circumstances and live within its means." Veilleux still maintained that in spite of the sweeping structural changes and loss of programs the budget cuts delivered, the CBC "will remain a balanced, national public broadcasting service, offering distinctive, high-quality, predominantly Canadian programs that appeal to the full range of tastes and interests."

But even then, the numbers did not add up. Looking back across the graveyard of Canadian public broadcasting from 1993, it would appear that someone might have miscalculated—about the extent of the 'surprise,' about how solid the advertising revenue numbers might be, and about how the Board's 1990 lay-off decisions would begin to stir a massive fiscal vortex that would draw into it most of the correct numbers, intentions and evidence. The sharp pencil may have turned out to be a bludgeon.

The more the corporation stomped money into that awful and indeterminate auger that was the cost of downsizing—the tens of millions the CBC had to pay after December 1990 to reduce its staff complement—the less certain anyone could be about whether the CBC was actually facing an extra $30-50 million 'shortfall' or not. The depth set for the auger would be $108 million. If any of the numbers making up $108 million were soft or speculative and might change—like an educated guess that advertising revenues eighteen months down the road at the end of 1992 might be short $30 million—the auger would not stop or care. It would always churn as if that $30 million 'loss' would eventually materialize, even if it did not. In the end, the machine would grind and chew and spit out people and station bits and pieces of numbers that made it look embarrassingly as if there hardly had been a problem at all. "In the CBC it is probably easier to hide a $10 million mistake than it is to hide $1,000," Bill Jones, a much respected regional finance manager once told me.

Veilleux announced on December 5, 1990 that the cause of the 1991/92 shortfall was government restraint ($32 million in cuts and $18 in non-funded inflation costs), "unavoidable" new costs in taxes and statutory expenditures ($16 million), a return of $12 million the CBC had effectively borrowed from its share of contributions going toward the CBC pension fund and $30 million caused by "declining television advertising revenues due to poor market conditions." Despite talk of surprises, the $32 million Tory cut had been known for over a year-and-a-half. The $18 million for inflation was no Jack-in-the-Box. Neither the Liberals nor the Conservatives had been forking over off-setting funds to fight inflation, except for salary increases. The 1991/92 fiscal year would be no exception. Some of the $16 million in statutory extras had been circling CBC Head Office for the previous year or so—pipers waiting to be paid. And the $12 million dip into the pension fund (something the corporation would ironically do again two years later to the tune of $96 million over two years or more) was a well-known fact of fiscal reality for at least two years, although Veilleux claimed it was a bit of a surprise to him. The CBC was due to pay it eventually. Where was the surprise?

National media attention focused on the "sharp drop in advertising revenue" as the outstanding cause for the $108 million budget cut. "There was never a [advertising revenue] shortfall of the magnitude of $30 to $50 million," claimed former English television vice-president Denis Harvey. "The biggest surprise was French television at about $10 million [in 1990/91]." Indeed, the tracks show that the CBC ended fiscal year 1990/91 with $297 million in net advertising income from its English and French networks. In the next year, 1991/92, the fiscal year in question when base revenue projections would be "down by $30 million," CBC net advertising income on the two networks was $312.5 million, or $15.5 million *more* than the previous year. Where was the revenue shortfall?

If the answer to the shortfall was supposed to be in losses that developed because the two networks could not meet their increased revenue targets for fiscal year 1991/92, the two networks, together, actually over-achieved their revenue budget projections according to CBC records—coming in at 101.2 percent of the targets set for them. "The $30 million was a target," said senior vice-president Tony Manera. "It wasn't a loss. It was a revised target. We revised our target [for 1991/92] down by $30 million." In 1990/91 the French network advertising revenue target had been revised downward twice, resulting in a projected shortfall in that fiscal year of roughly $20 million. But the next year, the year of the $108 million budget cut, French television made $10 million more than it had the previous year and English television exceeded its target by $2.5 million.

Taking the simple number analysis from CBC's own statistics—the anticipation it would be short at least $30 million in advertising revenue in 1991/92 and the fact they actually increased net advertising revenue by $15 million—and the total swing between estimate and reality comes eerily close to the amount of money ($46 million) cut from regional broadcasting budgets. If, as some say, the corporation was looking at going into fiscal year 1991/92 with a net advertising revenue target as high as $330-340 million, someone was either not paying close attention to the state of the Canadian economy or had forgotten how unsuccessful the last few revenue prognostications had been. The best year to date had been 1988/89, when the ETV network turned on the sales burners to cover the $20-million extra cost of Canadianization. Corporate net advertising income that year went up $30 million. But revenue growth fell the next year (1989/90) by fifty-seven percent to $19 million—the year the ETV network fell $16 million short of its revenue target. It should have been the first clear sign that the salad days of constant advertising income growth were over. The second clear sign came early in the next year when French television revenue projections started going into the tank. To forecast one of the largest revenue jumps in history in this shaky economic environment said you were probably one of the most courageous public corporations on record or were not tracking reality.

It might be difficult to follow, but it is not too difficult to speculate that by starting up that giant meat and aspiration grinder called the "downsizing exercise" based on, perhaps, a mistaken need to find millions more than was necessary, the CBC ended up cutting substantially more out of its body than was required. And like the spooky, never-ending downward spiral Veilleux talked about, the CBC cut more than it needed, then cut more to cover the new costs of cutting and laying off, then cutting more than it needed . . . and then . . . Like my dear friend in finance once said about $10 million inside the CBC, the margin of error got so big and everyone got so used to it, no one could see it.

While the auger was chewing it all up, few people noticed that, far from starving the CBC, the Tories were actually keeping it alive on life support. Certainly, they were responsible for their $32 million cut plus inflation shortages in 1991/92. But when Tory largesse is added up since 1991/92, CBC management has little to complain about. In fact, one could speculate that by the time the panic had subsided the CBC had more money than it had anticipated. It certainly had enough to give Windsor back its local news.

Although the $108 million downsizing exercise ended up at $170 million in 1990/91—$108 in cuts plus $62 in downsizing costs—a large part of that total was offset with Tory deferrals. The CBC received $50 million out of the government's Toronto Opera House pot. It was allowed to convert $25 million in capital funds to help out. The Tories included a $10 million loan, to be repaid with any money made from the sell-off of equipment or properties for a benevolent total of $85 million. Add this to Beatty's $46 million gift from the consolidated revenue fund in 1992/93—effectively negating that year's portion of the Conservatives cuts to the CBC—and it comes to $131 million worth of aid and assistance over two years. It would seem the Tories were paying for the damage they wrought.

To paraphrase Charles Dickens, the CBC would have enough money, and it would not have enough money. Even if the numbers did compute accurately, the simple margin of error on $1.3 billion should have been sufficient to offset certain embarrassing decisions. To stand on absolute dollar numbers to match absolute principle, such as the need to close Windsor, in a corporation with a budget of more than a billion dollars, was a sucker's game.

An old corporate adage says the CBC can always find a few million here, a few million there. It depends on how badly you want the money spent on what. Five million dollars—or the $2 million Veilleux suddenly and gratuitously erased from the targeted budget cut to regional supper hour operations in early 1991—is chicken feed to the CBC.

The tiny net amount gained by closing Windsor's regional production operations ($3 million a year by 1992) would have more than been covered by the amount the corporation saved when inflation began dipping in 1991. A more accurate prediction about the cost of inflation by Head Office planners could have saved the citizens of Windsor their loss and their grief. Inflation would track down monthly from January 1991 until it hit thirty-year lows in 1992. The $18 million 'loss' due to inflation did not stand up.

The amount the CBC would lose in advertising income in Windsor and Calgary after December 1990, as much due to the commerical backlash as the state of the local economies, could have kept the Saskatoon television station open. The net amount the corporation increased its publicity expenditures in 1992 ($5 million) would have, on an annual basis, covered Calgary's costs of station operation. Instead of spending an extra $2.5 million on new computer equipment, CBC could have kept the Matane station up and running.

Maybe the problem was in trying too hard to do the right thing—balance the books and clean off CBC's messy fiscal desk. However, the net result was to irreparably crack the foundation of Canadian public broadcasting while at the same time, strangely enough, maybe even prop up spending tombstones like the Toronto Broadcast Centre, among other things. Given the extra spending breathing space, the CBC was able to put $16 million aside for "productivity and efficiency measures"—money used partly for assisting staff to voluntarily leave the corporation. More significantly, the money is also being used, in a public broadcasting corporation where people, creativity and programs should be the top priority, to invest in new equipment and computer hardware for better 'productivity' and efficiency. And, of course, there is money for renovating cafeterias and washrooms. By the end of the 1991/92 fiscal year, the downsizing costs ("expense reduction and restructuring activities") totalled $93.4 million—largely to be able to achieve a cut of $108 million. And with little flourish, the CBC also predicted it would now, in this fiscal year, advance $58,108,000 towards the cost of Toronto Broadcast Centre, "in order to minimize the future interest costs associated with the lease." The money apparently would come out of "land revenues" gained from the Front Street site.

"Still another factor was how human 'logic'—ego, vanity, anger, pride, even panic—sometimes triumphed over business logic."
—Ken Auletta, *Three Blind Mice*

In what seemed like a moment, Veilleux went from being the public service's good soldier, relatively anonymous, working diligently in the dark caves of the federal bureaucracy, to standing all but alone in the glaring klieg lights of full national disapproval. The day after Black Wednesday, the *Ottawa Citizen*'s Tony Atherton wrote: "Gérard Veilleux failed to deal with the CBC's mounting problems. In the end, he had little choice but to slash his way out of financial catastrophe . . . the future sneaked up and knocked Veilleux head over heels this fall. Veilleux failed the nation's chief communications link by failing to communicate. He played things too close to the vest for too long. By not continuing with the public discussion of the CBC's problems, Veilleux had hoped to sway government opinion. Instead, he lulled his own troops into a false sense of security."

Only a handful of Head Office executive managers and vice-presidents and other managers knew in advance what to expect. No one talked to the people who ran the television stations, the directors of television. It was like trying to take Omaha Beach without talking to your colonels and captains and making them part of the plan—even though they would be the ones first out of the boats and on to the beaches. This small Head Office group, along with the Board, laid the public broadcasting map of Canada on the table, and left out huge chunks of the country and our aspirations. And then with all the holes and contradictions, they called their plan "symmetrical." The move was unceremonious, peremptory, gave no opportunity for CBCers to bid their audiences goodbye and, as Gerald Caplan wrote in the *Toronto Star*, provided "the private sector with some nice lessons in insensitive, merciless management techniques."

Calls went out for both Veilleux's and Watson's resignation. The NDP accused Veilleux of "buying the government line," of not fighting for the corporation, and were "furious" that Veilleux had briefed the Tories before other MPs. Sitting before the House of Commons Communications and Culture Committee on December 11, Veilleux was verbally roasted by Liberal MP John Harvard, a former CBC broadcaster: "The CBC is the symbol of Canada. It is the heart and soul . . . and damn it, Mr. Veilleux, we can't have someone with a deputy minister's mentality running the corporation." The attacks in committee became so nasty that a "harried and often emotional" Veilleux lost his composure and swore, suggesting that the blame should be directed "to the people who keep criticizing the goddamned CBC." He blamed ministers and politicians for abandoning their responsibilities for survival of the CBC: "Somebody else has decisions to make," he challenged the MPs. "and they should bloody well make them."

Veilleux had been stonewalled when he asked for government assistance to offset the financial pressure. He told the committee he spoke with Treasury Board president Gilles Loiselle and deputy communications minister Alain Gourd, "but did not press the issue with any politicians." However, he was "sure" the message got to "all levels." To his critics it was like Charlie Brown explaining why he had lined up again to kick the football. He always trusted Lucy to hold it, even though she would always pull it away just as Charlie ran up to kick it. Charlie seemed to be saying that it was okay. He did not resent Lucy. This was just how the game was played. On the same day he was being publicly humiliated by Liberals and the NDP (he was also attacked by PC Geoff Scott, who called the closing of the Windsor television station "insensitive and insane") and being vilified in the press across the country, Veilleux received Canada's highest civil-servant commendation—the Outstanding Achievement Award.

Writing a year-and-a-half later, the *Globe and Mail's* Hugh Winsor thought he could put his finger gently on the dichotomy. Veilleux had committed a lot of blood, sweat and tears to the organization, Winsor wrote. He had done the job during one of the most difficult periods in CBC's history. No one could question his commitment. "But throughout all of this, Veilleux has not been able to change his spots and make the conversion from civil servant to public broadcaster. He is still the model deputy minister working the way deputy ministers work to serve ministers." He accepted the massive cuts and closings imposed on the CBC "as an expression of the will of ministers and implemented them with bureaucratic symmetry that looked good on paper but made no sense with regard to CBC audiences."

Christmas of 1990, and the months that followed, were a bit of hell for Gérard Veilleux. He was trashed in papers across the country and on radio phone-in shows. Many Canadians cried for his removal. He was listed on a 'Wanted' poster in St. John's. He considered quitting, a number of times. No one knew how hard it had been, he said many times, for both him and his family: "the pressure, the criticism, the abuse. . . ." Those who met him at social events in 1991 found him distant, nervous. His eyes would mist when he talked about the budget cuts. He used the term "betrayed" frequently. He drew tight his circle of confidantes, so tight that he could have held meetings in a medium-sized bathroom. He told one: "'I can trust you . . .' but then he never tells me anything." Outside consultants started roaming the halls of the CBC. Somewhere in the fog of personal bitterness he chose to cut rather than run. He would stay.

At that point, he certainly did not have the staff and management of the CBC on side. Morale after December 5 was probably worse than it had ever had been in the history of the corporation. Senior managers talked openly about "no strategy for the future." In fact, there seemed no longer to be a future. The January-March 1991 period was one of sheer confusion within the CBC: more fighting and bickering between the regions and Head Office; the regions and the networks, and the networks and Head Office; harsh words aimed by Veilleux at regional managers; confusion over what programs might exist and which ones would not. No one seemed to know where the CBC was going or what it would do along the way. The rules seemed to change daily. Head Office slapped an embargo on local managers speaking to media. Producers and regional managers used terms such as "callous," "secretive" and "Orwellian." A deep veneer of cynicism and fear spread across the CBC. No one seemed safe from retribution and dismissal. Everyone seemed now to be working in terror of Head Office. In an address to the Empire Club at about this time, Veilleux saw "the genesis of a new CBC" within this turmoil: "We have a clear and shared sense of where we are going, why we are going there and how we intend to get there."

In 1988 Veilleux co-authored a paper for Canadian Public Administration. It was titled, "Kafka's Castle: The Treasury Board of Canada revisited." Veilleux and co-author Donald J. Savoie took as their starting premise the theme of an article written in 1971 by former Treasury Board head, and later CBC president, A.W. Johnson, about Treasury Board being much like Kafka's Castle. The powerful government agency was, Johnson wrote, "the apparent, if unknown, source of authority which governs the village [the Public Service]." It was "remote, mysterious, all-powerful, beyond comprehension . . . above all beyond the reach, let alone the influence, of the ordinary mortals governed by it."

But Veilleux and Savoie pointed out that things had changed in the Castle; the move over the years had been in favour of decentralization of decision-making, putting authority and the responsibility to manage in the hands of today's public service managers. "Letting the manager manage" would be a hallmark call of Veilleux's style after he joined the CBC. However, rather than a corporation where managers were set free, robust and confident in their independence, the CBC was still the sort of place where Kafka's main character, Joseph K, might be most comfortable—the main street from the village always pointed in the direction of the castle, but never did it lead there, and strangely enough, never did it lead away from there; the castle was always unassailable. There was not one purpose to the organization. There were many. The goals were always distorted by politics (external and internal), the ebb and flow of funds and the debilitating effect dreams that crash against reality have on the human psyche. The CBC was a better example of the 'before' in Kafka's Castle than the 'after.'

Al Johnson worked the drawbridge at both of Kafka's Castles, as secretary of the Treasury Board and president of the CBC: "It was not at all difficult for me to understand that you had to manage the CBC a little bit like a benign anarchy. If you know anything at all about management in the broader sense, you know you have to have independence within the cells of the CBC. Because it is the creativity of this production here, that unit there, that has got to be preserved. And that means you are going to make some mistakes on air, and you are going to get into trouble. But you must not become a manager in the conventional sense. You must allow that freedom, because freedom and creativity go hand-in-hand. And good organization and creativity don't necessarily go hand-in-hand." But Al Johnson's CBC did not exist any more. The Castle was back in charge.

"The only way to achieve a successful transition from the old culture to the new is to change the style and amount of communication from one that treats the employee as a child to one that treats the employee as adult."
—Katherine Gay, *The Financial Post*, November 7, 1992

When the March 1991 CRTC hearings were over, it looked as if the worst was over. Veilleux would tough it out. He survived the December 5 aftermath, the 'Wanted' posters and the berating at the CRTC hearings. As his managers stumbled through the last few weeks of settling who got gaffed and for how much, Veilleux fixed his vision to the one polestar still in his heaven—the absolute need for long-term, stable funding for the CBC. It would turn out to be a good move and a bad move: good in the sense that he would be addressing the issue that was the corporation's principal structural weakness; bad in the sense that he would have to play football with Lucy again.

By May, the time looked ripe to go for the gusto—long term, stable funding for the CBC. The Holy Grail. The one legacy that Veilleux would be satisfied to leave behind. He felt he had two challenges to overcome if the CBC was to survive. He had to start making CBC television, especially on the English side, look distinctive, offer a service Canadians would perceive to be different, not virtually the same as private broadcast offerings. If the CBC was not perceived to be different, and valuable, he thought, it would not be worth funding, let alone existing.

Long term, stable funding had always been the CBC's *elixir vitae*—the thing that would solve all the corporation's problems. It had been promised by a number of governments. In good economic times, the thought of a yappy and intrusive CBC, poking critical sticks at the government of the day while hiding behind a guaranteed annual appropriation of funds, was just too unnerving. In bad economic times, the question became: how can you guarantee the CBC a billion dollars a year when the nation was running $30 billion-plus deficits?

No modern CBC president had ever gotten a federal government close to changing their minds. Some did not even bother to try. Perhaps with the exception of Al Johnson, no one else had known how to pull the complex levers of political power in the proper sequence. If Veilleux could do it—either through appropriation, a licence fee, or even simply allowing the CBC to borrow funds to smooth out the spending bumps over more than one year at a time—he would go from chump to champ in one swing. They would chisel his name in the shaky concrete that held up Bronson Avenue.

He began by corralling bureaucratic support for the idea. He got Finance on side; then Treasury Board; then Communications. Finally, the Privy Council Office—the most important and most powerful federal agency, coordinating the activities of cabinet and cabinet matters—agreed to support the measure. It was now a government issue—with the CBC assisting and guiding the deliberations down the reasonable avenues of political power.

Veilleux's reputation and contacts opened friendly doors for the CBC. The fact he had orchestrated the budget cuts without anti-government rancour won him points. The CBC had been a good soldier. It cut more deeply than any other department of the public service. The lack of whining and finger pointing helped win the backing of at least a dozen cabinet ministers.

A document outlining how long term funding would be implemented was prepared for cabinet approval in July. It was summertime, when adversarial attentiveness tends to wilt in the muggy heat of Ottawa. The plan was to go before Parliament with a direct license fee on cabled households to cover CBC's funding problem. The secrecy was holding. The issue was evolving into one of those moments when faith, patience and perseverance all line up like stellar bodies to help make something profound happen. The cabinet document was signed, sealed and ready for cabinet consideration. It was to be presented the week of July 28. On July 24, the *Financial Post* quoted Patrick Watson as saying the CBC was looking at direct license fees on television households to help the corporation lessen its reliance on advertising revenue, and solve the problem of declining annual appropriations from Parliament. Bang. Dead. The cat was out of the bag. Maybe forever.

Critics of the license fee crawled out of every conceivable corner. The Canadian Cable Television Association threatened an anti-licence fee advertising campaign, aimed right at communications minister Perrin Beatty. The CAB's Michael McCabe mumbled reactively about the move to license fees being reminiscent of the "radio police." The Consumer Association of Canada's Don Axford talked about the fee being just another tax. Even the Friends of Canadian Broadcasting thought the idea an unworkable notion. "I was on my way on my holidays," Veilleux recalled, slowly, in almost a whisper. "I was in my car, in the parking lot of the Ste. Foy Shopping Centre in Quebec City. The phone rang and someone read to me what was in the press. I turned to my wife and I felt like crying. I said, 'This is not possible'. It was totally, totally, totally unexpected. I just thought I'd die. I knew at that very moment it was done—gone. I know how [Ottawa] works. It had just [fired] the starting gun for all the opposition." Lucy had done it again.

The Tories got instant cold feet and backed off the idea. Although the Veilleux plan would still have had to overcome a large hurdle in the Tory cabinet, he had clearly not been discouraged in his efforts to lasso long term, stable funding by even powerful Tory ministers. He would have bet money on the fact the CBC would have gotten some form of stable funding agreement—if not for Watson's ill-timed public utterance. Veilleux was reportedly "infuriated" with Watson's *faux pas*. Their relationship went into deep chill. The days of 1989, the merry camaraderie between the two, the days of back-slapping and togetherness were over.

"So, that's really when the notion of Repositioning came to mind," an increasingly resilient Veilleux recalled of his battered efforts to get the corporation out of its continuing fiscal mess. "We won't be able to try this one again. So we'd better try something else." This time he would try to remake public television into something Canadians would recognize as distinctive and respect enough to support reconsideration of a solution to the CBC's cash shortage problems. In August 1991, Veilleux "streamlined" the ETV network's senior management structure (the term sat well in Tory bellies grumbling about "top-heavy" CBC), filling the gap he made by forcing ETV network vice-president Denis Harvey out of the CBC, splitting authority for running the CBC's No. 1 operation between Trina McQueen and Ivan Fecan. "This restructuring is an important element of CBC's commitment to a more dynamic and streamlined administration . . ." Veilleux announced. McQueen would run ETV news and current affairs and Fecan would look after arts and entertainment and both would report directly to Ottawa, in effect, draw their deepest creative cues from Veilleux's office, and be forced to listen just as attentively to complaints coming the other way. Harvey had been a buffer between his managers and the politics of Head Office, often frustrating Veilleux with his protection of the network, its management, its programs, its advertising revenue information and its journalists. Less than a year later, in *L'Actualité* magazine, Veilleux would admit he had no problem in telling a CBC journalist how to do his job. The "streamlining" would also give him the reach he would need to smooth out the issue of "accountability."

Veilleux was still facing an estimated $50 million problem for fiscal year 1992/93. Another major round of cuts was predicted if the money did not materialize. Not relishing the idea of another public maelstrom, and possibly facing a federal election, Perrin Beatty coughed up $46 million, saving the CBC, for the moment, from a second round of budget cuts. But it was only for the one fiscal year. The longer term issues of where was the CBC going and what might it look like when it got there became a sort of *quid pro quo* between the Tories and Veilleux. Where are you going to position the CBC for the broadcast future? Where are you taking the organization? Are you properly 'accountable' in your journalism? Research shows that you are not valued by Canadians; what are you going to do about that? There were as many as eight principal questions that could be asked. With next year's financial problem out of the way for the moment, the way was clear for Veilleux to start reconfiguring the CBC so it was worth the public money spent on it. The right answers might lead to another run at long term, stable funding. Veilleux set up committees to discuss the questions and make recommendations. They would deliberate and return their findings back to him. He would then decide what pieces would eventually float out onto the Tory sea.

> *"CBC facing 'massive' changes"*
> *"Under a project called "Repositioning," CBC president Gérard Veilleux is planning sweeping changes in the corporation. . . . Generally speaking, Veilleux has expressed a desire to move toward more centralization, greater cooperation among services, fewer commercials, and greater use of such technological innovations as 'superstation' broadcasting . . ."*
> —H.J. Kirchoff, *Globe and Mail*, February 18, 1992

Veilleux's first answer came on February 13, 1992 with an all-staff memorandum called "Repositioning." It appeared to be a manifesto for the future. As a piece of written communication, authored by the nation's largest broadcast communications organization, the memo was all but incomprehensible. Managers called it "unreadable," "the biggest joke in town" and something that "scared the hell out of people." It was, said one senior manager, "one of the dumbest things I've ever seen Head Office do." It began by telling CBC staff that their organization was "embarking on a project that will ultimately define, for years to come, what we are and what we do, as Canada's national public broadcaster." From there, you would have to hire a clairvoyant to try to figure out where the CBC was going.

The document immediately drifted into a swamp of unspecific phrases: "It will equip us to face the future with a clarity of purpose. . . . The CBC faced cuts and now contemplates change imposed by the new shape of the broadcast landscape . . . a strategic initiative designed to enhance both the Corporation and the Corporation's programming." It was full of the latest corporate jargon: "Repositioning is leadership . . . a single image of shared purpose . . . a demonstration of corporate definition and values that will address the variables influencing revenue appropriations. . . . Repositioning is not a cost management exercise . . . is not a philosophical framework through which the Corporation will undertake another round of budget cuts . . . is not a move away from 'broadcasting'. . . ." It almost appeared to be a message meant to not say what was going on, while trying to look like it was saying something. Two days later, in a clearly written article by Peter Pearson in the Montreal *Gazette*, including comments from an interview with Veilleux, "Repositioning" was explained. Head Office suggested that communication departments across the country circulate copies of the Pearson article so staff might understand, one could only presume, what repositioning was all about.

It was Veilleux's formal plan for a renewed CBC, one that would be ready for tomorrow's 200-channel television universe. It called for a CBC television service with as many as ten channels, new strategic alliances with other broadcasters, greater cooperation between the French and English services, increased internal efficiency, a lessening of the dependence on commercial revenue, and the trotting out of the CBC's old one-trick pony, a "superstation" beaming CBC programs into the U.S. The article also said the move called for greater centralization of corporate money and resources in Toronto and decision-making in Ottawa—even though Veilleux had just spent the first two-and-half years of his mandate pledging the CBC to be "rooted in the regions." It allowed that this centralization of resources and program decision-making would take place even it meant closing more regional television stations. Radio was not to be played with, Veilleux was quoted as saying. This "piece of crystal, fragile and beautiful" had to be looked after, not changed radically or taken apart. But television was in for big change.

Many CBC employees saw repositioning as "a secretive and top-down process." Although the major questions posed about the corporation's future had been sifted through a committee process, little of the final stamping about where the CBC was going had been the subject of any detailed discussion with staff or managers. As far as many of them were concerned, the final decisions were made at The Castle. As former *fifth estate* executive producer Robin Taylor noted in SCAN magazine, repositioning was going to be imposed "by diktat." The producers were having a hard time trying to find out what repositioning was all about, what its real values and goals were. They knew that it was "partly political," something to convince policy makers that the CBC "is in motion," according to David Kaufman, writing in SCAN. They could also see a fundamental contradiction—no new programming ideas were being presented, "other than cooper-ation and co-production with the same private sector from whom we are striving to be distinct."

At the same time, the average Canadian's impression of CBC English television was becoming more and more poisoned with commercials and U.S.-look-alike programs that they honestly felt there was little distinctive about the system—and were leaving it in droves. Something had to be done to stem the life-flow. In June, Veilleux severely rattled the corporation by dumping a number of vice-presidents, among them, the much-respected Trina McQueen from the ETV's news and current affairs seat and replacing her with CTV's former news head, Tim Kotcheff. The move came with no advance notice, no broad consultation. Vice-presidents and directors were simply told to change chairs or titles. McQueen was summarily marched out of her news post—one she had been appointed to less than a year earlier in Veilleux's "streamlining"—into the corporate backwater, as vice-president of regional broadcasting.

Many CBC journalists saw the McQueen ouster as another tightening of the Tory screws. A number of the Tory-appointed Board members had been urging more "journalistic accountability" for years. In May 1991 it had come to light that the ETV network's Ottawa news bureau chief, Elly Alboim, had expressed scepticism about the PM's motives in pressing for the Meech Lake constitutional accord. The comments had been made years earlier to a small academic gathering at the University of Calgary. Copies of an article critical of Alboim's comments were circulated in Ottawa newsrooms and eventually brought to Veilleux's attention. He was angry that a lower-level civil servant had broken protocol and expressed an opinion. He wanted Alboim fired. McQueen and others defended him until the issue was settled with a letter of reprimand. As Hugh

Winsor wrote in the *Globe and Mail*: "Deputy Ministers are not used to being confronted by subordinates with such loyalty and cohesiveness. It's taken a while but Veilleux had dealt with his 'problem' in the classical bureaucratic way—an executive reorganization."

The acquisition of Kotcheff and assorted other new appointees from outside the CBC also made good on Veilleux's promise to bring new blood into the tired, old corporation. The move stunned the entire CBC. But as dramatic as it was, it did not fix any of CBC's problems—did not appreciably reduce the size of senior management, did not save slabs of money, did not make the organization any more efficient. It was, according to the *Globe*'s Hugh Winsor, Veilleux's move "to exert direct control over the most feisty and politically sensitive part of his empire—news and public affairs." He grabbed the news service by the throat and shook it. It might not have been the way of the professional public broadcaster, as Winsor pointed out, but it was the way of "the model deputy minister."

The fact that fewer and fewer Canadians could distinguish between CBC television and the competition annoyed Veilleux. Playing with the prime time schedule might, like smoke, make the CBC look different in the mirror. It also would attract the attention of the Tories, show them that the CBC was on the move, beginning to change for the future. He also envisioned a new, more cost-efficient news hour. One of the simmering internal irritants was the fact that *The National* and *The Journal* used separate crews and production staff to put together what Canadians saw simply as an hour's worth of news at 10 P.M. each weekday evening. Barely two weeks on the job, Kotcheff announced that the ten-year-old *Journal* was toast, and a whole new 9 P.M. news show (later titled *Prime Time News*) was now in the planning, including more efficient use of crews and production staff.

The schedule change was greeted with derision. As it would turn out, the new repositioned television schedule would not only not stem the alarming loss of audience. It would actually increase the flow, triggering a numbers haemorrhage the sight of which the English side of CBC television had never seen before. *Prime Time News* would settle in at a twelve percent share of the audience compared to *The Journal*'s fifteen percent share, and the bottom would fall out of audience numbers for most other prime time CBC programs. CTV, on the other hand, enjoyed an audience bonanza as viewers changed networks, with a two-point jump in its weekly share. CTV News would also enjoy a monstrous twenty-two percent leap over the previous year to 1.2 million viewers. The new repositioned schedule for CBC's ETV network was turning into an unmitigated ratings disaster. But it was enough for Perrin Beatty to say at the time how pleased he was with the new direction the CBC was taking.

The bleeding just got worse by January 1993. In Toronto, one of the regional supper hours that were not supposed to lose audience, according to the president, lost more than twenty-five percent of its audience from the previous year. In total, across the country, the supper hour shows were off more than forty percent from 1990, the year the Board announced the new regional news mandate—that leaky tarp of rationalization they had lain over the embarrassment of the cuts. CBC's "regionalized" news service drove Canadians away from the ETV network in hordes. As Edmonton executive producer Richard Bronstein said in the January 30 Globe and Mail: "The mandate we've been given is an impossible mandate. Actually, we're achieving the mandate. What's wrong with it is that the audience doesn't want it."

Repositioning continued ever onward. Other announcements included the news that the CBC was still wandering around trying to follow the needle on its compass in search of "Project Northstar," a decade-old idea that would see CBC television programming sold and delivered by satellite into the U.S. It had about as much chance of making money or breaking even as the Toronto Broadcasting Centre had. It also had absolutely nothing to do with CBC's mandate. Nothing in the Broadcasting Act urged the corporation to go looking for work outside the country. But it had sex appeal—it would make it look as if the CBC were a large player in the international television field and fit right in with the Tories drum-beat of "going global."

With start-up costs estimated to be more than $20 million, and many more years of corporate budget cuts to come, Northstar was an idea, again not unlike the TBC, whose timing was bad and whose possibilities were worse. In late May 1993 the CBC announced that the corporation and its Northstar business partner, Power Broadcasting Inc., had agreed to supply two channels of programming to, of all things, Los Angeles–based DirecTv—the "deathstar" satellite service set to launch its 150 channel invasion of Canada and the U.S.A. in 1994. The CBC–Power partnership signed a five-year deal to provide

DirecTv with a 24-hour news channel and a family oriented entertainment channel. A rattled Canadian cable industry spokesman termed the deal "signing on with the enemy." In laying down new broadcasting regulations in early June, the CRTC claimed jurisdiction over foreign satellite services and held out the threat that Canadian suppliers of programs to foreign satellite services such as DirecTv could be prosecuted for, if you will, trading with the enemy. Once again, the tired old Northstar seemed stalled, perhaps thankfully.

"He's trying to position the CBC as the central force in Canadian culture," claimed one senior Head Office manager, "as a global producer of programs." But this was a broadcaster making fewer of its own English television programs each year, filling the entertainment hollows in its network schedule with programs made mostly with other people's cash and ideas, a 'national public broadcaster' that could not apparently afford to produce a series about the information contained in *The Canadian Encyclopedia*, and one that could refuse to pay the repeat rights to hundreds of hours of *Beachcombers* programs— but it could afford to buy the repeat rights to *Taxi* and *WKRP*. And it was now going "global?" What did this have to do with public broadcasting?

Astoundingly, the push for CBC to "go global" was driven largely by the naive belief in Head Office that playing in The Big Leagues would bring in bundles of much needed revenue from the sale of CBC programs. But in 1992, the CBC made more money from renting out its equipment than it did from exporting its programs. "He's really caught up with the new technology," said another Ottawa manager. "He's got this little portable dish sitting on his windowsill, which ostensibly is going to pick-up 180 channels, so he's really thinking 'global,' which theoretically helps the revenue stream." So, the repositioning heralds began trumpeting even relatively insignificant announcements, perhaps in the hope the Tories were watching and listening.

"Repositioning," said one regional manager, "*is* the search for stable funding." But the gift of long-term stable funding could also be the bonding agent in the Tory concrete. As it set with each new initiative, the CBC started to look and act the way the Mulroney Conservatives wanted a public broadcaster to act. By mid-1992, a powerful member of the Mulroney cabinet mused over cocktails while on the west coast that Veilleux was on the right track—finally turning the obstinate CBC around.

"The Valour and the Horror and the shame"

"The CBC's journalistic reputation lies in pieces today, slit wide and deboned like a fresh-caught trout. It has been left in this condition not by the many criticisms, lately including those of the CBC's ombudsman, levelled at the controversial three-part documentary The Valour and the Horror, but by the craven efforts of the corporation's senior executives to appease the program's enemies in Parliament. This is the stuff of resignations . . ."

—*Globe and Mail,* November 12, 1992

By 1993 Gérard Veilleux was probably ready to find another place, other than the CBC, to serve the Canadian public. He looked tired, and as many senior managers pointed out, he was not particularly enjoying the job. It was doubtful the CBC logo stickers were still on his luggage. He could take the day-to-day crises that seemed to come with "the bloody job" but every now and then one of them cut right to his heart, saddened him greatly, and probably made him question his resolve. *The Valour and the Horror* controversy was just such a crisis. It would knock the wind out of him, as one senior manager said, "really hurt him."

"In the more than three years I've been here, that moment was the most difficult moment, the worst moment," Veilleux recalled in January 1993. He gave a huge sigh and stared out the window. The memory seemed to deflate him suddenly, his enthusiasm and energy seeping quickly away. "Why is that?" he responded. "Geez, it would take hours to explain—because of the games that were played, because of the misrepresentation, the lies, all sorts of things that I'm not very good at dealing with. It sort of depressed me to no end. And in that sense, I found it more difficult [than the 1990 budget decisions]."

The public debate over the CBC's broadcast of *The Valour and the Horror* in 1992 was an issue that went to the centre of Veilleux's rigid belief in the definition of public service. It became a convergent battleground between his principles, the distorting effect his continued pressure for greater accountability had on CBC journalists, and the public's need for vigilance in ensuring the CBC's freedom from the boarding house reach of government. It also was a horribly demoralizing affair for staff. To many of them, the CBC had capitulated to government and lobby group pressure and had timidly tried to placate angry veterans and senators rather than defend its programs, its journalists and its integrity. To Veilleux, it was nothing of the sort.

FADE TO BLACK

He was not bowing to political pressure. "In fact, I was doing exactly the opposite. I told the Senate Committee to go f—— itself. We [the CBC] have to have a process of accountability. Not them! If we're wrong, we admit it. So we can go on with our lives."

The Valour and the Horror was first broadcast by the CBC on the main network in January 1992. A second broadcast took place on Newsworld in March. The three-part series, produced by Galafilm Inc. of Montreal and the National Film Board, focused on three major World War II battles—the Allied bombing campaign over Germany, the Normandy invasion and the despatching of Canadian troops to Hong Kong. It was bitterly attacked by veterans' associations and individuals over what they saw as unfair and demeaning portrayals of Canadian servicemen. The series was accused of defaming the memory of many and for being filled with factual errors. In May, Veilleux instructed CBC ombudsman William Morgan, a former head of ETV network news and current affairs, to investigate the accusations. At the urging of powerful veterans' associations, a Senate sub-committee on veterans affairs was set up to investigate the allegations. It held hearings in June and November.

The Senate's investigation of a work of journalism sparked a furious media outcry across the country. It was called a "witch hunt" and an extremely dangerous precedent for freedom of the press. As the Globe and Mail put it, this was no innocent encounter intended to shed light on a dark subject; the Senate was arraying "the machinery of state against a free press, and the sole design is intimidation." The series' co-writer and director, Brian McKenna, accused the committee of "sheltering a politically correct view of history."

While the issue percolated around the Senate hearings, the corporation's ombudsman was investigating the accusations and testing the strength of The Valour and the Horror's credibility with a number of historians. Morgan's report was made public on November 10, 1992. He pointed out that the CBC certainly should be broadcasting programs which raised legitimate questions about our history and he had no reason to conclude the producers "deliberately set out to distort facts or to mislead their audience." Still, he found the programs failed to measure up to CBC's policies and standards. The main problem was the use of dramatized segments, a practice that Morgan stated was "discouraged" by the CBC as a general principle because, to the audience, it could "lend the appearance of reality to hypothesis."

On the same day, Veilleux released a statement that pointed to the ombudsman's findings and stated: "To the extent that these programs fell below acceptable standards, the CBC accepts full responsibility." He expressed "his sincere regret at any distress the programs may have caused members of the audience." Like Morgan, he felt the series "had considerable merit as a contribution to the portrayal of Canada's experience in the Second World War," but unless the series could be amended to comply with journalistic policy guidelines the CBC "will not rebroadcast the series." The CBC could not be afraid of controversy, he went on, but programs had to be "fully defensible" and meet journalistic policies and standards. "The principle of freedom of expression absolutely requires that we continue to deal with controversial subjects," but in the future there would be stricter adherence to journalistic guidelines. The CBC would be more accountable. The public had spoken. The CBC had listened. It had been wrong. It admitted it. In Veilleux's mind it was case closed.

But it wasn't. Galafilm's response was immediate and vocal. They denied any allegation of error, accused the CBC's report of being "manifestly unfair," even a miscarriage of justice. They—co-writer and director, Brian McKenna, co-writer and narrator, Terence McKenna, and producer, Arnie Gelbart—had not been given a proper opportunity to respond to accusations. They claimed the historians used by Morgan had not been entirely impartial. Morgan had ignored "voluminous documentation" they provide him. And as far as the drama techniques were concerned, there was no proof that the segments had confused the audience.

The general media reaction was swift and extremely critical: the CBC had hung out journalists to dry before a Senate inquisition. The ombudsman's process had been secret and arbitrary. The CBC could not air programs and then "turn on their reporters or producers," said Arnold Amber, the president of the CBC's Association of Television Producers and Directors. The ombudsman had too much power: "Who died and made him king?" The CBC had "sacrificed its programmers for reasons of political expediency," said Jack Gray, head of the Writers Guild of Canada. *Prime Time News'* Pamela Wallin asked Patrick Watson if the matter looked like the CBC kowtowing to political masters. Watson's response: "You bet it does." William Thorsell, writing in the *Globe and Mail*, accused the CBC administration and ombudsman of taking "the radical position that revisionism is not good journalism . . . they seem to be saying that only conventional wisdom measures up to the 'CBC's demanding policies and standards.' By this measure of measuring up, the CBC will turn itself into an intellectual and social eunuch forever safe from controversy or significance."

The paper editorialized about the "servile timidity of the CBC" and suggested the corporation had gone along with the "shameful" Senate process as a way to get "the $50-million supplementary allocation it has been angling for since the spring." They saw "nothing here so egregious as to warrant CBC President Gérard Veilleux's abject disavowal of the series." And they castigated the CBC senior management for sending "an emissary crawling to the lead kangaroo with an offer to plea bargain." As reported, CBC's vice-president of communications Robert Pattillo "met with Senator Jack Marshall more than a month ago, 'asking what the CBC might do', in Mr. Marshall's words, to satisfy the veterans he claims to represent, who are offended by the program's account of the Canadian war effort."

The issue was no longer *The Valour and the Horror*. It was the CBC's bungled handling of it. Although Pattillo would later deny that the sub-committee's chairman had seen an early draft of the ombudsman's report, the inference taken from the accusations being thrown back and forth between Marshall, National Council of Veteran's Associations chairman Cliff Chadderton and Pattillo, was that, while its ombudsman was going through the motions, the CBC had been trying to make amends with the Senate sub-committee. Morgan, who Chadderton claimed allowed him prior access to the report, stayed out of sight. Pattillo claimed Chadderton never saw anything resembling the report and that he met with Marshall only to find out what the senators were trying to achieve with their hearings. "But the notes of meetings and telephone calls kept in the usual way by two of Senator Marshall's aides indicate that Pattillo offered the subcommittee the McKennas' heads," Anne Collins wrote in the May 1993 issue of *Saturday Night*. "In the meeting before Labour Day he promised to give the subcommittee the ombudsman's report before its general release. . . . In the next meeting on October 2—with the release of the report delayed—Pattillo filled in Marshall and two aides on the ombudsman's criticisms, showed them the press release that contained Veilleux's pledge not to broadcast the films without corrections. . . ." Patillo refuted Collius' version of events concerning him, but from the streets, it looked as if CBC management had been in such a hurry to apologize and look good in the eyes of its political masters that it tripped all over itself.

Producers and reporters pointed out that Morgan had operated for a number of years less like an ombudsman than an arbitrator. And where exactly was his beef? A previous Galafilm documentary about World War I, *The Killing Ground*, used dramatic sequences and ran on the CBC without complaint—while Morgan had been the head of the department (in fact, dramatic sequences had been a standard tool on *The Journal* under Morgan). The scripts for both documentaries had been vetted by CBC current affairs management. Add to the problem the fact the CBC ran *Valour* twice and it was not until the veterans' associations and Senate inquisitors began making noises that the CBC checked its navel. And then, months later, the corporation apologizes? Who was running the place? Where were the standards of consistency, never mind journalism?

It now had little to do with the series and more to do with the clandestine and incompetent way the CBC ran its business. Veilleux was chastised for trying to be too early out of the gate with an apology that was not seen as necessary. Morgan was being hammered for his conclusions and handling of the process. Pattillo was accusing Marshall and Chadderton of playing fast and loose with the truth. How did Pattillo get in there anyway, staff were asking? What the hell was a communication v-p doing messing in a major journalistic issue? Although Watson was reportedly trying to support the journalistic side, Rick Salutin mused in the *Globe and Mail* that his relative absence from the battleground caused CBC employees to speak of him "as Russian peasants once talked about the czar: if only he knew, surely he'd do something. . . ."

Calls went out again for Veilleux's resignation. Management had sacrificed its programmers "for reasons of political expediency." More than a thousand CBC employees signed a petition criticizing management for its handling of the controversy. The seeming effort to appease the senators had "put a chill on controversial documentary production" for the future. Veilleux met with producers to try to iron things out, promising they would be part of a review of the ombudsman process. As one senior CBC journalist said at the time: "the CBC was at war with itself again."

From inside and outside the corporation, staff and critics saw the imprint of a more "activist" and intimidating Tory-appointed Board of Directors. The ETV network news and current affairs department had been rocked by the dumping of the popular Trina McQueen and eventual demise of *The National* and *The Journal*. *The Valour and the Horror* only increased the "chill" at the CBC. The Board had unanimously endorsed the ombudsman's report. What did that say? They were putting on the pressure. Patrick Watson denied that any political pressure had been applied to the Board from the Tories. But why would there have to be? The Board was Tory-appointed. Who needed to send a message? It was telepathic.

The debate over the 1990 budget cut decision was nowhere near as rancorous a matter "as dealing with the tremendous emotional cloud that blew up over *The Valour and the Horror*," Watson said in January 1993. "That's one of the worst experiences I've ever been through in my life, because there was such passion and such division over it. It was so difficult to arrive at consensus; the conflict and the bare philosophies coming out [within the Board], yes, and the perception of patriotism and idealism, the conflict of ideas, so deeply rooted in people's guts, that it caused tremendous anguish. It changed the whole tone of discussion for a substantial number of months. . . ."

The passion and the division continued. Later in mid-March 1993, the Gemini awards won by *The Valour and the Horror* would spark another public fight between 'team' members, this time between Watson and right-wing Board member, John Crispo. Crispo called the awards "a disgrace and a travesty." He termed the CBC's reaction to the massive media criticism "meek, mild and muted." Watson responded publicly by disassociating himself and his Board colleagues from Crispo's "extravagant" remarks, going on to point out that Crispo's outburst was "entirely inappropriate" and his comments "on *The Valour and the Horror*, the Gemini Awards, media accountability and related matters, do not represent the views of the board of directors of the CBC nor of management nor the programmers of this corporation."

Like the stubborn remnants of a smouldering forest fire, the issue flared ugly again in mid-July. The Bomber Harris Trust, an association of 25,000 veterans of the Canadian Bomber Command, announced they were filing a $500 million class-action lawsuit for defamation, citing forty-one errors and distortions in one of the series' episodes. In what one would hardly call 'precision bombing', the air veterans indiscriminately unloaded their lawsuit on anything that moved near or on the surface of *The Valour and the Horror*—the NFB, the McKenna brothers, Galafilm, the federal Attorney-General, the Secretary of State and Minister of Communications, Harper Collins Publishing Inc., which produced a book accompanying the series, and, of course, the CBC. The veterans' saturation bombing tactics seemed to fit nicely into the whole *Horror* war game, again sparking media outrage across the country. Brian McKenna warned that the lawsuit was "profoundly undemocratic" and an example of the "ultimate libel chill." For Veilleux, if he found the relentless nature of the debate depressing in January, by July he must have been wondering if this crazy war would ever end.

What depressed Veilleux most about the issue was the fundamental misunderstanding that existed about the concept of public broadcasting. "To me, public broadcasting is public service," Veilleux maintained after the first fires had cooled in January 1993. "Public broadcasting belongs to the public. It's public airwaves. It means they don't belong to the government. It doesn't belong to a Parliamentary committee. It doesn't belong to a Senate committee. It doesn't belong to any particular interest group in society—veterans or others. It certainly doesn't belong to a group of journalists. And therefore we have to place a process of accountability on the use of those airwaves."

To him, there was no process for an aggrieved public to have its say on public broadcasting: "They can't even write a letter to the editor! They can do that with most newspapers but not with the CBC! So when I came here, knowing this concept—I believe very deeply in it—I said we have to have a process for the rendering of accountability. . . . So I set up the ombudsman. Well, you saw what was generated—somehow there were accusations of censuring, not supporting journalists, all goddamn lies! And that really depressed me to no end because I have a feeling the goddamned journalists think the airwaves belong to them! They don't think they are working for the public. . . . The Canadian taxpayers are paying for you, therefore they have a right to every point of view and they have a right to objectivity and accuracy and balance and fairness . . ."

But what Gérard Veilleux was missing with his interpretation of public broadcasting, and the thirst for a formalized accountability mechanism, was that he was pitting his rigid definition against a generation of CBC journalistic methods and practices which had, for the most part, performed remarkably well. There would always be the odd dust-up over a particular CBC program. But it was not the appearance of a CBC journalistic policy book or guidelines or ombudsman that had suddenly rocketed the CBC's reputation into the upper reaches of Canadian journalism. It was CBC journalists—researchers, writers, reporters, producers—operating with as much fairness and as much objectivity as they could muster. The important thing, in their minds, was to make the citizen smarter and more aware. Veilleux seemed to be saying the journalist's job was as referee in a polarized world, where issues were balanced between opposing viewpoints by, ultimately, letting each extreme have its say and leave it at that.

As loudly as he tried to proclaim his will to make public broadcasting more responsive to its citizen bosses, all the journalists and producers and many managers heard—rightly or wrongly—was the heavy breathing of a highly partisan Board of Directors, and perceived the long, grasping right forearm of an angry and irritated Mulroney government. Veilleux's hardened view of public service broadcasting would only help drive a growing wedge between the Board, a few of his appointed senior managers, and the rest of the corporation. Whatever trust and teamwork with which he had hoped to re-energize the corporation, would be shattered once and for all, the chances of reconciliation, like the chances for long term, stable funding from the Tories, just another missed opportunity.

10 / The Empire Strikes Back

"I know what reputation I lost."
—Patrick Watson, February 1, 1991
"The strongest guard is always placed at the gateway to nothing."
—Dick Diver in F. Scott Fitzgerald, *Tender is the Night*

AS OFTEN AS NOT, RUNNING the CBC at the Board of Directors level must be to managerial science what hitting a home run is to space travel; what stumbling along a dark hallway is to Olympic sprinting. Few of the members have a lock on how the corporation runs. Information about the inner pulses of the corporation has occasionally been doled out in political dabs to the Board by management, often leading to their frustration and, occasionally, erratic decision-making—like the "symmetry" in their $108 million budget cut. Sometimes they just did what they were told.

Most Board appointees approach their new jobs with a true sense of mission. Very few of them walk in the CBC door indifferent about the organization. Buoyed with enthusiasm, flattered that they have been called upon by a senior cabinet minister—or heaven forbid, the PM himself—most enter primed for bear. Unfortunately, to be chosen as part of the guidance system for one of the nation's most complex cultural institutions does not require a knowledge of how public broadcasting works. Most simply bring their non-broadcast skills, the imprint of their political gene pool and, in a lot of cases, an overwhelming urge to "clean up the place." They can always see from the advantage of distance that the CBC is "fat" and needing radical surgery applied to its billion-dollar budget. But once they are on the Board, they're damned if they can find where most of the fat is. The CBC is in trouble, and has been trouble, for decades. But it is their sworn duty to correct the errors of history, get the darn place "moving again" and prove to their factional friends that they were worthy of

206

the trust. And then, the Marshmallow Lady would slowly ease her arms around them, embrace their enthusiasm, and huddling deep inside her soft and mysterious bosom, most were never heard from again.

Some look to the task in minute detail while others no doubt look to it in very general terms. They do not like the chummy way Peter Gzowski chats with Stephen Lewis. They like the music on *Stereo Morning*, but they cannot stand the guy who talks between recordings. There are too many commercials on television. There are too *few* commercials on television. Some cannot understand why, with the continuing corporate financial problems, and with CBC radio so popular, the CBC cannot just sell commercials on radio. Somebody's wife hates the local morning show host, thinks Vicki Gabereau is too saucy and is convinced that her husband's seat on the Board can be screwed up high enough to tower over all those little bureaucrats and public servants and show them what's what. "Everyone has two careers," a former regional director once said: "Theirs, and running the CBC."

"It is either the voice of the people," Andrew Borkowski wrote in the May/June 1991 issue of *SCAN* magazine, "or it is a gathering of professional elites, a tool of the party in power, and the dupe of an entrenched bureaucracy. It represents the regions but defends the national interest. It controls everything. It controls nothing. It is the CBC Board of Directors, and no one seems quite sure who they are and what the hell they do."

The majority of the appointments—for all their professional qualifications, social standing and political influence—are about as appropriate for the protection of the interests of public broadcasting as putting a finishing carpenter on the Atomic Energy Control Board. They did very good work in their own field, exceptional in some cases, but once inside the CBC, they are forced to fly by the seat of their pants a lot of the time and rely on instincts.

Few will have bothered to trace in detail the troubled history of the organization, in an effort to get to know how it came to where it is today. Their primary understanding of the CBC seems to come from their personal experiences, their political leanings, from conversations among themselves and from a small group of senior Head Office managers. They often end up working on some issues in a bewildering fog, peering out suspiciously, anxious that they will not be able to do the job their political peers hoped for. They have been known to panic. They are professional amateurs in public broadcasting, occasionally embarrassed or defensive about their politics, their lack of real knowledge about how the corporation works, and always just a little frustrated because they came to tame the Marshmallow Lady and can't get their arms around her to measure her girth. They always know she's hiding something.

The Board consists of fifteen members, including a president and a chairman, appointed by the Governor in Council. The criteria for the job are not what one would call demanding: you must be a Canadian citizen and you cannot be involved in a broadcast undertaking or making money from one while in office. Other than that, it is who you are and who you know. A seat is held for up to five years, with some chance for re-appointment. The Board is responsible for the "management of the business, activities and other affairs of the Corporation" and reports to Parliament through the Minister of Communications. Board members receive a fee and travel expenses for their trouble. The Board is supposed to be guided primarily by Sec. 3 (l) and (m) of the *Broadcasting Act*. As the national public broadcaster, the CBC should "provide radio and television services incorporating a wide range of programming that informs, enlightens and entertains." And that programming must follow eight considerations. First, programs should be "predominantly and distinctively Canadian." Second, the programming should "reflect Canada and its regions to national and regional audiences, while serving the special needs of those regions." Nowhere is there any mention about a network. Nowhere does it say that programming decisions have to be driven from metropolitan centres such as Toronto and Montreal. Nothing in this legislated mandate seems to have a higher priority than regional programming. In consequence, the position taken by some Board members—that their job is not to represent regional interests but the national interest—would indicate they might not understand their job description. It can be argued that if you are not "serving the special needs of those regions," you are simply not doing your job properly.

A number of things happen when new Board members cross the threshold. First, most inevitably become enamoured with the corporation. Like going through a cultural and even ideological pre-frontal lobotomy, some of their rage is tempered, their attitudes change. They begin to realize how large a responsibility the corporation has, how sweeping its mandate is, and how delightful life can be rubbing shoulders with the people who help make up the creative heart of the country—internationally acclaimed producers and writers, well-known Canadian actors and actresses, brand-name television executives. Their doctrinal ties get stretched between their allegiances to the party and their new-found infatuation with the CBC. In good times, that kind of Damascus-road conversion was helpful to the corporation. Members lobbied with their friends to improve its health, perhaps even raise the budget. In bad times, however, when the call came for them to either stand behind the corporation come-hell-or-high-water, or line up with their political soul-mates, the Marshmallow Lady tended to be left without a dancing partner.

They also begin to recognize that this is not going to be a romp through the fields of personal taste and the politics of cut-and-slash. They are in charge of baby-sitting this big, white, expensive beastie, but they cannot get a real handle on what's inside all the padding. Every time they start to think they have it aced, up pops another situation or statistic that flummoxes them. We own a building and a parking lot, where? We have *how many* employees in finance and administration? We're tied to how many millions in long term leases? She signed a contract for how much!? You mean we own art, too?

The Marshmallow Lady never gives up all her secrets without a tussle. She sits on most of them, doling them out at Board meetings through the management presentations, like little chocolates—a surprising sweet, but where do they come from and how many more are still hidden back there? And as a result, many members get suspicions, not over what she said she's delivering, but what she must have left out. It can drive members into a them-and-us thinking that can result in harsh and punitive decisions. The frustration can give you, as one member once put it, a "Sicilian kind of memory."

It is not really manipulation with intent. All boards are manipulated by management, even controlled to a some extent. That is the way the game is played. Management go to the board to get the decisions they want. They do not go asking for leadership. They want endorsement. Former CBC President Pierre Juneau was a recognized master at Board control. He would listen to everyone in a very democratic way, then go off, as one member recalled, and largely make the decision himself. Where some members under Juneau wanted wholesale facilities cuts in all areas of the country, Juneau would not agree. He felt the move would be seen by the government of the day as punitive—a deliberate attempt to embarrass. He also sensed that what was cut on the facilities side, particularly stations, would probably never reappear again. Juneau wanted to preserve the base of the corporation as it was. Many of the others felt that "saving the base" was like "buying a ticket on the Titanic."

> "The CBC is not a crown corporation like any other. It is not primarily a business to be judged on the narrow grounds of managerial efficiency. It is the core of this country's communication system, sharing with education the critical role of transmitting our nation's heritage and expanding our knowledge and cultural horizons. The CBC must be in good hands, and governed by a group of persons who are ready to answer for their stewardship."
> —Frank W. Peers, CBC: The Big Picture

Everybody talks about how the CBC belongs to the people—"the folks" as Patrick Watson likes to term it. But it is like saying Revenue Canada belongs to me. The Canadian Broadcasting Corporation, as much as anything, belongs to Head Office, the senior management executive and the Board of Directors, few of whom represent the interests and tastes of mainstream Canadians. The directors belong spiritually, not to Parliament or to the rig worker in Grande Prairie, Alberta, the Jamaican immigrant living in Toronto or the women's activist in Winnipeg, but to the people who have given them life and significance—the government of the day. Canadian public broadcasting is guided by the decisions of a group of like-minded ideologues who could be shoe-horned into a good-sized elevator. In the case of the present Board, an inordinate number of them have been active in Conservative party organizing and fund raising, at either the provincial or federal level, or have worked for federal PC politicians. They are well-meaning and dedicated, to be sure. In 1993, the group consisted in part of a disproportionate number of lawyers, an interior designer, a government lobbyist, a former Conservative premier, a car dealer and businessman, a former freelance journalist, two former private broadcasters, a philosopher-historian, an author-filmmaker and a university economics professor best known for his vehement attacks against the CBC, particularly its journalists.

For the most part, their political roots go deep and their doctrinal allegiances are strong. As former Board member and Liberal appointee Howard Aster said in *SCAN* magazine, this group brings to the job "a kind of single-mindedness to execute the government's views in opposition to being the arbiters of a public interest." The view from inside the elevator is a bit more forbearing. "There are people on the Board with a very, very strong business orientation, whose natural instincts come perilously close to privatizing the place," says chairman Patrick Watson. "And others who have a very strong sense of public service and think we are far too deeply into the commercial advertising business as it is." But one thing is for certain, since getting blind-sided in 1990 by circumstances and management, they are also a much more active Board, more involved in management decision-making and policy setting than ever before. They are not taking much on trust these days.

To say that this relatively well-heeled group "represents the country, represents the folks . . ." as Watson said in a CBC radio interview, is astonishingly naive. It is doubtful whether any of these folks have ever been laid-off from a permanent job, cleaned someone else's home or worried too long about the next month's mortgage payment. Watson must have forgotten what he said in the summer of 1991, that the Board's members came to a larger extent than he would like "from the political, financial and professional elites." The truth is they simply represent a right wing, upper middle class elite.

The current Board shares a conservative philosophy, just as previous Boards took their cues from whoever appointed them—Liberals or other Conservative governments. It is one of the saddest and most undemocratic realities about Canadian public broadcasting. Politics prevails over public service. The citizen can only hope that their ideological hats are not tipped too much one way or the other. On the one hand, true conservatives are disposed to preserving means and institutions, promoting reasoned and gradual development. They are realists for the most part, and recognize "the marketplace" can only take things so far. Given time and place, they can find room beside themselves on the ideological spectrum for many things others might find discomforting: from public investment in the economy to the need for broad social programs, from protecting cultural programs to promoting political freedoms. This is conservatism that used to build things—like the CNR and the CBC.

But modern conservatives are singularly dedicated to the health and growth of the private, not the public sector. Their belief systems are filled with the romantic notion that the private sector, let loose on the fields of the marketplace, can provide solutions for all of society's problems. They are the new, tough political elite, neoconservatives weaned on mythology spun by the patronizing economic thoughts of people like Michael Wilson and Ronald Reagan. They talk about "level playing fields" and yet they mean advantage in their court. They talk about "accountability" but they mean point of view. Where traditional conservatives used reason as a tool for building, neoconservatives are just suspicious. They are more comfortable taking things apart than they are putting them together. As John Ralston Saul wrote in the October 1992 edition of *Report on Business Magazine*, "This isn't conservatism at all. This is classic right-wing ideology."

As a group, as at least one study has shown, today's average Progressive Conservative Party member does not rely on the CBC for information and entertainment. Some of the CBC Board would probably be an exception, given their responsibilities, but today's PCs tend to watch private television and listen to private radio. They resent, more than is democratically healthy, that CBC journalists feel they have a responsibility to question the way in which members of their party perform in government. The only thing that makes many of them pause momentarily in their dedication to the eventual unravelling of the CBC is fear of general public reaction and the unsettling possibilities it holds for the party in any subsequent election. Nevertheless, at the 1991 PC convention, delegates voted to privatize the CBC.

The CBC Board has occasionally been likened to the Senate. Their appointments are purely political. It is assumed they vote the party line. But at least senators try to work in the best interests of their regions. They look after their backyards. But when the deliberations about massive budget cuts to regional operations were going on in late 1990—and taking fully into account the embarrassing shortness of time management had allowed them for decision-making—the Board weighed their options and ended up nuking large portions of their own backyards.

In some cases, they did not even know what regional programs were being cancelled by their actions—or so some said. Michael Power, the member from Nova Scotia, and a former executive

FADE TO BLACK

vice-president of the Nova Scotia PC Association, admitted, according to *SCAN* magazine, that he had no idea he was contributing to the "killing" of *Land and Sea* or the local telethons when the Board lowered the boom in December 1990. One other member did not even know the names of the CBC programs produced in his region. Don Hamilton, a former private broadcaster who thinks the CBC "has strayed quite a bit from its mandate in recent years," stated that his job was not to look after his particular region; that a Board's interests, unlike a senator one would suppose, should be focused on the "national" issues surrounding the CBC. "We are sworn to support the mandate, not to represent regional interests," Hamilton told *SCAN* magazine, thereby demonstrating a lack of familiarity with the *Broadcasting Act*.

In a December 6, 1990 interview with CBC-TV's Cecilia Walters about cuts to regional programming, at first Hamilton denied there would be cuts, stating, "no, the regional programming, I think, will be as strong as ever. I think the regions will be an integral part of the development of CBC. And I don't think the president has any intention of cutting regional programming, and certainly there's going to be no cuts that I'm aware of in British Columbia." When Walters asked about the loss of at least fifty jobs in Vancouver and the cancellation of a number of B.C. regional programs, Hamilton waffled defensively.

Hamilton: I am not exactly sure what you mean.
Walters: Those are the local programs here at CBC Vancouver.
Hamilton: Name me one. I don't . . .
Walters: *Diversity, Down to Earth.*
Hamilton: No, but I mean . . . what kind of program . . . I don't know what you're talking about. I mean, help me a little bit. What kind of programs aren't going to go?
Walters: These programs have been cancelled now.
Hamilton: Name one.
Walters: *Diversity.* That's the name of the program.
Hamilton: Okay. Another . . . [laughing]
Walters: And *Down to Earth.*
Hamilton: Eh . . . I have seen *Down to Earth*, yeah.
Walters: And CBC *Forum.*
Hamilton: I'm frankly not aware of that. . . . None of this is contained in the release that I got on the fax this morning.

Historically speaking, the regions were once supposed to be the dominant program players in Canadian public broadcasting. They were built and expanded between 1936 and roughly 1983, largely on the cooperation and strength of the working relationship between regional Board members and regional directors. In keeping with the intentions of the legislation, Board members lobbied for, and obtained, new production facilities, programming funds, increased schedule time and increased staff allotments for their particular regions. That relationship was a major factor in perpetuating the original premise of the "national public broadcasting service"—that program making should be in the regions or provinces. Nothing changed fundamentally over the years in the CBC's mandate. Only the people on the Board of Directors changed.

The mandate that members like Hamilton like to believe in, containing some abstract notion of "national interest," does not exist. Where the CBC is concerned, the *Broadcasting Act* focuses the CBC's priority—as "the national broadcaster"—on programs that reflect the regions. In fact, in espousing a national mandate for the CBC that chopped out large portions of the regions, the Board twisted itself into political pretzels, even contradicting one of the contemporary Tory beliefs in Canada as a nation made up of "a community of communities." By cutting regions instead of the networks—in effect making a simpler, economic decision rather than a cultural one—the Board deviated even from PC policy.

What happens in this fog of shifting subjective opinion is that the corporation's mandate becomes an organic thing, changing and being adjusted on the felt impressions of a majority of those people riding in the elevator, rather than a statement of purpose that leaps uncontested out of the *Broadcasting Act.* At least one member, Ontario's William Neville, wondered out loud in a 1992 Board meeting about why regions had to exist at all. In his eyes, the CBC was simply "a national service" and in his mind a program did not have to come from a region to reflect what was happening in that region. You could tell stories about the regions without having the storyteller live there, he opined. But his thoughts put a shudder through the entire regional management structure of the CBC. This was not the vision they had of national public broadcasting. And neither was it the vision old time Tory R. B. Bennett had when he gave life to the CBC. "The statement made my hair stand on end," said one senior manager.

In fact, as far as the 1990 budget cut decision was concerned, Neville would have taken advantage of the situation to cut even more deeply so the CBC could both solve its nagging financial problems once-and-for-all, and make an overdue fundamental change in the way the corporation provides public broadcasting services. "I don't want to create the impression I don't place importance on regional broadcasting," Neville said in January 1993. "But frankly I'm not so sure that chasing a fire engine in Vancouver for the six o'clock news is unique for us."

The Board also does not have much contact with the Canadian public. Many years ago, they used to hold their meetings in public, entertaining submissions and comments from the general public. Now they meet with "the public" (usually composed of such common folk as premiers, business and cultural leaders and assorted CBC employees and ex-employees) most often by invitation only, for cocktails and canapés (the food and beverage bill for a meeting in Vancouver in May 1993 was reportedly $16,500, or the equivalent of one-half year's salary for a researcher or a production assistant), usually after Board deliberations are over. Most members simply draw their information on reaction to the CBC from the particular elite they circle with. Many of them move in the rarefied air of politics, money and social power. Do they really know what the elementary teacher next door feels about the CBC, or the fisherman at the wharf, the mechanic in the garage, the trucker out of Estevan? When was the last time a Board member solicited your input into decision-making concerning the public's CBC? The public may be an abstract consideration, but not the principal one. Where public access to the CBC policy and program decisions are concerned, the CBC is truly Kafka's Castle. The villagers pay the taxes but they have little say in how their lives are run.

The Mulroney government's search for a new role for the CBC in the broadcast firmament has not been based on any profound understanding of the original foundations of Canadian public broadcasting, a construct moulded not by political whim but by the changing forces and needs of a culture. They want to see a corporation that fits, if it has to exist at all, as a non-intrusive player on the deep sidelines of the broadcasting "business." Their pursuit has little or nothing to do with history, or with the social and cultural role of public broadcasting. Today's CBC, then, ends up almost like any other large, over-mature institution—a functioning reflection of the thinking of a small group of individuals who, through a process of assimilation or collation of experience, partisan personal history, power, manipulation, emotion and gut-instinct, steer toward an obscure objective that may or may not fit with the public interest.

As seen from outside the castle, the CBC now tilts ominously toward a Tory view of things. Although rumours abound, there is no evidence that the traditional "arm's length relationship" between the corporation and the government has been openly breached by the Tories. There is no need. The influence is tacit, not direct. If it were within their power, it was clear in many minds that a number of them wanted to see the CBC eased from the national broadcasting picture. William Neville disagreed: "My view is that this government is as committed to public broadcasting as any and I don't simply buy the notion that there is some plot going on to 'get' the CBC." But looking back after his tenure as co-chairman of the Tory-appointed Caplan-Sauvageau task force on broadcasting, Gerald Caplan said: "I have never had any uncertainty about how much most Tories hate the CBC and hate public broadcasting." Members of the television producers' association talked about their lobbying meetings with a broad range of Tory MPs after the December 1990 budget cuts: "We came away from two days of sitting in their offices, getting abused," said CTPDA president Cathy Chilco. "They *hate* the CBC!" Chilco's experience brought to mind the caution from Emerson, that "there is always a certain meanness in the argument of conservatism, joined with a certain superiority in its fact."

The most troubling part of the tilt to the right end of the political spectrum is what some of the Board are achieving with persistent demands for "journalistic accountability." Somewhat surprisingly, there are varying degrees of intensity on the Board about the matter, from the thumping irrationality of a John Crispo to the occasional uncomfortable defence thrown up for CBC journalists by Patrick Watson. But overall, the mood still leans toward the wrathful. As Stephen Godfrey pointed out in a *Globe and Mail* article on Veilleux, "journalistic accountability" was used "as code for interfering in news management, particularly when there is coverage critical of government." Patrick Watson has tried at points to act the conciliator and defuse the attack. In responding to a question about the distance between the Board and news management, Watson told the CBC's radio audience in B.C. on September 14, 1992 that "We're trying to bring the Board *juuuust* as close to programming as is safe and comfortable so they're not trespassing, so they have a chance to say: 'we feel that the country—remember, the Board represents the country, represents the folks—we feel the folks would benefit if you went in this or that direction . . .'."

The issue that laid bare the Board's 'accountability' pursuit for Canadians was *The Valour and the Horror*. It cut to a delicate quick: whether journalists had it within their terms of reference to stimulate as well as inform the citizen. This Board unanimously supported the ombudsman's critical findings and the president's apology. This is probably not a Board which would comprehend the insightful essence of what famed U.S. newsman Walter Lippmann said to the Washington, D.C. National Press Club in September 1959: "If my country is to be governed with the consent of the governed, then the governed must arrive at opinions about what their governors want them to consent to. . . . Here, we correspondents perform an essential service . . . we make it our business to find out what is going on under the surface and beyond the horizon, to infer, to deduce, to imagine, and to guess what is going on inside, what this meant yesterday, and what it could mean tomorrow. In this we do what every sovereign citizen is supposed to do but has not the time or the interest to do for himself." As a professional edict, Lippman's words were light-years away from most Board members' perception of what journalism was all about.

In the *Valour* issue, the Board had run up a telling flag to the corporation's journalists. Although they seldom stopped talking about balance, the issue was point of view; a point of view that caused no political strains, seldom questioned, never investigated and seldom took risks. The Board members did not understand they were, in effect, the custodians of an organization with one of the highest journalistic standards in the world. As Patrick Watson pointed out in the summer 1991 issue of *SCAN* magazine, "when really [rigorous] analysis is done, the CBC tends to come out with flying colours compared to anyone else in terms of fairness and comprehensiveness." Writing in the October 31, 1991 *Globe and Mail*, Watson went further: "As for the apparent contradiction of having a public broadcaster free of state control, the rules governing the CBC confer upon it a right, indeed the obligation, to broadcast dissent: It must explore the dark as well as the light side of things," Watson stated eloquently, "and expose the broadest range of opinion, interest and experience." I guess the Board just forgot.

> "John Crispo's appointment to the CBC board of directors illustrates the inadequacy of the appointments process for federal agencies and commissions. . . . it is not safe to entrust so ideological a government as Brian Mulroney's with the unchecked power to name directors and chief executive officers to agencies and corporations owned by the people."
> —Michael Valpy, *Globe and Mail*, April 5, 1991

One of the most offensive appointments ever made to the CBC Board of Directors, in over five decades of its history, has to be the selection of John Crispo for a three-year term. It told Canadians what the Tories really thought of the corporation. Just before Crispo was appointed by Brian Mulroney, he told the CRTC at the March 1991 hearing that the corporation was intellectually dishonest in its news and public-affairs programming and was little more than a propaganda agency for its news and public affairs producers. The shockingly quick appointment of Crispo came about after Mulroney and chairman-designate Patrick Watson crossed public swords. Crispo was appointed "in a fit of Prime Ministerial pique," as one insider put it, over Watson's temerity to argue with the PM over the size and appropriateness of the CBC budget. Watson had been given "an undertaking" by Mulroney when he agreed to take the chairman's job "that names the government wishes to submit [for possible Board appointments] will be run by me for my comment." With Crispo's appointment, it was not the age of enlightenment for public broadcasting in Canada. It was another dark night of an already tortured cultural soul.

Crispo said the CBC was a "lousy, left-wing, liberal-NDP-pinko network," although he later admitted that he might have gone a tad "too far" on the "NDP-pinko" part. It was the corporation's journalism he despised so passionately. He advocated tying CBC budget cuts to his version of journalistic balance and accountability. The 1991/92 budget cuts were little more than "a down payment and a warning" that unless the corporation ended its bias and inefficiency, it would face further cuts and "eventual shutdown." He later wrote, in a full page feature in the *Globe and Mail* on May 18, 1991, as a response to the nation-wide criticism over his appointment to the Board, that the media in general and the CBC in particular are potentially the most dangerous and evil force in our society.

Crispo's idea of journalistic balance for the CBC would see every panel discussion of political issue stacked in the Tories' favour, the *Globe*'s Michael Valpy wrote. One Tory, one Liberal and one NDPer was an imbalance to Crispo, leading to twice as much "anti as pro." He evidently wanted numerical balance, rep-by-pop journalism; the more members your party had, the more coverage you should get. He criticized "stacked panels," like Peter Gzowski's discussion group "with that red Tory, Dalton Camp; that pink Liberal, Eric Kierans; and that mainline NDPer, Stephen Lewis." His world of ideological "balance" did not even have room for members of his own party whose thoughts might differ from his.

He quoted the right-wing Fraser Institute's "definitive study" that said the CBC was "anti-free trade." He said he "couldn't believe" how the CBC covered the GST debate, and for their coverage of the Gulf War (which others had claimed was superficial and cloying toward the U.S.), Crispo called the CBC "Radio Iraq." He did not know, he went on, why we just didn't "ship it to Baghdad." The CBC almost "killed Meech Lake, then reversed themselves in the last three sickening weeks and were so pro-Meech Lake that it was equally appalling." Radio-Canada had done more to "undermine this country" than any other radio or television network. *The Journal*, a program that roughly a million Canadians watched and enjoyed each weekday night, was, in a burst of Crispo's revisionist Socratic logic, just "lousy."

By the middle of 1992, this hounding was having an effect within the CBC: tally sheets for news stories, minutely timed coverage, loyalty oaths, an ombudsman and even a vice-president overseeing "media accountability," and a president who believed that CBC journalists "are not at arm's length from me." The pressure the staff felt was immense, and demoralizing. These moves were not votes of confidence for public broadcasting. They were not initiatives that built anything. They checked initiative. They destroyed things—ideas, beliefs, enthusiasm, dreams, morale.

Crispo's ranting reminded me of an incident in 1975 while I was executive producer of the radio documentary series, *Concern*. We had commissioned a documentary from a Latin American freelance journalist, to analyze events that led to the overthrow of Chile's

Marxist Allende government in September 1973 by a right-wing military *junta*. Among other issues, the program dealt with the CIA's involvement in the coup and its efforts to destabilize the Allende government. The death of Allende was surrounded by rumour, but little was explained about the incident. The freelancer offered new information and details about not only Allende's assassination but also complicity of certain military officers, and maybe even foreign agencies. We felt the documentary was factual and revealing, with many of those interviewed relating first-hand information about events leading up to the overthrow, and how Allende had been apprehended and, as the boys in Viet Nam used to say, "dispatched with extreme prejudice."

The theme of the documentary was centred on the fact that an elected leader of the Chilean people—yes, a Marxist and not a very accomplished governor, but hardly a despot or a dictator—had been assassinated, and the leadership replaced with a non-elected military government. We were not talking political stripes, or waving flags for a leftist movement. We were talking about democratic principles, law and then we were talking about murder. We were pleased with the program because it provided new information for the public to analyze events and went a great distance in countering the relatively unquestioning coverage of the coup by U.S. media.

The day after the broadcast, we received a long-distance telephone call from London, Ontario. The caller was furious about the documentary, berating us for broadcasting such lies. He claimed to know the real details behind the coup. Chile would, he argued, work much more efficiently under military authority. We asked him where specifically he might find errors or omissions in the program so that we could take his points into account in analyzing the program to see if, in fact, an imbalance in information or facts had taken place. He would not be specific. All he wanted, he yelled quite excitedly, was "equal time for the *junta*."

> *"I remember looking out the window [of the plane]. It was the day that a US Air DC-9 went off the runway at La Guardia and into the water. It was sitting there with its empennage above the water and half the fuselage was visible and it seemed to be a symbolic wreck. And my heart was very, very low . . ."*
>
> —Patrick Watson, January 8, 1993, on his return from New York in 1989 to rejoin the CBC

No one has suffered as much personal loss since December 5, 1990 as CBC chairman Patrick Watson. Gérard Veilleux went from shock to frustration, from bewilderment to anger over the way he was treated by the media and attacked by the general public. But once he got his hands on the corporation's levers of influence, he was back to what he was before—the good public servant and bureaucrat, pulling the controls and making people and the organization jump. The other relatively anonymous members of the Board suffered a bit of a singe on the backside of their reputations, but after the dust finally settled, they all strolled back into their cryptonymous existences.

Watson was left standing, the most obvious and the most exposed. And he lost the most. He ended up being accused of betraying public broadcasting, and being betrayed by the Mulroney government. He lost it both ways: from within and from without. Among the staff and the public, there were few expectations either way for the others, but Watson was different. When Watson was appointed in the fall of 1989, you could almost feel the morale rise among the staff. One of their own—one of the country's most recognized television broadcasters—was going to be "running the CBC." The Tories must have lost their minds. This was the Moses of public broadcasting. "If anyone can come down from the top of the mountain with . . . money for the CBC it's Patrick Watson," Larry Zolf wrote elatedly in the winter 1990 issue of SCAN magazine. This was Canada's very own renaissance man—brilliant host, insightful producer, author, writer, classical pianist, actor, "televisionary," one-legged pilot, bilingual intellect, a man who lived on a first name basis with the likes of Pierre Trudeau, Buckminster Fuller and Marshall McLuhan. He was "one of the world's finest broadcasters," Concordia University's Ross Perigoe wrote in the November/December 1989 issue of *content* magazine. "What he does best is dream."

In the eyes of most CBCers, and many Canadians, this man, along with his *Seven Days* friend and compatriot Laurier LaPierre, carried the same lustre that Paul Henderson carried for hockey fans. Where Henderson had his one-goal glory in the 1972 Canada-Soviet hockey tournament, Watson's brightest moments were with *Seven Days*, where he exhibited a shocking erudition and an in-your-face style of television journalism, especially it seemed, where governments and institutions were concerned. Together with LaPierre, Watson made a generation of public broadcasters believe that social good could come from your actions as a journalist. They were icons. Their reputation, based on two seasons on air, was handed down years after, like native folklore.

To a threatened CBC in 1989, Watson looked like the Babe Ruth of Canadian broadcasting. He was walking out to the plate in the bottom of the ninth, the team down three runs, bases loaded, two men out. For a moment, some of us could visualize that he even had a cocky smile on his face. This was the moment he was made for. He had come all the way from hosting a children's television show to chairman of the Board. In between, he chalked up major wins with *Seven Days, Witness to Yesterday, Some Honourable Members, The Watson Report, Titans, Venture, The Canadian Establishment* and *The Struggle for Democracy*. If there ever was a moment made for a man, this seemed to be it. But "The Babe" turned out to be "Casey At the Bat."

"There are more sightings of Elvis Presley than there are of Patrick Watson," said one disgruntled Vancouver television producer, long after the cuts were history. Watson had begun with such promise, as far as the CBC staff were concerned, and almost immediately slipped from view. They expected their man to take a high profile posture, publicly defending the integrity of the profession of public broadcasting before the heathen hordes of Tories, demanding the money they needed to make their programs; instead they got the invisible man. Although he would argue the point, to many staff he seemed hardly ever to appear among them. Many never saw Watson in the flesh until he visited CBC locations across the country after December 5, 1990, trying futilely to explain the budget cut, the closing of television stations and the cancellation of regional programs to a hostile and angry staff. He had been appointed at the beginning of October 1989. Veilleux covered more corporation territory and shook more employee hands when he came on board than Watson. "The other guy" quickly outdistanced Watson in appearances and public utterances, and captured the corporate spotlight. The staff could not figure it out.

But Watson's appointment was ineffective for what the staff expected. He spent the first twenty-one months of his part-time appointment in corporate purgatory, operating on the sidelines as "special consultant to the president" until the Tories finally passed the new *Broadcasting Act* in 1991. He was not sworn into the job until

June 14, 1991. Ross Perigoe had predicted in his *content* magazine article that Watson would face a big handicap: "Instead of functioning as a day-to-day manager, he will be working with the board of directors," making him "ineffectual at achieving any profound change." In the same issue of *content*, Robert Fulford also warned that as a part-time chairman, Watson's role was undefined and could be as marginal as that of a Canada Council chairman: "He could, in theory, be isolated from decision-making and turned into a public mouthpiece and solicitor of funds from the cabinet." But it was perfect for the Mulroney Tories. They were able to buy public relations peace by appointing Watson to the Board—showing the public how broad-minded they were where Canadian public broadcasting was concerned.

"Friends of CBC hailed Patrick Watson as their champion when his appointment was announced. Now they lament him as a lost leader," Antonia Zerbesias wrote in the *Toronto Star*. Part of the lament was that, where staff were concerned, Watson-the-king-saviour ended up not having much of a wardrobe. When he did speak early on, it was with assurance and confidence. "We're going to enlarge the resources that go into programming. . . . I wouldn't have accepted the job without the absolute, personal, direct and explicit guarantee from Ottawa that CBC could [fulfil] its mandate." Even though regional managers were sweating out the possibility of many more dollar cuts to come, Watson was quoted in the fall of 1989, after his appointment, as saying that he did not think the CBC would see "any more" cutbacks. "I've had an unequivocal statement of support from the politicians involved that they are completely behind the revital-ization of the CBC."

In an interview with the *Financial Times'* Sheldon Gordon, just after his appointment, Watson related that the "most important thing that both [the prime minister] and the minister, Marcel Masse, said to both Gérard Veilleux and me is, 'We want you to go in there and strengthen the institution and turn it into the first-class broadcasting organization that it's meant to be." When Gordon challenged that this was just a "motherhood" statement, Watson replied, "it's motherhood if it's not backed up. But it would be a very strange thing to say to a couple of guys if you knew as a politician that a year later you were going to have them come back to you and say, 'That's not the job that you asked us to do. You're trying to kill us.' Because they know that neither Veilleux nor I need this job."

As much as anything, words were Watson's worst enemy. And this was almost incomprehensible, considering that this was a man who had studied linguistics at the doctoral level and was the author of a number of novels and nonfiction works. His control of the language when he spoke in public—the terms, the metaphors, the pacing—was captivating, even entrancing. There was a sense of pleasant surprise as he released words. Some were like intellectual punctuation—"ineluctability," "renaissance," "motif," "electrifying." But somehow, when the words rolled together into explanations of issues or corporate politics, they often hinted at a strange lack of understanding. It was as if some words were only advertising sign-posts on the conversational highway, symbols rather than versions of reality. Hyperbole and overstatement began to flood his vocabulary. And the effect it had on CBC staff was devastating.

Watson told private broadcasters in 1989 that, "I could not imagine a future in which the CBC does what Parliament has asked it to do without . . . its local operations." On March 18, 1991, he told the CRTC that the CBC "would never go back to the kind of local programs that were cut even if the government comes up with the money." The Sunday before the CRTC hearings he announced "an electrifying new direction for the CBC," which turned out to be the very pedestrian and little-watched nightly current affairs magazine series *Newsmagazine*, and the scrounging of two hours of Newsworld for the ETV network's morning schedule. He inappropriately hailed the slashing of $108 million in budgets and the dismembering of regional television operations as possibly a time of renaissance in Canadian broadcasting.

He accused CBC managers under the Juneau administration of "cheating and lying." He maintained that under Juneau there had been a "destructive centralism" in decision-making, leading to domination by the network centres in Toronto and Montreal. Then his Board made decisions and applied budget cuts that would make the CBC under Veilleux and Watson the most centralized in living memory. Under the two, decision-making was now so centralized that day-to-day decisions were no longer left to senior media managers. "It got to the point," said Denis Harvey, the senior media manager in the corporation, "where we could not appoint a foreign correspondent without informing Ottawa of what our plans were and, in effect, getting their permission."

The savage 1990 budget cuts "were not the end of the world" to Watson. "We just have to tighten our belts and pull together as best we can . . . do what we have to do . . ." he informed staff. As regional station operations were being closed down after December 5, 1990, and thousands of hours of regional programming cancelled, he told staff that CBC television would now be more "regional" than ever before, that the ETV network would be putting people into the regions now to help them tell their stories and act out their dramas—which was what the people who were laid off were trying to do before the present administration took their jobs away.

Watson talked about how the ETV network would now be in the regions, "telling our stories, the singing of our songs, the dancing of our dances," but did not seem to understand that any production that might happen "in the regions" would now have to pass through the filter of Toronto. The emasculating cuts put the power to say what "our" regional stories said, what "our" songs sounded like and what "our" dances looked like in the hands of Ivan Fecan and the network's Toronto offices. Many staff, and even senior managers, began to wonder where Watson was getting his information and ideas. "One of Patrick's biggest problems was that the CBC he knew was the CBC of the 1960s," said one vice-president. "It had changed a lot since then, and Patrick made some pretty outlandish assumptions about how things worked today." Another acquaintance admitted that one of Watson's biggest frustrations as chairman of the CBC was lack of information, and that he had thoughts about setting up an information secretariat for the Board.

> *"Asked to single out his greatest weakness, Watson said, 'Impetuosity—it was the same kind of impetuosity that lost me my leg, an ill-considered tendency to jump into things'."*
> —*Maclean's* magazine, January 16, 1989

At a meeting in Vancouver on February 1, 1991, Watson made a number of statements that unnerved the staff, started heads shaking and convinced others that the Board had just gutted the regions without fully understanding what the regions did and what they had to contribute to national public broadcasting. On the very touchy point about whether there would be any more cuts announced, Watson somewhat testily shouted: "No! No . . . No . . . No. There are no more cuts on the way. . . . Who told you that?" When it was pointed out that there were rumours of a "shortfall" in reaching the $108 million cut target and I, as the station's senior television manager, was in Ottawa at that very moment meeting with other managers to find money to cover the "shortfall"—which would inevitably result in further cuts, Watson recanted and said: "Okay, okay. A million and a half bucks." But the figure was actually somewhere between $6 and $12 million. It was a big issue to staff. They were badly beaten up already and the fact the CBC was still looking to cut budgets meant that even more staff might have to be let go before the end of March. Watson was trying to say that the worst was over and yet the staff knew there were other shoes still to drop.

Watson termed the idea of having two television stations in Alberta—with that province's very diverse North-South character— "a wasteful, foolish rivalry." He told the Vancouver staff—people who had just lost their jobs, who would soon step into unemployment lines—that "television was now a national service rooted in the regions." He talked about doing "more" regional production than ever before, and that "we will not turn this into a 'Toronto or Montreal corporation'." He might well have been talking in Swahili, for all the sense his words made to them. He was immediately reminded that the 'regional' CBC network production of the 1991 Juno Awards show—to take place in Vancouver the following month—would be created, nurtured and produced, not by Vancouver staff, but by Toronto staff who would be flown in for the occasion. His response: "That doesn't sound very good to me. . . ."

When he told the gathered staff that now that the cuts across the country were over, there would be a new emphasis on encouraging co-productions with the private sector, there was incredulous silence. One employee sighed, stood slowly, and informed Watson that CBC Vancouver had been the biggest "co-production" centre outside of Toronto. More than 117 hours of co-productions had taken place in the year prior to the budget cuts, helping to contribute nine television series to the ETV network and attracting more than $2 million in outside cash to the CBC. The Board's budget cut had just effectively killed much of that co-production activity. A somewhat confused Watson admitted that the information about Vancouver's co-production successes "was new to me." But he would go, he said, and ask the Head Office finance people about it. Nevertheless, he would like information and input from staff to help him on matters like this, he continued. The whole room sagged noticeably. "What is horrifying," said one CBC staff member, "Is that you are asking for this information—now—after the damage has been done."

Watson's version of how the Board reached its December 5, 1990 budget cut decision was as appalling to staff as it was confusing. His persistence in interpreting the regional programs that had been cancelled as simply "local" programming—the kind even the private stations were broadcasting—revealed a misunderstanding of both the role the regions played and the history of its relations with the ETV network. What he could not seem to comprehend was that the programs which were cancelled were actually the last remnants of a regional network exchange system that was all but snuffed out by the ETV network. When Watson talked about how the CBC could now better "reflect the regions" of the country to each other—using tired adjectives like "mirrors" and "windows"—people rolled their eyes and shook their heads. He stood there and was talking words at the staff that had no match for their reality. "There's a way of doing everything—and that's how Patrick thinks," said his friend Robert Markle in *Maclean's* in January 1989. "Maybe he's just one of those smart guys who you'd love to punch in the nose once in a while."

How come you didn't howl to high heaven to the Tories? "We needed a plan we could execute . . . we agreed to (a) do the work and (b) to shut up about it. What good would it do to have been saying: Look out folks. . . ." Complementarity did not exist between radio and television audiences. They were two different audiences. Who was giving you advice? And you were trying for "symmetry" in your implementation of the cuts? That idea had about as much balance and elegance as the agenda at an anarchist's convention. Ontario and Quebec now had two stations, less than two months after the decision. And the plan was also supposed to have regional CBC televisions remain in each city where legislatures were located? What about Victoria? Gawd, the staff seemed to be muttering. Who's running this circus? Would you just quit trying to make it up as you go along? "The corporation has had its roots sliced," producer Cathy Chilco said icily to Watson. "It is a disaster. There is no future any more, no chance this region can take initiatives in making programs . . . your position is just not acceptable!"

Patrick Watson's stature among public broadcasters eroded with every contradictory statement. In Vancouver, one staffer talked about her pain, her anger and her sense of betrayal. "You've been as quiet as a church mouse," she said to Watson. "Where was Patrick Watson when the cuts were going on?" He had betrayed journalists within the CBC, a young staff member said to him in Calgary. "You used to be one of us. You're not one of us any more." "He didn't stand up when he was needed and then had the gall to say the CBC will be better than before," said Liberal communications critic Sheila Finestone, calling for his resignation. Staff began asking puckishly: "Have you heard about the new Patrick Watson television series? It's called *Struggle for Hypocrisy* . . ."

For a time it seemed everyone was calling for his resignation. Most thought a resignation, some form of public broadcast *hara-kiri*, was in order. "What possible good would that do?" he asked, puzzled. But he could not seem to understand, that was exactly what his supporters wanted of him—demanded—a fiery personal sacrifice to properly singe the beard of the malevolent Tories. After all, Watson was the one who had said he would walk if things did not work out: "We've got better things to do with our lives," he told the *Financial Times* of his and Veilleux's inclination to resign at the appropriate moment. But he did not seem to understand the moment, how he was perceived by Canadians, especially public broadcasters, or what was expected of him.

Watson was once quoted in the *Toronto Star* as saying that he felt his personal power was "of high visibility, of my acceptability to the industry and the country, of the irremovability of the position." His job was not to throw his body across the cultural tracks of the nation. It was to move closer to his new political constituency in and around the suspicious grey East and West Blocks on Parliament Hill, work to overcome their impressions that the CBC was fat, troublesome and badly managed; show them that the CBC, as he once said, is "in motion." It would be an impossible, thankless task. He would have been better off resigning.

Three years later, when asked jokingly how he was enjoying the job so far, he replied with a tired shrug: "Twenty-two months to go . . . [until it would all be over]." It was the phrase of a man who could hardly wait to get off the stage and out from under the glare of the spotlights.

11 / Radio—The Tiny, Fragile Crystal

"Our tendency has always been to make programs like we were living in tree houses. We climb up, get in and pull the rope ladder up after us. Then we shout down at the audience: 'We're going to make you real smart'!"
—a CBC radio manager, 1992

CBC RADIO (AM) AND CBC STEREO (FM) together form the nation's most significant cultural institution. No other organization compares in breadth, scope or effectiveness. It is the entity we talk around when we try to defend the entire CBC as the valued cultural service we would like it to be. We like to pretend CBC television is in there somewhere, but its shortcomings outperform its potential. Only radio truly performs as that paramount cultural purveyor, offering a service so unique that no other broadcasting company, no other organization, no other institution can say it does as much for Canadian culture. If there is a survival message for CBC English television, it is in CBC radio's service—the service of the past, not necessarily the present or the future.

Where the ETV network struggles for identity, appreciation and a role in the nation's cultural firmament, CBC radio is that firmament. Where CBC television executives watch in confusion, and occasionally horror, as their parade of North American-styled, commercial entertainment glitz attracts fewer Canadians each year, radio's aggregate audience remains relatively stable, even growing occasionally. In the fall of 1986, CBC radio's share of total anglophone listening was eleven percent. Six years later, in the fall of 1992, it was 11.5 percent, with a reach of over three million listeners. In roughly the same period, the ETV network lost a third of its audience. Television's audience freefall would continue into April 1993—more a meltdown than a freefall now. If the trend continued throughout the 1993/94 broadcast season, CBC English television could very well end up having a lower audience share than CBC radio.

CBC radio stands out as our cultural touchstone in a country fast losing national symbols. Its sound is absolutely distinguishable from the mindless cacophony of private radio. It delivers a startling range of programs, with a balanced emphasis on informing, enlightening and entertaining. Unlike CBC television, radio has its roots firmly planted in the regions of the country, with seven hours of CBC-AM weekday programming emanating from local stations. Radio's success comes in large part because it provides alternative programming and is a real, as opposed to gossamer, presence in the community. Those seven hours can be heard and appreciated Monday to Friday. They are 'the rock' on which all CBC radio services perch. CBC-FM delivers an absolutely distinctive service of classical music and information about arts, culture and the performing arts.

Although CBC-AM attracts more than twice the share of CBC-FM, both services are supported by large, vocal groups of listeners who view the CBC as a manifest part of their communities. On the other hand, CBC television's failure escalated when it started giving up on the communities, on the regions. CBC television no longer had a constituency. CBC-AM talks about the issues, the personalities and the events through the marvellous prism of our communities, linked like cultural sausage, with the network news service, and some of the most invigorating and informative national programs offered on the continent. It is a crystal that, for the moment, makes up the cultural soul of our nation. But it is a crystal in danger of losing its lustre.

What CBC radio delivers best is knowledge. CBC television delivers sensation. One can be substantive, reflective and intellectually challenging. The other can be visceral, spatial and often intellectually impoverishing. One has the potential for building concepts and understanding. The other can distort and undermine reality. One is reality. The other is distraction. Garrison Keillor, quoted in the December 3, 1991 issue of the *Globe and Mail*, declared that radio, perhaps even U.S. radio, "has a gorgeous future now that television is drowning itself . . . [television] has become a vague, diffuse appliance, an immense, squat passive beast that has a calming effect on people." Pictures and words are enemies, Keillor continued. "When they are brought into proximity, the picture destroys the word. Radio is the most powerful medium there is for talk, for human voice, for storytelling, for drama. Eventually, these things have to come back." In Canada, we have been enjoying a large part of that neural renaissance for more than twenty years.

The strangest thing of all is that, when it is done well, with forethought and planning and intellectual vigour, the information that CBC radio leaks into our minds can conjure up more vivid images and pictures than television ever could. If the 'technique' of information on radio is properly applied, it can be a phenomenon of insight, a transformation of words and energy that converts our way of thinking about things and doing things. It can enlighten and massage our stronger opinions, shedding light upon the perplexity caused by contextless news. It can sensitize and relax the mind at the same time, providing each of us with recesses from the stress of the unknown. It can entertain in a way that television can only hope to emulate, providing you through its sounds with a personal paint box of inventive imagery that has you laughing and crying and applauding and sitting and thinking and wondering—all while you listen.

CBC radio contains something few other media can claim—character. It is so distinctive that it is not really 'radio' in the contemporary, North American sense. It is an active media phenomenon. It is about making choices. It is the medium for people who treasure words and the thoughts they conjure. It is for people who have an urge to know, to understand. And it is not just 'information.' It is words that inform, stimulate, dramatize, analyze and provide a more positive rhythm for our lives.

A good early morning of your local CBC Information Radio program can open a more hopeful door into the problems of your community. *Morningside* can tie you infinitely closer to your country and your neighbours. A good day of *Mostly Music* or RSVP can stroke the soul. A good afternoon of *Gabereau* can leave you shaking your head in bemusement. A good evening of *Ideas* can pour so many new and astonishing insights into your packsack of thoughts and perceptions that it does not get heavier; it gets lighter. And if the week has been hard and the content of the weekend's *World Report* runs across the blackboard of your sanity like screeching chalk, there is always *Double Exposure* or *Royal Canadian Air Farce* to make fun of it all, and *Quirks and Quarks* to rewind the clock of fascination for the yet-discovered. When you sit down, and run your finger back and forth over that magical list of program events that CBC radio offers—on

AM and on FM, during the week and on weekends—and you think about each contribution—*Sunday Morning, As It Happens, The Arts Tonight, The World at Six, Brave New Waves*, and on and on—you are looking at one of the most forceful and compelling radio services in the world. It is truly, as Gérard Veilleux once called it, "a crystal, fragile and beautiful." Fragile.

My time in radio was the most stimulating and the most emotional of my time with the CBC. We were allowed to play with more images than a filmmaker, more visuals than a television producer. There were moments when our eyes moistened with the sudden understanding of how inadequate film and videotape really were when compared to radio's power to build images. They had to think about, then make up, images for us to see. Our images, the ones radio presented to us, came out of a soft, colourful ether, shifting and changing with each word, phrase, sound, rhythm or echo. The thing about good radio is that it gets better when you close your eyes.

But as good as the moments were—as high as each hallucinatory creative spike of colour and form took us—we seldom could ever keep it all up there in the higher reaches of the phenomenon; never able to drive the upper levels of radio's expectations as surely, as vigorously and as frequently as we wanted. Perhaps, because we were so in love with the tiny crystal, we kept trying to make it greater than it was capable of being. But when we hit those spikes, when the better radio experiences passed through the time-space equation that was a program in the air, the thing we knew we each had in common was the risk the CBC allowed us to take.

But strangely, as the clock ticked past the first anniversary of the December 5, 1990 budget cut announcement—a bullet that radio was able to dodge—the CBC's radio services seemed as full of misgivings, low morale and lack of purpose as their ravaged television counterparts. Anonymous staffers talked about CBC radio as "a totally dysfunctional organization," with an "irresolute" senior management group overcome with "indecision" about where radio was going. People were apprehensive about their jobs. Change was in the wind, but what change? Talk spread about a movement to "popularize" and "homogenize" the distinctive radio services. Another lumbering, massive navel-gazing process—"Creative Renewal"—had been taking place under then-radio vice-president Donna Logan's guidance. Creative Renewal raised more questions than it could answer. What the spooked staffers did not understand or appreciate was that CBC radio was just going through one of its half-decade soul searchings.

There are three forces which have the potential for permanently damaging the crystal. It will be seen to be standing too close to that bonfire of egos, vanities and misunderstanding that has finally begun to consume English television, and be terminally singed by the public heat. It will continue to allow its sound, especially its information sounds, to become more and more derivative, lacking in courage and risk—lacking "rigour" as Joan Donaldson, one of CBC's finer news and current affairs minds, used to say—and watch the audience dwindle away. Or the inhabitants of the tree house will try to change it by playing with form instead of substance; try to make it better by playing with things—formats, modulations, personalities, program slots—instead of understanding that it lives or dies by the strength and vigour of the spoken word.

The CBC radio you hear was roughly twenty-three years old last May. Except for an initial impressive burst of brave new programming initiatives in the early 1970s, nothing dramatic has happened in the way of bold, new programming ventures on CBC-AM in the almost two decades. *Sunday Morning* was the last large, successful new program venture, and it is more than fifteen years old, and shows it. *As It Happens* has been around since the 1960s ended. The local programs, all seven hours a day of them, are conceptually a good twenty years old in most cases. *Morningside* is really just *This Country in the Morning*—here again, a program born out of the radio revolution of the 1970s. The large scale 1980s efforts were *Gabereau* in daytime and *Prime Time* in the evenings. On weekends, the more recent titles included *Quirks and Quarks* (dating from the late 1970s), and programs such as *Basic Black* (early 1980s), *Double Exposure* and *The Radio Show*.

But few of them cuts the swath in audience share of a *Sunday Morning* or an *As It Happens*. In comparison, the audience for the younger *Prime Time* before it was axed in 1993, plummeted every week night after *As It Happens*, from a ten-share to a six-share. In the spring of 1992, the audience drop was from 740,000 for *As It Happens* to 325,000 for *Prime Time*. More than half the CBC-AM radio audience disappeared when Enright and Maitland signed off their more than two decade old format. To add insult to embarrassment, the venerable old *Ideas* series that followed *Prime Time* each night had slightly better audience numbers (326,800) in the spring of 1992, than the new program-kid on the evening radio block.

Nevertheless, approximately every six years, on average, a strange, torturous event takes place within CBC radio. Large numbers of radio people bend forward gently, open one or two buttons of their hair shirts, and search for public radio truth and understanding among the lint embedded in their navels. This cyclical exploration sets out to discover what, exactly, it is that fuelled radio's success, and how they can make it even better and more popular than it was. Radio staff, management and invited guests gather in large, concerned masses to try to change things—to tinker with the crystal. Unfortunately, they seldom meet their own expectations or agree on major structural change. The one thing they have not been able to do in over twenty years of ritual is come up with a significant and compelling new way to do radio programs. It was the curse of the munchkin failure. It was always a brave and laudable search.

They did it when CBC radio was in crisis. They did it when things were going well. They did it when they were bored, when they were elated, when they felt they were doomed. They even tried to do it when hardly anyone noticed they were there. Like unhappy Druids, these keepers of the public broadcasting light gathered to run their hands over the marvel of CBC radio, trying to plumb the mysteries and discover enough new secrets to draft a new catechism. The fact that most times it was doing quite nicely was almost neither here nor there.

> "It is precisely because some three million listeners are happy with the service, Parliament is impressed with it, CBC management is content with it, our staff is successful with it, Applebaum-Hébert praises it, the press respects it and the commercial sector envies it that we are in trouble."
> —The English Radio Development Project, 1983

Sometimes it was one or two folk, maybe a half-dozen, criss-crossing the country, talking to CBCers, taking notes, seeking inner revelations. Sometimes there were hundreds, meeting in meeting after meeting, musing over "the problems" of CBC radio. Occasionally—only God knows why—one or two would touch base with people in the U.S. and talk to them or quote them on their version of where public radio was going. They would share their notes and observations, tack their ideas up on flip-charts, draft reports, copy reports, distribute reports, spend tens of thousands of dollars searching for new light, seeking out the recipe for the elixir, the universal solvent to minister to the ills of national public broadcasting.

This tendency to go wandering in the conceptual radio desert began humbly in 1969 with the work of two insightful CBC programmers—Peter Meggs and Douglas Ward. Their work resulted in the 1970 English Radio Report, or the "Meggs-Ward Report" as it would be commonly known. It was followed by the 1975-76 Arts Report, followed by the 1983 English Radio Development Project, followed by the ill-fated deliberations of "Creative Renewal." Meggs-Ward was the trimmest and the most effective effort. The most costly and belaboured had to be the English Radio Development Project. That eighteen-month extravaganza involved 220 people, divided into fifty-four project groups, four standing committees, resulted in 2,000 pages of reporting and fifty-one briefings across the country. The process resulted in a 218-page report examining "why we exist, what we do, why we do it, how we do it, where we fit now in the spectrum of broadcasting" and ninety-three recommendations as to how CBC radio could position itself "for the future." The report ended up, largely, being a book on the shelf.

The 1970 Meggs-Ward report virtually turned CBC radio around. It laid out the road map for what those inside the tree fort called "the Radio Revolution." It eventually was the reason why three million Canadians appreciated CBC radio services. The 1983 English Radio Development Project resulted in a bunch of new tablets but no new commandments. It could not do what it was supposed to do: plan a CBC radio service that was even more loved and appreciated by even more Canadians. It had concentrated on things—technology, social trends, cultural relations, government—and ignored the word. The bureaucratic failures of the 1983 report piled up until 1989/90 and Creative Renewal. Creative Renewal was nine months of staff sessions and meetings in trendy hotels, six task forces, ten "Do-It-Now" workshops, six program department three-year plans and thirty-one station plans—resulting in fifty-six pages of oral briefing notes on a proposed three-year "strategic plan" that got shot down in the blink of a Druid's eyelash by the Veilleux administration.

The Druids kept trying to plumb the holy truths Meggs-Ward discovered, trying to do it one-better, and kept coming up woefully short, even losing ground. Meggs-Ward did a lot of marvellous and positive things to get a tired, old CBC radio service back on track. But one of its tiny tragic shortcomings was that it seemed to imbue many with the belief you could always make radio just that much better, more complete, more precise, more popular just by changing things. These two prophets implanted new DNA into the gene of successful public radio and, unfortunately, also implanted the Bug of Change. Each time the Druids went lint hunting, they ended up trying to remake CBC radio in their own image, time and space—with little reference to what elements had been successful in the past, or what the audience might want in the way of programming.

By the end of 1992 though, CBC radio management began to sense big trouble on the horizon. It hung by its generational fingernails, praying the reputation of a stumbling, misguided public television sibling did not rub off too noticeably on it, and fighting against the urge to change. But the threat to the fragile crystal was as much from within as from without. The beast called Creative Renewal still lurked in the antechambers of CBC radio, waiting for the moment it could begin to turn the face of public radio toward a more demographically-correct audience, into even more chatty conversations than programs, more "dance" than Dante. There was no Creative Renewal plan any more, but change would still come over time, except that it would not be widely recognized. By the time in the summer of 1992, when Gérard Veilleux put the skids to the official effort to "renew" CBC's popular radio services, the gene pool had already been infiltrated with the latest manifestation of the munchkin deviation.

The munchkin deviation is that phenomenon of generational change that always bubbled within CBC radio after Meggs-Ward. Each new froth was similar to the last in one sense. Each was based on hope—as Goethe termed it, "the second soul of the unhappy"—that you could make good radio just a little better, a little more popular. In today's case, it came to the ear, innocuously, in the form of what one might call "post-modern" information radio. It was the succession to CBC radio of a generation nurtured more by images than words in print, television more than books, music more than spoken word. They were a generation with multi-track sensibilities, but with little real understanding of the "technique" of CBC radio's information-based success—how the revolution started, what sustained it and how much it meant to Canadians who valued it. They were also a generation which, without a reference check of radio history, believed they could match or improve what went on CBC radio before them. Unfortunately, they often had, as one radio executive put it, "no collective corporate memory"—about what went on before, why, when and with what success. They would eventually try to create a new and different CBC radio. And the Canadian audience would not like it at all.

The current crop of Hansels and Gretels were so committed to marking their own trail through the forest of national public radio that if Peter Gzowski, Vicki Gabereau and Michael Enright were to resign from CBC radio tomorrow—or perhaps slip out for a lengthy sabbatical, with the hope of returning to CBC after their intellectual jets were refuelled—the odds are quite strong the munchkins would not hire them back. Like many other CBC hosts, journalists and interviewers, most stars harbour a deep and real nervousness about munchkin intentions. They know they would be toast if they slipped away for more than a season. These radio luminaries would not, in the eyes of today's radio programmers, have the necessary broadcast and personality qualifications to make it back into the CBC, once they were out from under the cover of tenure. When the moment came, the munchkins would gladly attempt to stuff their personal version of a new Canadian radio star into the vacated seat.

Stars aside, by 1992, the munchkins had their hands on the throttles of the CBC radio service and were probably not even aware that they had already been slowing down the pace, changing the vibration from vigorous to decorous, from challenging to chat, changing the attraction of CBC radio from personal to universal. Where once CBC radio produced a range of programs that offered, for the most part, well-crafted words and ideas and tones, we now had descended over the years to 'magazine' radio—talk and chat and snippets of music and subjects all strung together in the broadest mainstream of information imaginable. On January 29, 1993, the new radio administration announced that next season CBC Stereo listeners would be receiving four hours of seamless arts and culture information every weekday evening. It would be a magazine of culture, and we all knew what trouble the magazine industry is in. That was not to say there was no room for magazine program formats. It was just that whenever the munchkins were in doubt about how to make a good radio program, they inevitably trotted out another 'magazine.' As much as anything, this infatuation with the magazine format comes out of the success achieved by the seven local daily hours of loosely structured talk, interviews, information and the odd music disc or cassette slipped in for relief. National magazine format successes such as *This Country in the Morning* gave the idea credibility. Some managers described it as "seamless" radio, as if breaks in tone and theme and flow were dangerous or distracting. Well, if you don't have seams, your pants can fall down.

> *"You figure out some way of staying on the system, because if you go off the air you will be yesterday's radio host in five minutes. And you will spend, like I did, eight years with your nose pressed to the window saying: 'Let me in!'"*
> —Vicki Gabereau, March 25, 1992

The 1970 Meggs-Ward report was a clairvoyant internal document produced for the CBC Board of Directors. It eventually redefined radio. CBC Radio had been, to put it politely, languishing in the 1960s. It was a highly centralized operation with no solid, distinctive focus. The audience was rapidly dwindling. The service's format had deteriorated into a not very exciting mélange of classical and elevator music, predictable programs, officious news, spasms of sloppy dead-air and stiff-sounding BBC voices droning on ponderously about the efficacy of Renaissance public works projects. One of the most exciting moments was the National Time Signal. CBC radio carried schools' broadcasts, a program for stamp collectors and Gaelic-language offerings for the folks in Cape Breton. The CBC radio service, Ward and Meggs wrote in 1970, "defies all current and future trends in listening."

There was serious talk that perhaps the CBC should save itself some money, grief and embarrassment and put the entire radio service out of its misery. With the supremacy of television, and with increased competition from the private sector, CBC radio had lost its nerve, its momentum, its audience and its reason for being. On May 6, 1969, the Board asked for an urgent, "detailed, exhaustive study . . . into all aspects of radio operations." In effect, the Board was asking management to justify CBC radio's existence. After six months, over 400 interviews, and a perceptive analysis of a blizzard of paper on societal change, economic trends, technological advances, audience listening and modern viewing tendencies, and holding a damp finger to the winds of the future Canada, Meggs and Ward came up with the design for the foundation of one of the most important and valued public broadcasting services in the world.

Their conclusions were based, not just on how to fix a radio network, but how best to serve a changing Canada. In an eerie echo of today they wrote: "The issues before Canadians in this decade are not only economic. Regional disparity and a growing sense of separateness in several parts of the country jeopardize Canadian unity." They sensed a national feeling of "individual helplessness against decisions of government (on all levels) and large industrial conglomerates, the widening gap of understanding among generations and, most importantly for CBC, the lack of information upon which to base individual and community decisions." They accepted that "the age of anxiety is likely to remain with us." And they asked: "With the fragmentation of mass audience in a pluralistic society, what role is left to radio?"

They concluded, in effect, that Sir John Aird, Dr. Augustin Frigon and Charles Bowman had it right in 1929, that a national public broadcasting service had to be Canadian, had to be sincerely rooted in the regions and had to understand its mandate to "serve" Canadians with programming that was not available elsewhere: "Our exploration of alternatives over the past six months had led us repeatedly back to the mandate which was given to CBC Radio at the beginning and which no other medium has usurped, namely to enable Canadians to achieve their full potential in a changing society by sharing across Canada their problems, their hopes and the best creative talent this country can produce." For regionalists, the operative term was "sharing," not "network."

Although they covered myriad considerations—from programs to union relations, from transmission to promotion and public relations, from commercials to morale, and called for two if not three separate frequency services—the essence of the Meggs-Ward recommendations were that CBC radio, to survive and serve Canadians well, had to concentrate its priorities on delivering information, and do it principally in the communities of Canada, in the regions; not do it all from Toronto: "In the minds of many regional and local broadcasters the term 'network' in its present context is synonymous with 'Toronto,' with all the images that accompany that name in our country. The present English radio network emanates largely from Toronto and control decisions are made there. . . . the 'Toronto syndrome' seriously aggravates our proper response to the network mandate. . . . We found a real desire on the part of local CBC stations to be freed from many regional and national network constraints in order to probe more deeply their own community.

"We conclude that there is but one alternative open to the Corporation. That is to renew radically the present radio service to meet the new demands of the mandate in the seventies. Such renewal will involve a new understanding of a network service; one which is truly national rather than Toronto-oriented. . . . We envisage radio services rather than merely a rigid network. . . ." They were saying that if CBC radio was to survive, it had to get back to its roots. It had to start living and working *in the communities of Canada.* You could only serve and reflect the real Canada—perform as the nation's public broadcaster—by functioning in the regions. The CBC had to open up the entire radio system to more regional voices, and give Canadians a say in what was going on in their country. Program control had to be largely in regional, not network, hands. Only then would CBC be a 'national' service and be valued by Canadians—a lesson the Board, senior management and television network moguls still have not fully comprehended.

Just as significantly, Meggs-Ward swept away the ancient, arthritic hobby horse that, to be true to the mandate, the CBC had to be "all things to all people"—seek a mass audience as opposed to a minority audience. The days of the mass, national audience were dead, even in 1970. Once again, they laid out the lesson for television as well as radio: given that CBC's role as the sole heart of national broadcasting had long ago been usurped, pick your public broadcast niche and serve it well. Meggs-Ward set a radical tone for radio. They wanted radio as an "alternative" service. And by embarking on this courageous and fruitful path—that audience of 300,000 in the 1960s went to three million in the 1980s—carved into CBC's backside the reality that it had to be different, and valuable—if it were to survive. Television never got the message. It continued off on its own path, competing with private stations and networks for a place on the spectrum of entertainment mediocrity. Radio heard the message: "We must recognize the role of CBC Radio as a service of live information for those people who want to know more about the events, goods, services and movements that impinge upon their lives," Meggs-Ward wrote, "in order to help them to assume control of their lives and environment and become more aware of choices which affect the shaping of a just and human society. . . ." The setting was the community. The service was information—news that mattered, followed by explanations that made sense. The concept: local empowerment.

"We must respect our audiences," they wrote. "We must stop telling the people of Wawa about the traffic on Toronto's Don Valley Parkway. . . . We must not force a Dominion-Provincial Conference on the residents of Smithers, B.C. at 6:00 A.M. just to have it live across the country. . . ." The section on the evils of traditional networking read like a scary day in the 1993 life of CBC's English television network. Meggs-Ward was defining a solution, not only for radio in the 1970s, but CBC television in the 1980s and 1990s, providing it had paid any attention. The report pointed out that, coming out of the 1960s, the Canadian population was better educated than ever before. If TV had done anything for the citizens, it had helped sensitize them to a world of confrontation: students versus administration, workers versus management, citizen versus government, the individual versus special corporate interests. They were more politically aware. The age of consumer-fights-back was no accident. Meggs-Ward stumbled upon a basic reality that we are only now beginning to fully comprehend—that better-educated, intelligent and publicly sensitive people tend to use information as "currency." And the bank they would most likely draw from would be CBC radio.

They used information to make their lives better. The right information in the correct context allowed them to plan their lives better, understand society's myriad competing issues, raise their families more sensitively and perhaps even improve their careers. "Information Radio" was what CBC should be all about, Meggs-Ward trumpeted. It should be the backbone of an entire service aimed at satisfying an intelligent slice of Canada's population. It would not be for everyone. Just for those who could use it, and for those who eventually would come to almost not be able to live without it. "The real point is that the 1970s call for a new kind of radio programming spiked with confrontation, concern and exploration of the things people are interested in," Meggs-Ward quoted Jack Sturman, in *Stimulus*. "I call it Boutique Radio. It's programming designed for the minority audience—not for the mass audience, whatever that is. It reaches out for the specific-interest listener . . . talks to the consumers about things that concern them . . . food prices . . . new products . . . [it] reviews last night's opening of the new play in town, picks up the phone and goes after an interesting or unusual story that the newspapers didn't carry. . . ."

Meggs-Ward "boutiques" started springing up across Canada, with regional stations churning out seven local hours every weekday of community news, interviews, coverage of special events and personalities, and a local context for national events. A large part of the backbone of this new information steed—who spoke on air, what they said, how they said it—was not built from inside the CBC. It came from outside, from a new information species—the citizen-journalist. "The principle of the Meggs-Ward report was to open up the whole radio system and give the audience a say," former radio vice-president Margaret Lyons stated.

As suggested by Meggs-Ward, the door to the reclusive CBC crypt had to be thrown open to a nation-full of freelance writers, broadcasters, performers, actors, musicians and radio documentary makers if Canadians were truly going to have access to their national radio service. Public access to public broadcasting was paramount. The difference between these outsiders and television's later independent co-producer was fundamental and revealing. The former made public broadcasting better by contributing new-found ideas and material that enhanced public broadcasting. The latter made, and makes, programs that deviated from it and adulterates it.

This mercenary radio army of intellectual reinforcements did not contribute their skills and ideas and talents just to local programs. For almost a decade after 1970 their prose, their discoveries and their passion helped stem the tendency to talk . . . talk . . . talk rhetoric-radio that we are subject to today on most CBC programs. Their voices, their words and their techniques blossomed from the local program soil onto network programs and series—*This Country in the Morning, Ideas, Concern, Tuesday Night, Sunday Morning, Identities, Commentary, Shoptalk, Between Ourselves* and *Five Nights*. And in between and over and under, a seemingly endless cornucopia of two-to-three minute insights into our society on everything from politics to the modern fur trade, from rapeseed to the Judeo-Christian ethic, from performance and the arts to cemeteries in Nova Scotia, from medicare problems to defence, from the meaning of holidays to environmental activism. It was an audio version of *The Canadian Encyclopedia* ten to fifteen years before its time. The words and thoughts and ideas painted vibrant pictures about that mass of land and humanity that existed east of Scarborough, north of Uxbridge and west of Mississauga.

And their voices were not muffled by the comfortable existence of CBC staff-for-life positions, regular pension contributions or guaranteed long-term contracts. These people were selling their ideas about Canada to the CBC on a fee-for-service basis; money in exchange for the ideas of the citizen. "I think that's one of the real bonuses of *Ideas*," Vicki Gabereau pointed out. "[It's] a different person everyday presenting their God-help-me ideas, and much more of radio should be like that." Following the advice of Meggs-Ward, CBC radio opened the door to the crypt and in flowed hundreds of journalist/artist/citizens who energized CBC radio with their ideas, their observations and their aspirations. But the Ward-Meggs monument started melting in the late 1970s and early 1980s with the tightening of corporate budgets. By 1983, the impact of inflation alone meant that CBC radio was providing more services with less real dollars than in 1975. Most tragically, fewer and fewer dollars were available for freelance talent. With less money to spend on freelance talent, local programs began using more of their own staff. Weber's laws on bureaucracy were being activated once again.

The size of program production crews—even on local morning and afternoon shows—blossomed with bureaucratic predictability. Where a local drive-home program was once put together with a producer, a host, a technician, perhaps a part-time researcher and a revolving door of freelance contributors, staff sizes expanded with additional researchers, 'associate' producers and production assistants. Even with ensuing budget cuts, program staff rolls increased, along with individual salaries, while fewer original program opportunities, and opportunities for freelancers, took place. Where once some network programs got along with a handful of staff, now there were executive producers, with senior producers, producers, associate producers, production assistants, as well as researchers. When the nightly documentary series, *Five Nights*, was produced out of CBC Winnipeg for a short time, the only 'staff' on the program was the producer. When the weekly, one-hour network documentary series *Concern* was produced in Halifax, it had a 'staff' of one producer (made up of two producers contributing half their time to *Concern* and half their time to local Halifax radio productions) and a researcher on a six-month contract. In both cases, the backbone of these two network programs was freelance contributors.

By 1992, on some network series like *Stereo Morning*, the crew would eventually get so large (as many as sixteen people credited weekly with putting the show together, not including the administrative back-up) and diversified (where once a single executive producer supervised an entire program, area or station, *Stereo Morning* alone had two of them) that management admitted the crew did not always talk to one another about the show they were being paid to produce. By the time we got to 1992, *Stereo Morning* employed more people than an individual CBC station would have needed in 1975 to produce *seven hours of daily current affairs programming, five days a week*. To make current matters even worse, the sixteen people on *Stereo Morning* were there to put together a show that was hardly taxing— intellectually or journalistically. It was essentially recorded music— specialized music to be sure—interspersed with light, non-immediate information about arts and culture. On May 12, 1992, the big news on the daily "arts report" was whether Chinese porcelain would sell on the international market—plus eight minutes of chat with a whistling champion.

When people left all those newly created positions, it was only natural to expect that they had to be replaced. Few radio managers or administrators, or even producers, paused to ask themselves: "What if we *didn't* fill that job? What if, in these tightening times, we used the money for that position to hire two or three freelance contributors? To add variety to the program? Vigour? To bring in new ideas? Journalists who would even do their own research?" Information started to sound less varied, certainly less controversial, and became more chatty, predictable, structured and cautious. We had gone quickly from rhetoric to ideas and back to rhetoric again, in barely a decade.

On network programs, fewer freelancers meant more talking heads, magazine format shows and fewer documentaries made from outside the crypt. Management began a quest for a "star" system. It became almost mandatory that the host of a program did most of the chatting and asking of questions. We got guest after guest chatting with our genial host, as if Canadians were not capable of listening to the sound of an uninterrupted voice with a stream of thoughts. Fewer documentaries explaining backwater Canadian issues appeared—from the backwaters—on programs such as *Morningside*, *As It Happens* and *Sunday Morning*. The intrepid documentaries and mini-documentaries that once dotted these sorts of programs began to be produced, not by regional-based freelancers, but by Toronto employees flown in to the site of the weekly Big Issue, staying just long enough in places like Edmunston, Canoe Lake or Brandon to tell us their version of the local story, before hustling back to the warmth of their offices in Toronto. Somewhere in the early to mid-1980s, that revolutionary CBC radio service—concerned, inquisitive, aggressive, hustling for Mother Canada—started to take on the tone of IBM. CBC radio began to sound like Corporate Radio. And the telephone calls started coming again from Toronto to the regions: "What exactly is potash anyway?" "Is the well-head price of oil what we pay at the self-serve?" "How many native people live in downtown Regina anyway?" And "Is No. 1 Northern the name of a CNR train . . .?"

The crystal's demise would be hastened, like many a traditional institution, unwinding, as we lurch to the end of this century, by the centrifugal force of generational change and taste, and by the collective lack of memory that new generations have for what many knew to be 'public broadcasting.' It was neither sinister nor was it vindictive. They were just children of their experience. Nor would they understand the 'technique' of public radio. To many, it would be just a job. A particularly stimulating job, one with a fair degree of prestige attached to it and very well paying, but a job nevertheless.

It is one of the unfortunate and costlier truths about life in CBC; everyone is hell-bent, with the odd exception, on doing public broadcasting his or her own way, with little or no reference to the past. In *Turn Up the Contrast: CBC Drama Since 1952*, author Mary Jane Miller drew attention to this very problem, only on the television side of the CBC: "It is an absurd, regrettable and perhaps quintessentially Canadian fact of life at the CBC that almost no one making television drama in the 1980s remembers with pride, reviews with interest or ever reflects upon [the CBC's] remarkable record. . . . It should be a condition of employment that directors, designers, cinematographers, producers and writers look at a dozen or so plays selected from [the] rich store available. Would a filmmaker confess ignorance of the work of Welles? Ford? Eisenstein? Bergman? Would a theatre director be unaware of Stanislavsky? Meyerhold? Brook? Not knowing a national history and an aesthetic context makes for shallow cultural roots. Unhappily, this CBC obsession with the present and the immediate future is universal."

> *"Creative Renewal had nothing to do with renewing* CBC *radio by being 'creative.' It was a process."*
> —a CBC radio network senior manager, 1992

Except for the corporate *hara-kiri* carried out after December 5, 1990, and the rolling debacle that was Repositioning of the network television schedule, nothing raised the ire of CBC radio fans and editorial writers more these past few years than the concept of Creative Renewal. Creative Renewal was radio management's effort to renergize a moribund radio service—let loose the deadly Bug of Change. It ended up being a concept for change, not in the way programs were made, but in the way CBC radio went about delivering them. Creative Renewal took on a life of its own. Staff across the country were solicited for their ideas on programs and transmission and society. More than a half-dozen task forces were struck. Hundreds and hundreds of staff were consulted. It was proudly said to be one of the most gratifying examples of radio democracy ever embarked upon. The munchkins were cooking. They were going to re-make CBC radio.

If implemented, Creative Renewal would have made CBC Stereo the "main network" and filled the FM schedule with a mix of talk programs off the AM service (*Morningside*, for instance), more "mainstream" music (read: popular, less classical), and try to lasso "the whole listener," relegating the loyal CBC Stereo classical listener to second-class, pump up the percentage of pop music and make CBC–FM attractive to "family" listening.

Despite the controversy, Creative Renewal had some things right. The CBC certainly did need more network licenses if it hoped to deliver as many services as the politicians had saddled them with. Moving to FM as a main service was just keeping pace with the audience shift to a quality signal, although why they would suggest it at a time when digital radio, providing roughly the same listening quality as FM, was on the horizon, was a mystery. The sudden urge to be politically correct—to cater to an audience that demographically represented today's Canada—made some philosophical sense but was a broadcasting death wish; something that would throw the CBC audience appreciation back to the Dark Ages of pre-Meggs-Ward. And to suddenly suggest that CBC-FM might go from classical music and coverage of arts and culture to chat and more mainstream music was like poking a stick in the ear of over a million loyal, articulate and politically adept listeners.

The CBC-AM service would have remained essentially local, but the seven daily community hours would be swaddled in an ill-defined series of open-ended "responsive" programs relying on the telephone to cover issues and events—feared to be a "radio magazine-from-hell." The philosophical foundation for this renewal was the announced urge to make CBC radio more properly reflective of the "new Canada." CBC radio would become more "authentic" by focusing on the interests of the urban listeners, a younger audience and the needs of a more multicultural, rather than a White-Anglo-Saxon-Protestant Canada. "Authenticity in the 1990s means addressing audiences instead of constituencies," Donna Logan said in November 1990. The Meggs-Ward report had manufactured a survival premise for CBC radio: find out what Canadians were missing, and serve that need. Creative Renewal was saying: "Find out what Canada looks like and try to deliver programs they *all* might listen to." It was public radio trying to be sociologist.

Creative Renewal was also the victim of horrid timing. The first major presentation of the concept came barely three weeks before the $108 million budget cut and the massive damage inflicted on the regions of the country. CBC became a 'four-letter word' after December 5, 1990 and Creative Renewal very quickly climbed the charts to nestle right next to it. Radio management later protested that Creative Renewal was never meant to be "earth-shaking," but shake the country's radio firmament it did. By the spring of 1990, when the wheels for Creative Renewal really began to spin in the hallways of Bay Street and offices across the country, the two CBC services—Radio and Stereo—would be reaching 3,400,000 listeners each week, a figure that converted to 12.8 percent of the English language radio audience. Both figures represented the highest ever recorded number of listeners between 1986 and 1992, and perhaps the highest aggregate audience average in recent CBC history. CBC radio management were going to begin reassembling the national public radio service at just the moment when it was most popular with Canadians. They were, as Peter Trueman wrote in *Toronto Starweek* on January 26, 1991, about to shoot themselves "not merely in the foot, but in the head."

Of course, change always should be a principal consideration in any creative field. Change is a challenge to the spirit and, in this case, to public service. It was recognition of the need for turning over the stale and predictable sod and unearthing new seedlings. But where public radio was concerned it had to be led by vision—in programming, not by switching networks, or moving programs back-and-forth. "Where I think the big mistake was," said one senior radio network manager after the fact, "it looked as if it was a repudiation of everything that had gone before . . . and also it took into no account the hierarchical structure of the organization. As soon as [the presentation for Creative Renewal] came out with the *imprimatur* of senior management, people forgot how much of it had come from the bottom. They thought these were dictates." Nevertheless, the sheer urge to see CBC radio renewed failed also to take into account a number of traditional radio maxims, including the one offered by the 1983 English Radio Development Project: "CBC Radio's success is not the success of grand strategies. . . . Rather its success is the success of individual and collective talent creating fresh concepts, adapting the tried and true formats and taking chances." You 'renewed' the CBC by making better and more challenging programs that fit with the times and the interests of the Canadian audience. You did not do it by playing social scientist.

Until this present generation came along one might have said that it was impossible to live and work in public radio, enjoying the awesome power of The Word, and the delivery of a multitude of images, without suddenly waking up some day asking: "How does it all work? How can word and sound and rhythm perform so metaphorically? And how can I keep it working?" It was also a profound mystery to many why three million Canadians continued to tune in to a service that was less than it should be. The reason? It was all they had.

By 1993, CBC radio was either a stalled, rudderless, dysfunctional, mediocre entity, badly in need of vision, or it sat on the very edge of its own magnificent renewal. Most of us would like to agree with Garrison Keillor, that the potential exists for radio to blossom again. Keillor's belief that today's radio has a gorgeous future now that TV has succeeded in drowning itself, could only be realized if those who guided it understood the proper use of the technique of The Word, as Meggs-Ward did. Talk would not make radio great again. The proper use of words would. As author Sven Birkerts suggested in Harper's magazine, there is a huge generation out there which is just now beginning to understand "a McLuhanesque wrinkle in the collective sensibility" that, as an increasingly literate society, we are moving inexorably backwards—toward even ancient oral traditions: "Everything in creation has changed, but the triad endures: the voice, the story, the listener." The future for CBC Radio and Stereo—its 'renewal'—could be found in the past, in the very soil Meggs-Ward watered years ago. The Word.

Nothing would galvanize the interest of Canadians so vigorously as the intelligent use of words, of information, of thoughts, of reality, of fiction, of discovery, of ideas. Instead, we get to listen to conversations, not the form of words that always surprises, stimulates or challenges. Words on today's CBC radio are largely formulated with an absence of respect for the medium—that sense of awe at the power and influence an ancient oral tradition can have over our thoughts, as the words tumble through space to rest in our imaginations. Instead of wonder and awe we were often forced to eavesdrop on three-way conversations; between a host, a 'writer-broadcaster' who did not write and did not broadcast and the scattered and random third-party voices he or she had gathered while interviewing people in the street with a tape recorder's microphone shoved in their face.

We are reentering the age of storytelling, of trying to communicate with one another in words and phrases that are important, not frivolous. There is a huge intellectual hunger abroad in the land. A more literate and better educated society—the young, the middle-aged, as well as the old. They are the new consumer; hungry for ideas, thoughts and stimulation. CBC radio sits in the middle of a huge market demand for people to talk to them—about their aspirations, their fears, their weaknesses, their strengths, their spiritual beliefs. The thirst for words is strongest, oddly enough, among the very generation CBC radio had been pursuing, with such lack of discipline, the past decade—the baby-boomers. But they do not need to be pursued.

They will come, to an intelligent, informative radio service, but only one providing the same oral and literary stimulation newspapers and magazines and books do for most people now. Radio is the ideal future medium for them.

The post-modern baby-boomer, "reared on music and visual media, have reflexes and combinatory capacities that are something new in the world," Birkerts wrote. "They perform acts of multitrack cognitive juggling that leave their elders tied in knots. . . ." The newspaper's, publisher's and printer's loss would be Canadian public broadcasting's gain—a generation, walking in its own information wasteland, just looking for a modern matrix of aural stimulation to tell things, teach things, to entertain with words. CBC radio again has the potential to be the trinity around which the post-modern citizen gathers: the voice, the story, the listener. All they have to do is teach the munchkins how to more properly use this epiphenomenon that presently rests in their hands.

If a life-secret exists within the crystal for the struggling dinosaur called the English television network, and perhaps for the crystal itself, it is in CBC radio's past, not its present. Survival messages for both can be found in the Radio Revolution spawned by Peter Meggs and Doug Ward. No public network can be sustained unless it is rooted—truly, not falsely—in the communities or regions of the country. Local programming is the national rock upon which true public broadcasting is built. Centralization is death. Programming must be unique, distinctive and surprising—programs and experiences unobtainable elsewhere. The corporate mandate must be reinterpreted to mean: *inform* with the unknown, *enlighten* with the unexpected and *entertain* with the different, even the provocative. In the crystal's case, there is still hope.

12 / The Last Fandango

"It seems obvious there is little future for the CBC as we know it. It was a noble experiment, but conditions have changed. It is time to give the CBC a respectful burial and remember the good it has done."
 —Stanley Burke, former CBC-TV correspondent and news anchor, *Globe and Mail*, April 18, 1991

WHEN I STARTED OUT TO WRITE this book in the spring of 1991, I still believed in one survival option for CBC English television—the theory of "The Nine Percent Solution." Instead of continuing to compete in the seedy and indistinguishable world of commercial television, the CBC, so the theory went, should recognize the inevitability of audience fragmentation and offer Canadians one, clear option—a public television service that looked authentically Canadian, was non-commercial, with programs no other broadcaster provided. Television should decentralize operations into five equally resourced and independent regional production centres—with Toronto just one of them—and get closer to its real roots in the regions of Canada. The ETV network should take a tip from CBC radio and aim for a solid and appreciative audience share of about nine percent, and be satisfied with that number—hell, even glory in it—while all the private broadcasters and cablecasters fought it out for the tiny remaining clumps of television audience, with programs that mocked each other.

But by the time I started wrapping up this book in the spring of 1993, The Nine Percent Solution was probably no longer possible. The argument was not whether a nine percent share of the audience was a good target to aim at, but how could CBC stop the share figure from sliding even further below nine percent—into complete and utter irrelevancy? The only other thing that would be certain at that dismal future point would be the ETV network would cost more to run than it did today.

By April 1993, the CBC, especially English television, was sitting on the edge of disaster. The moves of the Veilleux-Watson administration—in scalping the regions rather than the networks or the Sports departments, in 'regionalizing' supper hour news, in allowing Toronto to set the tone and style for Canadian public broadcasting, in continuing to nurture a tired and arthritic bureaucratic structure, in chasing their advertising revenue tail—had begun the march to public broadcasting Doomsday. Audience figures were spiralling relentlessly downward. The recession and repositioning together had begun to contribute to revenue losses estimated around the industry at more than $30 million. There would be $50 million less in Parliamentary appropriation for the CBC in 1993/94. The future was even more dimly prescribed in late April when finance minister Mazankowski applied further budget cuts of $100 million through to 1996/97.

In June, one vice-president was heard to mumble about the corporation facing a funding shortfall as high as $180 million within two years, but the problem could go as high as $300 million by 1996/97. This was a corporation that could not find $4.5 million to provide Windsor with local news, and they were looking for $180 million?

ETV network audience share figures had now fallen to the low teens. Rumours began circulating about rating averages for *Prime Time News* on some nights now as low as 600-700,000 viewers, and 300-400,000 viewers for the combined seventeen-station supper hour news programs. If true, it meant that between $40 and $50 million was still being spent across the country to attract an audience less than half the size the supper hours had before the 1990 budget cut announcement. Vancouver news ratings dropped 30 percent between April 1992 and April 1993, meaning the CBC was paying about $7 million a year to produce an evening news program for an average of 80,000 viewers, or half the number of viewers before the 'regional' news concept was introduced on December 5, 1990. Nervous CBC managers began speculating the next logical move by the ETV network would be to have the supper hour news programs wiped out, and the last of the regional money and the time turned over for a national news show at 6 P.M. each weeknight—produced from Toronto. It could make business sense. But it would be the final lights-out time for public broadcasting.

In the midst of this viewer evaporation the ETV network trotted out its "new" fall schedule in early June 1993. In an interview with the *Globe and Mail* Ivan Fecan announced there would be no major changes to the controversial repositioned network schedule: "We're staying on our course because we think it is working," he was quoted. "We're reaching our objectives of having distinctive, complementary programming." Unfortunately, Fecan's claim that CBC's programming was "complementary" and did not look like their private competitors' was a can that had trouble holding water. One of the few "new" programs introduced on the CBC-ETV network's "distinctive" 1993/94 schedule was *E.N.G.* The network had acquired the "strip" or repeat rights to old *E.N.G.* episodes—a series coproduced and previously shown on, of all things, the CTV network. Come the fall, Canadian viewers could watch new episodes of *E.N.G.* on CTV, and old episodes on their "distinctive" public broadcaster.

Fecan also announced that he was convinced the ETV network rating debacle was now being reversed. "Whenever you change something as dramatically as we did in the past year, you have to accept an initial drop in your audience," he told the *Globe and Mail*. "But the numbers are rebounding and we're very confident in what we're doing." Fecan was speaking during the Stanley Cup final series between the Montreal Canadiens and the Los Angeles Kings—teams drawing an average 2.8 million viewers a night, a number that was up significantly over the previous year's final. But NHL hockey aside, it was difficult to see where Fecan's audience rebound was taking place. A comparison of the 1992 and 1993 television seasons to the beginning of March revealed that CBC's 24-hour share had gone down almost sixteen percent. Even taking into account a higher than average audience for the Winter Olympics on CBC in 1992, the network was still off more than 12 percent from the previous season. If there truly was a "rebound" in audience on the ETV network, it might have been from the disastrous week in late October during the Toronto Blue Jays World Series mania on CTV when CBC's prime time audience share slipped below ten percent into the single-digit range.

While the audience numbers continued to tumble and the revenue numbers stalled, the CBC communication wunderkinds were plastering the term "Public Broadcasting" on anything that moved in hope they could somehow protest their purity enough and stem the audience outflow. Like the little bunny in the battery commercial, the corporation began pounding on the message incessantly—"Go Public"—while ratings and prospects for increased commercial revenues continued to slip. The root problem had not been addressed: CBC television was not unique, its programs largely looked like Hollywood, it was full of commercial messages, between which the "This is Public Broadcasting" messages were squeezed. And perhaps worse yet, the growing audience indifference began to show up now toward CBC radio services. The malaise was evidently catchy. After years of being able to hold their consistent share of Canadians, English radio services' audience figures started to arch slowly downward. Perhaps not surprisingly, the downturn began in the fall of 1991, a year after the Veilleux-Watson administration put the cultural torch to regional television.

In mid-March 1993, Head Office released a second effort at explaining Repositioning, a sixteen-page tabloid-size brochure in English and French. This new repositioning brochure was an awkward, cryptic publication, with a message that was only slightly more comprehensible than the 1992 version. The brochure's colours—purple, claret, black, with patches of plums and pinks and reds—were the colours, as one CBC critic put it, "of a giant bruise, or haematoma."

The prose was uninspiring and every single photograph in the brochure was of a bureaucrat, either from Head Office or from the networks—one photo after the other, mostly smiling faces, their fingers gesturing at one another, some looking very business-like, one scratching his head, one peering professorially over the top of his Ben Franklin bifocals. Nowhere in this strange, dark document was there evidence of any people who made CBC programs or were of a colour other than white. Of the fifteen faces, three were women. The visual focus on senior managers may have been an effort to convey Veilleux's "team" in action, but the general reaction among staff ranged from cynicism to outright anger. The expected number of copies made their way into CBC wastebaskets.

The document did lock on to one of the major threats facing the tired, old corporation—to survive in the new technological age the CBC would have to present a programming service that was distinctive. David Ellis, broadcast researcher and author of a trenchant study, *Split Screen*, on the future of home entertainment and new technologies, commissioned by the Friends of Canadian Broadcasting, was predicting at the same time the bunnies were drumming and the brochure was hitting the halls of CBC in March that Canadian culture and the CBC were about to take an even more severe battering. "How we express our culture is going to be quite drastically affected by this two hundred channel universe," Ellis told the *Vancouver Sun*. Ellis predicted that the ETV network share of Canadian audience would drop "by half" in the next three or four years, an estimate that would barely put the network on track for less than a seven percent audience share future, let alone The Nine Percent Solution.

"We're looking at a situation in which globalization has really taken hold of television culture. We're never going back to the golden era of television in the 1950s when we had a cadre of very fine playwrights and performers and directors who put live drama on television and really spoke to Canadians and Canadians watched in droves. We're not going to go back to a situation like that, if only because our most successful producers have to make their living today by doing deals with producers in dozens of other countries around the world."

> *"I sense people are in a very different state of mind, than even two or three years ago. It's almost every guy for himself. We were all shocked when the ground was pulled out from under us. It's hard to see the big picture and commit yourself to the organization. It just feels like survival now. . . . Producers are a commodity. When they've finished with you, you're tossed out. You can't build loyalty like that. There are a lot of disillusioned people out there."*
>
> —Cathy Chilco, regional producers' association president,
> February 1992

From the outside, the CBC looks fairly normal. And to some extent, it is. Programs get made. Transmitters hum. People walk in and out of CBC buildings carrying their briefcases, sit at their desks, chat on the telephone, flip through files, edit tape, sign documents and make plans for next year. If you read chairman Watson's words in the 1992 annual report, you would think you were seeing a message from some peaceable kingdom: it had been a "pivotal year" for the CBC, the corporation was now "leaner, more muscular" and it was a year "in which we returned to our roots." In January 1993, Gérard Veilleux energetically cited no less than twenty-three "major things" the CBC had accomplished: "I think we did more in 1992 than any other year in the history of the CBC!"—from a new "productivity initiative" (some of it money spent to convince people to leave CBC) to "delayered management," from a seven-year license for Newsworld to French radio in Toronto, from repositioning two new television schedules to a senior management shuffle. "Any other corporation would be proud to do two of those things!"

But 1992 was to the CBC, as it was to Her Majesty, *annus horribilus*. It was a year that brought more confusion, senior management shakeups, the end to radio's Creative Renewal and television's *The Journal*, falling ratings and commercial revenue prospects, the expanding spectre of the Board's quest for journalistic accountability and the crisis of confidence and staff-management schism that was *The Valour and the Horror*. It was also a year in which the corporation had been forced to decide that it would again dip into the CBC Pension Fund, so that it could get its hands on $96 million in surplus funds just to be able to survive the next two fiscal years. It was a year in which the CBC began to devour itself.

"Morale has never been worse in this corporation," admitted one Ottawa manager bitterly in 1992. "There is complete and utter mistrust of everyone. The people who work for me don't trust me. We do not know where the organization is going." Said one other Toronto manager: "Everybody seems to want to leave."

"How good are your numbers?" is the conversational sign that someone would like to leave the CBC with the best financial package possible. A lot of it can be chalked up to emotional exhaustion, stemming in part from the effects of the budget cuts, but also from the lingering tension between senior management and middle management. "I'm certainly scarred," admitted one regional manager of the firing duties he was forced to carry out on December 5, 1990. "And I'm scarred as much by the scars of others as I am by my own."

Despite Veilleux's pronouncements that there now existed a clear and shared sense of where the CBC was going, many staff saw a different reality. The corporation's direction—the vision thing—seemed to get made up by circumstances. No long term stable funding? Okay, we'll reposition. What does that mean? A lot of things. Not moving fast enough for you? Bang! New senior management in place. Want us to be more accountable? Slap! Let's apologize for *The Valour and the Horror*. And with all the semantic gyration, the tension that exists between the Board and senior management and the rest of the corporation, and the staff's call to resist the building political pressure from the Conservatives, the Tory-appointed Board capped 1992 by telling everyone in its annual report, "We do not believe that shouting is good use of public money." Slap! Get back in the corner, be quiet and correct, and sit there until we tell you how to live out your public broadcast lives. Statements like that just continued to open more divisions between the administration and staff, blocking any real hope for any shared vision of the future.

A second tabloid sized brochure on 'media accountability' was circulated by May. It contained recommendations from the media accountability committee on improving journalistic standards, making the CBC more accessible to the public, correcting errors and increasing journalistic training and personal development. The recommendations came from more than 400 journalists and producers, many of whom were the most respected in the CBC. Despite the note that the CBC would also hold large public gatherings to showcase its new accountability initiative, the document made a lot of sense. Concentration on excellence in reporting, new money for recruitment, training and evaluation, dialogue with the public and an improved ombudsman process were all positive gestures. But in the minds of many CBCers, journalists and others, the CBC Board was still the Board. The memory of *The Valour and the Horror* would not dissolve with the introduction of new accountability standards.

The pall of mistrust that envelopes the CBC is largely a product of style. It is a style that says there is little time for a previously understood corporate culture. It is also one that, unfortunately, does not attract much loyalty. Some people would argue this destructive atmosphere is simply just desserts for a lazy, indolent CBC staff and management. But the test lies in results. Is the CBC any more efficient and appreciated in 1993 than it was in 1990? Have costs gone down? Have more programs been produced? Does the CBC have more or fewer Canadians watching or listening? Are there 120,000 Calgarians watching the CBC evening news each week night or 14,000? Has respect increased for the corporation's journalistic standards? Is the Renaissance upon us after almost four years under the present administration, or Armageddon?

Internally, the bleakness of the current corporate circumstances dictated a need for a quick shared vision, like it or not. In May 1993, the CBC officially recognized it was in big trouble. A travelling road show of vice-presidents and assorted managers set out across the corporate desert, like good Israelites, in search of a consensus plan for the future. The venture was modestly titled "Opportunity for Change: Creating a new operating framework for the CBC." But hidden deep within the venture's discussion paper lay the harsher reality: "The New Operating Framework for the CBC envisaged in Opportunity for Change is a blueprint for survival. . . ." Change or die.

It was hoped the exercise would involve almost all CBC staff, solicit their opinions, ideas and cooperation. Although the general guidelines for this odyssey seemed positive enough—examining work practices and production methods in all areas, finding more efficient ways of doing things, providing employees with opportunities for growth and career development—the overall tone and thrust was pre-terminal; the CBC had to massively and fundamentally change the way it did business or it would be out of it. They had about two years left to get it right.

Beyond the threats posed by a 200 channel universe, falling income, increasing competition for advertising revenue, new technologies and new forms of entertainment competition, the major challenge for everyone lay right inside the structure of this tired old corporation. Citing observations on this theme from the 1986 Caplan-Sauvageau task force on broadcasting policy, the discussion paper pointed out what many had known for decades—the CBC was poorly organized and badly structured. It was a creative organization modelled after an industrial organization. The CBC had more in common with a 1962 General Motors plant than it did with a twenty-first century broadcaster.

Efficiency was hampered by a rigid organization and unyielding labour agreements. There were too many unions, too many job categories and too little flexibility to help the corporation adapt to new technologies and new ways of doing things. In 1990 the Canadian Labour Relations Board told the CBC to squeeze its bargaining units down from twenty-plus to three. This CLRB-driven consolidation of bargaining units opened the door to the possibility of task sharing, greater job versatility, accompanying increases in efficiency and lower costs. To the CBC, this "new operating framework" represented "a profound change in the way we organize and carry out our work," the discussion paper stated. "It describes a fundamental change in the relationship between the Corporation and its employees. Implementing it will cause a fundamental change to the Corporate culture."

Initial staff reaction was cautious, even pessimistic. The one thing most staff always knew, even if senior management ignored it, was how awkwardly the CBC was organized and operated. The loudest feedback call from staff was for more training. Some managers saw this new venture as the first smart move out of Ottawa in a long time, even if it took three years for them to get the ball rolling. On the other hand some employees saw the new message as a corporate admission the whole place was going down the stinker. Some even suspected another corporate "done deal," that even with the soliciting of their opinions and suggestions by the travelling road show they were convinced there was already a glossy, completed report on the subject hidden away in an Ottawa drawer, "telling us what they intend to do anyway."

Some union heads saw the document and process as just another Head Office ploy that preceded the next round of management-union negotiations. Some talked about militant action, perhaps even strikes. But if "Opportunity for Change" galvanized any one common thought, it was the clear understanding that this exercise in corporate democracy and renewal underlined, once and for all, how bleak the corporate future really was. Don't change now, and you were dead meat.

"Opportunity for Change" was, without doubt, a good management initiative on the part of the Veilleux-Watson administration. Unfortunately, it was coming at least a half-decade late. Perhaps the wheels on Bronson Avenue could begin turning quickly enough to help put together a new, vibrant plan for a public broadcaster for the twenty-first century, but one was not given over to optimism. The coin of public broadcasting had already been so sullied and devalued, the changes outside in the real world of broadcasting so profound and so sky-shaking, that a future CBC rule that said a producer could now move a host's chair on a set, rather than a stage hand, was not likely to have much real impact on things. It would still end up being a corporation with too many tasks, too many people without them, too much old thinking and too few citizens outside Kafka's playground who really cared any more.

"Part of me says 'What's TV? It's sucking shadows and it's genocide.' If it's hell, at least it's purgatory. . . . I'm a compulsive TV watcher myself

*and I hate it. I sit and change channels and I watch and watch and it's
really upsetting me. You slept with your brother and was it good? And the
audience is cheering? Freud would be rolling in his grave. It's all so
dehumanizing."*

> —Louis Del Grande, of *What Are Families For?*, an Alliance
> Communication-CBC co-production, *Globe and Mail*,
> March 25, 1993

All institutions, even nations, have their time; mines run out of ore,
football teams grow old and weary, businesses get inattentive and run
out of customers. In this case, both the CBC and traditional television
broadcasting were fading away together. In March, the ETV network
kicked off its latest North American style, co-produced sit-com pilot,
What Are Families For?, to high indifference. The pilot could have
been another microcosm for the network's many ills.

In a strange, quirky way the trotting out of another tired,
derivative 'CBC' sit-com pilot took place just as the CBC was taking
part in "the mother of all hearings," as CRTC chairman Keith Spicer
put it, on the death of television broadcasting. The future was to be
a wide open sky but the CBC would probably be stuck on the
ground—with its rigid bureaucracy, its burdensome hardware and
assets, its 1960s management thinking, its tired and blatantly commercial television programming and its antiquated transmission systems.
The future the CRTC was trying to get a regulatory handle on was
termed the "Dinosaur Wars," for the way the private broadcasters,
cablecasters and broadcast traditionalists tried to preserve their profitable pasts. But the No. 1 dinosaur was surely the CBC.

"We are witnessing the death of broadcasting as we know it,"
Split Screen author David Ellis warned, "and the culprit is new
technology." Ellis wrote that "new technologies like digital video
compression and computerized TV sets will undermine the established
ways of making, financing, distributing and watching TV. They will
also make concepts like 'broadcasting' and 'TV program' largely
meaningless." The world is going "transactional." We are headed
toward "digital computerspace"—as George Gilder wrote in *Life After
Television: The Coming Transformation of Media and American Life*—a
"convergence" that will meld broadcast TV with data, fibre optics,
telephones, new technologies, market forces, changing tastes and
home service demands that would probably lead us to the tele-com-

puter as a replacement for the passive TV set. "It's not even going to be television," Tufts University's E. Russell Neuman pointed out: "Using a term like 'television' is like using an awkward term like 'horseless carriage'." For television, the days of the mass audience were dead. Narrowcasting was all about us. Any moment now we would be into "microcasting."

With satellite "death stars" and the 200-channel world moments away from our consuming grasp, North America's entrepreneurs trotted out their version of the ultra-fragmented television world of 1994. An astonishing host of specialty channels, commercial networks, educational TV, Pay-TV and cable networks would be joined by a channel for, seemingly, any subject in the encyclopedia—including a golf channel, a military channel (endless re-runs of John Wayne war movies), channels for food, porno, game, romantic classics, comedy and crime, a Golden Age Network channel, a Global Village Network, a 16-hour TALK-TV channel, the rumour of a Frank Sinatra channel and a 24-hour channel full of commercials. The prospects only became more surreal when it was announced from Los Angeles in late March 1993 that former junk bond king and prison guest Michael Milken planned to join business forces with Michael Jackson to launch a cable education network.

We are on the edge of a "multiplexing" world in which digital compression techniques will be used to transmit a multitude of channels over the electronic space on a satellite usually reserved for one channel. It is the dawn of "universal addressability"—all citizens with a box or keyboard attached to their television monitor which allows them to design their own program choice, even make up endings to movies and stories they prefer over the writer's efforts. It is the beginning of the interactive world in which the consumers of both television programming and personal services will ask their 'television' for anything from retrieving business data to buying a new suit, from playing video games to taking a home tutorial course, from movie-on-demand to deciding when they—not the CBC—want to see *Prime Time News*, from voting on national referenda, or for their favourite political candidate, to celebrating Christmas by having the entire family—from Port Hardy to Come-By-Chance—chat on a video conference call.

For Canada's cultural pirates—the private broadcasters and the cable operators—who spent decades championing their role in providing Canadians "with more choice," the idea of *this much choice* scared the actuarial hell out of them, shook them right down to their bloated annual report net profit pictures. The Canadian consumer was now on the edge of having more choice from the skies alright—enough to throw these cultural bandits right out of business. Typically, the boys in the shiny suits began sounding the cultural and political alarm bells. Long protected in their monopoly positions by the federal regulator, loathe to divert any but the required minimum of their profits to the making of Canadian programs, these two groups of brigands started pounding each other out in front of the CRTC over, of all things, the carcass of Canadian nationalism and culture.

At the CRTC hearings of March 1993 it was as if the ghosts of Aird, Frigon and Bowman had wandered into the debate and set down a problem sheet photocopied from 1929. By 1990, only 4.4 percent of television drama that Canadians watched was Canadian. As TV Ontario's chairman Peter Herrndorf told the CRTC, a UNESCO study discovered that, out of seventy-nine countries, Canada ranked last in the amount of broadcast time devoted to its own cultural programming. Canadians had been sold out again by their own broadcasting system. The American cultural threat was even more severe than in 1929. And a majority of Canadians, as Aird and his friends had pointed out, still wanted *more Canadian programs.* In February 1993, the Friends of Canadian Broadcasting announced that a national survey found that after all the American schlock that had been driven down Canadian throats by its broadcasters, sixty-five percent of Canadians supported rules that impose a minimum level of Canadian programming. More than six decades after Aird, most Canadians—with collective patience that must exceed that of Job— were still asking for their own, authentic programs. The only groups who seemed to oppose their request were the politicians they elected, their broadcast regulator, the private broadcasters, the cable companies and the CBC.

All most Canadians wanted—in 1992 as in 1929—was more programming that told them who they were. And they got less. It had not been, nor was it now, a great bargain by any measure. Taxpayers *paid* for the CBC. They *paid* for a regulator to regulate the industry, less to their benefit than the industry's. They then *paid* for independent producers to make their Canadian programs, which had to look American to make any money for the independent. They even then had to *subsidize* a pack of wealthy Canadian private broadcasters to convince them to produce Canadian programs. They then *paid* for those subsidized programs to be delivered to their homes on cables. And now, Canadian cable operators were coming forward to ask the CRTC if they could not convince Mom and Dad Canada to pony up another $2 billion in increased subscriber fees so the cable industry could get even richer by competing with the "death stars," principally by providing even more programming most Canadians did not want.

In June the CRTC announced its mother-of-all-decisions. It failed to break up the cable operator's monopolies. Although it took a juicy morsel off their profit plates—the existing guaranteed return of 23 percent on net fixed assets and automatic rate increases tied to the consumer price index—it again opened the wallets of Canadian consumers for the cable operators to tap. They would not get their $2 billion from Mom and Dad Canada to defray new technology costs, but they would get about $525 million through increased subscriber fees.

The CRTC had once again allowed the cable operators to pick the public's pockets.

> "'So forget everything else I said about television and remember this,' says Del Grande, with mock seriousness. 'This is an important show and a good show. It will employ a lot of people, and if we're lucky, it just might save the universe.'"
> —Louis Del Grande, *Globe and Mail*, March 25, 1993

While this latest ridiculous regulatory fandango went on, the CBC, in comparison to the sweeping but slightly warped vision of the cable industry, and the exciting technological challenge of filling a meaningful niche in the multi-channel sky, had trotted out Repositioning and renewed *Friday Night with Ralph Benmergui* for 1993/94. Yes, they were going after a French-language news channel, and, yes, they were going to play smoke-and-mirrors with Northstar, but if you stood back and looked at the whole package for public broadcasting of the future, there was little there.

Instead of looking inside for the solution, and starting to make more distinctive programs that were clearly identifiable as "Canadian public broadcasting," the Veilleux-Watson administration continued to pretend CBC English television did stand out, as if to say, as Veilleux did in an interview published in the April 12, 1993 *Globe and Mail*, that "there is a need for a strong recommitment to public broadcasting in the face of this massive number of signals." Recommitment? To what? *Street Legal? Romeo and Juliet?* Grand Prix auto racing from Monaco? *E.N.G.? Fresh Prince of Bel Air?*

They did not get it. Instead of pointing to a new line-up of exciting and challenging Canadian programming, Veilleux pointed with pride to the CBC's new aggressive strategy to link up contractually with private sector companies, domestic and international. The CBC was combing the world looking for co-production deals. But none of what they would bring home from their global jaunts would ever truly speak to Canadians about themselves. A joint venture with Power Corp. would attempt to get that tired, spruce-goose concept of Project Northstar broadcasting into international skies and profit-ability. Montreal's Astral Inc. would take over CBC program distribu-tion and, it was hoped, help rub out the sad and costly memory of CBC Enterprises. An "alliance" with Cadillac Fairview Corp. had brought us the Toronto Broadcast Centre. A "strategic alliance" with Australian Broadcasting Corp. would ultimately lead to more Aussie programs to watch. A deal with the BBC had us now watching British interpretations of international news events. Canadians were crying for new and different programs from the CBC which truly reflected who we were, and we got international business deals.

The corporation was bankrupt left, bankrupt right. It was running short of vision, energy, initiative and bucks. Viewers were disembark-ing the good ship ETV network. And a few listeners started to slip away as well from CBC radio. Advertisers were watching the rolling seas splash into the open holds. The captain had circulated the ship's navigation charts and almost everyone could see they would never make it past the satellite shoals. The ship was old and creaky and leaked all over the place.

Daryl Duke, a Vancouver-based, Emmy-award winning director, and one of the CBC's most daring television producers in the 1950s and 1960s, wrote in the March 1993 issue of *The Canadian Forum* about the ETV's loss of cultural purpose. Duke had been a significant player in the golden years of CBC television. He had produced and directed three of the corporation's most acclaimed documentary series:

Close-Up, Explorations and *Quest*. He went on to produce internationally, including *Tai-Pan* and the TV mini-series *The Thorn Birds*. At CBC, Duke had been part of the days that included Eric Till's *Pale Horse, Pale Rider* and Bill Gough's *Charlie Grant's War* and many, many other stirring television works—days all gone now, according to Duke.

Duke's criticisms prompted a mild firestorm of response from the CBC. Fecan termed his arguments "selective reminiscences of the good old days." The network's head of movies and mini-series, Jim Burt, tabulated an impressive list in *Forum* of recent prime time accomplishments—Eric Till's *Getting Married in Buffalo Jump*, John N. Smith's *Boy's of St. Vincent*, Anne Wheeler's *Diviners* and many others—and took umbrage with Duke's accusation about the network being "Toronto-centric."

But Burt, like many others, missed the point. Citing fifteen titles produced over a couple of years, no matter how high the creative and technical quality, was to point at the network's weak spot, not its strength. Burt should have been heralding fifteen different dramatic *series*, not one-off movies and a couple of short mini-series. This was pretty spindly stuff if the ETV network was truly in the culture business. While Burt was pointing with justifiable pride at the accomplishments of his department, across the hall the Sports department of our nation's public broadcaster was still producing 700 hours a year of play-pen television.

As far as Torontocentricity and Canada's diverse cultural needs were concerned, he was missing the point as well. As long as Toronto network management called the final shots on production projects—whether produced in Estevan, Saskatchewan or Yellowknife—Canadians would never witness truly diverse and reflective programs from the regions.

And Adrienne Clarkson also took Duke to task in *Forum* in a rambling and not wholly accurate defence of the ETV network and its centralized programming control system. Somehow in Clarkson's reasoning, television technical and presentation standards were more important, in the context of Canadian public broadcasting, than programs made by people who live in the region. She was saying that good looking TV was more important than authentic public broadcasting: "Nobody, not even the regions themselves," she said quite loftily, "would want the national network to broadcast programs just because they come from certain regions. Excellence and aesthetic judgement and audience appeal must always come into play in any decision of that kind."

Duke had articulated in tone and substance what many Canadians were now thinking about the corporation's bleak and contracting future. In Duke's Canada, CBC's strident promotional message about "The CBC and You" made no sense. It was delivering Toronto-made, commercial white-bread programming back to a nation of diverse cultures, ideas and regions. Who was the "you," Duke kept thinking?

"In the CBC of Veilleux and Fecan, our public television service is defined as a middle-of-the-road commercial enterprise, with no duty to achieve other cultural or social goals. . . . Yet those of us who live in various parts of Canada have cultural rights as compelling as any put forward by the national 'centre.' Our sensibilities across this country are varied. Our opinions coast to coast differ widely. Our directors, actors and writers build up unique outlooks and temperaments. If the word 'public' is to mean anything in broadcasting, then one program boss acting under the orders of one president and his board of directors cannot be permitted to dispense judgments across a Canada as diverse as ours."

Duke's words surely left many Canadians wondering again what the whole thing—Canadian public broadcasting—had been about. Did we really have a common fix on what it was supposed to be, or had it been hijacked by many forces and many individuals as we went along, to the point where the concept was whatever anyone in a position of authority said it was? Repositioning was "not some piece of theology," Duke wrote. "It can and must be debated."

That brilliant cultural template that Aird, Frigon and Bowman crafted for us was now so corrupted, so distorted, that it was probably better to take the remnants, toss them out and start all over again. If we were looking for a new mandate for Canadian public broadcasting, I thought, perhaps it would be best to make it simpler than those we have awkwardly tried to follow over the years. I recalled the words of another former CBC producer, who had left the CBC in bitterness over the missed opportunities and crippled corporate purpose. When asked what he thought public broadcasting was all about, he responded sadly: "All I ever wanted to do was make Canadians more aware of their wonderful country and the people in it, and when that was done, make them laugh."

Epilogue

GIVEN THE CONTINUING MISINTERPRETATION of what public broadcasting is and was supposed to be, and the events and crises of the past four years, both delivered and self-administered, it was no surprise that Gérard Veilleux decided in July 1993 to jump the good ship CBC. The voyage simply wore him out. The corporation was a sinking vessel. The captain might have made mistakes in navigation, but he was no fool. It was time to find another command.

If the CBC is to remain afloat, the vision we need calls for a radical disassembling of the corporate structure so dramatically more, not fewer, indigenous CBC programs can be made: more original, regional-based drama, not programs made for production partners and advertisers, or for ratings successes; more programs simply about life in Canada—flooding us with stories about our history, our people, our personalities, our performers, our writers, our artists, our musicians, our ethics, our morals, our problems, our solutions, our books, our theatre, our issues, our institutions, our varied cultures, our differences, our similarities—not deals with Disney, the BBC or Power Corp. To do it, the new captain will have to clearly convey that programs—not the administrative structure, not co-production partners, not bricks and mortar, not people raking leaves and fixing air conditioning equipment—are the most important reason for the CBC's existence.

The entire corporation must be overhauled, torn into functioning parts and modernized in a reassembled form that frees up hundreds of millions of dollars for new, better and more reflective programs, especially in English television. Decision-making, and the entire organizational structure, must be decentralized. The first move would be to radically downsize that huge, in-built administrative bureaucracy attached to Head Office and the networks and strip Head Office down to a liaison role with government, including a financial audit function; audit, not control. The inefficient and expensive Engineering department would be phased out, the distribution system modernized. Capital asset administration would be left to the people in charge of making programs—letting them say what they needed, why, at what cost and where they would go in the private sector to acquire the most suitable equipment or service.

The traditional networks must be eliminated and control decentralized back to regional Canada. Networks, as they exist, would be disbanded and program design, production decision-making and the establishment of a "network" schedule for Canadians left in the cooperative hands of five main regions—east coast, Quebec, Ontario, west and west coast, with room for northern services as well. Regional administrators would be guided in their deliberations over what programs Canadians want by regional advisory councils, whose public members would be nominated and elected from the communities. The five-region concept, as controversial as it would be, would go a great distance toward repatriating public broadcasting for Canadians.

Television should get out of commercial advertising, leaving about $350 million in potential revenue to the private sector—who would be required to contribute a portion of that largesse back to help fund a leaner, more identifiable public broadcaster. The CBC would leave the sports broadcasting field to the private sector. It has always been argued by network and Head Office managers that these initiatives were impossible to undertake—the lost revenue would cripple the CBC. But they also argued that if the CBC filled its schedule with more Canadian content, advertising revenues would fall. In fact, the best revenue years for English television occurred, strangely enough, when they dropped American programming and replaced it with Canadian. Also on the credit side would be the millions saved with the elimination of the nation-wide advertising sales infrastructure. And the myth of awesome revenues generated by CBC Sports is, if not a sham, at least worth testing to save a public broadcasting system heading for demise.

Economies and efficiencies within the CBC have seldom come from the top down. When CBC managers and producers are left to truly manage, when given clear objectives, creative support and an uncompromised vision, they can be remarkably adept at stretching taxpayers' dollars. With the right goal in mind, there is still a shocking amount of money to be found in the CBC. But in a corporate nether world, with confused priorities, rigid and archaic management thinking, departmental conflicts, centralized control mentalities and a corporation unreasonably committed to being "all things to all people" in an era of specialization, neither the money nor the purpose can ever be realized.

Gérard Veilleux must have understood all this. He did his best, but in the end the Parliamentarians he so admired would throw him no lifeline. Not surprisingly, it is those same Parliamentarians who must decide whether there will even be a CBC any longer. They are the ones who must set aside their crude partisan intentions, amend the *Broadcasting Act*, and put this unique and important organization in the hands of a more publicly responsible Board of Directors, to ensure the CBC is, as Frank Peers wrote, "in good hands, and governed by a group of persons who are ready to answer for their stewardship."

A move to save the CBC—make it better than it is and more like it was meant to be—requires an immense amount of courage and determination. A revitalized Board of Directors and administration must sculpt a new, dynamic vision for public broadcasting, one drafted with citizen input and implemented on their behalf. Management must work with new rigour and purpose; become radical in their thinking, take risks that challenge, even raise personal fears, if they are to do best by any renewed mandate. Producers must be given a new testament, one that reaffirms the importance of their creative roles *within* a public broadcast institution. It is only these creative people working inside the organization who can truly define public broadcasting for us. The staff must adjust expectations and realize that the days of jobs-for-life are over and roles in public broadcasting must be infinitely more flexible. The rewards will come in renewed pride and purpose.

It is a daunting challenge in total. But if it is not accepted, and dealt with intelligently, with a strong guiding principle foremost, the only alternative for Canada's public broadcasting future is to reach for the switch, hum a few bars along with Willie—and turn out the lights.

Index

FADE TO BLACK

PRINTED IN CANADA